The Adventures of Johnny Lovebus

Book I
The Heart of Everything That Is

The Adventures of Johnny Lovebus
The Heart of Everything That Is
Copyright © 2020 by John Robert Mernick Sr.
Cover art and photograph copyright © 2020 by John Robert Mernick Sr.

All rights reserved. No part of this book may be used or reproduced in any manner whatsoever without written permission except in the case of brief quotations embodied in critical articles and reviews.

Published January 1, 2020 on the **Centennial of the Suffragette**
by John Robert Mernick Sr.
Edited by Jamie Bryce Mernick
ISBN: 9781660732128
Imprint: Independently published

Dedication

This book is dedicated to:
My wife Jen who will always be on my buddy seat

Special thanks to:
Nici Tietjen Derosier, Timothy Mahoney, Jamie Mernick,
Johnny Mernick, Tara Mernick, Jon Horne & Sevilla Love

Thanks to my friends for the use of their names and likenesses:
Chris, Brian, Chicken Jim, Ursula, Pak, Sue, Tessa, Mark, Big
Dave, Marian & Gavin, Jewels, Yülia, Sandrine, Sheila, Sarah,
Michelle & Josh, Berndt,
Juliano, Kyrah, Joyce, Vera
& drivers Hal, Raoul, Gaunt, Kevin P & Kevin Q

Based on a True Story

The events described in this book were inspired by true stories. The details of the author's life history and family are true to the best of the author's recollection. Character names and physical descriptions have not been changed. However, the actions, words, and opinions expressed by the characters are fictional and should not be attributed to anyone other than the author. In many cases, space and time have been rearranged to suit the convenience of the narrative. Any historical references to the Green Tortoise or the owners, Gardner Kent and his son, should be treated as fiction, but you are welcome to do your own research to sort out the facts.

Chapters

THE RENAISSANCE OF WONDER — 1

THE ART OF ADVENTURE TRAVEL — 10

BUDDY CHECK — 32

SKINNY-DIPPING IN CONNECTICUT — 47

THE MOON OVER MANHATTAN — 77

THE DRIVER'S APPRENTICE — 124

INDIANA DUNES — 163

THE CHICAGO BLUES — 198

BREAKFAST ON THE MISSISSIPPI — 226

PARTY ACROSS THE GREAT PLAINS — 255

BADLANDS NATIONAL PARK — 280

SCENIC, SOUTH DAKOTA; POPULATION:12 — 297

CUNY CAFE — 320

SHEEP MOUNTAIN TABLE — 333

AMERICAN PRAYER — 346

CHAMPAGNE FOR BREAKFAST — 353

MUD FOR DESSERT — 365

WOUNDED KNEE — 376

THE RETURN OF CRAZY HORSE — 386

1
The Renaissance of Wonder

    Clouds coated the Boston sky like cataracts in the eyes of an insane old dog. The wonderful blue that had once shined behind the clouds seemed lost forever on the hounded features of the city. As my father fifty-fived his Oldsmobile up Route 93 toward the Boston skyline, raindrops crocodiled down the windshield like tears, distorting the foreboding pillars of capitalism, concrete, glass, and steel. With tear warped vision I imagined myself working in one of the countless office buildings, doing the same thing every day for the rest of my life. I wanted no part of that mindless routine. I had just turned twenty-two a month after graduating from college with a degree in sixties literature.

    You see, I was finished waiting. I was finished waiting for the movie to begin, for the rest of my life to get started. I was finished waiting for somebody to really discover America. I was ready to wail. I was ready to go On the Road to discover my own America. I was not going to sit back and wait for a renaissance of wonder. With great resolve, I bought a one-way ticket to San Francisco on the Green Tortoise Adventure Bus for a ten-day tour of the northern United States.

    My father parked his car on the corner of Essex and Atlantic Streets near Boston's South Station. We sat silently waiting with my mother on the cold leather seats of his Oldsmobile. "I don't love what you're doing," he told me in the rearview mirror, "but I will always love you." My reflection nodded acknowledgement. My mother had been prodding him to apologize before I left. That was as good an apology as I was ever going to get.

It had been a rough few months at home, ever since I told him I was moving to San Francisco. He wanted me to have a job lined up before I left, but that did not happen. Fighting with him the previous year had soured me on the world. I had lost that quintessential sense of wonder I had always felt as a child, but I aimed to get it back.

Through the misty rain-streaked windows, the only person I could see outside was an overweight Hippie wearing blue denim overalls, sitting on a suitcase under the overhang near the door to South Station. He looked like a Hippie, almost cool, but I could not tell if the pile of bags next to him was his luggage or the worldly possessions of a street person. I could not stand the silence in the car, so I offered to get my parents coffee. They declined, so I went inside the train station to see what I could find.

The second I opened the door I could smell marijuana, so I shut the door quickly and crossed the street. The man in blue overalls held a pipe to his lips and blew smoke out his nostrils as I approached. The massive man was as solemn as a lone Buffalo atop a treeless plateau. Except for the smoke billowing out his nostrils he remained motionless until we made eye contact. I lifted my chin and he did the same. For an instant I saw myself in his eyes, as if I was him seeing me walk past. I was just a kid. I could not help but imagine myself in his position, whatever that may be.

Back in the car I was sipping burned coffee when my father looked in the mirror and said, "That looks like your bus behind us."

"Oh, my goodness!" my mother reacted in the side view mirror. "What an interesting bus!"

I turned and looked out the rear window at the face of the ancient Tortoise bus. In the destination window the words "COAST to COAST" were written with magic marker on white cardboard. I had secretly hoped that the marquee would read "Further," like the Merry Prankster's bus, but "COAST to COAST" in a rainbow of colors was even better. The rain had stopped, so I rolled down my window. "That's definitely my bus," I said with a wide-eyed laugh. I watched as the forty-foot-long, hand-painted, lime and forest green adventure bus passed outside my window. I could hear the music blasting inside the bus as it rolled past with all its windows open. It was Love Shack by the B52s. As the bus crawled to rest in front of my father's car, I heard the lyrics, "Huggin' and a-kissin' dancin' and a-lovin' Wearin' next to nothing 'cause it's hot as an oven."

A slogan reading, "Arrive Inspired, not Dog Tired," was hand painted on the back below a pair of paisley curtained windows. The air brakes gave out a loud hiss and the engine grumbled to a halt. The steaming blacktop was pockmarked with puddles that reflected puffy

The Renaissance of Wonder 3

white clouds. The clouds that had loomed in the sky for so long seemed to dissipate as the bus arrived like cataracts removed from my eyes.

My mother seemed suddenly inspired. "I'm so proud of you," she said. "It's such a brave thing to go out on your own into the world and live your dreams. I was like that myself when I was your age, and I know it's not easy when you've got your whole life in front of you. It's wonderful that you feel free to experience new things, to challenge yourself and get out of your comfort zone. Just remember to take your time and think before you act. Life goes on, but your dreams may not."

"What's going to happen if he can't find work?" my father chastised.

"He'll do just fine," my mother assured him. She turned to me and soulfully said, "If I could give you one thing," she told me as a glow came into her eyes, "I would give you wings so you could fly."

"Oh, for Christ's sake honey," my father scoffed. "The boy needs a reality check, not a flight lesson. Sometimes I just want to tie an anchor to his foot to keep him on the ground."

The bus door opened, and two very casual looking young men emerged. The black-haired youth wore blue jean overalls and the red-bearded guy wore a loose-fitting t-shirt over shorts. Both of them seemed incredibly happy and full of energy. I could sense good vibrations emanating from them. These were no ordinary people. I imagined that vibe to be the childlike energy that had been missing in my life.

"I hope that's not the driver," my father complained. "He looks like a Hippie."

"That is the driver, dad. It's an adventure trip, like I told you. It's not a normal bus."

"I never should have agreed to this," he derided. "God forbid you end up like one of them." He glared at my mother and said, "I should have insisted he have a job lined up."

The two men assumed the same posture, swinging their arms like apes. The first figure stood 6'3" and had a huge red beard that fell to his chest. He was carrying a blue Igloo water cooler on his shoulder. The second figure had glasses and black curly hair. He was reading something aloud off the pages of a spiral notebook, speaking over the shoulder of the red-bearded man. Out of the side compartment of the bus, the red-bearded man pulled out a five-gallon water tank and began filling the water cooler.

From around the corner of the bus station a group of five backpackers, the kind I had seen all over Europe, made their way to the bus. A guy carrying an acoustic guitar wearing a Lou Reed leather jacket followed behind them hesitantly, holding a duffel bag, acting cool, smoking a smoke. The clouds were now gone, and the morning sun cast a gorgeous shaft of light that illuminated the travelers as they approached the bus.

An angelic looking girl with a golden-blond ponytail started a conversation with the guy who had been reading from the spiral notebook.

The black-haired youth looked up when she asked him a question, but instead of answering her, he read her something from the notebook.

The red-bearded man stood up from filling the water cooler and interrupted when the reader looked up to make approval seeking eye contact with the girl.

I felt a huge smile beaming from my face for the first time in months. Through the tinted glass I could see the group of travelers congregated at the door of the dark-lime and evergreen bus. The passengers and the reader of the spiral notebook exchanged greetings. They exchanged hugs rather than handshakes. In harmony with their rhythmic body language, I felt the warm peaceful feeling of the sun breaking through the clouds, heating my skin through the open window of my father's car.

Unlike Lawrence Ferlinghetti, I was finished waiting. I was finished waiting for the storms of life to be over. I was finished waiting for the great divide to be crossed. I was finished waiting for the American Eagle to really spread its wings, straighten up, and fly. I looked at my parents, thinking about our lives together and what would soon be mine alone. I spoke my thoughts aloud, "It's time for me to fly."

"Hold still for just a minute, John," my mother said, "I want to remember you as you were before you leave."

I held her hand one last time and kissed her. "I love you mom."

My Father reached across the space between us and took my hand, squeezing in his nonverbal love with the contraction of his fingers. "Take care of yourself son. Call me as soon as you find a job."

"I will dad," I told him. "I love you."

He advised me, "Remember, you should only believe half of what you see and none of what you hear. Nothing more."

"Okay dad," I said somberly.

"Do me a favor and stay out of trouble," he recommended.

"I'll do my best," I told him.

My relationship with my father was love hate at that time in my life. I would tell him I loved him, but both of us knew my heart was torn. He practiced what he called tough love, claiming it was for my own good, but I saw his anger and frustration with me as intolerance and disappointment.

I stepped out of the car and removed my mountain bike from the rack. The sun had risen above the clouds and the warmth of its touch on my skin heightened the good feelings. I shouldered the weight of my largest duffel bag and took my first steps toward the bus, feeling instinctively anxious about the unknown. I got a sense that the course of my life was about to change drastically and forever.

Without another moment's thought, I joyfully rolled my bike down the sidewalk toward the bus. I took in a deep breath at the sight of my mother waving and smiling from behind the windshield as I passed. At least she was happy for me despite what my father thought.

My mountain bike had accumulated a year's worth of stickers, style, and attitude, like a two-wheeled collection of adventure stories. I had completed a fourteen-hundred-mile cycling tour of the Pacific Northwest one year previously. I had started that trip alone too, riding from Seattle to San Francisco along the Pacific Coast on Route 101 for twenty-three days.

I leaned my mountain bike against the bus and walked back to the car to get two more heavy duffel bags full of gear. I had to make a separate trip to get a large cardboard box that held an incredibly special object. On my cycling tour through the Redwood Forest along the Lost Coast of Northern California, I found the skull and rack of a Roosevelt Elk. Immediately upon discovering it, I felt an overpowering compulsion to take it with me, even though it might be against the rules. Regardless, I cleaned off the dried skin and strapped the massive rack to the panniers on the front of my mountain bike.

A Canadian cyclist I met at the campground objected. He insisted that I ask the park rangers for permission to take the elk skull. To be honest, I felt a bit ashamed and irresponsible for removing it from the forest in the first place. I had yet to learn that you are supposed to take nothing but pictures and leave nothing but footprints.

To my surprise, the park ranger at Elk Prairie told me I could keep the elk skull. He explained that the felt was gone from the rack, so the field mice were finished munching on it, and if it was left on the ground much longer it would just turn to dust. He pointed out all of the skulls hanging on the walls of the visitor center and said, "We already have so many. We can't save them all."

Even still, I had always felt badly about removing the elk skull from its resting place in the Redwood Forest. It seemed like a sacred object to me and exuded spiritual power that I did not fully understand. So, I was planning to return the skull to the Elk Prairie after I arrived in California on the Green Tortoise.

Once all my gear and the large box holding the elk skull lay beside my bike, I walked toward the group of people gathered at the bus door. Cat Stevens was playing inside the bus. The curly black-haired guy with glasses turned his head and lifted his chin with a smile as I approached. He wore thin metal-framed glasses, with an Ozzy Osbourne concert tee shirt under his suspenders.

The others were clearly foreigners. I could hear the anthem of at least three different countries in their accented voices. Two British girls who appeared to be traveling together were introducing themselves to the Australian girl with the golden ponytail. There was a German guy with an artificial leg. A white sock covered the top part of a Velcro brace that went all the way up his thigh. His prosthetic limb had a hinge at the knee with a plastic kneecap, but his knee appeared to be working. I lifted my chin to him as I drew closer when he made eye contact with me. He did the same.

"Are you on tour?" asked the young blond English girl.

"No," I answered her, "I started a tour from Virginia Beach to San Francisco two months ago, but my knee blew out on the first day." I displayed the freshly stitched buttonholes on my left knee. "I had to have surgery, but I'm still going to San Francisco. I plan to live there."

"Hey man..." The curly-haired guy interjected. He paused and looked puzzled as if he had forgotten what he was about to say. "You're moving to San Francisco?" He stood up from filling the water cooler and walked toward me with his rolled-up notebook protruding from the pocket of his overalls. His kinetic body movement was even more pronounced up-close.

I looked into his eyes, "Yes," I said.

He lifted his chin with a nod of approval and said, "I moved there last year."

"Cool," I responded. "I guess you could say the Green Tortoise is my moving company." I gestured toward my pile of gear.

"Oh no dude!" His eyes got as big as saucers. "That's like, way too many bags man." He looked over his shoulder with concern at the driver whose back was turned. "Space is usually limited to one bag per person. So, do not let the drivers see your stuff. They get upset when people have extra bags," he explained. "If you don't mind putting your stuff on the roof, I'll help you put it up there before they catch on."

"That would be great," I replied with raised eyebrows. He understood my circumstances. For me, this trip was more than just an adventure tour.

He paused again and looked lost in thought. He bobbed up and down slightly with his neck and shoulders. "People call me Chicken Jim," he told me.

As he said this, the red-bearded man startled him from behind with a hand on his shoulder. The red-bearded man's eyes glowed and he smiled like a leprechaun. "I'm Chris," he said in a mellow tone, "one of your drivers on this trip." I thrust my hand out and he shook it. He thumbed over his shoulder, "You can load your bag under the back platform through the side door on the other side of the bus." He looked at my bike and pile of gear and winced. "Holy shit! You can't be serious," he reacted, shaking his head. "That's a fuckload of shit," he observed disdainfully. "We only allow one bag per passenger."

I felt a knot in my stomach, and I looked to see if my parents had left. I was relieved to see that they had not.

Chicken Jim spoke up in my defense, "I told him we'd help him load his extra stuff up on the roof with his bike."

Driver Chris tilted his head with a sigh of apprehensive approval and said, "Make sure you help the other passengers first," then he walked away without another word.

I was dying to see what the bus was like inside, so I grabbed my clothes bag and carried it around to the small, green emergency exit door on the driver's side of the bus. I grabbed the handhold next to the small door and used the recessed foot hole in the side to climb up. I loaded my duffel bag in the open space below the foam cushions while I listened to the music of Cat Stevens.

> *I was once like you are now, and I know that it's not easy,*
> *To be calm when you've found something going on*
> *But take your time, think a lot,*
> *Why, think of everything you've got*
> *For you will still be here tomorrow, but your dreams may not*

Just then, I heard the distinctive horn of the Oldsmobile. My mother was gone from the passenger seat and my father pointed frantically in the air toward the front of the bus. I jumped down and ran around headed for the door, just in time to see my mother's floral-patterned dress going up the steps. "Oh my God," I thought, "my mother just went inside the bus."

I walked quickly to the door and stepped in behind her. Several people were sitting up-front with their backs against the windows with their legs facing center. My mother was introducing herself to the massive blond-bearded, long-haired man sitting in the driver's seat.

I overheard him saying, "I'm Driver Brian, and yes, I'll be sure to take care of your son, Mrs. Mernick." My mother was speaking to a man with longer hair and more earrings than she had ever worn in her life. I tapped her on the shoulder.

"I just wanted to sneak a peek at the inside of the bus," she explained. "I haven't seen a bus like this since I was a teenager. How old is it?"

"It's a recycled 1954 Seattle Transit bus," the driver explained. "It's the same kind of bus Ralph Kramden drove on the Honeymooners. All of the original seats have been stripped-out of course."

"Oh, I just love it!" My mother said fondly.

Driver Brian continued proudly, "These benches in the front up here, slide out like futons and meet flush in the middle, so everyone can sleep while we drive through the night. We call it the Miracle Conversion."

"I love it!" My mother exclaimed.

The antique bus was the coolest thing I had ever seen. It reminded me of the forts my brothers and I built as children, using the couch pads to add comfort to our little caves. The thick foam cushions in the bus were covered with faded tie-dye sheets, laundered soft like a favorite shirt worn thin. The whole interior looked totally comfortable. It was like a rock-and-roll motor coach for Hippies.

There were no seats or anything like that, only communal areas where passengers could relax and hang-out. A wide center aisle ran between two built-in couches under the windows on either side. The original support bars for standing room only passengers were bolted to the roof above the front platform. The center of the bus featured a blond hardwood table with a pair of fixed benches across the aisle from a huge built-in ice chest. A foam cushion on top of the ice-chest made the space into a double bed, but the ceiling was too low for sitting.

There were no physical boundaries in the seating areas, but if you needed to be alone, take a nap or whatever, there were semi-private sleeping bunks hanging from the ceiling. These sturdy handmade wooden bunks ran above the dinette table and ice chest all the way to the back of the bus. The entire rear of the bus was one big bed where people could relax on tie-dye cushions stretching from window to window. A few of the foam cushions had been cast aside and the wooden hatch doors were propped open. The two British girls were rifling through their rucksacks under the enormous bed where I had stored my duffel bag. The whole bus was indeed one big bed. Nothing was cooler than this. For the next eleven days, the passengers would live, eat, sleep, drink, fuck, party, dance, discover and play, all within the confines of this crazy bohemian bus.

I was looking at the dashboard behind my mother's back while she inspected the rest of the bus and said hello to the passengers up front. The dashboard overflowed with cassette tapes, a stained map, flashlights, coffee mugs, a toothbrush, a dirty spoon, a brown paper lunch bag, scattered change, and various pieces of clothing including a towel and a pair of panties wrapped inside a bikini top. Beside the bikini top lay Chicken Jim's spiral notebook. The cover had been torn off. On the front page were words that read, "We LOVE with LOVE; Therefore, LOVE is LOVE." It was a mantra. Below these words it said, "You create your own reality!"

After taking this all in, my mother seemed satisfied, "It looks like you're going to have a wonderful time with all of these young people." She slipped a folded bill into my hand as she kissed me, whispering, "I didn't want your father to see this."

"I love you," I said. "Thanks."

"I love you, Johnny," she said back.

I felt reluctant to keep the fifty dollars, but she was off the bus and gone before I could muster a protest. Chicken Jim and his overalls came bobbing up the steps while my mother's expensive perfume still hung in the air. "Was that your Mom dude?" I flashed the folded president. "Hey man, that's cool," he said, bouncing to his internal rhythm maker, "I wish I was closer to home. I could sure use a cash injection right about now." He gave a knowing look to Driver Brian. "Help me with your bike and stuff," he instructed.

"Sure," I said.

"Then you can help me load the rest of the luggage," he added.

Driver Brian's shoulders dropped with a sigh.

Over his shoulder out the window I saw my father's Oldsmobile turning the corner of Essex Street, wheeling out of sight.

2
The Art of Adventure Travel

Inside the bus, Driver Chris had taken off his shirt and he was sitting at the dinette table reading from a business ledger. An incredibly attractive girl with flowing brown hair sat on the mattress close behind him massaging his shoulders. His red-bearded face exuded joy. There was a look in his eyes like that of a wise older person, like travel had taught him much about life. I longed to experience that kind of joy myself, to gain such wisdom and to learn about life on the road.

The huge man I had seen standing by the station door took up the rest of the bench next to him. He was setting up plastic pieces on a tattered chessboard. There was a pack of playing cards on the table next to him. It was a dirty deck of cards made in the seventies with a different half-naked woman on the face of each card.

The guy with the acoustic guitar had removed his leather jacket and was now sitting across the table from the man-mountain chess player. They introduced themselves to each other. "I'm Johnny from England," he said in a British accent.

"My name is Dave," said the big man in an incredibly slow, deep, and mellow voice. They shook hands. "Do you play chess?" he asked.

"Yes, but I'm crap," answered the Brit.

"Do you play to win, or do you play to play?" Dave intoned. His hairy jowls, massive body and broad shoulders reminded me of a buffalo.

"Err... to play," he responded.

"Then we can play," resolved the big man.

The black-haired guy who called himself Chicken Jim sat around playing songs on his guitar while the driver sold tickets. "So, you work here?" I asked him as I took a seat across the aisle.

He answered in a hipster voice. "Correctamundo," he said pointing his guitar pick at me with a nod. "I'm training to be a driver."

"That's awesome bro! I would love to be a driver. Do you get paid for training?" I asked him bluntly.

He kept using his hipster voice. "It's a labor of love bro!" He began plucking the chords to Ticket to Ride.

A cute American girl with light-brown hair came up the steps out of breath holding two reusable shopping bags and a soccer ball under one arm. She stopped before the top step and smiled at the huge blond-bearded driver. She was sporty and cute with an endearing sparkle in her hazel eyes. "Is this the bus to California?" she asked.

"Indeed, it is," the driver answered gregariously. "Welcome to the Green Tortoise."

"Wicked!" she said enthusiastically, looking inside the funky old bus. She gestured with her chin to her shoulder lifting her thumb under the strap of her bag. "Where do I put these?"

"Jimbo!" the relaxed driver called out. "Help this young lady with her luggage. Will you please?"

"I have more bags outside," she told the reclined helper, but he did not move.

A young kid wearing a San Francisco Giants baseball cap rushed up to the Bostonian and shouted, "Awesome! I love soccer!" He tried to grab the ball under her arm, but she turned away out of reflex. When he jumped for the ball, she raised it high above his head. "Awe! Come on!" he complained. She put down her bags so she could hold the ball in both hands.

A woman that appeared to be his mother scolded him. "Josh! Leave that nice girl alone." She had been combing her hair with a brush and a handheld mirror. She seemed annoyed at the interruption.

"It's okay." The soccer player softened. "As long as you don't mind."

"I don't mind," she replied.

She gave the ball to the boy.

"What do you say, Josh?" his mother prodded.

"Thanks," he mumbled. He winced when he licked his severely chapped lips. He tossed the ball in the air to himself, dropped it to the floor and kicked it down the aisle. He seemed overjoyed by such a little thing. Chicken Jim kicked it back and forth with him while the Bostonian stood there watching.

The driver smiled at her. "I'm Jen," she told him.

"Nice to meet you, Jen. I take it you're from Boston."

She answered with a distinctively native accent. "I'm from Arlington, outside Boston."

"Sounds nice!" he replied. "I'm Driver Brian."

"Where are you from Driver Brian?"

He smiled beneath his abundant blond facial hair. "I'm not really from anywhere at the moment," he told her, "but I grew up in California."

"Oh cool," she responded. "North or south?"

"Huntington Beach," he revealed.

"Awesome," she said. "I love Huntington Beach. I go to Cal State Northridge."

"Woe! Were you in the earthquake?" he asked.

"Not the big one but lots of aftershocks," she answered.

"How was that?"

"Pretty rough," she revealed.

"I hear that," he responded knowingly under his breath.

"Do people call you Driver Brian or is it just Brian?" she asked cutely.

"Driver Brian is my bus name," he said matter-of-factly, "but you can call me whatever you want." He smiled with shining blue eyes. "With forty people on board things can get confusing," he added.

"Everybody gets a bus name," interjected Chicken Jim.

"It's a Tortoise tradition," Driver Brian informed her.

"Everybody gets a bus name?" she puzzled.

"It's like a tribal name while you're on the bus, he explained. "We have our own way of doing things on the Tortoise," he told her with a smirk. "It's like a social experiment in communal living." He nodded contemplatively. "If you've never experienced life on the bus, it can be like living on the Moon. It's got a unique atmosphere." He chuckled knowingly. "That's the remarkable thing about adventure travel," he told her. "It gives you the opportunity to redefine yourself. It takes you out of your comfort zone. It inspires people to take chances, if you're willing." He nodded with her in agreement.

"Bring it on!" she cheered, pumping her fist in the air. "I'm always ready for adventure."

"Right on!" He pumped his fist in kind supportively. "With great risk comes great reward."

"I've been out of my comfort zone ever since I moved to Northridge last fall," she confessed. "Every day has been an adventure."

"Ha!" He laughed. "I'm right there with you. My life's been off the hook ever since I became a Tortoise driver." He shook his head in dismay. "I've redefined myself so many times, I don't even know who I am anymore." He checked a quick look in the mirror. "People used to call me Baja because I lived in Mexico." He explained, "I was the caretaker of the Green Tortoise Baja Beach Camp."

Her eyes lit up. "Wicked cool!"

He shook his head. "I don't think I look the part anymore. I totally lost my tan."

"I guess the name didn't stick," she observed.

He looked in the mirror again. "I've been on the road for so long, I'm not even sure who I look like anymore."

"You look like a Hippie," she remarked happily. "I love Hippies." She turned to me for confirmation. "Doesn't he look like a Hippie?"

I confirmed with several quick nods. "Hippies are cool."

"Are you a Hippie?" she asked him.

"No," he said, "not so much. I grew up thinking Hippies were cool though, so I will take that as a compliment. The Hippies were open to anything and everything. I'm open like that."

"Were your parents Hippies?" she asked.

"I guess they were 'Bohemian' enough to be called Hippies," he answered. We lived in a cooperative when I was a kid. My mother did yoga, reiki, and shit. My dad wore tie-dyes and followed the Grateful Dead, but I wouldn't say they were Hippies exactly."

"They sound like Hippies to me," Jen opined. "Compared to my parents, at least."

I spat a laugh and agreed with my eyes and a nod.

"Na," he disagreed. "If anything, they're Neo-Hippies."

"Neo-Hippies?" wondered Jen.

His shoulders moved back and forth in a cool way as he nodded. "The original Hippies had ethics," he expounded. "They did shit for a reason, you know. Neo-Hippies are way more apathetic," he scoffed. "My mom greets people with 'namaste' when she meditates at the yoga studio, but she doesn't acknowledge Buddhism. She's vegan, but it doesn't have anything to do with protesting the dairy industry." He shook his head no. "She's lactose intolerant." He chuckled. "My dad's cool enough, but he smokes weed that costs four-hundred dollars an ounce. I got so high with him once; I could almost see what he sees in the Grateful Dead."

"You smoke weed," gasped Chicken Jim. "Do you have any?"

Our blond-bearded driver continued without answering. "The Hippies may not have ended poverty, but their ideals are pervasive in today's society and around the world. I mean, we all wear blue jeans, everyone meditates and lots of people do yoga. I could go on for an hour all the good the Hippies did, but sadly, the real Hippie Movement died off after the counterculture got commodified."

"What do you mean commodified?" Jen asked.

He expounded. "Everything became a product like blue jeans. Everyone wears jeans nowadays. You can wear them in the office on Fridays."

"Blue jeans started out as a Hippie thing?" asked Jen.

He nodded in confirmation, making eye contact with her. "The Hippies wore blue jeans to promote solidarity with women working in Russian factories who were forced to wear denim dresses."

"Straight up," Jen cheered.

"Someone told me that once," he revealed. He went on speaking passionately. "Organic food is super popular now, but hardly anyone grows their own food, so no one can afford it."

"Seriously!" Jen agreed.

"There's a lot of image-consciousness among Neo-Hippies too. I suspect most of them would not be caught dead wearing a bumbag at WOMAD. They think they're dressing like Hippies when they wear Birkenstocks, but they cost a hundred bucks a pair."

"Aren't those Birkenstocks?" Jen asked gesturing toward his feet.

"Indeed, they are," he admitted. "Technically, they're recycled." He smiled as he lifted his legs and wiggled his deformed toes. "Someone left them on the bus awhile back. They're in surprisingly decent shape, considering all the hiking I put them through."

"So, you're not a Neo-Hippie either," she surmised.

"Nope." He shook his head. "I like to think I defy categorization."

"You do," she told him.

Chicken Jim had grown weary waiting for the conversation to end. "You can load your bags through the back door under the back platform," he told the Bostonian. He started playing soccer with the boy again.

"Jimbo!" The blond driver responded sharply. "Get out there and make yourself useful."

"Yes sir," he responded dolefully, but then he took the ball away from Little Josh again and started playing Monkey in the Middle.

"Jimbo!" The big blond snapped.

"On it," said the trainee, still not relinquishing the ball to the kid.

"Dude!" shouted the driver.

Finally, the trainee stopped playing and headed outside.

"I can load my own bags if you show me where to put them," the cute Bostonian said as she followed the black-haired youth down the steps. "Just show me where they go," she called after him. She hesitated on the bottom step and turned around to address the driver. "Do you need to see my ticket?" she asked.

The Art of Adventure Travel

"Ask Chris," he told her. "He's taking tickets in the back."

She disappeared for a few moments and came back up the steps totting even more bags. She now carried two larger reusable shopping bags along with the two she had earlier. "My ticket is in here somewhere," she told Chicken Jim. "I just don't remember which bag."

He followed her inside with a smug expression. "When you're ready you can put your bags under the floorboards in the back," he told her. The driver gave his apprentice the hairy eyeball, but he just tilted his head with a shrug.

I heard my name called. Driver Chris waved for me to come. I quickly checked my pockets, but I could not find my ticket either. I dug my hands into each pocket in turn, frantically searching each one as I walked up to the table. "I can't find my ticket," I told him in desperation. "I know I have it, but I'm not sure where it is."

I held my breath as I watched his hand move down the list of names in the ledger. I cringed when he made a mark next to my name. "It's all good," he said. "You paid-in-full. You're all set."

"Thank you," I huffed with a sigh.

"He needs to sign the waiver," said the girl behind him with a French accent.

"Ah! The waiver," the driver recalled. "I almost forgot."

"I need to sign a waiver?" I asked tilting my head.

"Everyone has to sign the waiver," he explained. In one fluid motion he pulled a sheet from a stack of dog-eared papers tucked in the back of the ledger. He tossed it on the table and slapped his pen down. "You can read it or just sign your rights away," he advised.

"What rights?" I inquired.

"Basically, you can't sue us if the bus breaks down or if you do stupid shit," he informed me.

"What happens if the bus breaks down?" I wondered aloud.

"You can wait around for the bus to be fixed, or if you need to be on time somewhere, we'll pay for a Greyhound to take you the rest of the way."

The British guitar player voiced his concern. "Isn't there a replacement bus?"

"No," he responded. "All of our buses are out on adventure trips. We'd have to put you on a Greyhound."

"What happens if the bus can't be fixed?" I asked.

"I don't expect that will ever happen," he said matter-of-factly. "She breaks down all the time, but we always get her running again."

"She?" I asked.

"We call her The Ark," he informed us proudly.

"How many miles are on the odometer?" I asked.

"No one knows," he informed me. "There's no odometer, but she's crossed the country more times than you could ever imagine. Some estimates put her at over 5 million miles."

The Australian girl with the golden ponytail dropped into the seat at the dinette next to the British guitar player. "That's a liability waiver? We don't have those in Australia," she said before I could answer. She snatched it out of my hands and read while talking. "We Australians accept the fact that it's our own damn fault if we do stupid shit."

"Be nice," I commented.

She slapped the waiver down on the table, gesturing at me with an upturned hand. I handed her the pen and she signed it. "Fair Dinkum," she concluded.

"Americans sue way too much," the Irish driver agreed. "It's true." He raised his voice for all to hear. "People have tried to sue us for stupid shit."

"Like what?" she asked.

He addressed the Aussie and said, "Like taking mind-altering substances and getting themselves killed." He tucked the signed waiver underneath his stack of papers and told the Aussie, "You're all set." He handed me another waiver.

She asked, "Do people get killed often on these trips?"

I laughed and listened as I perused the document.

Driver Chris smiled a big smile and laughed a little, "As far as I know, only two people have ever died on a Tortoise trip."

"For fuck's sake," the British guitar player voiced his concern again. "What are you getting on about?" The big man was resetting the chess pieces, having won the game.

Driver Chris seemed to like the attention drawn to him. "One passenger died after he sucked hot spring water into his nose to clean out his sinuses." He demonstrated by putting a finger on one nostril and inhaling deeply through the other. "He died from microbes that ate his brain."

"Oh God!" exclaimed the Australian girl. We all laughed.

"I've done that before!" said Chicken Jim, sounding worried.

"You ate a guy's brain?" teased the red-bearded driver.

"No, I cleaned out my nose with hot spring water."

"How revolting," remarked the Australian girl with the golden ponytail.

"Is it going to kill me?" Chicken Jim pleaded.

The French girl rolled her eyes and said, "You will be fine; you don't have a brain."

We all laughed. "How did the other passenger die?" I asked.

The Art of Adventure Travel

Driver Chris smiled like a leprechaun. "The other guy died on a Baja trip in Todos Santos, Mexico." This had us all listening intently. "There's a notorious riptide there, but this guy was a lifeguard, and he insisted on testing the water."

"I see where this is going," said the British guy. "Poor fucker went balls-up and lost the plot."

"Well, I'm not sure about that, but he died," said Driver Chris chillingly. "That's for sure. The rip tide carried him right out."

"Out to sea?" I asked.

"No," he answered. He gestured with his arm making a semicircle to the left. "The current brought him out to the reef where the surf pounded him against jagged rocks again and again until he was chewed to shreds."

"Oh my God! How awful," reacted the Australian girl. She looked away. She had heard enough, but I kept my eyes on the driver, suspecting that his story was bullshit.

"Are you serious?" I asked.

The red-bearded guide looked at me, nodding. "The last time we saw the guy he had gotten up onto his feet. He was covered in blood from head to toe, but he was waving like he was going to be okay. Then this huge wave came and swept him off the rock and we never saw him again."

"Holy shit!" I said. I was starting to believe.

"So much for being a lifeguard," miffed the British guitar player.

The driver nodded.

"Did he sign the waiver?" inquired the Australian girl.

"He must have," Driver Chris concluded. "Everyone signs the waiver." He motioned with his eyes for me to sign my name. I signed the waiver and took a seat next to the Australian girl who was now playing chess with the three-hundred-pound man in overalls.

Her accent bounded up and down, hopping on syllables like a kangaroo in a verbal mosh pit. She was telling him about her experiences as a scuba diving instructor working on an island off the coast of Honduras. She went there on vacation with her boyfriend, seeking to dive one of the world's greatest reefs before it dies from global warming. They ended up working for a dive shop. Over the next few years, they became managers and ended up running the place.

With dismay in her tone, she told us, "You can already see the tips of the coral bleaching."

"That sucks," I observed. "I guess it paid to be in the right place at the right time when you landed that job."

She explained, "When we first got to Honduras the dive shop desperately needed instructors so they could offer dive certification.

That is where you make the big bickies. People love to get PADI certified abroad. It is easier in a place with good visibility. We brought in so much income, we turned that place around. Our boss was a bit of a mongrel, so when we got the chance, we bought him out."

"I looked into getting scuba certified," I told her. "It's wicked expensive."

"That's a bloody oath," she agreed. "My boyfriend and I were skint when we started out, but we got certified for free in Australia. That's the only way we could have afforded it."

"How did you manage that?" I asked.

"We worked for a dive company on Fitzroy Island off the coast of Cairns," she revealed. "We got unlimited free training as long as we worked there. We were both Certified Dive Instructors by the time we bailed two years later."

"Where's Cairns?" I asked.

"On the Great Barrier Reef," she informed me.

"I can't believe you got paid to get certified," I marveled. "That's just awesome." I was blown-away. This girl was no older than twenty-five and she had seen parts of the world I never dreamed of. "I would love to do that," I enthused.

"You should do it," she told me.

"Yeah right," I scoffed in disbelief.

"Trust me," she advised. "People do it all the time. Dive operators hire as many people as they can find in the high season. You can never have enough dive-buddies for resort dives. You have to start out as a snorkeling guide, but they train you while you work so you can do resort dives."

"What's a resort dive?" I asked.

"That's when a tourist pays to dive side by side with a certified diver. It's the only way you can dive without having your certificate. You only have to sit through one fifteen-minute video and spend a half hour in the pool."

"That's awesome," I huffed.

She spoke passionately. "I'm telling you. They will hire anyone in the peak season. Just show up. Go to the docks, ask around, and I guarantee you will have a job by the end of the day. You might want to bring your boardies because they'll probably have you in the water before the end of the day."

"Where would I live?" I wondered aloud.

The answer was on the tip of her tongue. "There's a ten-dollar youth hostel right on the waterfront in Cairns, but we lucked out. We got to live in a bungalow on Fitzroy Island. We started as snorkeling guides and worked our way up."

The Art of Adventure Travel

"That sounds like the perfect job," I marveled. "Why did you leave Cairns?"

"Cairns was getting old," she remarked flatly. "The company we worked for visited the same reefs day in and day out, so we bailed. A lot of people in the dive scene work their way around the world. We met a lot of divers in Cairns who had worked as dive instructors in exotic locations." The golden-blond Aussie was a force-to-be-reckoned-with below the water, but not so much on the chess board. The Old-Growth-Hippie already had her on the ropes.

****

The soccer player with light-brown hair was still rummaging through her reusable grocery bags, searching for her ticket. She reminded me of Sporty Spice from the Spice Girls, wearing sweatpants and a tight purple three-quarter shirt. She was petite but solid. Her abdominal muscles were not discernible, but her fitness level was evident in the way she held herself. Her eyes sparkled with enthusiasm and her smile reflected an inner joyfulness that inspired me.

"Need help?" I asked.

"Yes," she exasperated. "I brought way too much crap. I know my ticket is in here somewhere, but I forget where I put it." She was about to pour out one of the bigger bags.

"Just so you know, you don't need your ticket if you paid in advance," I informed her. "I had the same problem and it was no big deal."

"Jeez, thanks," she said with a sigh. "I was worried there for a minute. I'll go ask him now." She seemed resolved to go but kept searching anyway. She poured out the big bag and began sorting through the items. She set her purse aside, a hair dryer, an extension cord, and two folded reusable grocery bags. "It doesn't make sense. I swear I put it in this bag." She removed a journal and flipped through the pages. "It's not here," she huffed.

"Do you want me to ask?" I offered.

"No," she said with a smile. "I got it." She began repacking her bags. I took a seat next to her on one of the couches. After her gear was re-packed, she stood up with all her bags and started toward the back, but at the last second, she hesitated, stopped, and rummaged through a different bag. "I found it!" she proclaimed.

She brought her ticket to the red-bearded driver and the French girl helped her load her bags under the floorboards in the back. After a little small talk, he checked her name off the list.

"She needs to sign the waiver," the French girl reminded him.

"This is my friend, Sandrine," he told her, stressing the word friend. He handed her a waiver and a pen.

The kid up front shouted, "We call her Sardine! She's a fish!" His mother physically constrained him with a tight hug and whispered something with her lips by his ear.

The French girl cast the boy an evil look. She extended her hand to shake and said, "I'm his girlfriend," she said, stressing the word girlfriend in a strong French accent. "Sandrine."

"That's a pretty name," gushed the Bostonian trying not to laugh.

"Merci," responded the driver's girlfriend. "You may want to read that before you sign it."

"I'd like to read it first," she told the driver.

"Knock yourself out," he responded.

"What happens if I don't sign it?" she asked him.

"You won't be allowed to ride the bus," French Sandrine revealed.

"Really?" she questioned the red-bearded Hippie-looking dude.

He just shrugged.

She read for a moment and sighed. Then without reading another word she put the paper on the table, signed it, and returned to her seat up front. She kicked-off her flip-flops, tucked her legs beside herself, and leaned in to listen to the driver-in-training strumming his guitar. It was endearing how attentive to his efforts she appeared, like she admired him just for holding the instrument before ever hearing him play. He saw her watching him and gave me a knowing look.

The German guy with the artificial leg came aboard and stepped up to pay for his ticket. He wore the classic garb of the Teutonic backpacker, sporting heavy duty hiking boots, tight shorts and a royal blue V-neck t-shirt with a German flag stitched to one arm. The logo of the European sportswear company on his lapel was a brand unknown by the average American. He looked like he was ready to go rock climbing or mountaineering. His hiking boots looked like none I had ever seen before, made of genuine leather, and heavier looking than normal hiking boots. He was well groomed and athletically fit like most of the other Germans I met in Europe. He was handsome enough to be popular with the ladies, but he lacked the chiseled jaw and bulging muscles of a model. He seemed well-educated from the way he spoke, and he was good-mannered, like his parents had done an excellent job teaching him respect for others.

"You're German," our red-haired driver deduced. "You must be Berndt." He made the youthful backpacker's name sound wonderful, pronouncing it like it rhymed with 'yearned.'

The Art of Adventure Travel

"Hey!" Berndt exclaimed joyfully. "You got my name right the first time." The German guy seemed genuinely impressed. "Americans never get my name right."

"It's terrible, isn't it?" our driver commented, shaking his head. "Americans always butcher foreign names. It's embarrassing." He traced his finger down the page. "Here you are," he said.

"What's your name?" I asked with an inquisitive tone, not wanting to be one of those Americans. "How do you say it?"

"I'm Berndt." He pronounced it slowly with deliberate purpose. His tone suggested that he had become accustomed to having to enunciate his name for ignorant Americans.

I was determined to pronounce his name correctly the first time and every time thereafter. "It rhymes with yearned," I said matter-of-factly. "It's good to meet you, Berndt." I put out my hand and said, "I'm Johnny." We shook hands.

"Likewise, Johnny," he said. He was unusually handsome with the bearing of an athlete.

Driver Chris spoke up. "You haven't paid anything, right?"

"No," the German confirmed. "I have paid nothing."

"So, you owe the whole fare then, four-hundred eighty bucks."

"I have travelers checks, if that's okay?"

"Yeah, for sure."

"Should I make them out to the Green Tortoise?"

"Please leave them blank. Sometimes we need to use them if we run out of cash," the driver said nonchalantly.

As he signed the checks he commented, "My college friends kept calling me Bernie until I couldn't stand it anymore. I finally broke down and told them it sounds like burned toast, and just like that, everyone on campus started calling me burned toast."

Chicken Jim stopped playing guitar and sat forward. "Dude, people call you burnt toast?"

"It's burned not burnt," he said, "and yes, my American friends call me burned toast."

The motley fool spread the word at once. "Hey Little Josh," he called to the twelve-year-old kid in earnest. "That dude's called burnt toast."

"Ha," the boy laughed. "That guy's burnt toast!" he announced so his mother could hear. "That's an awesome bus name." The boy's body sprung like a rubber band, lunging toward the dashboard. "I'll get the notebook," he trumpeted.

Chicken Jim sat back and strummed his guitar while the boy ran to the dashboard.

Driver Chris collected the German Guy's money and logged it in the ledger. The boy returned with the notebook and told Chicken Jim, "I need a pen."

"It should be in there," insisted the guitar player. He pushed his glasses on his nose with a finger and ran his digits through his curly black hair.

"It's not here," complained the boy. "Driver Chris!" he called out. "Do you have a pen?"

The red-bearded Irish driver responded patiently. "There's only one pen, and I'm using it."

"I have a pen," offered the German guy.

Little Josh went to his side by the dinette and took the pen. "Thanks," he said vaguely in thought as he put pen to paper. He eyed the German guy's prosthetic limb. "What happened to your leg?" he asked abruptly.

The hearty German's eyebrows jumped. "It had to be removed," he informed the boy. "I had bone marrow cancer in my tibia."

The kid cringed and said, "Sorry." He gave up writing and scratched his head as he asked, "How do you spell burnt?"

"It's burned. The German spelled it letter by letter, "B-E-R-N-D-T."

The boy looked puzzled, then he offered the German the notebook and the pen. "Why don't you just write it yourself."

Berndt looked at the notebook and asked, "What is this?"

"It's a list of bus names," declared the boy.

"Everyone gets a bus name," declared Chicken Jim.

"Yours is burnt toast!" shouted the kid with a laugh and a smirk.

"It's Berndt Toast," he corrected. "You don't pronounce the T."

"Ha! That is so funny," the kid laughed again.

"Where do you want me to write it?" he miffed.

"You can put it anywhere," he answered. "Put it next to mine." He pointed at the list. "That's me."

"You're Little Josh?" he asked.

"Yup," the boy confirmed happily.

"Who is Sardine?" the German guy asked.

"Ha!" cackled the little boy. "That's French for fish," he said, holding his nose.

"Josh!" The French girl scolded him, then she addressed the German directly. "My name is Sandrine," she told him with a flourishing hand.

"Smells fishy to me," spat Little Josh. He snickered with Chicken Jim.

"Guys!" the red-headed driver barked at them.

"Nice to meet you Sandrine. You're very pretty," the German guy complimented the French girl.

A blond and a brunette girl were next to pay for their tickets. I heard the driver say their names, "Sue and Tessa," but I could not tell who was who. I watched him check their names off the list. "Looks like you owe three-hundred and eighty dollars each."

"Bloody hell, we couldn't owe that much," the blond girl objected in a strong English accent. "You must have gotten your numbers in a jumble. We should only owe three-hundred each." She looked to her traveling partner for support.

"Yes. That is right, three hundred each," the brunette confirmed.

Driver Chris remained completely relaxed, "It says here you both paid a hundred-dollar deposit."

"Yes, that's right," agreed the blond.

"So, it's all set then," said the brunette. She tried to pass the driver a handful of money.

"No," said the driver, "there's the small matter of the food fund. That's an additional eighty bucks."

The girls seemed shocked.

"The food fund brings it to three-hundred-eighty dollars each," he confirmed.

"Oh, bloody hell, I forgot about the food fund," the blond looked at her friend in disgust.

"Yes, it seems we've dropped a clanger," said the brunette. She held up her hands in surrender and said, "I've got bugger all."

The blond girl started searching through her waist pack. "I've got four twenties, a ten and four fives," she said. They handed all their money to the driver.

"You're short fifty dollars," he said, putting the money into a folder without counting it.

When I heard they needed fifty dollars my hand instinctively went into my pocket to make sure I still had the money my mother had just given me. "I can loan you fifty," I offered.

"That would be smashing," said the brunette.

The blond's face lit up as she spoke. "That would be tickety-boo."

I handed her the folded president.

They both said, "Ta," and returned to where they had been sitting.

"We're good to go!" Driver Chris called forward to his partner. "I've got seven counting Michelle and Josh. It looks like everyone else gets on in New York." He went forward to speak with him.

I watched the chess battle going on at the dinette. Big Dave's moves were swift, but the Australian girl took her time with each move, occasionally biting the tip of her golden ponytail. She lost eventually, but it was impressive how she managed to hold her own against a more advanced opponent. He suggested a rematch, but she declined and got up to sit somewhere else.

I took a seat next to Little Josh's mother on the front platform. She was reading a novel called *The Gate to Women's Country* by Sheri S. Tepper. "Hello. I'm Johnny," I introduced myself.

She closed her book and looked up at me fondly. She rose to her feet to hug me. "I just met another Johnny, the guy with the guitar," she said, looking around back at the Brit. "I'm Michelle and this is Josh."

The boy did not respond. He was using her mirror to adjust his filthy orange brimmed San Francisco Giants baseball cap. He kept fidgeting with it. He bent the stained orange visor and put it on. He would not settle down and it seemed to be getting the best of his mother.

"Josh! Please sit down," she implored him. The boy gave in and rested on a cushion in front of her. I sensed him eyeing me with contempt under the brim of his hat.

"Hi Josh. I'm Johnny," I offered. He did not respond, so I asked, "How old are you, Josh?"

"I'm twelve," he answered quietly, tilting his head, "twelve and a half."

"I think your hat needs a bath," I commented.

The boy seemed annoyed. "Hats do not take baths," he snapped.

Michelle asked, "Is this your first time on the Green Tortoise?"

"No," I said, "I took the Tortoise from San Francisco to Seattle last summer, but that was not really an adventure trip."

"Oh, you took the commuter." She nodded and smiled. "Did you stop at the Green Tortoise Commune at Cow Creek in Oregon?"

"Yes," I told her. "It was amazing."

She nodded in agreement.

"I met a bunch of cool people in the sweat lodge down by the river," I told her. "It was awesome!"

"That's so cool," she said. "I heard about the Tortoise Commune. The drivers were talking about that last night, actually."

The Art of Adventure Travel

"You were on the bus last night?" I questioned.

"Brian and Chris picked us up at the youth hostel yesterday, so we didn't have to worry about getting here on time this morning," she answered.

"That was nice of them," I said.

Little Josh was fidgeting again, so she resorted to hugging him with one arm. She struggled to keep him contained in her arms, but he wiggled loose.

"I didn't know there's a youth hostel here in Boston. How was it?" I asked.

She replied, 'It was good to sleep in a real bed for a change, but Josh couldn't wait to get back."

"You were on the bus before?" I asked.

"We've been on the bus for weeks," she confirmed. "We took the Sunny Southern trip from San Francisco before this one."

My eyes widened, "Wow, that's cool."

"Yeah, it was a really great trip." She smiled. "I can't imagine how this trip could ever match up to the last one, but one thing is for sure. These guys are full of surprises."

"It sounds like it's going to be great," I said hopefully.

"I'm sure it will be. It's been really great for Josh," she said, looking off into infinity. "We live in Oakland and just needed to get the fuck out of Dodge. If, you know what I mean?"

"Yeah, I can relate," I told her. I needed to get out of Rhode Island, myself. I was living at home with my parents, you know. I'm twenty-three and my dad can be a real," I whispered, "asshole." I sighed. "I couldn't take it anymore, so I had to leave."

"My dad was my best friend," Josh said with a sniffle.

"That's great," I told him. "I remember loving my dad that way when I was your age, but that was a long time ago. Sorry to say, we are not really friends anymore. I guess it's normal to fight with your dad at my age," I added. I paused to wait for her to agree, but she did not.

"I don't think that's true," she said. I know plenty of kids who have great relationships with their fathers. You should be thankful your father is still alive," she said. "Good or bad," she hugged Josh with both arms. Her face appeared a bit haggard, and her eyes darted from my face out the window. "Josh's dad passed away last year."

"Oh, I'm so sorry to hear that," I swallowed hard.

"Thank you," she responded. "We miss him." I examined her expression. It seemed like being a single parent was taking its toll on her. She reminded me of a Rolling Stones song. She was the girl with the far away eyes. She was always off somewhere in thought, it seemed. "My husband was a workaholic," she revealed. "He hardly got a chance to spend time with Josh because he was on the road so much. He had been planning to take us on a cross-country trip for years before he got sick. I promised him I would still do the trip, but there was no way I was going to do it alone. Thank God we found the Tortoise."

Josh looked back at me with his hat in his hand and said, "This was my dad's favorite hat. He was a big Giants fan."

Michelle leaned in and kissed the top of her son's head. Michelle's husband had not been a perfect father either, but his son clearly loved him anyway, and that started to eat at my heart. "You're right," I admitted. "I should be glad my dad is still with us. I just wish we still had a good relationship."

Michelle smiled fondly, looking right into my eyes, "It's never too late, you know, until he's gone, and then that shit's forever."

I nodded contemplatively.

"We don't believe words are bad; It's all in how you use them. So, you can feel free to swear in front of Josh."

"Wow!" I made an expression like I was impressed. "I couldn't agree more." I was happy for the change of subject. "When I was training to be an English teacher, I had to teach a class in profanity," I told her. "I'm sure the administrators intended me to teach the kids to not swear, but instead we looked up the etymology of the word 'shit' in the Oxford English Dictionary. It turns out the oldest reference to the word shit appeared in the Bible."

"No way!"

"It's true. They replaced it with the word dung in the King James version during the Elizabethan era."

She seemed impressed. "See that Josh," she told her son. "How can the word shit be bad if it came from the Bible."

"Shit!" he shouted joyfully. He turned to Chicken Jim. "You're full of shit. Shit head."

"Now Josh," his mother rebuked him while we all laughed. "Remember the rule."

"Yes mom," he said.

"What's the rule?" He said nothing. "Repeat it to me," she demanded.

"Never use swears against people," the boy said.

"Now say you're sorry," she demanded.

"Sorry Chicken Jim," he said. "You're still full of shit."

"Sorry, I brought it up," I said.

"No worries," she responded. "He usually never swears."

****

The Art of Adventure Travel

Driver Chris casually took a seat on the cooler in the aisle next to the dinette. "Okay everybody please listen up," he shouted. "I need to explain a few things." After waiting for the passengers to quiet down he continued. "I'm Driver Chris."

"Hello Driver Chris," came back from the group in a mixture of accents. "You have all met Driver Brian." He gestured toward the other driver at the front of the bus. "Hello Driver Brian," came back.

Brian sat in the driver's seat facing backwards, relaxing one arm on the wheel with one leg draped over the wooden seat next to him. "Hello everyone." He waved. He spoke over the sounds of city traffic. "I've been driving for the Green Tortoise for three years."

"I've been driving for six," Driver Chris continued. "We also have a special guest on this trip. Most Tortoise trips only have two drivers," the red-bearded driver explained, "but Jimbo here is training to be a new driver." He motioned with his hand. "Stand up fool," he said with a chuckle.

The group spoke together, "Hello Jimbo!"

Jim stood up awkwardly. "Hello," he said with a wave. "People call me Chicken Jim. That's my bus name."

Together the group said, "Hello Chicken Jim."

The French girl hit him in the arm with the back of her hand. He looked back over his shoulder at her, like he suddenly remembered her. "This is my friend Sandrine," he reported.

She lifted her head to see everyone and said, "Hello."

There was a chorus of, "Hello Sandrine," but Little Josh clearly yelled, "Hello Sardine!"

Driver Chris waited for the laughter to trickle off and continued. "There are a few things you need to know about adventure travel on the Green Tortoise. We don't have many rules, but there are a few rules you will need to follow." His voice rocketed over our heads, too fast to understand every word, like a plane traveling faster than the speed of sound. There was a rumble of verbal recognition a few seconds later. "The Green Tortoise uses the buddy system," he informed us. "So, when you get off the bus to go to the bathroom or to go on a hike or to go shopping, or whatever, we use the buddy system to make sure everyone gets back on board before we leave. We are never going to do head counts or stupid shit like that. That's not how we roll."

Some mild concerns were voiced.

"Hey, you all need to pay attention." He cast a look at the fidgeting twelve-year-old. "Even you, Josh."

His mother hissed, "Shush," putting her fingers to her lips.

"When other bus companies stop at rest stops, they give you a time to be back on board, and if you're not there in-time the bus leaves without you. Then, you must wait for the next bus. On the

Green Tortoise, there is no next bus, so if you get left-behind, you're screwed. I must warn you. The Green Tortoise has left people behind before, sometimes in the middle of the night by the side of the road in the desert."

Most of us chuckled and smiled nervously, as Driver Chris continued. "The way the buddy system works is simple. Before we drive away, we will call for a Buddy Check. So, when you hear one of us yell 'Buddy Check, the rest is up to you. If you do not see your buddy, yell 'Buddy Check' back to us again until you find them. If your buddy is missing just let us know and we will wait. If no one objects when we yell buddy check, we will assume everyone is on board and we will leave."

More nervous chatter was heard.

Driver Chris sounded serious. "Each of you will need to make at least two buddies before we make our next stop," he instructed. "We encourage you to make at least two buddies, but feel free to make more. Remember, it is not our responsibility to make sure everyone is on the bus. So, choose your buddies wisely. Don't go choosing a buddy that you're traveling with, because then you both might get left behind."

There was another murmur of comments among the passengers.

I made eye contact with the boy's mother and asked, "Do you want to be buddies?"

"That's fine," she said tiredly. She was struggling to keep her son still.

"I'll keep an eye out for him too," I offered.

"That would be great," she said with a sigh.

Driver Chris waited for quiet and spoke again in a serious but mellow tone, "Once again, I repeat. Make your buddies right now. We will be stopping for a bathroom break somewhere between Hartford and New York in a couple hours, and we'll do our first buddy check then." He sat down at the dinette table. "This brings us to the second rule, the Pee Scale."

The German guy who Chicken Jim insisted on calling Burnt Toast asked, "Pee Scale? What's a Pee Scale?"

Our red-bearded driver continued, "As you may have noticed this bus does not have a bathroom." He paused, "But we cannot leave the highway to go searching for a bathroom every time someone needs to take a piss. Especially east of the Mississippi, we cannot just pull over and piss on the side of a highway. It is against the law. That is why the Green Tortoise uses the Pee Scale. The Pee Scale gives drivers enough time to schedule a bathroom stop before it is too late."

A nervous giggle rippled through the group of passengers.

What Driver Chris was saying sounded a bit like a disclaimer, like the one written on fireworks, except this one involved the potential

The Art of Adventure Travel

explosion of the kidneys and bladder. "The Pee Scale is a scale of one to ten. How badly do you have to go? A one on the Pee Scale means, I just went, and I feel fine, but a ten means it's already too late and I've pissed myself."

Many of us laughed at this point, but it seemed good to have a system. Who would want to have to stop every few miles when someone had to pee?

The red-bearded driver explained nonchalantly, "If you come to us when you are already at a nine on the Pee Scale, we probably won't be able to find a rest area before you have an accident. So, let us know when you're at about a four or five so we can plan ahead."

At that moment, the young boy stood up and yelled, "Tell them about the funnel!"

Driver Chris slowly turned his head toward the boy and gave him a look. His expression was like someone had smacked him in the face. The boy looked slightly embarrassed, although still delighted and amused.

The boy's sprightly mother grabbed his shoulders and sat him down on the tie-dye cushion in front of her. In one theatrical movement the boy tried to stand up again, but now the grip of his mother's hands held him in place. He kicked his legs up and banged his sneakers against the bench in surrender. "Josh, Chris is speaking, please don't be rude." It was a tired plea. The boy looked annoyed, but then he smirked mischievously and settled in to listen.

"Well," Driver Chris said, "Josh is right. We do have a pee funnel." He looked around at our faces. "For those of you who are brave enough," he turned his head as he spoke, "or desperate enough," he looked at the British girls, "you can always use the pee funnel in case of an emergency."

The whole group leaned in to get an ear-load of this. There was a cacophony of accented questions thrust into the silence after these words. "Pee funnel?" people from around the world asked, "What is a pee funnel?"

Driver Chris stood halfway up in his seat and looked toward the front of the bus. "Brian, can you show them the pee funnel and explain how it works?"

"Yeah," Josh snickered, "Show them how it works!" Josh's mother hid her frustration in her hands.

Driver Brian dropped his leg off the dashboard and slowly unfolded his other leg from beneath him. He stood up and stepped down into the stairwell. He was a mountain of a man. The bus was silently shrouded in a moment of mysterious wonder. I asked myself 'What would this curious twist reveal?' Most of us have probably read about the lack of a bathroom on the Tortoise bus in the brochure, but now, our six-foot-five, long blond-haired driver opened a small hinged door below the dashboard. He turned to us and smiled behind his huge blond beard. He stood there for a moment with his hands inside the glove box making some clunking sounds. To my dismay he turned around to show us passengers what was in the glove box. In his outstretched hand he held a large red funnel attached to a long black rubber hose. "This," he proclaimed, "is the pee funnel!"

"Show them how it works!" shouted the boy.

The driver held the funnel in front of himself to demonstrate. "It's really simple to use," he explained. His eyes widened with sudden insight. "Come to think of it, I have to go right now," he said flatly. "Excuse me one second." He stuffed the hose back in the glovebox and turned his back to us. He centered himself in front of the glovebox and appeared to unzip his shorts.

"Do it!" shouted the boy.

Sure enough, the driver of the Green Tortoise bus put his hand down between his legs like he was urinating. Little Josh was going crazy with laughter. The laughter was contagious. It looked like our bus driver was peeing in the glove box. The girl from Boston looked horrified, but she was laughing just the same.

"I didn't expect you to actually demonstrate, but that's cool," said Driver Chris, looking around at all of us incredulously.

Driver Brian responded with a shrug. "When nature calls, there's no sense in pretending," he said over his shoulder.

The thing that threw me off the most was the driver's completely relaxed attitudes. I thought, 'He cannot possibly be pissing in a funnel in the glove box, parked in the street in front of South Station.' My mind was simply not ready to believe it. My father's words echoed in my head. I didn't even laugh at first. Then, I saw him shake himself. I mean, I didn't actually see anything, but I certainly saw him make a shaking motion. Realizing that it might be true made me cackle. Then, he spun around dramatically revealing that his shorts were still zipped. He had been pretending for the sake of the boy.

"Stop!" cried the British girl. "I nearly peed myself laughing."

At that point, every reluctant bone in my body let go. My proverbial hair was let down. Everyone on the bus broke out in an unrestrained burst of heartfelt laughter, including Berndt Toast, the British girls, Driver Chris, Chicken Jim, Big Dave, Jen from Boston, Little Josh, and his Mother Michelle. Our drivers were off-their-heads, and this was certainly going to be an interesting trip, maybe the greatest trip of my entire life.

Driver Chris stood up after the laughter ebbed and he said, "I have a great idea." He sounded genuinely excited. "There's a swimming hole in Connecticut in the town where I grew up, and if we

The Art of Adventure Travel

get going right now maybe we can squeeze in a swim before we get to New York."

Everyone cheered.

Driver Brian slid into the driver's seat. He strapped himself in with the seat belt, flipped the run control switch and pushed the starter button, bringing the Tortoise bus to life. I watched as he stomped the clutch with his left foot, palming the stick shift with a masterful touch, waiting until the gears meshed inaudibly into the zone with a gentle push forward. Our journey began as we merged into Boston traffic.

I felt like I had shifted into a zone myself, meshing with these new people in this new reality, merging with my new friends. Everyone played along with our zany drivers with natural fluidity. Judging from the laughter, the high-fives, squeamish giggles, and good, happy conversation, everyone was on the bus.

3
Buddy Check

While driving west of Boston through the woodland hills of Massachusetts, I sat behind Driver Brian listening to him speak with the soccer player from Boston. "Where did you live when you were a kid?" she asked him earnestly.

"In a cooperative," he informed her.

"Is that like a commune?" she asked.

"Ha!" he laughed. "I should hope not." His eyes lit up with his smile. "A cooperative is a place you live with other people, typically in a place you could never afford yourself, but instead of owning your digs, you share the whole property. It's a bit like rent control."

"Like a condo?" she questioned.

"Not really," he informed her. "We were all about sharing resources with our neighbors. We lived in a yurt on a communal farm in Cupertino.

"Hell yeah," said the soccer player. "That's so cool." She had an athletic spirit to match her build. Just like Sporty Spice from the Spice Girls, she was a kickass brunette with an empowered attitude. She was smart and fun altogether.

"There are several types of co-ops in the Bay Area," Driver Brian explained. "Some are just apartment buildings, but there's almost always a monthly fee. In ours we could not sell our share when we left. We loved it there, but someone else started paying the fee and we lost our right to go back. The fees are stupid expensive in the bay area."

"Wicked!" I said. "I wish I grew up in a place like that."

"It was great," he gushed. "I would still be living there now if I could."

"Why did you leave?" asked Sporty Spice.

"There was a parting of ways between people living in the woods and the established people living in more permanent structures," he explained. "So, my parents fought against them, and we eventually moved away. They wanted everyone to pay the same fee regardless of where you were living. It was totally unfair. It did not make sense to pay the same money as someone in a house with running water and electricity, and heat for that matter. Some of the old-growth Hippies were still living in lean-tos and tents, sometimes just a hammock."

"I love the term Old-Growth-Hippies. I never heard that before this trip," I told him.

"They're still out there," he said. "There's no shortage of old-school tie-dyed-in-the-wool folks from the sixties in San Francisco."

"We walk among you in disguise," the boy's Mother Michelle suddenly interjected. She had a cool way about her. "We don't get the respect we deserve for trying to save the world," she opined. "The word Hippie isn't even capitalized in our language."

"It should be," voiced the Bostonian.

"I'm going to start capitalizing it," I told them.

"It's sad," observed Mother Michelle. "Many of your generation have lost sight of us Old-Growth Hippies and what we stood for. We fought for women's rights, we fought against the war, we were idealists, anti-materialistic and very much seeking out innovative ideas. We had a sense of purpose, like we were doing something good with our lives," she told us. "All that remains is a terribly commercialized relic of what was once a pristine and beautiful thing. Young people see us as desperately conventional because we value frugal living and buying wholefoods in bulk, instead of paying a premium for individual servings of frozen microwavable kale. That shit produces a shit-ton of waste." As she took a breath, the two women looked at each other and nodded in solidarity. She concluded, "If your rice comes in a box, you're definitely not an Old-Growth Hippie."

"That's funny," observed the Bostonian, "but I see your point."

"The kids today only love themselves," spat Michelle. "It's all about me, me, me."

Our driver's eyes smiled at the middle-aged woman in the rearview mirror. "I've got relatives in Humboldt who make a living building paths and doing farm work," he told us. "In my eyes, they're real Hippies, even though they don't have dreadlocks and wear bell bottoms. They are always very open-minded and welcoming. My Uncle once told me, 'It's not your position in life that matters most; it's your disposition.'"

"Right on!" I cheered.

"I can dig that," said Jen.

His shoulders rocked back and forth with the bobbing of his head. "Being a Neo-Hippie is more a badge of honor than a way of life. And when you are on the wrong end of it, it can feel less like peace and love and more like snobbery. I am always baffled by people who think growing up in a co-op carries social cache. I loathe that kind of bullshit; it's the antithesis of everything my parents taught me. We lived there because we were poor."

He looked from side to side, checking the mirrors and engaged the blinker. "Of course, I prefer to wear natural fabrics and eat organic food, but I do that because I'm worried about the impact my choices will have on other people and the environment," he told us. "Neo-Hippies are programmed to choose organic even though the word has become polluted by corporate greed to the point it's nothing more than a label used for advertising. It used to mean farming that was good for the soil, but it doesn't mean shit anymore."

"Not even manure?" I interjected.

"Sadly no," he scoffed. He smirked at the irony. "The fucking food conglomerates knowingly mislead customers by labeling their products 'All Natural' and '100% Natural' when in fact those products are riddled with pesticides. Food labeled 'natural' can still contain artificial ingredients, GMOs, antibiotics, and growth hormones. Just because food says it's natural doesn't make it good for the environment either. Yes, it is good that meat does not contain hormones, but that does not mean it is better for the planet. Humans have been genetically modifying plants through selective breeding since the dawn of history. The truth is, without GMOs a lot more people would starve to death each year."

He took a breath. His passion for the subject was evident in his fast-paced words. "Neo-Hippies can be so intolerant of other people's lifestyles too. Like, who are you to look down on me for eating a hot dog? Plenty of Hippies eat hot dogs without putting each other down."

"Someone dissed you for eating a hot dog?" I asked.

As the bus changed lanes, he turned his head nodding with his shoulders swaying. "I've seen it all, Hippie chicks calling each other out for shaving their legs, vegans who give you nasty looks for eating eggs." His eyes grew wide as he recalled, "I was once accused of being insensitive because I bought a non-vegan chocolate cake for a passenger's birthday party."

"That's crazy," commented the Bostonian.

"No way," I scoffed.

"We were in the middle of fucking nowhere, too," he reeled, shaking his head. "Do you know how hard it is to find a fucking vegan birthday cake in Buttfuck Minnesota?"

"I bet it's hard!" said Jen.

"It's getting there," he responded with a chuckle.

Jen's eyes widened and her eyes blinked repeatedly.

He continued. "I once got lectured for being in a monogamous relationship with my then girlfriend Mara, instead of being poly."

"What's poly?" Jen questioned.

He began by saying, "Polyamory is consensual, ethical, and responsible non-monogamy. We enjoy sex with multiple partners."

"Like an orgy," she gasped.

"No," he said with a smirk and a shake of his head. "I believe human beings are capable of loving more than one person at the same time romantically; at least I am. Polyamory is more of an agreement to be honest in a relationship while having the freedom to love everyone you want without the fear of being cheated on or betrayed like you can get with monogamy." He shrugged with a sideways glance. "As long as you're upfront and honest about it, you get to have sex with everyone you want without hurting anyone's feelings."

She shrugged halfhearted agreement before saying, "It still sounds like an orgy."

"The sex doesn't usually happen at the same time," explained the big blond-bearded Hippie-looking driver. There was a moment of silence. "Orgies don't happen very often," he told her.

"But they do happen," she said coyly.

"I've only ever witnessed one," he revealed, "and I spent most of my time that night discussing the benefits of polyamory with my fiancée."

"Who won that argument?" she questioned.

"She did," he said matter-of-factly. "That's the night I became polyamorous." He shrugged one shoulder.

She looked directly at him and gasped, "You're polyamorous?"

"Absolutely," he affirmed. "It works out really great for me as a Tortoise driver because I meet so many interesting people all the time, and I can hook up whenever I want."

"How's that not cheating if you don't tell her before you do it?" she questioned.

"It's all good as long as I'm honest with her when I get home. She has to be honest with me too, and we always require condoms."

"How do you know she's being honest?" Jen asked.

"I don't," he shrugged. "She can have sex with whoever she wants. We have agreed to keep it real, to be honest and open about our sexuality, our desires, and we agree to not hide anything, to keep everything out in the open in an ethical way that does not betray anyone. So, I don't worry about it."

"Isn't loving one person enough?" Jen argued.

"Is having one friend enough?" he shot back.

"You think it's normal to love more than one person?" she volleyed.

He shot back, "I think the real question is, 'Is it normal to love only one person?'"

"Don't you want to get married someday?" she pleaded.

"We're engaged," he told her flatly.

"No way," she said, rolling her eyes. "Is that illegal?"

"You're thinking of polygamy," he schooled her. "That's a religious thing involving one man and a bunch of subservient women. There is nothing natural about it. When you are polyamorous you embrace your natural desire for loving more than one person. Once you open yourself to it, anything else seems repressive."

"The Hippies called that free love," commented Mother Michelle.

"Awesome!" I cheered before turning across the aisle to ask, "How'd that work out for you?"

"I married the first guy I slept with," she revealed coyly.

"It always sounded so wonderful in the literature," I opined. "I studied sixties literature and the counterculture in college. You know, Ginsburg, Kerouac, Tom Wolfe, Aldous Huxley."

"What did that teach you?" she asked in turn.

"I was surprised to learn that there weren't as many Hippies as I originally thought. I mean, they were half-a-million strong at Woodstock, right?" She nodded. "I figured there were tens of millions of Hippies, but there weren't really."

"There was a shit load of us in California back in the day," she argued.

"Right on!" I said excitedly. "The Hippie stronghold has always been California." She smiled in recognition of her home state. "It was easy to drop out and live in the woods on a commune in sunny California, but dropping out wasn't as common in Boston and New York. It was too cold to live outside. The number of full-on-Hippies in the rest of the country, who genuinely dropped out, lived in communes, slaughtered their own chickens – true grassroots – was pretty small," I told her.

She smiled. "I'm proud to be one of the few true Hippies," she boasted.

Buddy Check

"Did you drop out?" I asked her.

"For sure! The movement was all about changing the world by withdrawing from it. There was so much corruption in politics, we set up our own little world where we could live organically and ethically and challenge capitalism."

"What did you do in the sixties?" I asked.

"I hung-out at the Hog Farm," she revealed.

"I heard about the Hog Farm," I expressed mounting interest. "It was a Hippie commune, right? What was that like?"

"Not much happened there, to be honest," she admitted. "We experimented with psychedelic drugs, we listened to lots of amazing music and we hung-out with other like-minded people from all over the place. I ended up living in a house with a shit-load of people in the San Gabriel Mountains."

"How many people?"

"There were like fifty of us living in a six-bedroom boarding house," she revealed.

"That's awesome," I praised.

"Not really," she spat. "Nobody had much money back then. We were able to eat, but only a few of us had cars or anything. At least gas was cheap, but we had to hitchhike a lot. Dropping out was less of a sacrifice than it would be today, but living a Hippie lifestyle, even for a little while, made people calmer and happier. Your generation could use a dose of that. Life has become so stressful and work is so demanding. You do not need to be on a spiritual path; you just need to yearn for fulfilment – that's what it's about."

"I can dig that," I told her. "I came on this trip because I feel like something huge is missing from my life. When I was a kid, I was so wide-eyed and full of interest and wonder. I guess you could say moving to San Francisco on the Green Tortoise is my way of dropping out."

"Right on!" she cheered.

The blond English girl that now owed me fifty dollars came forward to toss some trash. When I waved to her, she smiled, and on her way back she took the seat across from me.

"Hiya," she said. Her blond hair and wide-set eyes reminded me of Ellen Barkin in The Big Easy. "Thanks for the loan," she said, standing up to hug me. "Tessa and I will pay you back after we find a cashpoint in New York."

"No, problem," I said cheerfully as I reached across the aisle. "I'm Johnny."

"I'm Sue," she smiled. She was full of fun and had great energy. Her eyes sparkled with happiness and her whole face joined the party with her smile and adorable nose. You seem like a smart bloke," she said. "Are you at Uni?"

"I just graduated as a high school English teacher," I answered. "I'm moving to San Francisco to find a job."

"Jolly good," she said excitedly.

"I lived in London for a semester in college," I told her.

"Where in London?" she inquired.

"I had a flat in Emperor's Gate, near Kensington Park."

"Oh, that's posh," she said. "I bet it cost a bomb."

"Are you and Tessa traveling together?"

"Yes. We have been mates since primary school, when she moved to Brighton Beach. She has been dating my brother for years. She is family now. We are on our way around the world. We have work visas for Australia. We plan on getting jobs there for at least a year."

"That's so cool," I said admiringly. "You're so brave."

"We never would have done something like this without each other," she admitted.

"I did a solo bike trip last summer from Seattle to San Francisco," I told her. "Going out into the unknown alone scared the crap out of me at first. It was so far out of my comfort zone, but then I woke up one morning and I was so excited to get back to my bike. I loved seeing all that amazing stuff, the scenery, the coast, the people, everything. It was like my brain turned on. It was like I was a kid again all filled with wonder at every turn in the road."

"Where are you from originally?" she asked.

"Rhode Island," I told her.

"You come from an Island?" she gasped. "Is that the one near New York City?"

"No," I chuckled and looked around to see who was listening. I tried to not sound like I thought she was stupid. "That's Long Island," I said. "Rhode Island has a bunch of islands, like Newport and Block Island, but I come from the mainland."

"Oh," she said contentedly. "I'm from an island too," she said coyly. "An island with three countries on it."

"What Island is that?"

She tilted her head and looked at me like I was dumb. "Great Britain, silly." She shook her head affirmatively. "England, Wales and Scotland."

"I didn't realize Wales was its own country," I admitted to her. "Isn't Wales in Parliament?"

"Same government, different country," she explained. She looked to see if her friend was listening. She was.

"And you're from England? Right?"

"I am, but people from England prefer to be called British outside of Great Britain. English is what British people call themselves

Buddy Check

when talking to the Scottish, Welsh, or Northern Irish. 'British' is what British people call themselves when talking to Americans."

"I beg your pardon," interjected her friend. "I prefer to be called English no matter who I'm speaking with."

"I'm sorry if I offended you." I said, searching for something to say.

"No offence at all really," she said smoothly.

"And you are?" I proffered.

"I'm Tessa," she said demurely. "I'm Sue's best mate."

"Pleased to meet you Tessa," I said offering my hand. "I'm John from Rhode Island."

"Nice to meet you," she said offering me her fingers.

I grimaced at the guitar player. "I'll have to remember that you prefer to be called English, Tessa, and you prefer to be called British, Sue."

Thankfully, Chicken Jim rescued me. He stopped playing guitar and asked, "You're British Sue and English Tessa?" He chickened his shoulders back and forth three or four times like he thought himself cool.

"I am British Sue," acknowledged the blond.

"I'm English Tessa," acknowledged the brunette.

"Those sounds like bus names," he concluded.

"I beg your pardon," said the blond.

"British Sue and English Tessa," he said assuredly. "Write 'em down Little Josh." The boy proceeded to jot down their bus names in Chicken Jim's notebook.

Thankfully, British Sue asked me, "How did you get into cycle touring?"

"It all started when I broke my back," I explained. "An old man drove into my lane going sixty."

"Heavens!" she cried. "You could have died."

"I almost did," I informed her. "I broke my back in several places and I was told I would lose the ability to walk if I didn't take rehabilitation seriously."

"That's beastly," she remarked. "What did you do?"

"Desperate times call for desperate measures," I told her. "So, I bought a bike with the insurance money and rode fourteen-hundred miles from Seattle to San Francisco."

"I'm glad to see you have recovered," she remarked.

"I'm doing much better now," I told her. "I was in a lot of pain before I went on tour."

"When did you hit the road?" she asked.

"Two years ago," I told her.

"How did you like it?" she asked.

"It was the greatest thing I've ever done," I told her.

"You like to travel then?" she asked.

"I love to travel. It has helped me reconnect to a part of myself I thought I had lost."

"What is that?"

"When I was a kid, I felt like everything was more colorful and amazing. I had a really keen sense of wonder," I explained, "but something changed. It's like everything lost its luster."

"What's that exactly?" she asked.

I began to explain my theory. "When you are a kid, everything is new and fascinating, so your mind is awake and full of wonder. You are learning new things constantly, learning about the world, and your brain is turned-on, but as you get older your brain figures shit out. You get bored. You establish routines and your fascination with everything stops, your sense of wonder diminishes." I gazed into her eyes to be sure she was following. "Cycling the Pacific Coast brought my sense of wonder back for a while, but it left me wanting more. There's something about travel that seems to do it. It wakes up my brain. It lets my inner child come back to life like everything is new again."

"You're dreamy," she crooned.

I looked at her wide-eyed for a second. I was starting to really like this girl. "Did you spend much time in Boston?" I asked her.

"We just got back from Martha's Vineyard," she enthused. "We took the ferry with the English bloke over there." She pointed to the British guitar player seated at the dinette.

"Oh, you know him?" I asked.

"Hardly at all," she opined. "He was a bit ill-mannered when it came to saying hello."

"He didn't say 'ello a'tall," jabbed English Tessa. "He's a total prat," she indicted.

"He's probably just shy," I suggested.

"He's as skinny as a rail. He looks like he's got scurvy."

"He's not all warm and bubbly like you," crooned British Sue.

"We should be buddies," I declared, nodding at her enthusiastically.

Sue laughed and said, "Sure," she nodded in agreement, "as long as you look after Tessa as well. That would be just smashing. She follows me around like a sweet little moggy, I'm afraid. She goes wherever I go, that one does, and God knows she can't be trusted to stay dry in the desert."

"So, is that a yes?" I wondered aloud.

She got up to go tell her friend and said, "Thanks for the chinwag."

Buddy Check 41

****

The bus stopped at a roadside rest area on the highway somewhere near Hartford on Route 81 in Connecticut. The chess player in the blue overalls, Big Dave called me over as I exited the men's room door. His super deep voice suggested, "Would you like to go commune with the fish?" He pointed down a walkway leading to a gorgeous little pond covered in lily pads, surrounded by flowers, and manicured gardens.

I gave him a puzzled look, as I could not have guessed what he meant, and I wasn't in the habit of taking offers from strange men at the bathroom door.

He lifted a wooden cane and pointed his index finger at a stone-carved pipe hidden in the palm of his other hand. He clutched the pipe and hitchhiked his thumb toward the pond. He spoke so slowly it was a bit unnerving at first. "We mustn't keep the fish waiting."

I was not a big pot smoker, but I would smoke with the right people at the right time, so I said, "Sure, as long as we make it quick." We started walking and I casually said, "Nice pipe." He handed it to me as we walked.

"That pipe was carved for me out of soapstone by a Native American friend, a Navajo," he informed me. "I've had it for almost thirty years." The pipe was light blue in color and cool to the touch. The end of the pipe was carved into the shape of a fish head with eyes facing forward. Fish scales decorated the stem. It was perfect for a quick toke with a decent sized bowl. "It's my number one prized possession," he informed me.

When we got to the edge of the water, he passed me the lighter, I sparked up and passed both items back. While he smoked, I told him, "I have a number one prized possession." His eyebrows rose. I removed a red Swiss Army pocketknife from my pocket. "My father gave it to me when I was twelve, back when we used to get along."

"I can see why you like it," he observed. "That's a nice one."

"It has a locking blade," I told him.

He passed the pipe and I smoked. "Thanks for inviting me to commune with the fish," I related. "I've never heard smoking weed called that before."

"That's not what I meant," he told me before taking the pipe back. "I can speak to fish," he said matter-of-factly.

"Yeah, right!" I said.

"Would you like to see?" he asked. Smoke billowed from his nostrils.

I nodded and said, "Okay," with a tone of abject disbelief.

He closed his eyes for a second or two, then he leveled his raised hand. He waved it across the horizon of the pond like a magician waving his hand over a hat. Much to my dismay, fish broke the surface of the water at the precise moment his hand pointed in each direction. One, two, three fish jumped in various places along the path of his outstretched arm.

"Holy shit!" I gasped incredulously. At the last second before his arm fell to his side a fourth fish jumped out of the water, bending its body in the air. I put my hands on my knees bent over with laughter and amazement. "That was awesome," I marveled.

"Why do you laugh?" he asked.

"The fish jumped right where you pointed your finger," I said incredulously.

"Indeed, they did," he said. "I asked them to jump."

"No way," I spat. "That was just a coincidence. Fish jump all the time." I waved my hand across the pond slowly. Nothing happened.

"You need to open your mind," he suggested.

"I like to think my mind is open," I told him, "but I find it hard to believe you just made those fish jump simply by leveling your hand. My father always said, 'Believe none of what you hear and half of what you see.'"

"It's all in the mind, John. Your focus has a direct impact on everything in the universe. The outcome of your life is determined by it."

I was dumbfounded. "Okay," I said, "do it again."

"It doesn't work that way, Johnny. The Universe reacts differently when we observe it with a closed mind."

The words of Jim Morrison played in my mind.

> *Awake!*
> *Shake dreams from your hair*
> *My pretty child, my sweet one.*
> *Choose the day and*
> *choose the sign of your day*
> *The day's divinity*
> *First thing you see.*

"What kind of fish are those?" I asked.

"Brown Trout," he answered in an even deeper voice.

I chose the sign of the day, the Connecticut rest-stop Brown Trout.

I heard the air-horn and I looked up to see the Green Tortoise bus rolling across the parking lot. "That's our bus, Dave!" I yelled and ran as fast as I could, leaving him with the fish. I yelled for the bus to

Buddy Check 43

stop with Big Dave hobbling and yelling behind me. I heard the bus shift gears and I almost gave up hope. "No matter how fast I run," I thought, "there's no way I can catch the bus. My trip is going to be over before it begins." I felt a strong knotting in my gut and suffered a feverous plague of thought. How stupid of me.

Just at that moment, the bus stopped, and I heard the pop and hiss of the air brake. The air horn sounded again in two short blasts. There was Jen from Boston standing in the parking lot in front of the bus, waving frantically for us to hurry. Evidently, Driver Chris was serious about leaving passengers behind if you do not have a buddy looking out for you.

"Thanks Jen," I gushed with praise as I got near her.

"No worries," she said. She followed me up the steps. Inside the bus, I made eye contact with the British girl that was supposed to be my buddy. I shrugged but she just smiled dumbly.

"He's going as fast as he can," I told the driver.

"I didn't realize it was him," he admitted.

I watched out the open door of the bus as Big Dave's huge hand gripped his thick wooden cane, trying to move his massive frame as quickly as he could with great determination. He hobbled noticeably when he tried walking fast but he could not run, not even to save his life. "Thank you, Johnny," he said as I stepped off the bus to let him pass.

"We should be buddies," I followed him with my words.

"I'd like that," he intoned deeply.

"No problem, Buddy," I said and patted him on the back. "Nice job getting back here so fast." He was clearly exhausted from the short run. He checked his pulse with two fingers on his wrist. He asked the little kid to push over and flopped down at the dinette to rest. The bench across from him was empty, so I took a seat.

Having witnessed him communing with the fish, Big Dave and I were now on a similar wavelength. I always thought I had an open mind, but I started calling that assumption into question. I remained cautiously skeptical, but I was eager to learn more. I took out my pocketknife and started playing with the blades, extending all of them at once then closing them up one by one as I thought about everything.

The boy seemed fascinated. "Can I see?" he asked.

"Sure," I said, "just be careful.

"I promise," he said eagerly, grabbing for the knife.

Big Dave spoke in an incredibly slow, deep, and mellow voice. "Do you play chess?"

"I've played before, but I'm not very good," I said.

"Do you play to play, or do you play to win?" he intoned, as he went about setting up the plastic pieces.

"Ouch!" wailed Little Josh. He had cut his index finger with the knife. It was bad. The boy burst into tears. He was wailing crying. "Ahh! Ahh! Ahh!"

"Oh, that's just great," I huffed, angry with myself for letting him play with it. The big man took out his handkerchief and offered it to the boy. I asked, "Where's your mother?" Big Dave pointed over my shoulder.

She was already on the scene walking up behind me. "What is it now?" she demanded.

"I'm bleeding," he cried. He released the grip on his finger. The tip had a curved slit in it the size of a staple. There was an abundance of blood considering the size of the wound.

"Oh my God!" His mother was beside herself. "How did you manage to do that?"

The boy smirked at me and said, "I was trying to close this knife."

"How many times do I have to tell you not to touch other people's stuff?" she chastised him.

"He said I could use it," her son protested.

"Who?"

"That guy," he squealed, pointing at me.

"You let him play with your knife?" his mother asked flatly.

"Sorry," I said sheepishly.

She just rolled her eyes. Chicken Jim brought the medical kit and she bandaged his finger.

I spent the time cleaning up stray drops of blood with the handkerchief. It was everywhere. He had somehow managed to splatter blood in an arc like a rainbow. I had to clean blood off the chess board, the seat, the back of the seat, and the ceiling above the table. It was unreal.

Before we got back to playing chess, Big Dave told me more of his life story. "I'm just an old Hippie," he told me.

"Michelle said she's a Hippie too," I related.

"I figured as much," he intoned, "but that's good to know."

"She called herself an Old-Growth-Hippie," I confirmed.

"I'll have to introduce myself," he said with a tilted head looking for her up front. "I'd like to meet her," he mumbled in a deep guttural tone. "I hope she wasn't one of those long-haired Hippies they always show on TV protesting in Golden Gate Park. Most of those Hippies were just copycats and wannabes. That bullshit came long after us. We were the-real-deal. I was twenty-six at Woodstock. I worked security for Joe Cocker, Joni Mitchell, and Sly Stone."

"No way! That is awesome," I said, taken aback. "Holy shit!" I scrunched my face and nodded in amazement. "That's so freaking cool."

"It was an excellent job to have at that particular time," he concurred. "I eventually became a road manager and traveled with a bunch of really famous talent and I got to know a bunch of folks like Janis Joplin and Jimi Hendrix."

Hearing this got me totally excited. "Did Hendrix really drop acid all the time?"

He answered with his eyes. "We all did."

"Ha!" I laughed "You said we. It sounded like you dropped acid with Jimi Hendrix."

"I was there for it all," he revealed. "His crew ate a ton of acid, but they did a lot of hard drugs too. The establishment tried to tell us all drugs were bad, so when we figured out some drugs were good, we tried them all. That was before people started dropping dead. Obviously, some drugs are worse than others. Smoking weed is much different than popping butyl nitrite, huffing ether, and shooting heroin and crazy shit like that. Our generation paid a heavy price for those mistakes. Hard drugs killed so many great musicians."

"It's such a shame," I commented. I was blown-away. I was so excited to hear this. "I studied sixties literature in college," I told him excitedly. "I read all the books on psychedelia, the Doors of Perception, The Electric Kool-Aid Acid Test." I nodded enthusiastically. "I wasn't born until '68," I told him. "I've always loved he Hippies, but I feel like I missed out on it completely." I was all smiles. The sixties fascinated me. "So, what was it like being a roadie?"

"I was never a roadie." He heaved a big breath. "I managed security for bands. I spent a lot of my time in rock coaches like this one back when I worked personal security for the talent. I eventually became a road manager, but all of that ended when I got shot."

"You got shot?" I asked incredulously. I put my hand on his shoulder, "Holy shit! Sorry to hear that. Where did it happen? Was it at a show? Altamont?"

"Hardly," he scoffed, "I was in a convenience store in New York City, buying a pack of smokes," he explained. "This guy pulled out a gun and started demanding money. I reached for my wallet and he shot me right here." He pressed two fingers under his rib cage.

"Wow!" I said exhaling. "That fucking blows."

"I knew smoking might kill me, someday, but I never could have guessed it would happen this way." He straightened himself like he could still feel the pain. "The bullet is still lodged in my spine. The doctors said it's too dangerous to operate."

I looked at him in disbelief, shaking my head. "Are you okay? Are you in pain?"

"I'm in constant pain," he revealed.

"I'm sorry to hear that," I consoled.

"The marijuana helps," he claimed.

"That's good," I said.

His voice saddened. "The spine damage slowed me down at first. I had to quit my job as a road manager."

"That's too bad," I lamented.

"My physical therapist saved me. He started me on lower body workouts and I never looked back."

"That's great," I praised.

"Yeah," he concurred. "As long as I keep my spine isolated, I can leg press five hundred pounds."

"Holy shit!" I marveled. "That's incredible. Were you able to go back to your job?" I asked.

"No," he said. "Everything changed by the time I got back on my feet."

"That's too bad," I appraised.

"Do you ever think of going back?" I wondered.

"Na," he said, shaking his head. "I put on so much weight over the years; there's not a whole lot of jobs I can do."

"What do you do now? Do you work?" I inquired.

He looked glum. "I work part time," he bemoaned, sounding humiliated. "I push around a mail cart delivering interoffice mail. I'm not the sharpest tool in the shed either," he concluded.

"Why do you say that?" I questioned. "You seem smart to me."

"My friends are worried that the lead has started to affect my mind, but hell, I can't tell. That's what scares me the most, the thought of losing my mind and having no fucking clue all the way to the nuthouse."

"I don't see it," I informed him. "You play chess for-crying-out-loud. You're good at it."

"Do you want to play again?" he asked. So, we did.

4
Skinny-Dipping in Connecticut

About fifteen minutes after the rest stop, the bus pulled off the highway onto a two-lane country road lined with tall pine trees somewhere west of Hartford. Less than a mile later at a nondescript break in the tree-line we turned onto a primitive single-lane dirt road that ended in an open field at the foot of a hill. The bus listed severely on the grassy slope as our driver turned the bus around, throwing passengers side to side and back again as he made a three-point-turn. The bus came to a halt facing the direction we had come, and Driver Chris set the air brake with a pop and hiss.

The bus parked on a dead-end dirt road within sight of the highway. Pine trees populated a hillside between the highway and the pond, muffling the roar of engines and car horns, creating an oasis yards away from the motorized mayhem.

Driver Chris stood up next to the driver's seat to make a brief announcement. He bent down a little and pointed out the window. "The swim-hole is down the path over there. Just follow that trail. You can't miss it." He sat back down and stroked his red beard and tucked his long hair back behind his ears. "This place is completely private and we're only going to be here for about an hour. So, you do not need to waste any time digging out your bathing suits and towels or stuff like that. There's no place on the bus to hang wet clothes to dry." He reached over and opened the noisy door with a screech. "We will blow the horn when it's time to go." As an afterthought he advised, "Don't worry about the sunken car. It's been there forever."

"Sunken car!" shouted Little Josh enthusiastically. "Yay!" He pulled his mother's hand. "Come on, let's go."

The brunette soccer player from Boston remained seated while everyone else exited the bus. I sat across from her to put my boots on and asked, "Are you going to swim?"

"No," she answered abruptly. "I'm all set. My swimsuit is buried under the floor in the back, and there is no way in a million years I am going skinny-dipping. That's just nuts."

"I could help you find your bag," I offered.

"No, it's fine," she replied. "I'm good." She was so sweet, demure, and unassuming, with an assertive self-determination that told me she was trying to manifest independence.

I had to agree with her. Having grown up in Rhode Island, skinny-dipping in Connecticut sounded crazy, but I had to go along with it. I was swept-up in the excitement and swimming in the oppressive heat sounded great, suit or no suit. So, I said, "Stay cool," and stepped outside to join the others. The sky was a clear New England summer of blue. The heat of August in New England pressed down upon us, baking our hair and skin.

Chicken Jim led the charge, skipping like a stone down the path to the pond, taking off his shirt as he ran. Driver Brian walked with Mother Michelle and her son, followed by the other driver's French girlfriend and six of the new passengers. The footpath was well-worn and easy to follow, but it was obvious we would have this hidden sanctuary entirely to ourselves.

At the edge of the pond, we all stood around for a minute, not knowing what to think or where to begin. A blanket of thick orange pollen covered the surface of the water. Chicken Jim was already standing knee-deep in the water with his blinding white butt-cheeks displayed for all to see. A rusty old antique car that looked like it had been there for a generation sat submerged up to its missing windshield on the opposite bank about fifty feet away.

The big, old, American gas-guzzler had come through the pine forest on the hillside without hitting a single tree. It had careened down the hill off the highway, probably the result of an accident. The passengers speculated as to whether or not anyone had been hurt, or if the car had been stolen and was pushed down the hill to hide the evidence.

Big Dave was the first passenger to start undressing. When he dropped his overalls, I could not help but notice his lack of underwear. His calf muscles were enormous. Without thinking, I quickly followed suit. Soon, I was standing next to a three-hundred-pound naked Old-Growth-Hippie ankle-deep in the warm water. I was now ready to commune with a whole new group of fish.

Skinny-Dipping in Connecticut

Some of the other passengers started to undress as Big Dave waded in. He made a big wave as his chest entered the water, parting the pollen like an icebreaker in the Bering Sea. He moved slowly, clearing the pollen with his hands as he walked, leaving a giant wake of clear water behind him until he was up to his trunk in the divine liquid tranquility of the small pond. He rolled over on his back with his belly protruding above the water. He swam gracefully and majestically on his back, singing, "I feel like the Prince of Whales." Swimming seemed to be therapeutic for Big Dave, like fog for a redwood, relieving his massive body from the straitjacket of gravity.

A thin layer of mud squished between my toes as I took a few steps forward. I was knee-deep in the pond with little waves lapping at my knees as other swimmers began to join me in the warm water. The reflection of the blue sky and green pine trees made the surface of the water look as black as space.

Just then, Chicken Jim came bounding past me splashing, yelling, and flailing his arms. "Last one in's a rotten egg!" he exclaimed.

I dove in, keeping my head above the surface and rolling over on my back as soon as I was afloat. I had put on a few pounds, having just had surgery from a knee injury that had kept me inactive for several months, but the water in the pond seemed incredibly buoyant. Maybe it was the pollen, but the water felt wonderful on my skin, like I was experiencing something new, almost surreal, and magical.

The French girl stripped down without hesitation, revealing her deliciously feminine curves and voluptuous bosoms. When Driver Brian removed his shirt, one could not help but notice his nipple rings. He dove in and swam past me on his back, making loud clunking sounds as he kicked. He looked quite different in the water, more relaxed with his blond beard all wet like a sea otter. "Come on in! It's warm!" he called out to the others.

The British Girls undressed casually, but no one else got naked at first. The guy wearing the Lou Reed leather jacket kicked his heels for a while on the bank and slowly took off his black boots and blue jeans, opting to swim in his tighty-whitey-underwear. The German guy with the prosthetic leg took off his shirt and laid in the sun on the sloped bank, but he never went swimming. The girl with the golden ponytail swam topless but kept her panties on. Little Josh swam in his soccer shorts, while his mother modestly entered the water in her bra and panties. Although, she did toss her bra on the shore once she was in the water.

British Sue snapped pictures of the sunken car, standing up to her waist in the dark pond, naked and beautiful. She had an interesting body to match her accent, with curved hips, athletic arms, and large, naturally shaped breasts with button-sized nipples. She sounded worried when she asked Driver Brian, "Are there any fish in there?"

"Well, it's not the fish that you need to worry about," he explained. "The fish don't bite." He lifted his head out of the water, looking directly at her. "It's the beaver that you need to watch out for."

British Sue backed slowly up the bank, peering into the dark mirror of the pond. In her most prim-and-proper English tone she asked incredulously, "And what beaver might that be?"

Chicken Jim said, "It is true what they say about girls' eyebrows. The carpet matches the curtains."

"Don't be a pig," advised his boss.

Now, I could see the beaver myself. Her beauty surpassed that of the others right down to her blond hair. I kicked a backstroke with the heat of the sun on my face, beaming a joyful smile projected at the perfect blue sky.

I overheard Driver Brian talking with Chicken Jim. "Have you ever gone skinny-dipping before the Tortoise?" he asked the trainee.

"Yes," he answered with a laugh. "My first and only other time was a complete accident, in Yosemite."

"You went skinny-dipping by accident?" inquired the blond driver.

I swam through the orange pollen to get closer to Chicken Jim so I could hear his story.

"Yes," he began. "My college roommate and I got high and went swimming in the pools below Lower Yosemite Falls."

"That sounds awesome Jimbo!" said the driver.

"We were sliding down these super slippery channels in the rock and launching into the air like a water slide."

"Wicked," I said.

"The water is freezing in Yosemite even on the hottest day of summer," he told us.

"I didn't realize that swimming is allowed there," I commented.

"I think you can swim at your own risk anywhere in Yosemite, but I really have no idea. I was just following my friend." Chicken Jim turned toward me. When he saw I was listening intently he smiled before continuing. "So, a whole crap-load of tourists were watching us slide down the rockslides from behind the railing on the observation platform. Most people just follow the paved path and find themselves trapped and crowded on this little pressure treated deck, when, in actuality, they could hike anywhere they want."

"Every time we slid down the rockslides, we had to hike back up to go again," he continued. "So, I get to the top this one time and my friend comes up behind me laughing his ass off. He's like 'You're a funny bastard.' I had no idea what he was talking about, so he points and says, 'look behind you.' The tourists on the observation deck were all laughing and pointing at us taking pictures and shit. 'No not them! Look at your shorts,' he says, and I turn to see my shorts were ripped wide open, right down both sides leaving my ass flapping in the breeze.

"Ha," I laughed loudly. "What did you do?"

"I just took 'em off and threw 'em away," he told us.

"That's funny," laughed the Driver Brian.

"Were you embarrassed?" I asked.

"No," he stated proudly. "I couldn't have cared less. Ever since that day, I don't worry about getting caught with my pants down. I just walk like I'm not wearing any pants." We all had a good laugh at that. "People may laugh at my little yellow wiener, but I know, 'It's the little acorn that becomes the mighty oak."

"How about you, Johnny?" asked Driver Brian. "Is this your first-time skinny-dipping?"

"No," I explained, "My first time was at the Green Tortoise Commune in Oregon."

"Oh, cool you've been to Cow Creek," he said.

"So, let me get this straight," Chicken Jim interjected. "You know the Tortoise is a cult, yet you still want to be a driver?"

I laughed.

"Seriously," spat the curly black-haired trainee. It was like he was trying to dissuade me.

Before he had a chance to explain, Driver Brian scolded him with his eyes and changed the subject. "Cow Creek is awesome, he said. "Did you stay for long?"

"No, we just woke up there in the morning and split after breakfast."

"Ah, northbound," he said. "Where were you headed?"

"To Seattle," I explained. "I rode a bike tour around the Olympic Peninsula back to San Francisco on Route 101."

"What made you decide to do that?" he asked.

"I was in a car crash, and they told me I would lose the ability to walk unless I did some serious rehab, but I had no idea how radically different living on a bike would be. It scared the crap out of me, but it was the most awesome thing I have ever done. Every day I was blown-away by the most amazing shit. I learned so much. The exercise altered my body and I think it changed my brain chemistry for the better."

"That's freakin' sweet dude," said the blond-bearded driver. "That must have been quite a trip."

"I did some of my driver training on the Olympic Peninsula," commented the trainee. "It's impossible to shift on hills like that."

"It's not impossible Jimbo," commented Driver Brian. "You need to learn how to shift to pass your driver's test. You need to pass that test to get a license. You'll never get promoted without a license. You need to sit up front more so you can learn how to shift on hills."

"I'll get around to it. I promise," said the rookie.

"Are they still clear-cutting the Redwood Forest?" asked the driver.

"Yeah, pretty much," I answered. "I saw a lot of signs that said, 'This Home Built by Timber Dollars' and bumper stickers that said, 'I Eat Spotted Owl for Lunch.'"

"That's just sad," Brian lamented as he clunked his feet and drifted away.

The girl with the golden ponytail swam over and Chicken Jim asked her, "Are you from down under?"

"Yes. I'm from Australia," she told him with a strong accent. "I'm Sheila."

"Ha!" he laughed. "Like Crocodile Dundee?"

"Good on ya," she said sarcastically.

"Doesn't Sheila mean chick or something?" he pressed.

"Sheila is slang for woman," she informed him flatly.

"That should be your bus name," he declared.

"How creative," she said sarcastically. "Like I haven't heard that before."

"Australian Sheila. That's cool," he said. "It's easy to remember. What's wrong with that?"

"It's fine," she snapped.

"Is Sheila a derogatory term?" I questioned.

"Back home it is," she said, nodding, "but I get it all the time in the states."

"That's not cool Jim," I commented.

"Really, I don't mind," she restated.

"It's settled then," said the rookie.

She was strong yet adorable. I eagerly introduced myself. "I'm Johnny," I told her. "I'm from Rhode Island."

She dipped her hair in the water luxuriantly and said, "Nice to meet you, Johnny."

"Nice to meet you too," I told her.

"I'm from Pennsylvania," the driver-in-training told her proudly. "They call me Chicken Jim."

"How could I forget," she said vacantly.

"Hey Josh, he called out, "We got a new bus name over here." He swam away to tell the boy.

The Bostonian arrived at the end of the trail and stood by the water's edge with her hands on her hips, surveying the orange pollen

Skinny-Dipping in Connecticut 53

and the half-sunken car. Hesitantly, she hoisted her three-quarter shirt over her head, revealing a black sports bra. She untied her sweatpants, looked around, kicked off her flip-flops and dropped her pants. She had an athletic build. She hurried into the water. After her panties were wet, she turned toward the bank, unclipped her bra and tossed it ashore. She waded through the pollen, rolled over onto her back, and kicked with her strong legs.

The boy let out a yell, "Who wants to check out the car!"

"Be careful Josh," his mother called out, and she started swimming after him.

When he reached the car, he put his hand on the half-submerged hood and waited for his mother to get closer, then he swam around and tried opening the door. When that failed, he struggled up the bank and approached the car by land. He put his foot on the bumper and tried to push the car into the lake unsuccessfully. He climbed up onto the trunk.

"I said be careful Josh," his mother reminded him.

"It's fine," he answered back. With one big tentative step he mounted the roof of the half-sunken car. He looked triumphant. He was a little apprehensive at first, having to use his hands to steady himself as he climbed higher. When he realized the roof would hold his weight, he stood up and jumped off. He landed close to his mother and held onto her hand on the surface of the pollen coated water.

"That looks fun," I coaxed the Bostonian.

She smiled with a laugh. "You'd like that wouldn't you," she huffed.

"Suit yourself," I replied before swimming closer. With Mother Michelle an arm's length away, I submerged to test the depth of the water in front of the car. I opened my eyes on the way down and glanced at the older woman's nude body.

When I broke the surface she asked, "Whatcha think?"

"It's perfect," I responded without a second thought. "Perfectly deep," I clarified.

"I get you," she said coyly as if she knew I had checked her out.

I made my way to the bank and climbed onto the trunk and then stepped onto the rusted roof. The solid steel frame did not buckle beneath my weight like a modern car. I dove in. It was awesome, so I went back for another dive. On the roof of the car, I helped Josh up.

"Thanks buddy!" he said.

"No problem," I replied. He did a cannonball off the roof. I followed suit, doing my first ever naked cannonball. I repeated the process and alternated diving in and jumping off. A while later I joined the group of passengers drying off in the sun, choosing to lie down in the grass next to British Sue and English Tessa. I was happy to see Jen from Boston make a cameo appearance on the roof of the old car. After climbing up onto the roof, she modestly covered her chest and jumped in with her arms folded like Aladdin. Her legs were nothing but hard muscle.

Right about then Driver Chris came running down the trail to the pond with nothing on but shorts. He kept running until the edge of the water where he kicked off his sandals and dropped his shorts.

"What's the rush?" shouted Driver Brian.

"I've got to stay with the bus in case the cops come," he explained. "We can't afford to be late getting into New York."

He took a few steps through the orange pollen and dove in. He scrubbed his armpits and groin, then swam back to shore. He put his shorts back on, stepped into his sandals and started running back to the bus. Before he reached the trailhead, he turned back and yelled, "You'd better move your ass if you hear a siren. We may need to get out of here quick."

After a while I got dressed. The girls seemed content sunning themselves. I didn't feel like putting my shoes on, but the trail turned out to be far too rocky and painful for bare feet, so I donned my shoes and plodded uphill back to the bus.

****

Driver Chris was alone sitting in the driver's seat with his legs up on the small wooden buddy seat. He dropped his book hand to his lap and asked, "How'd you like it?"

I sat on the edge of the first seat on the front platform facing him and said, "It was really great. That car was incredible," I marveled. "I can't believe it's not completely rusted out."

"Yeah, they don't make cars like that anymore." He reminisced from the driver's seat. "It sits above the water-line most of the time, but it gets completely submerged when it rains. It has been there since I first started coming here with my dad when I was a kid. It was our secret spot."

"It's wicked cool!" I praised. "Thanks for sharing."

"You're welcome," he responded smiling gregariously. "I'm glad you liked it." He pinched his chin through his beard with two fingers.

"What's not to like," I said. "The pond is gorgeous. The people are cool, and I just went skinny-dipping in Connecticut. I mean seriously, who goes skinny-dipping in Connecticut? Nobody. I mean, my sister lives in Connecticut. She is a fucking Puritan. I call her the church lady."

Skinny-Dipping in Connecticut

He chuckled before scoffing at my broad generalization. "Not everybody is like your sister," he informed me. "Plenty of people go skinny-dipping in Connecticut."

"Like who?" I wondered aloud.

"Aside from myself, I happen to know a group of liberal minded Pagan folks from Oxford who call themselves the Forest Folk. They skinny-dip all the time."

"There are Pagans skinny-dipping in Connecticut?" I questioned. "Are you serious?"

"I'm part of their group," he revealed. "I guess that qualifies me as Pagan."

I had to ask. "What's it like being Pagan?"

"The word Pagan is a broad term," he began to explain. "It covers a wide range of non-mainstream belief systems that fall outside of the five major religions."

"Don't Pagans believe in multiple gods?" I asked.

"Some of them," he informed me. "Personally, I believe that Mother Nature reigns supreme. It's not that far off from what most people believe." He looked at me to confirm my understanding. Most of us acknowledge ourselves as being part of Mother Nature. We are but a handful of her dust."

"I can dig it," I said with a nod.

He continued, "We have all witnessed the incredible power of Mother Nature. I just choose to honor her as a Goddess. To me she is the Sun and the Moon. She keeps us warm and sets the tide. She bathes us with her rain and cools us with her breath. She is the container in which all of space and time exists."

"That sounds harmless," I said with a tone of surprise. "I thought Pagans were witches with brooms and shit like that."

"You're thinking of Wicca," he concluded, nodding.

"I've heard of Wicca," I confirmed nodding back. "When I was out west."

"Many of my friends are Wiccan," he acknowledged. "There are many aspects to it, witches being one of them," he acknowledged. "But there's much more to it than that. It's an ancient tradition based on timeless ceremonies where there's a male and a female goddess."

His book caught my eye. "What are you reading?" I asked.

He positioned the book so I could read the cover as he said, "*Black Elk Speaks*. It has been called the Indian Bible."

"Never heard of it," I confessed.

"It's a collection of visions recounted by an Indian holy man named Black Elk," he informed me.

"Never heard of him," I admitted.

"Black Elk was a Lakota Sioux," he explained. "He was the cousin of Crazy Horse."

"Right on!" I said. "I love Crazy Horse. I grew up reading a book my cousin wrote called *The Return of Crazy Horse*. It's a children's book. He sent me a signed copy when I was a kid. It was about this sculptor, Korczak Ziolkowski, who was summoned by the Indians by way of a spiritual dream to carve a statue of Crazy Horse out of a mountain. It's the largest sculpture in the world."

"I know!" Driver Chris enthused. "We're going there on this trip."

"We're going there!" I exclaimed. "No fucking way!"

"Yes Way!" he grooved.

I was in shock. "I've wanted to go there ever since I was a kid," I revealed.

"I'm glad you get to satisfy one of your life goals," he said approvingly, smiling with a glow in his eyes.

"It wasn't so much a goal," I stammered. "It was like an impossible dream." I blinked my eyes a dozen times in dismay.

"Your cousin's book sounds chill," he commented. "I'll have to pick up a copy. What's his name?"

"William Kotzwinkle," I told him. "He wrote the novelization of *E.T.*"

"*The Extraterrestrial?*" he marveled.

"The one and only," I boasted. "Stephen Spielberg liked his books so much he asked him to write *ET* based on a screenplay. The novel became the movie exactly like it was told in the book."

"The author of *Black Elk Speaks* was also called by the Indians. He had a dream calling him to the Pine Ridge Indian Reservation in South Dakota." He paused dramatically. "When he got there, the Indians greeted him like they were expecting him, and they rushed him up to the highest point in the Badlands where Black Elk had his teepee." He opened the back page of the book and pointed as he spoke. "It says it right there in black and white." He read, "All of Black Elk's visions were held in his teepee on Sheep Mountain Table on the Cuny Plateau."

"That is so cool," I marveled.

"You want to know what's even cooler?" he questioned.

"What?" I begged.

"We'll be camping on the Cuny Plateau on the third night of this trip," he revealed.

"In the Badlands?" I questioned. "That's awesome."

"Even better," he promised. "The Tortoise is friends with the Cuny family. They are Lakota Sioux. We will be having dinner with them, and they let us camp out on their land. The Tortoise has been going there for over twenty years."

"Oh my God!" I exclaimed. "We'll be there in three days?"

"Three days," he confirmed.

I was having a hard time following my father's advice to believe none of what I hear and half of what I see, but this put it over the top. This put my resolve to the test. I was blown-away. This news filled me with joy and expectation. It was like I had received a much-needed booster shot of childhood wonder.

"Speaking of Black Elk," I spoke up, "I have the skull of a Grandfather Elk in a box up on the roof."

"You have an Elk Skull on the bus? That's sick," he observed. "Where did you get that?"

"I found it in Elk Prairie State Park on the beach in California when I was on my bike tour." I checked his expression. He seemed skeptical. "I'm going to put it back," I added.

"Oh okay, cool," he responded. "You should leave only footprints and take only pictures in State Parks."

"I know," I said in agreement. "I feel pretty bad about it. It's the strangest thing," I revealed. "It called to me. As soon as I saw it, I felt compelled to take it. I just had to have it. I rode fifty miles with it strapped to my handlebars until I found a place to ship it home."

"It sounds like you still want to keep it," he deduced.

"Sometimes I want to keep it," I admitted. "The park rangers said I might as well take it. The skull would have disintegrated if I left it where it was, and the antlers had served their purpose as food for other animals."

"If they said you could keep it; why not keep it," he suggested.

After a long awkward silence, I asked, "So, you lived in Connecticut when you were a kid?"

"Yeah," he said. "I grew up in Manchester."

"No way, my sister lives in Manchester." I was beaming a huge smile. It tickled me to think that the driver of this bizarre bus grew up so close to my sister's house.

He smiled at me and looked up the hillside toward the highway. "When we first started coming here, we had to park on the side of the highway," he told me. "The police always kicked us out."

"That's too bad," I consoled.

"Nah," he shirked. "My father wasn't the type of man to give up easily, so he brought tools and a chain saw and we cleared the road in here."

"You made that road with your dad?" I gasped.

"And my brother," he confirmed. "He looked over his shoulder down the road we had driven in on. "The cops didn't bother us for the longest time, but it became a hangout for kids to drink, so we still have to be careful."

"I wish I had a swimming hole when I grew up," I told him.

"I love swimming holes," he gushed. "There are a bunch of cool swimming-holes in the United States," Driver Chris reflected with a joyful smile.

"Like where?" I wondered. "What's your favorite?"

He contemplated, seeming to drift away into fond memories. "I'd have to say, the hidden hot spring in Big Bend," he said definitively. "That's the coolest hot spring I've ever seen. Not the main hot spring, mind you. That one is on the map. The cool one is off the radar. Its location is known only by locals and a few Tortoise drivers, the ones who have been there and were able to find it. It's hidden in a bamboo thicket on the bank of the Rio Grande."

"That sounds incredible. Where's Big Bend?" I asked.

"Big Bend National Park," he informed me. "It borders Mexico at the bottom of the little hump of Texas, right where the Rio Grande turns north."

"Cool," I said in total admiration.

"It sure is," he spoke with wonder. "There's a hidden hot spring in a cave at the end of a twenty-foot-long bamboo tunnel." He was so excited to tell me about this. "Right there at the end of the tunnel sits an absolutely gorgeous hot spring, bubbling out of the ground at one-o-four, the perfect temperature."

"I didn't know we have bamboo in America," I commented.

"Yes, we do. It's called River Cane or Canebrake. It's native to Texas."

"Amazing," I marveled.

"The bamboo grew over the top of the trail, so it forms a tunnel and it makes a roof over the hot spring. The bamboo has grown so thick over the years that it keeps the rain out. It could be pouring outside, and you would never know it. It's the best thing ever. It can get cold in Big Bend at night. We once saw a fifty-degree shift in temperature. It was 104 in the daytime and 54 that same night with clouds and rain."

"Wicked," I said under my breath.

"Yeah. The Park Service doesn't want people going in there because the center of the floor in the hot spring is like quicksand."

"Quicksand?" I marveled.

"Oh yeah," he nodded. "It's so unnerving. Most people just stand around the edge and never go near the middle. As soon as you put your feet down in the center of the floor, quicksand starts sucking your feet down. Nobody actually gets sucked under because the edge

Skinny-Dipping in Connecticut 59

of the hot spring is always within arm's reach. The whole thing is only eight feet across, but it's scary as hell when your feet get swallowed."

"Quicksand would freak me out," I told him.

"It's extremely private, but you can fit about ten of the right people in there, but you gotta warn 'em about the quicksand before they go in unless you want to freak them out."

"That's crazy," I surmised.

"That's why the Park Service tries to obscure the trail to the tunnel. They piled rocks to keep hikers on the main trail. That keeps random hikers from stumbling on the trail accidentally, but the rock pile just makes it easier to find when you know what you're looking for."

"Where is it exactly?" I inquired.

"The Tortoise doesn't want us to give out that information, but it wouldn't help you too much, even if I was allowed to tell you. There's really no way to accurately describe its location. The rocks all look the same in the desert. I could draw you a map, but even then, you still wouldn't find it. It's best to have someone who's been there before show you the way."

"I'd love to go there someday," I commented.

"Take the southern cross-country route," he recommended.

"You take passengers there?" I asked.

"Sure thing," he answered.

"Then how do you keep it secret?" I wondered.

"We're only supposed to take them there at night," he revealed.

"Wow!" I marveled. "That's so cool." I could see the British girls walking back up the trail returning from the swimming hole.

Driver Chris' eyes lit up as he began to recount a story. "So, I'm down there once," he began, "with Gaunt Murdock, this other Green Tortoise Driver, right?"

"Right," I replied.

"Gaunt is this giant guy with blond dreadlocks circling his head. He's bald on top so he looks like the Predator in that Schwarzenegger flick."

My eyes grew wide.

"So, Gaunt decided to test to see if the quicksand in the hot spring is as deadly as everyone assumes, right?"

"Right." I nodded.

"So, he's like six foot five, right?"

I nodded again.

"He's planned to let the quicksand suck him under all the way until he's sure he would die if no one was there to help him. So, he gets these two big German guys to sit on the edge of the hot spring and hold his arms as he sinks into the quicksand."

"Oh, shit!" I gasped. "No way!"

"Yeah, this mother fucker's bat-shit crazy, we all think, right?"

"Right," I nodded again.

"So, the ladies start freaking out. They're like, 'No, no, don't do it! You're crazy!' But he does it anyway, and he starts sinking, right?"

"No way!" I was totally hooked.

"Yeah, and he keeps sinking and sinking and the girls keep freaking out and begging him to stop, but he won't." Driver Chris turns and sits up with one hand on the back of his seat. More passengers were on board now and everyone was listening. He continued, "Even the two German guys holding his arms wanted him to stop, but he wouldn't. He was already up to his armpits in the water and he tells the Germans to let go of his arms and to hold his hands. So they do, and everyone, including me is just losing it, but Gaunt keeps on sinking deeper and deeper into the quicksand. At this point we don't even know if the Germans will be strong enough to pull him out, but he kept sinking in the quicksand until his chin was in the water. Mind you he's six-foot-five, but half of his body was trapped in the quicksand." Driver Chris now had the attention of just about everyone.

Seeing this, he stood up to demonstrate. He bent his knees like he was sinking in quicksand with his one hand in the air like it was being grappled by a strong German. He put his other hand flat out in front of his chin to show how deep the water was getting. He kept bending his knees until his hand was at his upper lip. Then, he puts both hands up and says dramatically, "Then, Gaunt tells the German Guys, 'Let me go.'"

"Ah, no way," I reacted. Most of the passengers reacted too. We were all growing uncomfortable with the thought.

"So, you can imagine how everyone was freaking out even more." Driver Chris opened his eyes widely. "The girls were screaming at him to stop. The German guys say, 'No way,' but he fights their grip and he let go!"

"Holy shit!"

"Gaunt dips his nose below the water until his whole head disappears for a moment. We were all going nuts. The women were crying. It was so stupid. We all thought he was going to die, then he stands straight up and says, 'It's only this deep.'"

Then, Driver Chris stood up, lowering his hand to show the water depth returning to armpit height and he says, "It was only as deep as his nipples."

"Ha!" I laughed and smiled at him shaking my head.

Skinny-Dipping in Connecticut

Driver Chris sat back down in the driver's seat with a shit-eating grin. So, I sat next to him on the small wooden fold out seat.

"Big Bend sounds amazing," I told him. "How many times have you been there?"

He looked me in the eye. "Quite a few," he answered fondly, "maybe a dozen?" We heard a siren in the distance and the driver shifted position in his seat uncomfortably.

"Wow," I said jealously. I started thinking about what it must be like to be a driver for the Green Tortoise.

"Big Bend is pretty incredible," he explained. "There are fewer roads down there per square mile than any other place in the country."

"That's so cool," I said in awe as the siren grew closer.

****

We both bent over sideways to look up the hill at the same time. A police officer pulled a car over on the side of the highway right above us, not in a direct line-of-sight, but close enough to make Chris shrug. The flashing lights remained on after the wailing siren ceased.

"Should we get out of here?" I asked.

"Not so much," he said, "but it's about that time. We should be getting a move on." He threw his book onto the dashboard and the air-horn blew out a deafening note, calling the passengers back to the bus. I looked around wondering what had triggered the horn, and he coyly said, "There's a button on the floor."

"That's so cool," I said reverently, leaning over to look for the button. I found myself idolizing this crazy long-haired Hippie-looking dude.

"Want to give it a try?" he invited.

"Really?" I asked bashfully.

"Sure, why not?" He got up and took the first seat on the front platform nearest to the door.

I jumped into the driver's seat and bounced on the springs. I grabbed the huge steering wheel and turned it from side to side, pretending to drive. "This is awesome," I marveled zealously. The steering wheel was eighteen inches across. I struggled to turn it to one side until I could feel the wheels turn in the dirt. I looked down for the airhorn button on the floor and I positioned my foot on it. "Fuck!" I startled myself when I accidentally hit the horn.

"It's sensitive," he said.

The enormous long-haired, blond-bearded driver came running up the trail followed by Chicken Jim and a handful of passengers, including Little Josh's mother and Australian Sheila. The co-driver had a look of horror on his face. He came bounding up the steps and tossed his boots under the little fold-out seat next to the driver. "I told them the cops are coming and we need to get out of here as soon as possible, but the British girls seem to be taking their sweet time getting dressed."

"No rush bro," the red-bearded driver told his colleague. "That cop is not interested in us. He's just giving somebody a ticket. I just figured it was time to go anyway."

"Shit man," he huffed with a hand on his knee, trying to catch his breath while the other passengers passed behind him and took seats. "When I heard the horn, I figured we were screwed," he breathed.

He addressed his partner with a warm smile. "You should try to get some rest before New York if you can, brother."

"I'll try my best now that my heart's running a mile-a-minute," said the enormous blond from where he stood blocking the doorway. He picked up an empty Gatorade bottle off the dashboard and headed for the driver's cabin.

"He's going to bed?" I asked with a wrinkled forehead.

"He has to drive all night," he informed me.

"Really?" I marveled.

"Yeah, it's a long drive, like nine hours," he explained. "I'll take over if he needs me to, depending on how much rest he gets."

I watched him make his way past the line of passengers waiting to take seats until he climbed through a small wooden door over the engine at the rear of the bus. The British girls were back as was most everyone.

The red-bearded driver turned and lifted his chin at the driver-in-training as he boarded the bus. He had been standing at the bottom step. "Hey Jimbo," said the driver. "How was it?"

He did not answer. Instead, he asked, "Why are you sitting in the driver's seat?" He looked at me curiously. He snapped, "You seriously want to be a driver?"

"Absolutely!" I said happily, "I'd love to learn how to drive a bus like this. I fuckin' love this bus. I love everything about it. I love how old it is. I love the inside, the outside. I love how comfortable everything is. I just love this bus," I cheered.

"He loves the bus," Driver Chris said with a chuckle. A look of insight lit up his face. "Johnny Lovebus!" the Irish driver proclaimed. "That's a good bus name."

"Wicked!" Chicken Jim clucked. "Johnny Lovebus. Coo! Coo! Coo!" He smiled. "We got another guy named Johnny," he informed the driver. "The one with the guitar."

"Everyone gets a bus name," the driver said matter-of-factly. "We can call the other guy Guitar Johnny."

Skinny-Dipping in Connecticut

"Everyone gets a bus name?" I questioned.

"Yes," Driver Chris answered. "It's a Tortoise tradition. We do it every trip. It's an effective way to remember passenger's names," he explained. "He's Chicken Jim." He shook his head. "I don't even remember his real name."

"And you're Driver Chris," I interjected.

"Exactly!" he proclaimed. "Passengers always refer to us as, 'the drivers' anyway, and it works in case we have more than one Chris or Brian."

"Why do they call you Chicken Jim?" I asked the rookie.

"Coo! Coo! Coo!" he clucked and flapped his bent arms with his thumbs in his armpits. "I have no idea," he said as if he was dumb.

Driver Chris shouted, "Buddy Check!"

"Buddy Check," shouted Michelle. "Oh, there you are Josh," I heard her say. "Don't scare me like that."

"Buddy Check," I shouted, looking for British Sue and English Tessa. I could see them, sitting across from Big Dave at the dinette.

"Is everyone here?" he asked me.

"Yes, I think so," I said, psyched that he asked me to help. I cupped my hands around my mouth and shouted, "Buddy Check," as he sat down. No response came back. "Seems good," I said, and he started the engine. I sat down next to him on the little wooden fold-out seat, but then I remembered. "Where's the girl from Boston?" I asked rising to my feet to have a look.

"The girl with the flip-flops?" asked Chicken Jim.

"Yes!" She was nowhere to be seen.

"She was still in the water when I took off," he told me.

"Maybe she's still down there?" I suggested.

"Go check. Will ya?" the driver prodded.

I jumped up and ran toward the trailhead. I spotted her walking barefoot up the rocky trail. "We're going!" I advised her.

She was pissed-off. "What the fuck!" she mused. "These rocks are killing my feet. Someone took my flip-flops!" she complained. "I'm sure I wore them down there. I remember taking them off. Do you think someone stole them?" she asked me.

I waited until she caught up and walked with her. "I don't think so," I told her. "Maybe someone mistook them for their own?"

When she got to the bus, she stormed up the steps and shouted, "Has anyone seen my flip-flops?"

"My bad," shouted Chicken Jim from near Little Josh and his mother, Michelle. He was wearing her flip-flops. "I borrowed them, he confessed. "I had to run back to the bus." He kicked them off one by one, so they fell on the floor at her feet.

"What the hell!" she complained.

"I thought the cops were coming," he explained nonchalantly, not making eye contact with her. He pulled his Ozzy Osbourne t-shirt over his head and adjusted the shoulders.

"You could have asked," she snapped.

"Would you have let me borrow them?"

"No."

"There you have it," he said.

"You're such a jerk!" she mused. She clapped her flip-flops together and brought them with her to her seat.

Chicken Jim gave me a look like he needed to tell me something. So, I sat backwards on the wooden seat to face him. "Just so you know, if you're going to work for the Tortoise there are a few things I have to warn you about upfront," he divulged.

"Like don't borrow a passenger's shit without asking?" I chided him.

"No! Nothing like that," he scoffed. "No worries Flip-flop. She'll get over it." He shook his head without a care. "Shit happens."

"Did you just call her Flip-flop?" I questioned.

"It's a good bus name," he snorted. He took on a serious expression and hushed tone. "The Tortoise is notorious for getting people to work for free."

In two elongated syllables I said, "Oooh kaaay."

"They pay you with credit toward taking adventure trips," he told me, "but hardly anyone gets to ride because there aren't enough ride credit seats available."

"So, let me get this straight," I reiterated. "They get you to work for free by promising you trips you never get to go on."

"Exactly!" He waged a finger in the air like the town crier.

"It sounds like a cult?" I said with a smile.

"The jury is still out on that one my friend," he spoke disconcertedly.

I wondered aloud. "What kind of an idiot would be willing to work for free?"

"I did it for a while," he admitted sheepishly.

I looked at him skeptically. "You worked for free?"

"Yes." He tilted his head while speaking like he was ashamed for having been duped.

"How long did you do that?" I inquired.

"Six months," he replied flatly.

"How could you afford to live while you were working for free?" I wanted to know for future reference in case I did end up working there.

Skinny-Dipping in Connecticut

"I couch-surfed a lot with friends," he told me, "but they got sick of me pretty quick, so I moved into the warehouse at Tortoise World Headquarters."

I was incredulous. "How much do they charge you to stay there?"

"I live there gratis," he informed me, snapping his fingers like the word gratis was some amazing trick of magic. "Breakfast and dinner are gratis too," he snapped his fingers again.

"I thought you said you worked for free?"

"I did," he insisted.

"Room and board is a form of payment," I argued.

"Well, I guess you could look at it that way, but it's not like I get my own room," he contended. "We sleep together in common rooms."

"Who's we?" I spat.

"Everyone working for ride credit," he answered.

"So, all the workers get free room and board, not just you?"

"Yeah," he huffed.

"Are you sure it's not a cult?"

"It is what it is," he said with a shrug.

"Do they force you to live there?" I begged.

"They don't force you to do anything," he said, "but they make you work."

"So, everyone who works there lives there by choice," I confirmed.

"Where else would we live?" He spoke as if I was dumb.

"You make it sound like you're all homeless."

"I happen to be homeless, but hardly anyone else is," Chicken Jim whimpered. "Most of them are backpackers just passing through town. They work for a few days and move on before they have enough credit to book a trip."

"Oh, I get it now. They let you work for room and board, and if you work there long enough, they let you go on a trip." I looked at him for confirmation but got none. "That seems like a good deal," I contended. "I'm kind of homeless right now myself," I confided in him hoping he could relate.

"Right on bro!" Chicken Jim tucked his elbows in and clucked, "Coo! Coo! Coo!" Then he put his hand up for a high-five. "Here's to being homeless," he proclaimed.

I slapped it and said, "Working for ride credit sounds awesome, but I need a job that pays cash money so I can afford to stay in California. If I cannot find a job fast enough, I may need to work for ride credit too, so I can get back home."

"Don't do it brother!" he insisted. "Never work for ride credit."

"Are you getting paid while you're in training?" I wanted to know.

"I don't get shit-or-shinola," he told me, touching his thumb and forefinger together in the shape of a donut hole. "I don't even get money to cover my expenses."

"What expenses?" I asked.

"Weed and beer for starters. A cheeseburger now and then maybe." I could not believe he was serious. "I can always get lunch off the roof, but everybody needs a cheeseburger once in a while."

"At least you don't have to pay to go on trips," I consoled him.

"That's true!" he exclaimed, with a snap of his magical fingers. "All of my trips have been free since I started training. It just sucks to have worked all that time for nothing but ride credit when I will never be able to cash it in. They still owe me a shitload."

"How much ride credit do they owe you?"

"Enough to go on a cross country trip," he spoke with contempt, "but they won't let me book a trip while I'm in training."

"You're on a cross country trip right now and training seems like it's a blast," I marveled. "Aren't you having fun?"

"It's all fun," he complained, "but it's still work."

"So, let me get this straight. You just want to have fun without having to work?" I fathomed.

"You got that right bro!"

"It sounds like you need a vacation from all this fun," I jabbed.

"Exactamundo!"

"You're too much," I laughed with him.

As I rose and went to sit back on the buddy seat, he cautioned me one last time with a pointed finger, "Never work for ride credit."

****

The British guy with the leather jacket took the seat closest to the front and started strumming his guitar. He was a tall, thin, Englishman. He reminded me of a young Michael Caine, with his thick black framed glasses that dominated his face. Unlike most of the other passengers, who wore tee shirts and casual clothing, Johnny was wearing a button-down Oxford and blue jeans.

Guitar Johnny has one of those great big smiles, the kind that seems to stretch from ear to ear. His whole face got involved. His eyes squinted when he smiled, and his head would bob around a little as he spoke. He was the kind of guy who would kick his boots because he was shy and say, "Awe shucks," if he was American. Having heard him play

Skinny-Dipping in Connecticut 67

guitar so well, I felt like Guitar Johnny was one of the coolest guys on the bus. He seemed personable enough, despite the assessment of English Tessa and British Sue.

Emotionally honest and easy to read, he was a modest guy, with a discerning view of others. He was always commenting on what people did and said like you might expect from a novelist or a writer for a tabloid talking about the rich and famous. He stuttered horribly in front of women. He was always self-deprecating with a tendency to be a harsh critic of others.

I turned to him and introduced myself. "I'm Johnny," I said, "from Rhode Island."

"Bloody hell," he responded, "I'm Johnny too, from Birmingham."

"People have been calling me Johnny Lovebus," I revealed, "to distinguish between us." I gestured toward his instrument and added, "The drivers called you Guitar Johnny."

"I've been called worse," he reacted.

"I lived in London for a while in college when I went to Cambridge."

"G, g, good on ya'," he stuttered. "That, that, that makes one of us, you sodden Yank." Suffice to say he stuttered a lot. There is no sense in belaboring the point. "You don't look the academic type," he commented.

"I'm not," I confessed. "I just wanted to study abroad, and that's where I landed."

"Spot on," he assessed.

"What's it like in Birmingham?" I questioned.

"I don't fancy the city," he revealed. "I live on the outskirts, mostly for employment. I try to stay away from the city, but you have to go through downtown to get anywhere. I grew up in a fishing village called Grimsby on the northeast coast. It's one of those places you never actually go through to get anywhere."

"How'd you like the swim-hole?" I asked him, wiggling my eyebrows suggestively.

The other Johnny leaned forward and whispered, "You, you, you, cheeky bastard," he said, stuttering terribly, putting emphasis on the word 'cheeky' in a heavy British accent. "Have you no sh... sh... shame?" he stuttered.

"None at all," I said proudly. "Shame is toxic."

Guitar Johnny rolled his eyes, seeming a bit put off by our conversation, so I asked him, "What's up?"

"You're wasting the dawn worrying about the dark," he scoffed. "Life is hard everywhere. Everyone has a burden of one sort or another."

"What's your burden Johnny?" I asked.

"Besides stuttering like a daft imbecile," he said flatly. "My life was cursed from the moment I was born. Before I popped out of my dear mother's womb, God rest her soul, my family was planning a party for all of our relatives to meet the baby, but the moment I came into the world my father cried, 'Why is he so bloody ugly?' Then he said, 'Cancel the party!'"

I laughed, but at the same time I felt bad for him. He was a bit too thin, but he was not ugly at all. "That is the saddest thing I've ever heard," I commented.

At that point Johnny picked up his guitar and held it to his chest like a shield. "Do you know a song called Roadrunner?" he asked.

"The one from the cartoon?" I sang, "Roadrunner, if he catches you, you're through. Meep! Meep!"

Johnny wrinkled his brow, "No, not that song, you wazzock. Roadrunner is a bloody Sex Pistols song."

I shrugged. "Are you in a band?" I asked.

"Err... yes. I am in a band called the Chemists. I'm on holiday now, but we just finished recording an album back in England."

"Cool," I said.

He adjusted his glasses on his nose, then strummed the chords as he sang, "Out on Route one-twenty-eight down by the powerlines." He did not stutter once.

Guitar Johnny and I talked for a long time about music and other things. I gave him the highlights of the semester I spent in London studying at Cambridge, and he expressed his opinion about stuttering.

"I spent years in speech therapy," he revealed. "They were trying to get me to rehearse everything I was about to say. It was keeping me from living in the moment. I wanted no part of it. I'd rather spend my time rehearsing songs."

I agreed with a nod and said, "I learned to stop rehearsing from Neal Cassady of the Merry Pranksters."

"Who's that?"

"Did you read *The Electric Kool-Aid Acid Test*?" I asked. He had not, so I explained. "It's the original Hippie bus story. They drank Kool-Aid laced with LSD at parties with the Grateful Dead. Tom Wolfe was this writer who went to investigate. He embedded himself with this group of Hippies called the Merry Pranksters. They had this crazy bus all painted with psychedelic colors. They drove it across the country to Woodstock. You see it in all the classic counterculture news films and movies."

"Right-o!" he responded. "That's sounding a bit familiar. I've seen a bus like that on the telly with a bunch of Gypsies sitting on top."

Skinny-Dipping in Connecticut

"That's the bus," I confirmed, pointing at him. "Ken Kesey was their leader, but the driver was this guy they called Speed Limit. His real name was Neal Cassady."

"Ah yes," he acknowledged. "A friend of Jack Kerouac. He died of an overdose, if I'm not mistaken."

"That's right," I confirmed. "He took shitloads of speed and drank a whole bottle of booze."

"That'll cause you to snuff it," he concluded.

"They called him Speed Limit because he believed there was a biological limit that keeps humans from living in the moment. Even when you put your hand on a stove." I put my hand out toward my new friend's arm to demonstrate. I pulled it back the instant my fingers touched his skin. "The signal doesn't make it to your brain before your body responds. There's still a one thirty-second of a second barrier between the brain and the body. That's why he took speed."

"Ha!" The British guy scoffed. "So, the poor bloke figured he'd live in the moment if he got all jacked up amphetamines? Do you figure he got there?"

"We'll never know," I surmised.

"Do you take speed?" he asked me.

"No never, not once, nor would I ever," I denied. "I just try not to rehearse what I'm about to say. That puts me in the moment enough as it is."

Amazingly, Guitar Johnny sang song after song without stuttering once.

After that, Chicken Jim got his guitar and the two guitar players started playing side by side. At first, they took turns picking songs, but then they attempted to play together. Guitar Johnny kept stopping whenever Chicken Jim would screw something up. This annoyed them both to no end.

****

Driver Chris tapped my arm with the back of his hand. When I turned around in the seat, he told me, "If you really want to be a driver, you need to learn how to shift. That's the real reason Chicken Jim has not been promoted yet. He's still struggling to get comfortable behind the wheel. I can see why. Shifting is the hardest part of the job. I'll teach you how to do it while you're sitting here, if you like."

"I'd love that," I told him.

"You might as well start learning now. Otherwise, it'll scare the shit out of you, like it did me," he advised.

"It scared you?"

"Fuck yeah!"

"Why?"

"Well, if you can't shift, you can't drive, and if you can't drive you won't get the job. The Tortoise doesn't fuck around when it comes to their drivers being able to shift correctly, without grinding the gears. Sometimes it's downshift or die on a mountain road in the middle of the night in the middle of nowhere with no clue what lay ahead."

"Holy shit!"

"Still interested?"

"Yes." I nodded happily. "I love this bus."

"Johnny Lovebus," Driver Chris proclaimed. "I'll let Brian know you're in. He'll be psyched. Watch how I downshift here," he said as we approached a red light. "That's RPMs." He pointed at a big round gauge mounted on the dashboard. "When you downshift, you want to hit the top of the next gear, so watch what I do." He stomped on the clutch, put the bus in neutral and floored the fuel. He pointed at the gauge again. "See how it's pinned at twenty-two hundred?"

"Yes," I said. I could hear the engine roaring behind us.

"The engine has a governor, so it can't go past twenty-two hundred. Now, watch my hand," he gestured down at the stick shift. "See how the stick rattles."

"Yes," I said with a nod.

"I'm not pushing it; I'm just resting it up against the gears, right?"

"Right," I said.

"When the stick stops rattling, that's how you know when to shift," he explained. He swiveled his toes using his heel as a pivot and put his toes on the brake. I could feel the bus slowing down. "Here it comes," he said. He stomped the clutch as his hand moved forward and the shift was complete. It was like magic.

"Some guys don't use the clutch on downshifts, but this is how I learned." He took his foot off the fuel pedal, letting the engine slow down the bus. "It's pretty easy when you get the hang of it. Well, not when you're coming down out of the mountains and everyone's lives are in your hands. But you will learn. We all have to at some point."

"Whatever you say, man." It all happened so fast. To me this looked like rocket science. I knew right then that I would never master the no clutch downshift, let alone downshifting on a mountain road with a busload of passenger's lives at stake. I was eager to follow along because Driver Chris was the coolest person I have ever met to that point in my life. I asked him, "How'd you discover the Tortoise?"

He shook his red hair back like a rock star and fingered a few strands over his ear. "I was staying with friends in California scoping out the best places to surf, so I was always on the move. The Tortoise Commuter was the best way to get up and down the coast. They let you put your surfboard on the roof. It's dirt cheap and you can sleep," he explained with a chuckle and a wry smile.

"I stayed at the Tortoise Commune a lot," he revealed. He cocked his head and shot me a sideways look, "You know, the Tortoise has a commune up in Oregon called Cow Creek."

"Yeah, I went there." I explained, "I rode the Tortoise to Seattle to start that bike tour I was talking about before.

"So, you've seen Cow Creek," he marveled, casting me a knowing look. "What'd you think?"

"I loved it." I said, wholeheartedly. "The people were extremely cool, the food was phenomenal, and we made mad music around the campfire in the bubble dome."

"Ah, yes, the 'Thought-Provoking Structure.' That's the bubble dome's official name. I was there when they were building that thing. Was the new sauna open?" he asked. "The old one got swept away in a flood."

"Oh, man, that was the best part," I related with wide eyes and a smile. "The sauna was a real eye opener. The people there were so cool it was ridiculous."

"West Coast people tend to be more laid-back in general," he observed. "I think it's an East Coast thing to be uptight." He nodded his chin and shoulders. "People are way more uptight here. If you're not depressed and bored-to-death, they all think you must be doing something illegal. It's uncanny."

"It's like they're a bunch of Puritans who still wear buckles on their hats."

"That's for sure," I marveled. "The kids I met in the sauna were so cool, they even had cool parents. This dude Kyle and his sister were passing a joint around in the sauna. They said their mother grew the weed they were passing around, but that their father's weed was even better. Imagine that," I marveled. "I could never imagine smoking weed with my parents."

"Ha!" the driver laughed. "My father would disown me if he ever found out that I had smoked pot, even once. It's true. He has no clue what's going on in my life and he doesn't want to know."

"My old man's like that too," I related.

"My dad thinks I'm high all the time," the red-bearded driver revealed, "even after I told him that Tortoise drivers are subject to random drug testing." He shook his head from side to side. "I can't even be in a good mood on the phone without him accusing me of being on drugs. I swear to God." He nodded insistently. "Seriously, he asks me if I'm high every time I get excited about anything."

"What's up with that?" I asked with a furrowed brow.

"You can't make everyone happy," he told me. "If you try, you'll lose yourself in the process." He nodded and looked me in the eye for a moment. "At some point you need to start respecting your core values. You know, like your principles. You need to have autonomy and stand up for yourself."

"You're so right," I agreed.

"I've met a lot of West Coast kids that actually like their father, believe it or not. They act like it's normal for your father to be your best friend."

"Right on!" I reacted. "It probably is normal. Who knows?"

Driver Chris swallowed hard. "I'm a little jealous, if you want to know the truth. My dad was my best friend when I was a kid," he revealed, "but those times are long gone. He is way too stubborn to change. I've gotta live my life."

"Sounds just like my old man," I joined on.

"I'm afraid that ship has sailed my friend," he said pessimistically. "I have to face reality; my dad's never gonna accept me for who I am. That's okay. He can have it his way. He's the one who's missing out on knowing his son."

"That's so true," I agreed. "When was the last time you saw him?"

He had to think about it before answering. "I haven't seen him in over a year," he revealed. "Even though I am in Boston a lot, I don't go home unless I have somewhere else to stay. They run a bed and breakfast, so I can't stay there."

"That sucks," I commiserate. "I don't have a good relationship with my father either. God forbid I speak my mind or tell him the truth about what I think or disagree with anything he says. If I tell him how I really feel he tells me to go to hell and kicks me out of the house."

"He kicks you out?"

"Not for good, but it might as well be," I told him. "He eventually lets me come back. He once kicked me out for taking a tone with my mother. He didn't let me come back for a week."

"Sometimes I wish my old man had kicked me out earlier," said the driver. "Now that I've seen what it's like living on my own, I'll never go back. I'm so glad to be out of his house."

"So, you don't talk to him at all now?" I was curious.

"We talk on the phone once in a while," he revealed, "but it's mostly just exchanging pleasantries, that is, until he starts belittling me again. If he puts me down, I have to hang up."

"Right on!" I commented supportively. "I need to remember that one."

"I don't know why he can't just be nice. I'm his freaking son for fuck's sake."

"It's not your fault," I consoled him.

"I know," he reasoned. "If he disapproves of my lifestyle that much, he doesn't deserve me in his life."

"What's wrong with your lifestyle?"

"He said, and I quote, 'Living out there in la-la-land with a bunch of crazies is a complete waste of your life.'" He shook his head as he spoke. "He thinks being a bus driver is beneath me, just because I went to college. He says it's a blue-collar job. It does not pay enough. I should get a real job. He thinks I'm running away from my responsibilities, avoiding a career."

"I thought I had it bad," I huffed, blinking my widened eyes. "My dad was pissed off before I left Boston because I didn't line up a job in San Francisco. I mean, that's total bullshit, right? I can't go for an interview if I'm not there, right?"

"That's right," he reflected. "You're moving there. That's cool. Do you have a place lined up?"

"I have a friend with a couch in San Mateo," I told him.

"What kind of work are you looking for?" he asked.

"I have no idea," I admitted.

"You'll find something," he reassured me. "If not, you can always work for the Tortoise. They'll let anyone work for ride credit."

"Thanks for the tip," I said. "Sorry to bring up all that shit about your dad."

"Ah, no worries," he shrugged. "All of that is in the past. I have learned that now is the only time that matters. I used to waste time thinking about that shit, but you can't control the past, and you can't predict the future, and trying to do so only removes you from the one thing you can control, the present."

"That's deep," I concluded.

"Suffice to say I try not to let my father issues bother me anymore," he said. "I've met a lot of great teachers who have helped me get a handle on my feelings." He downshifted into first gear again. We were bumper to bumper in toll booth traffic. The bus stopped and he looked me in the eye for a second. "One of the greatest things about driving for the Tortoise is that you get to meet so many cool people on the buddy seat." He looked down where I was seated. "The buddy seat is a platform for wisdom," he proclaimed.

"That's what it's called, the buddy seat?" I asked, gripping the edge of the wooden slab between my legs. "That's awesome."

"Since I started driving, I've been exposed to the wisdom of so many amazing teachers and healers," he revealed. "I've learned a lifetime of lessons from people sitting on that seat."

"I could use some wisdom myself," I said with an enthusiastic nod.

"Ha!" he laughed. "If you came seeking wisdom, you're sitting in the right seat," he said with a smile. "Not that I have much to offer. I'm just starting to learn myself." He put on the blinker and changed lanes before he continued. He glanced at me in the mirror.

"I could use some words of wisdom," I said thoughtfully.

"I'll do my best," he offered.

"My father thinks I'm avoiding getting a job and starting a career, that I'm running away from my responsibilities. He thinks I should have had a job waiting for me before moving to San Francisco."

"Let me ask you this. Are you running away from something?" the driver asked me.

"Him," I answered flatly. "My father."

"What do you hope to find in San Francisco?"

"A job, I suppose, maybe happiness."

"Being obsessed with finding happiness is what prevents you from getting it," he advised me. "Happiness is always present in your life; you just have to connect to it and allow it to flow through you. It is challenging, but worth the effort. What makes you happy in your life right now?"

"Travel makes me happy," I told him.

"Why?"

"I don't know," I answered thoughtfully. "I was happy when I was younger, but I've lost the feeling I used to have. I was so full of wonder and excitement about everything when I was young. Travel makes me feel like that again."

"You're still young dude," he observed.

"I know," I agreed. "I just think I've grown pessimistic living at home with my father. He always tells me to believe none of what you hear and half of what you see. I used to be more optimistic, but I've been very depressed for the last few months."

"So, you're a seeker," the red-bearded bus driver surmised.

"A seeker?" I questioned.

"It sounds like you're seeking enlightenment," he suggested.

"Enlightenment? Ha!" I laughed.

"Your spiritual path in life," he explained.

"My spiritual path?" I wondered aloud.

"You want to get excited about life again," he deduced.

"That's my spiritual path?" I marveled. "Are you trying to hypnotize me?"

"Maybe," he questioned before telling me. "There are as many paths as there are people."

"Right on." I said.

Skinny-Dipping in Connecticut

"What kind of job are you hoping to find?"

"One that lets me travel," I answered with a laugh. "To do something that I love, something that lets me use my talents."

"Maybe you should be sitting here instead of there."

"I would love be a Green Tortoise driver, but I don't think that's possible. It seems way too far-fetched."

"You create your own reality Johnny," he told me. "Envision the path to get where you need to go and take one step at a time. Eventually, if your steps be true, you will get anywhere you want to go." The bus came to a complete stop in traffic. Driver Chris quickly unbuckled his seatbelt and took his shirt off. It was hot in the bus, especially when we were not moving. "My father thinks I have no morals," he shrugged shirtless. He quickly balled-up his shirt, threw it on the dashboard, and stomped the clutch so that the bus rolled fluidly along with traffic. "It's funny," he smiled and shook his head as he gestured to himself with a cocked wrist. "He called me a Hippie when he saw me drive up to his house without a shirt."

"Ha!" I laughed out loud, looking at him sitting there shirtless with his wicked long hair and no trace of inhibition. "You are a Hippie," I observed, "in the best sense of the word, of course."

"I'm no Hippie Johnny," he scoffed. His shoulders dropped with a sigh. "It just makes me sad to think that my father will never get to know the real me. He is too stubborn to forgive me for failing to meet his lame ass expectations. He keeps telling me to get a real job."

"You have an awesome job and he should be proud of you," I told him.

"Try telling that to him," he scoffed. "What's the big deal about driving with no shirt? People do it all the time in the summer. He said I don't care about my job and that driving half naked is disrespectful to our customers and the company."

"Why would anyone care?" I asked. "There's no air conditioning in here. It's better than reeking up the place with your body odor."

We stopped one car short of the toll and he looked at me seriously. "The Tortoise doesn't care if we drive naked for crying out loud. There is even a rule about driving naked in the driver's handbook. It's true." Driver Chris stopped the bus at the tollbooth and threw the coins into the basket. I watched him work the clutch and stick shift, getting the bus back up to speed.

"What's the rule in the handbook?"

"You're not allowed to drive naked on the first or last day of any trip."

"Ha," I laughed. "What about all of the days in between?"

"Exactly!" He smiled laughing. "They had to make that rule because someone's mother sued the Tortoise when one of our drivers arrived naked at the bus station in San Francisco."

"That's hilarious," I laughed and laughed. "Have you driven naked before?"

"Oh yeah!" he said.

I made a disgusted face and said, "That's just gross."

"Why do you say that?" he questioned.

"I just sat there, dude," I shuddered. "That's nasty."

We both laughed and remained silent for a while. It dawned on me how painful it would be to have a son that I would never know. For the first time in my life, right then and there on the buddy seat, I began to feel bad for my father. He was missing out on the best part of parenthood, arguably the best part of life. Not another word was spoken on the subject, but Driver Chris had inspired me to start thinking about the role of a son in his father's life. I turned and listened to the two guitar players battling through songs, and I lost myself in the music on the way into New York City.

5
The Moon Over Manhattan

When the Green Tortoise bus rolled down Broadway the citizens of New York took notice. As the antique bus maneuvered through traffic, horns beeped, and arms waved enthusiastically through open car windows. Cabbies leaned out waving and truckers blew airhorns. Pedestrians on the sidewalks stopped in their tracks, lining up along the curb as the bus rolled past, cheering, and waving like the bus was a big green float in the Thanksgiving Day Parade.

One passerby yelled excitedly, "The Hippies are back!" A young woman shouted affectionately, "I love your bus!" Someone asked loudly, "What's a Green Tortoise?" The passengers joined in the fun, shouting, and waving to fans. Much to his mother's chagrin, the little kid, Josh, pulled his shorts down and stuck his bare ass out an open window. The passersby cheered. Then, this hilarious guy on the sidewalk shouted, "Lord Jesus, I'm having a flashback." He held his hand to his chest, staggering backwards like Redd Foxx calling to Elizabeth on Sanford and Son. It was comical.

As the bus circled the George Washington Bridge Bus Terminal, we turned the second corner and saw flames under the bridge where street people and indigents in dirty clothing were drinking and smoking around a fire barrel. I noticed one of the dark figures shaking his head furiously in disbelief, as if the green bus rekindled a memory of some unfulfilled promise made in the Sixties. Driver Chris turned the bus onto the side street below the towering stack of iron decking leading to the massive bridge. A line of taxicabs and shiny limousines waited at the curb of the bus station across the street, ready to escape the city.

As the bus pulled into a loading zone on Fort Washington Avenue, a group of men with squeegees surrounded the bus and started washing the windshield and windows. The passengers quickly started closing the windows to stop the spray from getting everything wet. The old metal school bus style windows were hard to close. This created a commotion throughout the bus as passengers got sprayed as they struggled with the metal latches.

Driver Chris slid the driver's window open and hung his head outside. "We don't want our windows washed," he told the man at the windshield, waving him off with his hand. "We can't pay you," he shouted, shaking his head emphatically.

"We wash your windows and you pay us, yes?" the guy shouted in broken English. He sprayed the windshield with a bottle. "We do a respectable job."

"No," our driver shouted persistently, "we're not paying you." He waved the guy off again with his huge hand. "We don't want our windows washed." He slowed down his words. "We're not going to give you money!" The squeegee man kept spraying and swiping the rubber blade on the glass. When he tried pulling on the wiper blade, expecting it to lift off the windshield, Driver Chris yelled, "Stop!" Then, he drew his head back inside and removed his seatbelt. He was clearly upset. "Mother fucker's going to break our damn wipers and they'll still want money."

I stood up from the buddy seat and let him pass.

"If you refuse to pay, they threaten to smash your windshield," he told me, like a shot he was out the door.

Chicken Jim had been sitting up front, strumming his guitar. He tossed the instrument on the seat and followed the red-haired driver off the bus. Together they engaged in an intense argument with the squeegee man while the others continued to wash the side windows. After arguing for several minutes, the squeegee team finally backed down. He called his men with a loud two-fingered whistle and they disappeared.

Chicken Jim promptly lit a cigarette and leaned against the bus terminal wall, triumphantly puffing, and blowing smoke. An attractive passerby asked him for a light, and they engaged in a brief conversation. She did not seem impressed with his nihilistic attitude, and she scurried away like he had said something rude.

Our driver came back inside and stood next to the buddy seat to make an announcement, so I moved back to an open seat on the front platform. Chicken Jim stood outside the door to listen, causing smoke to blow in through the windows.

The Moon Over Manhattan

"Hey, everybody listen up!" directed Driver Chris. "We're here to pick up the rest of the passengers. They're supposed to be here for an eight o'clock departure, but we'll be staying until ten, so we don't have to fight rush hour traffic on our way out of the city." He looked at his wrist, but he had no watch. "Does somebody have the time?" he asked the passengers closest to the front.

"Four-twenty," blurted Berndt Toast.

"Very funny," he responded.

"It's seven-thirty," shouted Mother Michelle from the dinette. She went back to reading her novel.

He paused to do the math in his head. "That gives you two and a half hours to explore New York. You can take a walk here in Washington Heights, have a look around or get some food. Just don't go too far. If you feel the need to see Manhattan, be sure to leave plenty of time to get back. The subways can be unreliable. If you are not back by ten o'clock sharp, we will be forced to leave without you."

There was a knock at the bus door. An unlikely pair of female passengers stood outside. Based on how differently the two girls dressed there was little chance of them being traveling partners. The shorter girl had cropped black hair with maroon highlights and carried a worn-out lime-green suitcase. She was dressed-to-the-nines in a fancy getup with a frilly blouse and a short black pleated skirt rimmed with frilly white lace. Except for the lack of an apron, she bore an unmistakable similarity to a French maid or a housekeeper at a fancy hotel. The taller one had bright red lipstick with long flowing auburn hair, and she wore a backpack. She was dressed like an athlete in multi-colored, form-fitting, spandex workout pants and a shirt that said, JUST DO IT.

The driver turned to address them.

The athletic girl spoke with a clearly Canadian accent. "This is the bus going to San Francisco, eh?"

"I'll be right with you," the driver told them, holding up a finger. "It'll just be a few minutes. I'll let you know."

"There's at least a dozen people waiting inside the bus station eh," she informed him.

"Oh shit," said the driver. "I was wondering where they were all hiding. We're expecting a lot more people."

Chicken Jim was hovering close behind the girls in the doorway listening.

The German girl turned toward him with a start. "Put out that cigarette, dummkopf."

"Put it out Jimbo," chastised the driver.

"Hold my bag and we will tell them to come," the well-dressed German girl told the driver.

"That would be great," he responded with a smile.

"You will keep my suitcase here, ja?" the German girl asked him.

"No worries," the driver said as he stepped down one step to take the suitcase from her. He put it on the floor beneath the dashboard.

"I will change clothes when I return," she told him.

"No worries," he said. "It'll be right here when you get back."

He offered his hand to take the Canadian's backpack, but she declined. "I'll keep hold of it, eh," said the Canadian. "I need to get a few things organized, eh."

Our driver bent down to look around, briefly searching for other passengers. "Could you do me another favor please?" he asked them.

"Fuckin-a," she responded.

The other spoke in German. "Was ist es?" she said.

"If you see any other backpackers wandering around in there, let them know we're out here," he requested.

"No problem, eh," replied the Canadian.

"I'll go with them," volunteered Chicken Jim at the last second, and he took off hot on their heels.

Driver Chris turned to address us again. "Like I said you have plenty of time to explore New York, but there's plenty to see around here in Washington Heights and there are tons of places to eat within walking distance. Just don't go too far and try to be back here before ten, just to be safe." The noise of the city made it hard to hear him speak. Passengers had been whispering plans the entire time Driver Chris spoke. People were moving around, retrieving money from their daypacks, and putting on shoes. Driver Chris cupped his hands around his mouth and shouted over the noise, "I repeat, you need to be back here by ten sharp, or we'll have to leave without you. Of course, you're welcome to stay on the bus, if that suits you better. That's it. Have fun! Any questions?"

Everyone stood up all at once and crowded the front platform. I put my feet up on the cushion to make room. Driver Chris sat in the driver's seat answering passenger's questions one by one as they left, but I remained disinterested. I had experienced New York ad nauseam and it always left me feeling depressed.

The German guy with the artificial limb announced, "I'm going to the top of the World Trade Center if anyone wants to share a cab."

The Bostonian shouted, "I'll come!" She dropped her flip-flops on the floor in front of me. "Come with us," she suggested.

"I'm not a huge fan of cities," I told her.

The Moon Over Manhattan

"No way!" she gasped. "Everybody loves New York." She slipped into her footwear and said, "Come on! The World Trade Center is the biggest building in New York. The view must be amazing."

"I'm not big on heights either," I revealed.

"Suit yourself," she huffed.

Once most of the passengers had left, Driver Brian came forward from the driver's cabin and stood on the steps. "Hey boss." He greeted his partner with a nod.

"Good timing," the other driver commended him. "Did you sleep?"

"Somewhat," Driver Brian divulged. "It's always hard to sleep in traffic. It got stupid hot in there."

"Do you think you'll be good to drive tonight?" the redhead asked.

"I should be all right," the big blond answered.

"You don't have to drive the whole way," he advised him. "It's nine hours if you don't stop."

"I'll get us there," he touted. "You can cook breakfast."

"Do you remember the way into Crane Creek?" the Irishman asked.

"It will come back to me along the way," he supposed. "It always does. If I've been there once, I can always find my way back."

"Try to park in the shade near the lake," he recommended. "It'll be hot early. The weather looks perfect. You can wake me up as soon as we arrive, so you can get to sleep before it gets hot."

"Thanks," he said in response. "Where are all the new people? I'm surprised no one is here yet."

"Ha!" he laughed. "A bunch of them are waiting inside. I just sent two of 'em to get them with Chicken Jim. Other than that, I haven't seen anyone."

"Do you want me to round 'em up?"

"No, he replied. "Chicken Jim is with them. He should have that covered. I've got to piss, and I need to call the office to get a head count anyway, so I'll have a look around myself."

"I hope they show up," the Californian driver hoped.

"You're in charge until I get back," Driver Chris instructed him. "Chicken Jim can load the luggage and you can start checking in passengers. You can sell tickets; just don't exchange any money on the street."

"I know better," the co-driver avowed.

The two men nodded at each other. On the bottom step on his way out, the red-bearded man turned to speak to his friend behind the wheel. "I've decided to call my dad," he said flatly.

"Good man," his partner encouraged him. "I'm glad you finally made up your mind to give him a call. I know it's been a struggle."

"Thank you," he acknowledged his partners empathy. "It may take a while," he warned. "My dad and I have a lot of catching up to do."

I hope it works out this time," he said, "for the both of you."

"Me too," Driver Chris agreed. A second later he was gone.

Mother Michelle was getting ready to go somewhere, but Big Dave remained seated at the dinette. I slid sideways onto the bench across from him. We nodded at each other in acknowledgement. "You're not going out?" I asked him.

"No," he said somberly. "There's nothing here for me but bad memories." I understood his sentiment. He got shot in the back in a convenience store robbery in New York. It was on these mean streets that the course of his life had changed forever.

Surprisingly, the Bostonian came back on board. She kicked off her flip-flops and took a seat on the front platform.

"What happened?" I asked her.

"Nothing," she answered cutely. "It's just a lot of walking in flip-flops. I should have worn my boots. They said they'd wait up, but I told them to go on without me."

The Australian girl with the golden ponytail stood in the aisle next to her. "We're going to Time Square," she informed her. "Won't you come with us? I know which way they were headed."

"I'm all set," answered the Bostonian.

"How 'bout you?" she asked me again.

"No," I told her. "Thanks for thinking of me, but I'm going to stick around and see if I can help." I was content staying onboard, but I felt like I was missing out as I watched her golden ponytail bobbing happily down the sidewalk with the other passengers.

At the last second the girl from Boston scrambled to put her boots on. "Are you sure you don't want to come?" she asked me.

"I thought you were staying."

"I'm going now."

"I'm all set," I responded. "Have fun." As it turned out, there was not much for me to do to help. Chicken Jim asked me to help him prepare the back platform for the loading of luggage. He made it sound like it was a lot of work. Then he disappeared. So, I stacked the mattresses and removed the folding wooden platform doors. Even though I did all the work it only took three minutes.

Driver Brian leaned against the front bumper until the first new passenger arrived. He sat in the driver's seat while they came

The Moon Over Manhattan

aboard one by one. After taking tickets and money he made sure each person signed the liability waiver.

The German girl in the fancy dress came aboard to pay for her ticket. She looked amazing in her house cleaner outfit. She was wearing a flared black pleated skirt with white knee-high stockings and black shoes. Her skirt had a row of black buttons that rode up high on her stomach like a girdle. Her bright white socks featured a row of black sequins down the outer thigh. Her white blouse had frilly blossoms of lace on the breast and her neck was tied with a black bow.

Chicken Jim had her in his sights the second she picked up her suitcase. "Do you need help with that?" he asked her suavely.

"No!" she barked. "I don't need your help." She pulled her suitcase away from his extended hand and shooed him off with her flagging fingers. "Go away!"

"Geeze, what did I do?" he said out of the side of his mouth to me, then he wiggled his eyebrows suggestively.

The perturbed German girl tossed a big pair of hiking boots on the floor and landed her suitcase on the seat beside me. I had been relaxing on the comfortable cushions of the front platform, but it was hot just sitting there, so I grabbed my boots to go outside. She looked at me tying my boots and spoke to me in a German accent, "You will go with me for food, ja?" She kicked off her shoes.

I did not know how to respond at first. Was this a question or a command? "Yes," I responded dumbly. "I guess so. Sure."

"Wait for me while I get out of this stupid uniform," she instructed. Her green eyes smiled brightly behind her small, oval reading glasses. Her short-cropped hair was dark black with maroon highlights and her bangs swept across her forehead when she leaned over, hiding half of one eye.

"Sure!" I said. "I'll wait for you. I'm Johnny."

"Wunderbar," she said. "I'm Vera." She opened her suitcase and removed a pair of short shorts.

"Nice to meet you Vera," I said. "Did you come directly from work?"

"Yes," she answered harshly. "I just got off work."

"Where do you work?"

"I'm an au pair," she huffed.

"What does an au pair do?"

She smiled so I could see her cute dimples. "I clean their house and watched their children."

"Does that pay well?" I inquired.

"Not really." She elaborated, "I saved enough for this trip, but it's so expensive here. I could never afford to live in New York if I didn't get free room and board."

"How do you like it here in America?" I asked.

"It's been the greatest year of my life," she revealed, "but I've seen enough of New York. I'm excited to see more of the country."

"Do you enjoy being an au pair?" I asked her.

"Not so much anymore," she spat. "I work for a company that treats us like slaves. "I can't tell you how hard it was to get this time off approved. I have half a mind to tell them to go to hell, but I love the family I've been working for." She unbuttoned three buttons at her neck, turned on her heel so her back faced me and asked, "You will get the zipper?"

"No problem," I said rising to my feet.

"I have been living with a great family," she explained as she bent her neck forward, "but they just left for Europe, so they won't be needing me for six weeks."

I pinched my fingers on the fine fabric and unzipped the fastener all the way until I could see a strip of sexy white lace crossing her back. "If they don't need you," I asked, "why would they deny your vacation?"

She lifted her blouse over her head and began folding it as she spoke. "The family I work for wants me to travel. It's my agency that said no. Families hire us through them." She spun around and laid her folded blouse in her open suitcase, standing there in her provocative white bra. "They think they control our lives. Just because we're expected to act a certain way on the job does not mean that we have to act that way all the time."

She made a motion like she was scratching her back and her bra suddenly came loose, then she took it off right there in front of my face without a second thought.

I averted my eyes like a gentleman and said, "Excuse me." The moment was gone.

She tossed the garment in her suitcase and moved her hands to her hips.

Chicken Jim stood in the open luggage bays making googly eyes at me. I watched his face enjoy the show.

Much to my delight, the tepid East German girl snapped, "I don't care if you see me naked. I'm not a little girl."

I looked her in the eye and said, "Cool." Her breasts were small with small dark boyish nipples, but they were firm enough not to be too pointy when she leaned over. Just when I thought it could get no better, she put her thumbs in the waistband of her skirt and shook her hips as she shimmied it down. I was sitting on the edge of my seat, leaning forward with my elbows on my knees, so her face was close to mine when she lowered her head to balance with her skirt below her knee. Naturally, I put out my hand for her to hold in case she lost her balance.

She teetered with her toes caught in the folds of her skirt for an instant, so I made ready to catch her. She gave my hand a disparaging look before performing a quick hop to catch her balance. She scolded me with a look of contempt as she stood up. "You will not treat me like a girl!"

"Sorry," I said. "I was just letting you know I was there if you needed me."

Her provocative au pair skirt was quite revealing, despite the frilly white hem. I figured she had to be wearing a slip under there, right? Anything else would be dehumanizing. It would be unbefitting of a strong self-respecting woman, right? Boy was I wrong.

Suddenly, she was standing there in her sequined socks with my eyes stranded at sea level, shipwrecked on the skin of her sensational snatch. I sweat like a clam, helplessly trapped in a moment where I was eye to eye with the folds of her feminine flower. She sure looked great in nothing but her knee-high socks. I watched her fabulous body step into her tight shorts. She pulled them up snug against her crotch until her sock suspenders were visible below the hem. She looked amazing topless. She stepped into her hiking boots, took a seat, and laced them up.

"Nice boots," I commented.

"Vat?" she snapped.

"Those are some serious hiking boots," I clarified.

"I don't fuck around," she replied. "When I see a mountain, I climb it."

"Killer," I said, feeling hot and clammy. "I'll wait for you outside," I suggested.

"You will wait here," she commanded. "I'm almost ready." She removed a black halter top from her suitcase and pulled it over her head. She packed her au pair clothes and shoes into her suitcase and buckled it closed. "You will take this back there for me, ja?" She handed me her suitcase. "If he says anything to me, I will choke him out," she assured me.

"Sure," I said with a laugh. "No problem."

I brought her suitcase to the back platform and passed it to Chicken Jim. He put it under the wooden floorboards with the rest of the luggage. "That German chick is hot," he whispered conspicuously.

"What did you do to piss her off?" I asked him.

"I was just rolling out the romance," he answered. "She's got a great ass," he commented without answering my question.

"No comment," I said quietly, looking in her direction. She was watching us. I walked back toward her shaking my head.

Before heading out she demanded, "You will tell me what he said."

"He was just paying you a compliment," I tried to cover for him at my own expense.

"Tell me," she barked.

"He said you have a nice ass," I told her.

"Fucking schwein," she barked. "I don't need his compliments." His ears perked up. "You will tell him to fuck off," she insisted.

I gave her a bewildered look. "I think, I'll let you handle that one," I laughed. "I'm afraid it just won't sound the same coming from me."

"What are you looking at?" she chastised Chicken Jim.

"Nothin'!" He spat. He had been ogling her the entire time like a lonely-eyed puppy.

"Fuck off," she leered. She stormed off the bus and I followed. We walked toward the busy part of Washington Heights.

"What kind of food do you like?" I asked.

"Take me anywhere," she told me, "as long as it's not McDonald's."

We hurried across an intersection. As she walked, I noticed her muscular legs and arms. She seemed pretty tough, but she had a youthful manner and smiled often enough to keep my interest. At the next crosswalk, no cars were coming, so I started walking against the light.

"Halt," she commanded, scolding me with a harsh German accent. I froze in the middle of the road and walked back to the curb. "You seem nice," she told me while we stood there waiting. "I can deal with you, but that other guy is a fucking pig."

"Who's that?" I asked, knowing who she meant.

"The guy on the bus. He called himself the Chicken Man or Chicken Dick or something stupid like that."

"Ha!" I laughed out loud. "That's Chicken Jim. "He works for the Tortoise."

"Scheisse!" she spat. "I was hoping he was not coming with us. Is he a driver?"

"He's training to become one," I told her.

"He's foul," she remarked.

"Ha! Foul," I laughed.

"Seriously," she looked at me sideways, "he wouldn't leave me alone in the bus station. I told him to screw, but he followed me around reading me a stupid poem. He tried to grab my suitcase inside the bus, then he watched the whole time I was changing my clothes. Pervert."

The Moon Over Manhattan

The light turned and "Go!" was her next command. I was starting to like this girl. "Where are you from?" she asked me.

"Rhode Island," I told her. "How 'bout you?"

"Berlin," she said, walking briskly.

I struggled to keep up. Her ass looked rock solid in her tight shorts. I could tell she was an avid hiker. "I went to Munich, a couple of years ago," I told her.

"Ja," she said enthusiastically. "You got to taste some real German beer. Did you like it?"

"I was only there for a couple of days on a Eurorail Pass. Mostly, I remember the beer at the Hofbräuhaus and the concentration camp at Dachau."

"Ya," she seemed disconcerted, "everyone always goes to Dachau, but there's so much more to see in Germany than those stupid concentration camps. I wish they would just run them into the ground."

"The beer was awesome," I said. "What brought you to America?"

"I was an au pair for a family outside Berlin at university," she answered. "They asked me to come with them when the husband got transferred here for a job. They went back home, so I took this job, so I can stay until my work visa runs out next year, then I go back to university."

"What's your major?"

"Music."

"You're a musician," I marveled.

"I'm a singer," she answered. "I study voice, mostly."

"You sing. That is awesome. What kind of singer?"

"I sing alto."

"Is that like opera or something?"

"I am not a la-la-la singer; I am a ra-ra-ra singer. I like to sing loud."

"Are you in a band?"

"I was in a punk band before I came here, but I had to quit to come."

"Killer," I nodded. "That rocks." It made sense that she was into punk, I reconciled. Her hair was chopped short like a tomboy, her tone was gruff, and her nose ring matched her persona, all pure punk.

"I like hard-core punk," she responded, "like the Ramones, but mostly German bands. You know Die Ärzte?"

"No. What does that mean?"

"It's a punk band from Berlin," she told me. "Farin Urlaub is a mad guitarist you know. You will look them up."

"I like classic rock, you know, Springsteen, Pink Floyd, the Doors."

After peaking inside a few dark restaurants and pursuing several window menus, we found a place called Yummy Falafel and stood in line. We got our food and headed back toward the bus, eating as we walked.

****

The sun was below the horizon, but the western sky had yet to grow completely dark. The Green Tortoise bus was parked in the shadow of an apartment building, so that the sidewalk next to the bus fell entirely under the piss-yellow light of streetlamps. A bunch of people were congregated near the bus door with backpacks resting against their legs, but they seemed a bit put-off. These were not the happy-go-lucky passengers I had seen in Boston where it was all hugs and high-fives. This was a very eclectic scene.

Driver Chris was sitting with his head in his hands on the bottom step in the doorway next to French Sandrine. She had her arm around him, and I could tell by his body language that something was wrong. He had a blank expression on his face. Vera and I kept our distance for the time being. He normally smiled all the time, so having no expression diminished his aspect to the point where he looked sad.

The backpackers gathered on the sidewalk sounded angry. "This is bullshit," one of them complained.

"It's not fair!" shouted someone else.

One guy was talking to his girlfriend like he had a wild hair up his ass. "They gave me our deposit back!"

"What the fuck!" she responded.

"There's another trip leaving in ten days," her friend told her. "They said to call the office to see if any seats are available."

A late arriving backpacker walked up to the group and someone told him, "They're not letting anyone on." This was very disconcerting.

"Brian will explain your options," the driver pleaded with someone. "You just need to wait your turn." He shook his head in consternation. "Brian will discuss your options when it's your turn to go inside. It's out of my hands." He rose to his feet to get out of the way when a six-foot-tall backpacker came down the steps.

"Well, that fucking sucks," derided the young man as he folded and pocketed his wallet. "I didn't come all this way to take a Greyhound," he remonstrated. "I refuse to take a fucking Greyhound."

The red-bearded driver apologized repeatedly. "I'm sorry, I'm sorry, I'm sorry," he sobbed. "How many times can I say it. I'm terribly sorry, okay."

The Moon Over Manhattan 89

The tall backpacker lowered his voice as he shouldered his pack. "It's nothing against you personally," he said. "Sorry to hear about your brother."

"Thank you," Driver Chris' words followed him as he stormed off. Driver Chris moaned in defeat and his hands covered his face with a quick breath.

My heart sank for a moment.

Vera pulled my arm. "Tell me what this means," she demanded.

We turned away to speak privately. "They're turning people away, issuing refunds," I told her.

"Ja! I see this, dummkopf," she chided me.

"It sounds like there may be other options," I pointed out. "There's another bus leaving next week."

"I will not stay here another week," she said bluntly. "Ask about his brother."

"I don't think we should bother him right now," I told her.

She did not seem pleased.

I heard Driver Brian shout from inside the bus. "Who's next?"

"I'm going to ask the other one," she told me.

Before Driver Chris had a chance to sit back down, Vera tried to enter the bus, but French Sandrine blocked her with her arm braced across the threshold. She shook her head. "Hold up!" she told her, "You need to wait your turn."

"You will let me in," she commanded. "I need to get a tampon from my suitcase."

I stepped back and leaned against the bus, trying to hide in the shadows.

Vera's strong tone eradicated her free will. "Make it quick," she said sympathetically. She thumbed over her shoulder and ushered her inside with a sweep of her arm.

"You will wait," Vera said as she rose up the steps. She at once engaged the big blond driver in conversation.

As soon as her foot hit the first step the woman next in line complained, "Hey! That's not fair," she shouted with a thick New Jersey accent.

"Brian will be happy to help refund your deposit next," he told the uptight American woman.

She exploded in Jerseyese, "I don't want a fucking refund! I paid for a fucking adventure trip. I want a fucking adventure trip."

Driver Chris made an annoyed expression at his girlfriend, so she went inside to see what was taking German Vera so long. A few moments later they came out together and the Jersey girl stomped up the steps.

"Sorry," he said as she climbed the steps, then he sat back down to block the door.

I walked a few steps away with the German girl. "What did he say?" I implored.

"He said not to worry because I already paid my ticket," she revealed.

"That's great," I huffed.

The girl from New Jersey was yelling at the driver inside the bus. "Please calm down," he implored her. "I wish there was more we could do, but my hands are tied." He tried to soothe her. "There's another bus leaving at the end of next week. We can get you a seat on that bus for sure."

"I can't wait until next week," she said, sounding trapped. "I have a flight to catch in San Francisco in ten days."

"This is a bus station," he informed her. "You can take a Greyhound. They'll get you there in three days."

"Fine!" she exasperated in defeat. "Refund my credit card, so I can get the fuck out of here."

"That shouldn't be a problem," he told her. "As soon as we are done here, I will be calling the office and have them return your deposit." He took her name and number, and she stormed off.

Driver Chris was sitting on the bottom step holding his head in his hands again. More people were walking up as we waited.

Among the passengers gathered on the sidewalk, one exceedingly cheerful and energetic guy stood out from the rest. He wore a jungle safari hat, reminiscent of Indiana Jones. He was strikingly handsome, one of those rarified young men with rock star looks. He fell into a category of attractiveness above-and-beyond normal humans. He had all the suave of Ricky Martin, but he was even better looking.

He spoke with a beautiful-sounding South American accent. It was the kind of exotic tonality with the power to entice the ladies. He was young, muscular, short, thin, and apparently accustomed to the attention of women. He was already entertaining four of them simultaneously. He had the attention of the girls with Irish brogues and braided hair, the athletic Canadian with the bright red lipstick and her new friend, the Australian scuba diver with the golden ponytail.

He stood out not only because of his good looks and cool headwear, but also because he was neither commiserating with others, nor was he standing in line to be sent home. He looked relaxed, like he was planning on sticking around.

A black Town Car pulled away from the curb in front of the bus. An attractive olive-skinned girl approached the group of backpackers. She was followed closely by a small-framed Asian guy, who was carrying her fancy luggage. He was carrying a metal-framed backpack, but he was not dressed like a backpacker. He was slender, well-dressed in slacks and a white button-down Oxford, not tailored but form fitting. He had an obvious overbite that remained mostly hidden behind his upper lip. He wore conservative glasses that gave him the appearance of an intellectual. His boyish short hair rose high above his prominent forehead without the need for hair gel. He was clearly older than the rest of us, probably the oldest guy on the bus.

His traveling partner was clearly not the backpacking type either. She exuded a certain grace and elegance that reflected a higher station in life, or at least higher than most of the motley crew of slouching travelers standing before her. She carried herself like a lady. Judging by the way she held her shoulders, I could imagine her balancing a book atop her head. It was uncanny. "Put those down," she instructed her attendant, referring to the large brown Louis Vuitton suitcase and matching garment bag.

Her traveling companion set both of her bags on the sidewalk and removed his backpack. His backpack appeared to be as light as a feather, like there was nothing in it. When he set the metal framed pack by his feet, I noticed the sale tag was still attached. He caught me looking and discreetly bent down and ripped it off. He stood up and crumpled the tag in his fist.

"Hello everyone," the woman greeted those close to her with a pleasant tone of reverence. She spoke with a hint of an accent that I could not place. "My name is Ursula and I am simply delighted to be here." She huffed a sigh. "What an afternoon we've had."

A few greetings were exchanged but no names were offered in return.

"Why is everyone so frumpy?" she twittered. "Is something wrong?"

One of the backpackers informed her, "The trip's been canceled." He was clearly disgruntled. "They said there's another bus next week or we can catch a Greyhound."

"What in heaven's name is this nonsense?" She enunciated with an uplifted chin. "I say that's balderdash," she trailed off. "Who's in charge here?" she demanded.

"Oh shit," I whispered to Vera. I stepped back into the shadows leaning against the bus, pretending to mind my own business.

The outspoken woman was clearly upset. She approached the red-haired driver with her Asian lackey following close behind. "Do you work here?" she asked him incredulously. Before he could answer she looked over his head into the bus. "Oh driver," she called to the massive blond behind the wheel.

"There's a line," someone informed her snidely. "Wait your turn."

The red-haired driver looked up at her with wet eyes. "I'm the lead driver," he told her softly.

"Please tell me the trip has not been cancelled," she implored him. "I have a confirmed reservation."

"I'm sorry miss," Driver Brian politely consoled her. "I'll explain everything when it's your turn. For now, you need to wait like everybody else."

"Brian will be available to help you in a few minutes ma'am," said Driver Chris.

"Don't ma'am me," she shot back. "My name is Ursula and I demand an explanation." The Asian guy remained silent.

"You need to wait your turn Ursula," he told her. "Brian will explain your options when it's your turn."

"Qué mierda!" She objected sternly in Spanish. "That's unacceptable! It is imperative that we get to San Francisco on a private coach, not a public bus. Our only option is the Green Tortoise," Ursula spoke adamantly. "We cannot take Greyhound!" She looked pissed. She turned and barked something harsh in Chinese to her companion. He remained silently demure.

"You speak Cantonese?" the driver asked him.

"Yes," he answered, adding something in Cantonese.

"Cool!" said Driver Chris excitedly. "I've been taking lessons." He said something back in the foreign tongue.

The dignified woman ushered her friend forward to shake his hand. "This is my friend Pak Chan," she gestured with an upward palm.

Driver Chris gave her a shitty smile and said, "Nice to meet you Pak Chan." He did a little bow with prayer hands. I shook the Chinese guy's little hand and introduced myself.

"Pak is a flute player traveling around the world on tour with the Hong Kong Chinese Orchestra. As you know, China is not a free country, but the orchestra's top musicians are at times allowed to travel apart from the group as long as they get to the next performance on time."

"I have wanted to see America since I was a child," Pak interjected.

"Right on!" cheered Driver Chris.

"Your culture is very open and accepting compared to my country," the Chinese man continued. "I am thankful for the opportunity my government has provided, but they have ways of keeping us musicians on a short leash." He leaned in and lowered his voice. "They will detain my family if I don't get to San Francisco in time for our next performance."

"That's barbaric," declared Driver Chris.

The black-haired Peruvian beauty continued without pause. "It's nice they let the musicians travel unsupervised, but there's always a risk of never seeing your family again. If we do not arrive on time for the concert, Pak's family may be detained indefinitely. So, it is imperative that we make it to our destination on time," she asserted. "We specifically chose this bus because it gets to San Francisco exactly when Pak needs to be there, no sooner, no later. I'll rent a car and drive him there myself if it comes to that, but we cannot take Greyhound." There was no overt response from anyone. "Are you listening?" she demanded of the red-bearded driver.

"I hear ya," he said nonchalantly. "For now, you need to wait your turn."

She sneered with a huff. "Thank you," she said, seeming satisfied for the moment.

"Where are you from Pak?" the driver asked the man.

"Pak is currently living in Hong Kong," his friend answered for him.

He spoke up for himself. "I was born on the mainland, but I spent my childhood in Yantai, in the north."

The driver began speaking Chinese again. Soon all three of them were exchanging Cantonese phrases. The driver's grasp of the language must have been fairly primitive because they switched back to English after a few exchanges. "I've always wanted to visit Hong Kong. I hear it rocks," he said.

"Hong Kong is a modern city with beautiful architecture," the Chinese guy lilted girlishly. I was beginning to think he might be gay. "Hong Kong has many parks with good places to hike," he told the driver. "Chinese Hollywood has Avenue of the Stars and they are building a Hong Kong Disneyland. My apologies, my English is not so good," he admitted.

"Jeez, it sounds fine to me," commented the driver. "My Cantonese sucks." He remained seated in the doorway.

"I only had two years of English school," Pak revealed.

"Where did you learn Cantonese?" I asked the woman. "Are you from Hong Kong too?"

"I'm from Lima, Peru," she informed him. "There's a large Chinese population in Peru." She said this like it was common knowledge, so I tended to believe her. The conversation continued like that for a few more minutes until the Peruvian cut it short. "That's enough of the personal details," she snapped. "We might not even be taking this bus," she warned her friend.

"I'm sorry to hear about your brother," Vera told Driver Chris when they were face to face.

"What?" I asked stepping closer.

"My brother had a really bad accident last night," he informed us. "He fell off a parking garage and fractured his skull twenty-nine times." There was a collective gasp of horror, followed by condolences. "I just found out an hour ago. It happened last night. He survived the night, but he's still in intensive care. They don't think he's gonna make it."

I cursed under my breath. "I'm sorry to hear that."

"Thanks," he said sounding horribly dejected. "My brother is not the kind of person who gives up without a fight. If anyone has a chance of surviving, it is him. He's a tough guy, a firefighter."

"That's good," I responded.

He continued to explain in a dire tone. "If he dies, I'll have to go home for the funeral and the trip will be over for everyone. We'll have to put you all on Greyhound."

"No way!" My jaw dropped.

"I'll fill you in later once the rest of the ticketed passengers return," he talked to me on the side. "Once everyone is back, we'll have a sit down and discuss your options."

The petite olive-skinned girl consoled the grieving driver. "I am very sorry to hear about your brother," she said formally. "You need to go home to be with your family. You must be beside yourself. Surely, your employer must understand. They will have to send a replacement driver."

"Our dispatcher is working on sending a replacement, but all of our drivers are on the road or they have a trip coming up in the next few days and they can't be spared. They're calling former drivers to see if anyone is available, but that's a longshot."

Ursula pointed inside the bus. "Why can't he drive?" she asked bluntly motioning to the driver inside the bus.

"He can, but it takes two drivers to get where we need to go," he explained.

"Longshot or not," the diplomatic woman professed, "it is imperative that the two of us get to San Francisco on the Green Tortoise."

"Do you have tickets?" he asked.

"We have reservations," she clarified.

"So, you didn't pay-in-full yet?"

"No," she answered flatly.

His eyebrows lifted as he inhaled through his nose. "I'm sorry," he said blinking. "We can't help you. You have to take a Greyhound."

"Under no circumstances will we take a Greyhound," she insisted.

"If you don't mind," he said defensively, "Brian will explain all of your options when it's your turn to go inside."

She stormed away with a huff and her friend followed closely behind.

****

I got a whiff of ganja. Chicken Jim was hanging-out in front of the bus with a few of the Boston passengers. "Maybe they can tell us something." I motioned for Vera to come with me.

When she did not follow, I gave her an inquisitive look. "Fuck that!" she snapped. "I don't need any more chicken shit."

"Ha!" I laughed. "It's Chicken Jim, but you're right, he is completely full of shit." I did not want to facilitate any more animosity than was clearly deserved, so I spoke in his defense. "He's totally harmless," I told her. "You have nothing to fear."

"I have no fear of him," she objected to the supposition. "He will be the one who is afraid," she said forcefully. After a pause she added. "You will go. You will tell me what you learn." She walked off in the other direction and I passed through the angry mob to go stand with the others.

A semicircle of people stood around a barefoot girl in her mid-twenties leaning against the front bumper with a cocked leg. The brown-skinned woman radiated positive energy with an almost visible aura. Her long raven-black hair shimmered in the soft yellow streetlight like a mirror on the netherworld. As I approached, I heard her say, "The mind is like a bicycle. It's only stable when it's moving forward. If you stop thinking, you'll fall over." Over sweatpants she wore a loose-fitting hemp V-neck with visible bra straps. Above her voluptuous cleavage hung a carved bone figurine.

"Oh! I love your necklace," I crooned.

She greeted me with a bountiful smile and said, "It's the Fertility Goddess."

I joined the circle, standing between Chicken Jim and British Sue.

Flip-flop and the British girl's friend said, "Hi."

"I just heard some terrible news about Chris' brother," I said to Chicken Jim.

"Dude!" exclaimed the driver-in-training before lowering his voice. "It's a total nightmare."

"What is?" questioned Jen, the soccer player from Boston.

"Oh! You don't know?" I said.

"Know what?" she demanded. None of the Boston passengers seemed to know.

"Chris' brother is in the hospital," I told them.

Chicken Jim pointed his finger at the bridge of his glasses and pushed them on his face. "His brother fell from the third floor of a parking garage in Hartford," he confirmed.

"Scheisse!" exclaimed Berndt Toast.

"Oh no! That's terrible," gasped Flip-flop.

"Seriously," emphasized Chicken Jim, "he fractured his skull more than twenty times."

"He's still hanging in there," acknowledged the new girl.

"When did this happen?" questioned Flip-flop.

"Last night," he revealed. "His heart stopped three times, but they brought him back to life."

"Perhaps his journey on Earth is not complete." The raven-haired woman pointed out the positive. "The spirit must be strong within him to have survived the pull of the underworld. Three times no less."

"He's not out of the woods yet," warned Chicken Jim. "He's still in intensive care."

The soulful woman closed her eyes in a posture of silent prayer for a moment with three fingers touching on each hand. "May Goddess grant Chris' brother the strength to heal and to help him on his journey to wellness."

"Amen!" I said without thinking. I had never heard anyone pray to the Goddess before, but I can tell you it felt right coming from her, and I was happy with the way I responded. She was so chill, I felt more relaxed just being in her company.

"Is that's what all the commotion has been about?" Flip-flop wondered aloud.

"A lot of people are angry, but there's nothing we can do," the driver-in-training explained. "The home office told us we couldn't sell any more tickets, so we've been refunding deposits and sending people home." He was struggling to get a hit from the pipe.

"You're sending people home?" The Bostonian was discombobulated. "Has the trip been cancelled?"

"It's not cancelled for everyone," revealed the young woman with the carved bone necklace. "They told me I should just hang-out and see what happens because I paid-in-full for my ticket six months ago."

Chicken Jim confirmed, "Anyone who has paid-in-full needs to stick around until the office tells us what to do next."

"Wunderbar!" exclaimed Berndt Toast. "I paid in-full in Boston."

"That reminds me," the bubbly blond-haired Brit spoke to me directly. "Here's you fifty quid," she said softly as she handed me a

The Moon Over Manhattan

folded wad of money. "If you 'adden't done that," said the Brit, "it'd really 'ave thrown a spanner in it for us. Cheerio."

"Yes, nice one," commented the British girl's friend. "Thanks."

"It was the least I could do," I contended. "I'm so glad you're staying."

"Ain't he smarmy bloke," she whispered to her friend with a nudge of her elbow.

"Dude!" Chicken Jim raised his eyebrows and looked impressed. "Is it me, or do random chicks just give you money?" he asked jokingly. "That's twice today, man."

"Did you just call my mother a chick?" I asked in dismay.

The German guy interjected, "Is Chris leaving to go home with his brother?"

The driver's apprentice took the pipe down from his lips and said, "That's up in the air at this point." He checked to see if the lighter was working while he spoke. "The Tortoise is trying to find a replacement driver," he informed us. "We have to call the office to find out before we leave."

"Chris must be beside himself," Flip-flop empathized. "This might be his last chance to see his brother alive. They can't make him stay."

"We offered to take him home," Chicken Jim informed us. "Hartford isn't far."

"I was encouraging him to go home right away," added the brown-skinned beauty. "He can't seem to make up his mind."

"He said his brother would want him to stay if it means he would lose his job," revealed the-driver-in-training. "So, he's not rushing home at this point."

British Sue spoke up next. "What happens if he snuffs it?"

"Sue!" Her friend English Tessa said with a look of disgust. She was aghast.

"He'll have to go home for the funeral," blurted Chicken Jim.

"What then?" British Sue demanded.

He shrugged in thought. "He'll probably stick around Connecticut for a while."

"Don't be a daft cow!" British Sue chided. "What happens to us?"

"If Chris has to leave the trip will be cancelled," he stated flatly.

"That's bollocks!" commented the Brit.

He nodded confirmation. "You'll get your money back, or you can wait for the next bus."

"I can't wait around for the next bus," the Bostonian voiced her dread. "I have to be in San Diego to register for classes in two weeks. I need to get there by next Monday no matter what," she asserted.

"No worries, Flip-flop," Chicken Jim consoled her. "That shouldn't be a problem. The Tortoise will put you on a Greyhound, wherever you need to go."

"When will you know?" she demanded.

"We'll let you know before we leave around ten," he told her.

"You talked with them?" the Bostonian asked the raven-haired woman.

"Yes!" she revealed. "I'm in the same boat. I don't have the option of catching the next bus because I go back to teaching full-time in three weeks."

"Oh! You're a teacher." Flip-flop smiled approvingly. "Where do you teach?"

"I teach at a Dominican school right here in Washington Heights," she revealed.

"I've been toying with the idea of becoming a teacher myself," revealed the soccer player.

"That's awesome," praised the barefoot woman.

"I have a degree in secondary ed," I interjected.

"Where do you teach?" she asked me.

"I was subbing in Rhode Island, but I'm moving to San Francisco."

"Groovy," crooned the woman. Her brown eyes were like orbs of spiritual energy.

Flip-flop asked her, "What do you teach?"

"Everything," she responded. "All the major subjects, English, Reading, Math, Science, you name it.

"So, you're a primary school teacher," deduced the Bostonian. "I'm trying to decide which way to go."

"Yes," the woman enthused. "I don't think I could ever teach high school."

"Why not?"

"Secondary school teachers teach the same thing all day. I'm with the same group of children all day, so I don't have to teach from bell to bell."

"Your school doesn't have bells?" fathomed Flip-flop.

"I wish," huffed the Dominican schoolteacher. "There's a bell that rings between periods, but I kind of go with the flow and teach whatever's on their minds."

"You let your students decide what you teach?" inquired the fit soccer player from Boston.

The Moon Over Manhattan

"Not really," clarified the New Yorker. "They think they're in charge, but I point them in a general direction and encourage them to go a certain way."

"Do you ever wish you went for secondary ed?" probed the Bostonian.

"Never," responded the New Yorker. "The young kids have open minds. They get along with each other so well, it is incredible. There's no bias, no notions of wealth. Even though some cannot afford the tuition, the kids do not differentiate. Children don't see skin color. They know nothing of hate. If children were left to get along without adults, there would be no war."

She went on with a furrowed brow. "Primary teachers nurture and help shape children into wonderful little people. Even if it is only make-believe, we keep up the illusion of living in a perfect world, at least for a while they are young. The thought of teaching secondary school freaks-me-out a bit. I would never want to be the teacher who destroys a young person's innocent perception of the world. By necessity, older kids need to learn to defend themselves against would-be oppressors who would otherwise discriminate against them or seek to rob them of their dignity. I'm not sure I could shoulder that responsibility.

"Don't get me wrong," the New Yorker expounded. "I understand how important it is for young people to be vigilant against racism and sexism, especially as a woman of color." She nodded profusely. "We need to teach secondary students about the horrors of war and famine. They need to be aware of rape and human trafficking, drug addiction and crime. I just don't want to be part of it. I prefer to focus on the positive. Most of the people in the world are good upstanding citizens who care about each other. Most of them would lend a hand to those in need if given the opportunity to help the less fortunate. You see good people come out in force every time there's a natural disaster."

"That's true," agreed Flip-flop.

"I like to think my students are the kind of people who will grow up to help others when disaster strikes." The soulful schoolteacher smiled endearingly. "I hope they are part of the solution and not part of the problem." She corrected herself. "I know they will be part of the solution."

"Wunderbar!" cheered Berndt Toast.

"That's awesome," praised Flip-flop.

"I give up." Chicken Jim told the woman and he passed her the pipe. "It's cached."

The young brown-skinned girl tried to blow out the ashes, but the pipe was clogged. She said, "It needs a stir." She looked around at us. "I need something pointy."

I quickly reached into my pocket for my Swiss Army knife, but it was gone. I patted down my pockets.

"What's wrong?" she asked.

"I lost my knife," I answered with concern.

"Don't worry. You'll find it," she reassured me.

"I hope so," I fretted. "My father gave it to me when I was twelve." I figured I had left it on the dinette table when Little Josh cut his finger.

Berndt Toast pulled out a knife with even more blades than mine. "Here you go," he said. He opened the smallest blade and handed it to her.

The voluptuous New Yorker stirred the bowl, blew out the ash away from her bare feet, closed the knife, and handed it back to the German. She put the pipe inside her bag of weed and filled the bowl.

"Thank you so much. This weed is amazing," praised Berndt Toast.

"You're welcome," she responded.

"I love smoking pot," he touted. "It's like medicine to me."

"Me too," crooned the dark-haired woman. "Weed calms me down."

"That's funny," Berndt Toast said with a laugh. "You seem like the calmest person ever." We all agreed with nods and mumbled confirmation.

"Believe me; I'm a fucking mess," said the barefooted beauty. "I get extremely paranoid sometimes and I have terrible panic attacks. I'd be lost without marijuana."

"Smoking hash has the opposite effect on me," blurted the English blond. "It makes me bloody paranoid," she revealed.

"Weed gives me the munchies," said the German. "I started smoking to improve my appetite when I was on chemo for my leg." He showed-off his artificial leg.

"How did that work out?" I asked.

"It worked out well," he informed us. "I'm three years cancer free."

"Congratulations," cheered the woman.

"I can dance now, and I'm as fat as a mini-bear," he added.

We all offered him congratulations.

Without a word the teacher from New York reached out and offered me the pipe.

"Thanks," I said as our hands touched.

"Oh, you're welcome," she said soulfully. She locked eyes with me and nodded kindly, letting her fingers linger on my hand. She giggled.

"You're totally baked," I said. Now, they all giggled.

"You're totally right," the woman breathed. "We're totally baked." More giggles.

I stepped back, held the pipe up to my mouth, flicked the lighter, and studied the barefooted girl's face as I inhaled. Her features were simple and natural. She wore no makeup. The upturned corners of her prominent lips were pressed into the creases of her round cheeks, creating a pleasant relaxed expression. Her thick black hair, rooted low on her forehead, framed her face in the shape of a shield. Her deep-set eyes drew me in, radiating a spiritual energy.

I was so intrigued. I had never been in the presence of someone like her before. She was clearly an old soul, connected to the ancestors so deeply that it affected her outward appearance. I had never witnessed such radiant spiritual beauty. I imagined her to be grounded to the Earth like a lightning rod. In that moment, as I gazed upon her face, she appeared to me as a goddess of energy and light. I found myself enamored with soulful respect and homage. To me this was Gaia, the personification of the Earth.

I staggered back with a spasm of small coughs. The group giggled again. I wiped my eyes and handed the pipe to British Sue.

"I have to pass," she said waving her hand. "Wacky backy makes my skin crawl. I get mad paranoid, remember?"

"You just need to remember to breathe sweetheart," advised the owner of the pipe.

English Tessa took a small puff and passed it on.

Berndt Toast wavered, "I'm so hungry I can't think straight." His eyes rolled in his head. "I need to eat something."

"Ha!" Chicken Jim clucked. "You're not baked; you're burnt." He bobbed his shoulders and went, "Coo, coo, ca-choo!"

I chuckled. The raven-haired woman smiled with a contorted expression and a tilted head.

"How is it working for the Tortoise?" asked the teacher from New York.

"Being a driver's apprentice is the best job in the world," he proclaimed. "I just don't know how much longer it will last."

"Then you will become a driver?" she asked.

The wild-haired Pennsylvanian smiled at the notion. "I'm more worried about getting fired," he admitted.

"Why?" she questioned.

"Driver Chris hasn't been happy with me lately." He put a finger on the bridge of his glasses and looked directly at her cleavage. "He questions my prior-i-titties," he stammered.

I snorted a laugh.

"Imagine that," commented Flip-flop.

Driver Brian knocked on the windshield above our heads causing the soulful girl to jump away from the bumper. We all looked inside at the Peruvian woman and her Chinese friend standing next to the massive blond-haired person behind the steering wheel. He waved to the driver-in-training. "Come!" he shouted.

Chicken Jim jumped to it. The black girl propped her leg against the bumper again, and the conversation continued, but I remained distracted by what transpired inside the bus. Chicken Jim followed Driver Chris up the steps to speak with Driver Brian. The Peruvian woman flashed her ID at them like she was a police officer. They all shook hands as though they were in agreement, then the Peruvian proceeded to pay Driver Brian with hundred-dollar bills.

Suddenly, the groovy woman's eyes widened, and her chin lifted. "Look!" she exclaimed. "The Moon is out of its cave!" Her bent leg dropped to the pavement and she drifted past me. She gestured for us to follow. We all took a few steps along the sidewalk toward the intersection until we could see past the building on the corner.

"You gotta be kidding me," I marveled. A brilliant half orb of silver-white radiance unfettered by clouds hung low in the western sky. It was one of the brightest moons I had ever seen, shining in the sky over the Hudson River next to the towers of the George Washington Bridge.

"Wow!" commented Flip-flop. "It's enormous."

We all gazed blissfully at the glowing moon, slack-jawed in amazement.

"The Moon turns me on," the young brown-skinned teacher spoke in a velvet-soft voice. "When it comes out; I come out too."

Her long black hair sparkled like lake water under the spotlight of lunar radiance. She noticed me staring.

"You look amazing in the moonlight," I fumbled, turning red in the face.

"We all look better under the moonlight," She laughed. "Outward beauty is only a thin veil. I'm more interested in what lies beneath the surface."

"You're from out of this world," I gasped. "Where are you from?"

"I'm from right here in Washington Heights," she informed us. She opened her arms and gave me a hug that left me feeling warm and appreciated. "Do you mind going back?" she asked softly. "I feel safer over there by the bus." I stepped aside and she returned to her position at the front bumper, leaning with her back against the bus. I circled around her with the others and she said, "Thanks. Sorry about that. There are a lot of sketchy people around here. It makes me uncomfortable."

"No worries," I told her. "I'm Johnny from Rhode Island," I revealed. They call me Johnny Lovebus."

"I love it," she gushed. "Johnny Lovebus! That's such a fun name," she said approvingly.

"We have another Johnny too," I informed her.

British Sue interjected, "He's the thin white pasty bloke that plays guitar. We've been calling him Guitar Johnny to keep the two Johnnys straight."

"He looks like he's got scurvy," remarked English Tessa. British Sue snorted and they giggled together.

The Bostonian stepped forward with open arms. "I'm Jen from Boston," she told her as they embraced. "AKA Flip-flop."

Chicken Jim exited the bus and said, "She's not the only one with an alias." He gestured at the Chinaman.

The robust German guy announced, "I'm Berndt." With a slight bow, he leaned over to squeeze the black-haired woman with an arm around her back. "You can call me Berndt Toast," he told her. "All of my American friends do."

"Berndt Toast?" the relaxed New Yorker questioned.

"It's a nickname I got in college," he explained.

"It's your bus name," Chicken Jim declared.

"I want a bus name," crooned the groovy girl as she stood up straight, resting both bare feet on the blacktop.

"Everyone gets a bus name," confirmed Chicken Jim.

"What should mine be?" she questioned.

"Do you have a nickname?" Flip-flop asked.

"I've never had a nickname, but my grandmother used to call me Jewels," she offered.

"That's a good bus name," I commented.

"I'd love it if you called me Jewels," she rejoiced.

The driver-in-training sprang into action. He removed the left suspender of his overalls and magically pulled out his notebook from within. He hooked his arm back through the loop and told her, "I'm adding Jewels to the list."

I spontaneously took Jewels' hand in mine and kissed her knuckles. "Welcome to the Green Tortoise, Jewels," I told her. "You sparkle. I'm enchanted."

"Oh," she breathed. "You're too kind."

"He's a tart!" sanctioned the blond Brit. She stepped toward Jewels for a hug and introduced herself. "I'm British Sue," she said proudly.

"Nice to meet you, British Sue," said Jewels as they hugged.

"Pleased to meet you, Jewels," she returned.

Jewels turned to British Sue's friend, prepared to give her a hug with her arms open, but the English girl stopped short, looking hurt with a disgruntled expression. "I have no desire for a sodding bus name, but this one's been calling me 'English Tessa.'" She gestured at her friend.

"If my bus name is going to be British Sue, it only makes sense that yours should be English Tessa," declared the blond.

"Awe," Jewels sympathized. "Don't worry about it, sister." The two women shared a long full-bodied hug.

English Tessa stepped back in awe. "Your hug made me feel so much better."

"I'd like to talk to you about being a teacher," Flip-flop told the dark-haired New Yorker. "I've been thinking about becoming a teacher for years, but I keep going back and forth."

"Groovy," she crooned. "I'd love that."

British Sue spoke to me on the side, although her friend could obviously hear what she was saying. "She hates being called British," she revealed.

"It makes you sound like you 'ave a stick up your bum," English Tessa defended.

Jewels laughed warmly and asked, "Are you guys together?"

"Kind of," answered the English girl.

"We've been mates for life," objected her British friend.

While they talked, I watched Chicken Jim scratch the name Flip-flop at the bottom of the list in his notebook. The title at the top of the page said "Westbound." I happily spotted my bus name, Johnny Lovebus, near the top of the list right below Mother Michelle, Little Josh, and Berndt Toast. I read some other names upside down, Guitar Johnny, Australian Sheila. One name in particular caught me off guard. I suddenly closed my lips to catch a laugh, but my face farted, and I got my arm wet with spray.

"What?" the driver-in-training asked.

"Does that say FRAWLINE Vera?" I asked incredulously.

"What's wrong with that?" He questioned. "She said I could call her Frau Vera," he explained, "but that makes her sound like an old lady. Wouldn't you say?"

I pretended to cough as I laughed. "I'm not saying a thing," I said, pointing to the page. "I'm pretty sure you spelled it wrong." He handed it to me, and I made the correction.

He looked up inquisitively. "You were hanging-out with Fräulein Vera," he whispered reading my spelling. "What do you think of her?" He smiled like a deranged stalker. "I picture us making sweet love like mad," he said.

My eyes jumped open and I whispered, "You may want to lay off a bit," trying not to embarrass him "You're right about the mad part, but the love ain't happening."

"Aw. She'll come around," he scoffed. "Just imagine the possibil-i-titties!"

"She doesn't like you, dude," I told him flat out. "All she did was complain about you at dinner."

"Methinks the lady doth protest too much," he said with swagger.

"I wouldn't fuck with that," I warned him in a whisper. "She's a punk rocker."

Berndt Toast asked Jewels, "How do you like living in New York?"

"As a woman I don't always feel safe alone at night, but I'm working on that," she answered in a silky-smooth-and-soulful tone. "I was born here. I grew up here, and I'm still here. This is where my family is. It's all I know." She smiled broadly. "I have an awesome job teaching at a Dominican school," she informed us. It made sense that she was a teacher. She was intelligent, capable, and full of enthusiasm, a special person for sure.

"A Dominican school?" questioned the German. "Do your students speak English?"

"They're learning," she replied with a smile that conveyed it was a complicated story.

"So, you teach in Spanish?" he inquired.

"Yes," she answered mildly. "Most of my students come from the Dominican Republic, but some are from other places like El Salvador and Puerto Rico. They're all such amazing and beautiful kids."

"It sounds like you're a great teacher," suggested Flip-flop. "You have such a good energy."

"My students sure love me and we always have a lot of fun, but I don't know if that qualifies me as a teacher," she smiled, proving the Bostonian's point about good energy.

"It sure does," commented Flip-flop.

"It's easy to teach children when you love them so much," she opined. "I love every last one of them. Well?" She hesitated with an exaggerated expression of thoughtfulness, suggesting there might be one child she did not love. Then with a nod she said, "No! I love all of them." She smiled so deeply I could feel the warmth. "My job is easy.

It's hard to see it as work," she enthused. "I look at it this way. I get paid to spend time with all these incredible little people."

"That's awesome," the German observed.

"The world needs more teachers like you," remarked British Sue. "Boarding school was a bit of hell here on Earth."

"I second that," rejoined English Tessa.

"I hated all of my teachers," commented Chicken Jim.

"The kids relate to me because I'm Dominican," she revealed. "They see me as one of them, even though we've been here since the beginning. I'm still Dominican first."

"How long has your family been in America?" Flip-flop asked.

"We arrived on a slave ship," the powerful black woman put forth bluntly. "My ancestors were native Dominicanos descended from the Taínos."

"What are Taínos?" Flip-flop questioned.

"We are the Indians of the Dominican Republic," she informed us.

"American Indians?" begged the Bostonian.

"The Taínos were the first indigenous people to be encountered by Columbus. They were the first people to be called Indians," she explained assuredly. "Before Columbus came, the Taínos were ruled by women. They were a peaceful people with no crime or violence. They had to learn how to fight when the Spanish tried to enslave them. The resistance was led by a female Chief who was one of my ancestors," she informed us proudly.

"Your people fought Columbus?" asked Berndt Toast incredulously.

She struck a pose with a hand on her hip and said, "Honey, if we didn't revolt those fuckers-in-the-tall-ships would have enslaved every one of us. Many of our people escaped, but things did not work out so well for my branch of the family, being related to Chief Anacaona and all. As a punishment we were interbred with Africans, so our family tree gets blurry after being sold as slaves." She ran her fingers up her arm. "That's where I get my mocha complexion." She was enthusiastic about everything and her mannerisms were enchanting.

"You have beautiful skin," raved Flip-flop.

"African skin is gorgeous. It makes me feel all luvvly-jubbly," commented British Sue.

"I see myself as Dominicano, not African," the girl revealed. "We're a proud people, but it hasn't been easy living in New York. I often have to remind people who think the immigrants should go back to where they came from, that my people got here on the first boat.

Black people were some of the first Americans. Then I ask them, 'When are you leaving?'" We all laughed.

"I dig how you're so in touch with your heritage," I marveled.

"What's your heritage?" she asked me with a tone that could melt butter.

"I'm a McDonald's Hamburger with Mayo," I said with a laugh. They all looked at me with incredulity. "Seriously, check this out," I explained. "Half my family is from Hamburg, Germany and the other half are McDonalds from County Mayo, Ireland." I paused to let this sink in. "So, I'm a McDonald's Hamburger with Mayo."

"Ha!" Flip-flop laughed.

"I would love a cheeseburger right about now," miffed Chicken Jim.

We all heard Driver Brian shout, "All aboard!"

****

Driver Chris popped his head around the corner and called the rookie, "Jimbo! Bus meeting! Now!" Chicken Jim followed the other two drivers to a spot on the sidewalk some fifty feet away where they conversed privately with the Spanish-speaking woman and the tall Chinese man in the white Oxford. She did most of the talking with a stiff posture. He had a look of concern on his face while she talked, but he did nothing but nod. Judging from their body language the drivers were listening intently. When she was finished talking, they each shook the Chinese man's hand, seeming to congratulate him.

After the meeting convened, the Peruvian girl passed by me with a look of disdain and said, "What are you looking at?"

"Nothing," I said instinctually, taken aback.

When Driver Chris walked past, I motioned toward her with my head and asked, "What's up with her?"

He wiggled his eyebrows in abject disbelief. "I wish I could tell you brother, but you wouldn't believe me even if I did." He cupped his hands to his mouth and shouted, "Everyone inside the bus please!"

I started back to the bus with the others, but Chicken Jim pulled me aside.

"What's up?" I asked.

"Don't tell anybody else," he confided in me. "Even if Driver Chris has to go home, Brian will have to deadhead to San Francisco."

"Deadhead?" I asked him with a tilt of my head.

"That's when you drive a long distance with no passengers." He shrugged. "No matter what happens, we have to get the bus back to headquarters," he clarified.

"Okay," I said with drawn out syllables.

"If you really want to train to be a driver, he will probably let you stay."

"You think so!" I marveled.

"He won't kick you out on the sidewalk. Not if you agree to help," he advised. "Just relax. You're all set. Don't let them put you on a Greyhound."

"That's awesome dude," I breathed. "Thanks for letting me know." I gave him a pat on the back. I went inside to retrieve my knife, but it was neither on the dinette, nor was it underneath the table on the floor. I intended to ask Little Josh if he had seen my knife, but he was playing inside the driver's cabin, the big wooden sleeping berth suspended from the roof in the far back of the bus. He looked like he was having fun, so I took a seat on the front platform next to the boy's mother in the first seat behind the driver.

I did an inventory of the Boston Passengers. We were all still on board. That was good. I searched the bus for new passengers. The well-to-do olive-skinned girl with the fancy suitcases sat in the first seat behind the driver. Her Asian friend sat quietly by her side. I was relieved to see Fräulein Vera listening to music on her Walkman. She had paid before Driver Chris got the shocking news. I caught her eye and she smiled at me with a nod before going back to banging her head.

Mother Michelle saw me looking at her and asked, "What kind of music do you like?"

"Classic rock," I answered.

"I figured," she concluded. She tilted her head towards the German headbanger. "She's into punk."

"Yeah," I confirmed. "She was in a punk band in Germany before coming here."

"She leads a wild life, yes. You might find it hard to keep up," she surmised. "Relationships are much easier when you're in rhythm."

I gasped. "We're not in a relationship," I said, trying not to laugh.

"Well, save yourself the effort," she concluded.

"Well, thanks," I said vaguely.

A guy wearing a yellow soccer jersey that said South Africa was sitting across from me next to a woman who appeared to be his girlfriend. Their accents were remarkably similar. They were engaged in conversation with the sporty Canadian girl in spandex tights.

Chicken Jim came up the steps and fell into the closest seat by the door. He turned to listen to the Canadian talk about life in British Columbia. She worked as a snowboard instructor at Whistler. "It's the greatest," she raved.

"What's so great about Whistler?" he inquired.

"Ha!" She laughed at his American ignorance. "It's one of the greatest ski resorts in the world."

"So, you're a snowboard instructor at the greatest ski resort in the world?" he inquired. "How'd you land that gig?"

"Anyone can do it," she coaxed. "You just need to show up early in the season when they're training the new instructors. I just walked up out-of-the-blue, asked for a job, and they trained me on the spot. I was teaching kids how to ride two weeks later."

"Why did you leave?" he asked.

"It was hard to leave," she admitted. "I loved it there, but I wanted to travel."

"BC is incredibly beautiful," gushed the South African man.

"The ferry to Victoria Island was super romantic," remarked his traveling companion.

"I love the mountains," restated the Canadian. "My friends in BC call me Mountain Girl."

"That's a good bus name," spouted Chicken Jim. "I told you," he said to me across the aisle. "It never fails. Everybody gets a bus name."

The South African couple continued their conversation with the Canadian while Chicken Jim wrote her bus name in his notebook.

The bantering brogues of the two girls from the Emerald Isle delighted my ears and melted my heart. They were sitting at the dinette with their backs to me, each with beautifully braided hair. One had flowing dirty-red hair that flowed halfway down her back, with several thin braids wrapped in colorful yarn floating amongst the auburn waves. The other had blond hair with flaxen bangs with braids gathering at her temples, braided along the sides of her head, culminating in a bun weaved together like a monkey-fist behind her head.

Their clothing looked a bit ragtag at first glance, but they wore it well. It is cool to be poor in backpacker circles. As a team they seemed infinitely popular, eliciting rowdy laughter from those around them. They encouraged and supported each other at every turn in the conversation. They both kept the laughter flowing in equal measure.

The dirty-blond-haired girl appeared to be leading the hijinks. She was more outspoken than her dirty-red-haired accomplice with a growly voice that could straighten a man's spine like a scathing post. She wore three sets of studs with a silver star dangling from a chain pierced through the cartilage of her upper left ear.

Compared to her friend's demeanor the dirty-red-haired girl appeared to be more of a peacekeeper than a rabble-rouser. She was more withdrawn with a voice that soothed my Irish heart like hot breath melting Irish butter. She wore a headband with peace-signs that tied at the back of her head, featuring long tails that curved around her braids. She too had multiple piercings in each ear.

Suddenly, the dirty-blond turned and shouted, "Vera love! Come hither!" She cupped her hands and shouted again, "Vera!" Seeing that the punk rocking Fräulein Vera was rocking out with headphones, she called me. "Will you please tell her that the Irish Twins want her."

I tapped her on the leg. She took off her headphones looking put off. "Your friends want you," I told her, motioned with my thumb towards the back. She jumped up when she saw them waving her back. She dropped her Walkman in my lap and said, "You will listen to this until I come back."

I said, "Okay," and she went back to be with them. I donned the headphones but did not push play.

The Irish girls were obviously fraternal twins, but both girls possessed that unmistakable classic Irish beauty. Being Irish myself I was partial to such delights. The dirty redhead had freckles strewn about her face like fairy dust, and her friend had skin was so fair that the wispy hair on her sideburns glowed bright yellow.

When the German girl arrived the blond one whispered something in her ear, to which she scoffed loudly, "I'll ask him."

The South American hombre was sitting shirtless on the drinks cooler in the center aisle laughing along with the Irish girls. It was hot enough to justify the removal of one's shirt, but he was so good looking it seemed a bit over the top. He had removed his adventure hat revealing a thick black mane of perfect hair.

"How old are you, Juliano?" inquired Fräulein Vera.

"Eighteen," he reported.

"Ja!" she laughed.

"Do you date boys?" she asked him.

"No, no, no," he reacted coyly. "I date girls! I love one-and-all."

It was difficult to resist resenting him for his youthful appearance and infectious exuberance, but I was doing my best. It was precisely that kind of youthful excitement for life and new experiences that I was seeking to recapture by traveling and moving to San Francisco.

I adjusted Fräulein Vera's headphones and pushed play. About ten seconds later I hit stop. It was a screaming raw kind of music.

Driver Brian came up the steps and took the driver's seat. The Peruvian girl took the small wooden seat next to him. "That's a very special seat," he told her with a smile. "We call it the Buddy Seat."

"I beg your Pardon." She raised a hand to her sternum. "Am I not allowed to sit here?"

"No," he breathed a laugh. "It's not like that."

"So, I can be your buddy then?" she questioned.

"I'm actually not allowed to be your buddy." He checked his own logic. "Not that I have a problem with you."

"I see how it's going to be," she sneered.

"I can't be your buddy," he clarified, "for safety reasons."

"I see," she said curtly.

"You need to make buddies with other passengers," he told her, nodding to measure her comprehension. She was reluctant. "It's called the Buddy System. We'll explain that later."

"I'll be your buddy," Chicken Jim suggested with eyebrows a-wiggle. "You have to make friends on the bus," he blurted, sticking his face in close. "Your Asian friend can't be your buddy either."

Her eyes turned to steel, but she did not flinch. She ignored the interruption and remained focused on the driver.

"I'll be your buddy," he sputtered again.

She huffed, "That won't be necessary," then she addressed the driver with a tone intended to dissuade the hapless youth. "Please continue with what you were saying. I was trying to listen." She was exceedingly skillful at conversation, and she exuded an aura of confidence that made me assume she was good at everything she did.

The driver gave Chicken Jim the hairy eyeball over his shoulder. "I was talking," he stated with a long pause, "about the Buddy Seat."

"What's the Buddy Seat?" she asked.

"It's the board under your ass," snickered Chicken Jim.

"How crass," observed the cultured Peruvian, still not giving him the satisfaction of so much as a glance.

"You will shut up," Fräulein Vera shouted at him.

The driver shot him a look that finally silenced him. "Suffice to say," Driver Brian expounded, "a lot of very smart people have said a lot of very smart things on the Buddy Seat."

"I take it he's never sat here," she said under her breath. She talked with the driver for more than half an hour. She was remarkably interesting indeed. Among other things she told him that she was born in Peru, she lived in several countries around the world growing up, and she spoke seven languages. Her father was the Peruvian ambassador to the United States in Washington DC. Her Polish mother owned an art gallery in Old Town, Virginia where she once sold a painting to President Kennedy.

When I found out that she attended George Washington University, I let her know that was my alma mater. We compared years of attendance and discovered that we were there at the same time. She asked me what happened to my knee, and I ended up telling her about the cycling tour I did between Seattle and San Francisco the previous summer.

At one point Driver Brian referred to me as Johnny Lovebus and the subject of bus names was discussed. "Most people call me Ursula," she told us, "but my grandmother always called me 'Ita' because I'm tiny. It's a term of endearment," she said happily.

Chicken Jim looked completely puzzled. He strained his voice. "Say what?"

"Me apodo es Ita," she objected. "Su apodo es Pollo Jim."

He shook his head in ignorance.

"My nickname is Ita," she translated. "Yours is Chicken Jim."

"Yes, it is," he clucked proudly, "but I'm not feeling the whole 'Ita' thing," he told her making finger quotes. "I'll have to come up with something better."

"Pendejo!" she derided him in dismay. This made the driver laugh.

The driver-in-training looked the Asian man up and down before asking, "What's your name dude?"

The Peruvian spoke before he could answer. "This is my traveling companion." She put her hands together like she was praying and nodded at the man as a sign of respect.

"What's your name, dude?" asked the driver-in-training sounding kind of rude.

The Chinese gentleman answered, "Pak Chan."

"Ha! No way! Is that your real name dude?" jabbed the rookie.

"Yes," he said tentatively. "That's is my name." He looked to his friend for support. "Did I say it right?" he questioned. Chicken Jim and I both laughed, causing his friend to sneer at us. Perhaps something was lost-in-translation, because for a moment it seemed like he was unsure of his own name.

"You said it right," Peruvian Ursula confirmed.

"Ha! It sounds like, PAC-MAN!" spattered Chicken Jim.

"It's Pak with a K," the Chinaman told the rookie. "Pak Chan," he reiterated.

"Don't worry about him," miffed his Peruvian friend. "He's a jackass."

"That name's gonna stick." Chicken Jim looked around smugly. He told Little Josh, "That guy's called PAC-MAN."

"Ha!" The boy laughed.

"I am Pak Chan," the man objected mildly. Although, it seemed he was more proud of himself for having pronounced it right than actually having pride in his name.

"Don't you know who PAC-MAN is?" teased the black-haired youth adjusting his glasses on his nose. He spoke in a loud voice reserved for foreigners who might not know English.

"Of course, he knows who PAC-MAN is," scoffed his Peruvian friend.

"Who is PAC-MAN?" the Asian man asked cluelessly. This set Chicken Jim and Little Josh off on a laughing spree.

"Son of a bitch," spat the Peruvian. "Americans are the worst. They always fuck with foreign names."

"It's so true," agreed Driver Brian, speaking from experience. Several other foreigners agree.

I heard Little Josh tell his mother, "That guy's called PAC-MAN."

"Hello PAC-MAN," his mother said with a wave.

I wish I could say differently, but Chicken Jim was right. From that moment on the name PAC-MAN stuck like glue. This clearly pissed her off, but PAC-MAN did not seem to mind at all. They spoke together while we waited in what I assumed to be Cantonese, but she always listened and helped correct his English whenever he spoke to anyone else. He seemed delighted that Driver Chris could speak in his native tongue. He was polite when people said hello and introduced themselves, but he otherwise appeared standoffish, possibly reluctant to embarrass himself with broken English. As a result of his conspicuous silence, he remained somewhat of a mystery for the time being.

****

Driver Chris came aboard and stood next to the buddy seat to make an announcement. Mother Michelle shushed her son and silence fell. He spoke over the street noise. "I know things are kind of chaotic, hot, loud, and strange right now, but eventually, it won't be so loud. Welcome to the Green Tortoise!"

He continued in a serious tone. "I understand that many of you have concerns about everything that's been going on. I am sure there has been a lot of rumors and speculation. Rest assured. I am here to put your mind at rest. My apologies to the new people for making you listen to all of this again, but I need to bring the Boston passengers up to speed." He bobbed his head sympathetically as he looked at our attentive faces.

He reset himself by taking a deep breath followed by an open-mouthed sigh. "As you may or may not have heard, my brother is in the hospital with a severe head injury and we're not sure he's gonna make it."

Conciliatory comments were offered.

Mother Michelle said, "That's just terrible Chris." She got up and hugged him. "I'm so sorry," she consoled him soulfully. She was visibly distraught.

"Thank you, Michelle," he responded warmly as she returned to her seat. "What this means for me is clear," he explained, "If my brother dies, I have to go home to be with my family. What this means for you is a little more complicated." He gathered his red beard with his fingers and thumb at his cheeks and slowly slid his hand all the way down to the tip, constricting his hand along the way. "If you haven't figured it out yet," he shouted, "everyone here paid for a ticket in-full before we were told to not sell any more tickets. I found out that my brother was in the hospital two hours ago. When I told the office that I might have to leave, they made it painfully clear that we should not sell tickets to people who have not paid-in-full."

The petite pig-tailed German girl sitting next to Jewels asked him, "What happened to your brother?"

He tried to keep his volume up, but his heart was not in it. "He fell off a building and fractured his skull," he explained. The passengers leaned in to listen. "The last time his friends saw him he was watching a basketball game at the Providence Civic Center with a bunch of other firefighters. No one knows why, but he went back to his car and some kids saw him fall from the third story of the parking garage. The doctor said he would have died within minutes if those kids did not run for help. So, we're lucky he's still alive."

Driver Chris' face scrunched up as he fought away the tears. He steadied himself and blinked his eyes clear. He waited as someone closed a window to dampen the roar of traffic noise. Another passenger followed suit at a second window. He raised his voice in response. "I got an update ten minutes ago. Right now, he is going in for surgery to relieve the pressure on his brain, so as of this moment we are proceeding with the trip as planned."

More windows were shut as people struggled to hear every word, so the driver moved to the center of the bus. He motioned for the South American guy to make room for him to sit on the cooler. "If you don't mind, I'd like to sit there," he asked.

"Not at all," said the handsome young man with a velvet voice. "I'm sorry about your brother." His words rolled off his tongue. All the girls' heads turned to adore him with their batting eyelashes. The guy was unbelievable, but he did not seem to realize he was in any way special, not in the slightest. I found that endearing. He seemed nice enough, positive and in good spirits. He was hard not to like. He seemed like a conversationalist despite the language barrier, and before Driver Brian's speech, the Irish girls had been hanging on his every word.

Driver Chris thanked him with a nod, took a seat on the cooler and continued. "The Green Tortoise is currently searching for a replacement driver. If they find a replacement driver in time, he or she will be sent to our next destination, whether it is Cleveland or Chicago or someplace else. If that's how it goes down, you'll have nothing to worry about. I will go home, and the trip will go on as planned."

He looked at us with reluctance like he was prepared to drop the bomb. "However, if my brother dies before a replacement driver is found the trip will end at once. We'll take you to the nearest Greyhound station where the Tortoise will buy you a ticket to your final destination." There was a murmur of complaints and disappointment. "I know it sucks," Driver Chris conceded, "but it's the legal responsibility of the Green Tortoise to provide alternative transportation to our passengers if for any reason we can't get you where you need to go. Under those circumstances, we have no choice. Our hands are tied." He swallowed hard.

"When will you know if another driver is available?" Flip-flop wanted to know.

"As soon as I get an update from the office, you'll be the first to know." He looked her in the eyes. "Honestly, the chances of them sending a driver are pretty slim," he told her in a loud voice so that others could hear. "Our dispatcher told me that all our drivers are on the road or have trips booked in the immediate future. He's going to reach out to former drivers and he's considering hiring someone new, but the chances of that don't look good either."

He waited for things to calm down. The street noise diminished with the closing of the windows, but the heat was starting to rise from the lack of cross-ventilation. "What it comes down to is this. If you got on in Boston, you need to decide if you want to leave with us tonight or go back to Boston. If you choose to go back to Boston, you can either get a full refund or wait for the next Tortoise bus. We can hold you a seat on the next cross-country trip that leaves ten days from now."

There was a great deal of commotion as passengers talked through the decision and let each other know their thoughts. I had made my decision, so I did not say a word. I remained silently content, trusting in the knowledge conveyed to me by Chicken Jim that the trip would not be ending for me, even if it ended for everyone else.

He shouted, "If you decide to stay on the bus, you will ultimately get to your final destination whether I need to go home or not, you just risk ending up on a Greyhound instead of the Green Tortoise." He nodded around in a circle seeking confirmation that we all understood. "Does anyone have any questions?"

The chatter rose to a crescendo at this point. Pretty much everyone broke out in conversation about our options. Several passengers shouted questions. Answers were provided, but it all meant the same thing. It did not make any difference to me. My decision was made.

Flip-flop was seated across the aisle from me. She looked a bit distressed with a vacant look in her eyes. Her shoulder seemed to be causing her pain. She smiled when she caught me looking at her. I smiled back. "What are you gonna do?" she asked me.

My big eyes and smile surprised her. "I'm staying no matter what," I told her. I spoke with a degree of confidence intended to bolster her faith. "I think you should too." I winked at her conspicuously.

Chicken Jim looked at me cross-eyed.

I did not want to betray Chicken Jim's confidence by revealing my insider information, but I thought my positive attitude might help her make the right decision.

"What if the trip gets cancelled?" she quavered.

I lifted my eyebrows with a shrug and said, "I'm not worried."

"Easy for you to say," she scoffed. "I have a schedule to keep. I need to be at school to register for classes in Northridge in two weeks or I'm screwed."

"You're going to get there either way," I promised. "Even if it's on a Greyhound. Besides, what other choice do we have?"

Her shoulders sagged. "I can't risk missing registration. I'm going to ask for my money back, and I'll take Greyhound I guess."

"I'm sorry to hear that," I told her.

Jen from Boston jumped to her feet and approached Driver Chris. He stepped out of the way and directed her to speak with the big blond in the driver's seat. She told him her plan, he answered her questions, told his partner, and stepped outside with Flip-flop.

Driver Chris stood with one knee on the buddy seat and raised his voice. "If you need more time to make a decision, we can wait a while longer, but it's almost time for us to go. We need to know how many Greyhound tickets we need to buy." He waited for silence until all I could hear was the roar of traffic on the George Washington Bridge. The time had come. "Okay then," he shouted. "Who's going?"

Nobody said a word. "Okay," he started again. "How 'bout we do it this way." He cupped his hands at his mouth and yelled, "If you've decided to get off here, please come forward." The tension was high as we all waited silently. It was like watching a roulette wheel, as long as thoughts kept spinning everyone still had a chance to win. The ball dropped on the double zero with everyone's chip on green. "You're all staying?" he shouted for confirmation. After a moment of tense silence, a bunch of passengers slapped high-fives amidst a celebration of hoots and hollers.

"Good choice," announced the red-bearded driver with a glow in his eyes. With that there was a round of applause.

Chicken Jim bobbed his head and shoulders when I looked his way. He said, "Good move, bro!"

Driver Brian appeared in the doorway and said, "Let me guess. They're all staying."

"Yup," his partner answered with a happy nod.

"Right on," he said to his bearded partner. It appeared this was the outcome both of them had been hoping for. "Just one," he said. "That's not bad."

"I'll go with her to get the ticket," Driver Chris told him. He nodded his head and without another word he headed into the bus station with Flip-flop.

Driver Brian came inside and stood on the top step to speak. "Let me start by saying thank you all for your cooperation over the last few difficult hours. I expect there will be more difficult hours ahead, but I am glad we are all on the same page. Thanks for sticking in there and trusting us to get you where you need to go no matter what happens. Driver Chris feels really bad about all of this, but you've all been so cool, I'm sure that has made it easier for him."

He stepped up the last step and continued. "We can only hope that his brother has a speedy recovery and that the trip will go off as planned." He nodded left and right, making eye contact with me personally as if to say he was glad I was sticking it out. Of course, I nodded back. I was delighted to have his approval.

"Now," he shouted with new vigor, "We need to establish some Green Tortoise ground rules before we get moving. We do not have a lot of 'No' rules on the Green Tortoise, it is mostly 'Yes' rules, but there are a few 'No' rules. I'll explain in a minute."

"The most important rule on the Green Tortoise is to have respect for one another. That includes respect for each other as human beings regardless of sex, creed, color, or political beliefs. We expect nothing less, and we will call you out on it if we witness you being disrespectful."

"The Green Tortoise is like a social experiment. Living in such close quarters requires acceptance, open-mindedness, patience and, as you will see, a great deal of tolerance. Adjusting to this strange new world can be challenging. I like to look at life on the Tortoise as an opportunity for personal growth, to discover new things about yourself, things you may have never known. You may discover a new you or a long lost you."

"That's why we encourage the use of bus names. You may have already heard people talking about their bus names. A bus name is a name you take to show that you embrace this new world. Taking a bus name is optional, but it's a cool way to embrace this new way of life and the new side of yourself."

"For example, we should all need to respect each other's personal property. We are sharing this entire space with no assigned seats. So, if you leave your movable property where other people want to hang-out, chances are your stuff will get moved as soon as you turn your back. This happens all the time on the Tortoise, so please don't get angry when your stuff goes missing. Nobody is stealing your stuff."

I raised my hand when he looked my way. When he pointed at me and I said, "I lost my pocketknife."

"What color is it?"

"Black," I told him.

"Hey everybody!" the red-bearded driver shouted over the din. "Johnny Lovebus here lost a black pocketknife. If you see it, please pass it forward." He turned back to me and asked, "Where was the last place you had it?"

"Right there at the dinette," I informed him.

He looked over at the tabletop, but it was not there.

Then Big Dave spoke up. "I haven't seen it and I've been sitting here the entire time," he told the driver.

"You can't sit there all the time," he informed the Old-Growth-Hippie. "You need to give other people a chance to sit there." The big man nodded understanding.

The Irish driver turned back around to address the whole group. "That brings me to the first 'no' rule on the Green Tortoise, 'No homesteading.'"

"What's homesteading?" someone asked.

"Homesteading is when someone sits in the same seat all of the time. We try to discourage that. It's antisocial. You cannot reserve a certain seat or expect someone to hold your seat for more than a few minutes. As the saying goes, 'If you shuffle your feet, you lose your seat.' If you get up or move around and someone is in your space when you return, find another seat, and meet some new people. It's more social that way, it adds to the fun and it's a good way to experience the whole bus."

"The second 'no' rule is 'No shoes on the mattresses.' So, if anyone back there still has shoes on take them off and pass them up." Shoes were already being passed forward and thrown on the floor. He turned around to look behind him and added, "People have to sleep on these cushions, and no one likes sand in their bed."

"Are not these our beds?" the South American guy asked, pointing at the bunks above his head.

"The whole bus converts into one big bed at night," Driver Brian informed him. "We call it the Miracle Conversion. He gestured with his hand toward the benches on the front platform and said, "The whole front of the bus changes into a bed so people can sleep up there." He pointed at the dinette table. "That table converts into a bed."

"Everybody sleeps like sardines," Mother Michelle shouted from the dinette. She held up her hands with her fingers interlaced so her fingertips were in the webbing of the opposite hand.

"We all get to sleep together?" enthused the South American.

Driver Brian continued as he walked toward the back. "You sleep with your heads facing the windows and your legs in the middle." He put his hand on the pile of daypacks on top of the food cooler across the aisle from the dinette. "This bunk is reserved for daypacks during the day, but everything up here will get moved under the front platform at night." He pointed behind himself. He put his hands up on the wooden bunk over his head. "If you like privacy or you like to go to bed early there's room enough for at least eight people to sleep up here in the bunks," he explained. "Don't be afraid to sleep in the bunks. There are reading lights up there and all the speakers have a volume control knob." He walked forward down the aisle to the front platform. "If you like to hang-out late and listen to music, you should probably plan to sleep on the front platform. The whole area up there will be converted to a bed later tonight."

The blond-haired Californian driver reflected in thought for a moment, then he asked Chicken Jim, "Did I forget anything?"

The driver-in-training said one word, "Garbage."

"That's right!" Driver Brian remembered. "All recyclables and garbage go in the two trash bags tied to the handrail by the door. Trash goes in the black bag and recycling goes in the green bag."

The Canadian girl got up from the back platform to throw away a half-eaten sleeve of McDonald's French fries, but Berndt Toast stood up to stop her at the near side of the dinette. "What?" she asked.

He smiled as he took the trash from her. "If you aren't going to finish those, I'll eat them," he told her.

"Knock yourself out," she responded.

"You don't have to get up to throw stuff away," Driver Brian continued his announcement. "Just pass it to the person in front of you. It's a whole lot easier."

A lot of garbage came forward from the back platform and the driver had to pass stuff forward repeatedly. When the first of the trash reached Chicken Jim he stuffed it in the trash bag without complaint, but when he saw the load of trash coming his way, he said,

"I can't believe you people brought all that trash on the bus." As more garbage came to his hands he complained, "What a bunch of freaking hoarders." The trash was backing up I got up to help and started stuffing trash into the bag.

The German girl I had dinner with also rose to bring a bunch of trash forward. As soon as I took over Chicken Jim stopped helping and said, "Cool," with his back turned to the oncoming wave of trash.

The voice of Fräulein Vera struck, "Achtung Scheisskopf."

Chicken Jim took this as a compliment, and he winked at her coyly. "I told you she liked me, bro," he said to me.

Berndt Toast shouted, "That means, 'Pay attention shit head.'" He passed forward the now empty French fry container.

"I think that's everything," Driver Brian shouted, "If you have any questions, please feel free to ask either one of us, or our Driver-in-training, Chicken Jim. He gestured for the Pennsylvanian to stand up.

"I'm Chicken Jim," the rookie said with a wave, then he sat down.

"I will be driving overnight to a beautiful lake in Ohio called Crane Creek, where we will be making breakfast. We expect everyone to help cook or clean at every meal. So, if you wake up early you can expect to help cook breakfast, and if you like to sleep in you can expect to help clean up. It's always a group effort on the Green Tortoise. When everyone works together there will be more time for the good stuff." He clapped his hands and asked, "Any questions?" No questions were asked. With that he took the driver's seat.

Flip-flop climbed the steps followed by Driver Chris. "She decided to stay," he announced. There was a cheer.

"Right on!" said Driver Brian. The two men gave each other a knowing look as she took a seat.

This made me happy and I smiled at her broadly with wide eyes of encouragement. "Good decision," I told her. She smiled back.

"What's the word from the office?" asked the enormous blond-haired driver.

"There's nobody available on the East Coast," the redhead informed him. "They're willing to fly someone out, but it's not looking good out west either."

"Did you call home?" his partner asked.

"No change," he answered curtly.

"That's good news," his partner concluded.

"Let's roll," he said. "I'm fucking exhausted. I'm going to try and get some sleep." Driver Chris took his waist pack in his hand and headed for the driver's cabin with a wave and a nod. Passengers consoled him and said goodnight along the way.

British Sue and her friend went outside to brush their teeth, rinsing with a water bottle and spitting foam in the gutter, so I got my daypack and went out to join them. On her way past British Sue singled me out and said, "I'm off To Bedfordshire."

All I could do was shrug.

The wholesome Dominican woman had been getting on famously with the little blond German girl with pigtails. Their interactions and body language spoke to an instant kinship. They were talking so fast back and forth I had to wait to speak.

Jewels spoke with love. "I figured what better place than the Green Tortoise to go by a name I was called as a child. This bus is made for children. Just being here makes me feel like a kid again," she enthused. "I can't wait to explore the rest of the bus."

"It makes me want to climb on everything, like a playground," squeaked the tiny German girl in a super-excited high-pitched voice.

Jewels sighed with the fond admiration of memory and said, "The Tortoise reminds me of kindergarten. Everyone is just here to play and have fun. I feel like that is what is going on here. I've never felt so accepted and loved, and I just met you all."

"Ja!" burst the petite German girl with pigtails. "Kindergarten was wunderbar! I loved kindergarten!" The two of them together were so enthusiastic it rubbed off like chalk.

"Kindergarten was the favorite year of my life," proclaimed Mother Michelle. "The only thing we had to learn was how to share. There was none of this competition between parents that you see nowadays. Everyone wants their kids to be little Einsteins."

"Right on," Jewels agreed.

"Children need to be free to learn at their own pace," concluded Mother Michelle.

"You're so right," the German girl replied happily. "Children should be allowed to grow naturally."

"You're practically a child yourself," Mother Michelle commented across the aisle. She took a good look at the girl and guessed, "What are you, all of sixteen?"

"I'm eighteen," stressed the adorable German girl. From our perspective this was very young. Most of us were already in our twenties, either that or much older, like Mother Michelle and Big Dave.

"You could pass for ten, girlfriend," came the response from the Dominican. She chuckled in a way that made her bodacious breasts jiggle.

Mother Michelle interjected, "Don't grow up too fast, Yülia. You're perfect as you are."

"Oh, thank you," said the German Girl. She spontaneously rose to her feet and hugged Mother Michelle. "You are wunderbar! All of you! This bus is so awesome. Everyone I have met has been wunderbar. The people are so nice. I feel so lucky to be on this bus with all of you wonderful people. I'm so happy now!"

When she went to sit down, I said, "Hello again," to Jewels.

"This is my new buddy," she informed me excitedly as she hugged her friend.

I thrust out my hand, but the petite pig-tailed blond girl refused my hand and stood up to hug me. "I'm Yülia from Germany," she said.

"Nice to meet you Yülia," I told her as we hugged.

The spritely little white-skinned creature exuded youthful innocence. Even her hand felt light and ethereal. She reminded me of the fairy Tinkerbell happily zipping through the forest. Before I could introduce myself, she said, "You're Johnny Lovebus!"

"AKA John from Rhode Island," I acknowledged.

"Nice to meet you AKA John from Rhode Island," she said mimicking me stiffly. "I like Johnny Lovebus better!" she blurted.

"You gotta love the bus," I said with a smile. "What brings you to the states, Yülia?"

"I'm moving to San Francisco to enroll at USF," she enthused. "I'll be living there for the next four years. I'm so excited."

"I'm moving to San Francisco too," I revealed. "I don't have a place to live yet, but my friend Tim is lending me his couch."

"What good is a couch if you don't have a place to live?" she asked innocently.

I laughed. "He's not giving me the couch. He's just letting me sleep on it for a while."

"Don't mind her," Jewels advised me with a snort of laughter. "She's not high."

Yülia snorted and they both started cracking up. "I'm so not high," declared the pigtailed blond in a lovely German accent. "I'm having so much fun." Except for her use of the German word wunderbar, she otherwise spoke English fluently without thinking twice or being tripped up in translation.

"Yülia is a beautiful name," I commented.

"Funny you should say that," Jewels said, pointing a finger at me.

"Ja!" laughed the German girl. "Yülia is my name for the bus," she announced. "It was her idea," revealed Yülia.

"She's so cute I figured she had to have a pet name," Jewels explained.

"My real name is Julie," revealed the young German girl.

"We're both named Julie!" The New Yorker boasted in solidarity.

The Moon Over Manhattan

"My great grandmother called me Yülia," said the German girl.

"My grandmother called me Jewels," said the New Yorker.

"Goodnight Yülia," I said. It was nice to meet you." She returned the sentiment and I exchanged nods with the others and said, "Goodnight." Without missing a beat, they got back to their animated conversation.

As I passed the dinette British Sue reached out and touched my shoulder. "Oh, there you are love," she said happily. She was lying down in the bunk bed over the built-in ice chest. Her friend was in the bunk across from her. "It's quite cozy kipping up here," she said.

"Why don't you make room for 'im," English Tessa prodded her friend, and they both giggled.

"I just fancy a bit of conversation," British Sue protested. "You make it sound like I'm on the pull." I was a bit confused, but she did not make room for me next to her, so, I climbed up into the bunk facing the opposite direction so that our heads were close together. At least that way we could talk.

When the girl from Boston passed by, she eyeballed British Sue suspiciously and said, "Goodnight."

"Goodnight," I responded. "I'm glad you changed your mind and decided to stay. I know you made the right decision."

"Let's hope so," she said with a sigh before sitting down in the spot directly across from me on the back platform.

Our scheduled departure time had been ten o'clock. It was after ten-thirty when we pulled away from the loading zone at the George Washington Bridge Bus Terminal in Washington Heights, New York. The highway through Pennsylvania was under construction, and at one point in the night, the repetitive bumps in the road began resonating with the air-shocks on the bus. The bouncing grew to tremendous proportions. At times, we were lifted off the bunk into the air. It was a bit scary at times. At one point, British Sue reached out for my hand and we held hands while we bounced up and down on the bunks, for about twenty miles. When the exciting part was over, her hand released mine and we fell asleep. All night long, delightful strands of British Sue's hair blew in the breeze, touching my face as we slept.

6
The Driver's Apprentice

The engine was silent when I woke up, but I could feel the bus swaying slightly as passengers moved around below. I felt well-rested despite the bumpy roads and being kept awake by British Sue's wind-blown hair touching my face. The dinette table had been converted to a bed on which Michelle and Josh were now sleeping. I peeked over the edge of the bunk, trying to get a look out the windshield. Driver Brian was asleep in the driver's seat. Sometime in the night, the Miracle Conversion had transformed the couches on the front platform into a sleeping area. I observed the row of bodies in sleeping bags, trying to figure out who was who.

The South American guy was awake. He had his arm around the Canadian girl with the bright red lipstick. She was sleeping soundly with her head on his chest. He made eye contact with me, looked at the girl sleeping on his chest and his cheeks dimpled into a grin. I gave him a wide-eyed nod of admiration. His eyes closed blissfully.

An attractive couple in their late twenties sat-upright with their backs against the windows reading the Tortoise brochure. The young woman waved to me with a bent wrist and I smiled. She was quite pretty with upturned corners of her mouth and sculpted cheekbones that gave her a pleasant appearance. She wore a tan headscarf with a green tribal pattern over shoulder length brown hair tied up in a bun.

The guy next to her, who I presumed to be her boyfriend, lifted his chin to say hello and I did the same. A pair of sunglasses rested on top of his short, curly, black hair, and he wore a yellow soccer jersey with a green emblem on the front reading, South Africa. I could tell from his smile and body language that he was both educated and

The Driver's Apprentice

congenial. The way he affectionately leaned in reading over his partner's shoulder spoke to a deep connection.

I felt the bus shift as Driver Chris came up the steps. After some deliberation, he selected a cassette tape from the case on the dashboard. He put his hand on his sleeping partner's shoulder. It could not have been comfortable sleeping in the driver's seat, but the big blond driver awoke in a pleasant mood seeming rested. "Hey brother," he said to his friend. "I got us here."

"Great job," said the red-bearded driver. "I've already got breakfast started. It's time to wake the troops." He handed him the cassette.

He read the label and said, "Nice!" He pushed a cassette into the stereo and raised the volume slowly as a song began to play. The Latin sounds of wooden claves, shakers and tambourines rose to a crescendo as The Who's Magic Bus played on every speaker. Roger Daltrey sang the lyrics, "Thank you, driver, for getting me here."

Driver Chris looked at me with a knowing look. He smiled, but I could tell his mind was elsewhere. I wondered if his brother was still alive. He stood there for a while with one knee on the buddy seat, holding the support bar, waiting for passengers to show signs of life. Eventually, he persuaded the sleeping passengers to wake up in a creeping deep voice. "It's time to wake up," he urged. "It's time for breakfast. We need to start cooking now, or else we will not have time to swim in Lake Erie after breakfast. If you do not want to get up now, you can help clean up. Everyone needs to either cook or clean. Especially the guys. Don't you dare let the ladies do all the work."

This left me feeling somewhat offended because I have always done my share in the kitchen. I consider myself a feminist, so I was glad when someone spoke up.

"Hey now!" Jewels objected with attitude. "You're just reinforcing the stereotype. I hope you don't think cooking and cleaning is 'women's work,' because I won't lift a finger."

"No, no, no he said. "I'm not reinforcing the stereotype, I'm trying to encourage guys to take the next step, to take it to the next level. Men must own that shit because stereotypes are still forcing women do the brunt of the work when we should all be sharing the load. Men often default to women like when a doctor enters the room you step aside. Men need to carry their own weight. Even progressive guys on the bus will at times default to women in the kitchen. I've seen it a thousand times. Most guys have no problem letting women take over and do all the work."

"Damn straight!" proclaimed Jewels. "We need to get the men on board. If you let them, guys will walk all over you, especially when it comes to caregiver roles, like when a kid cries the woman usually gets the Band-Aid." She shook her head in disbelief and said, "I can't tell you how few men I see in parent teacher conferences."

"You're so right," agreed our driver. He spoke with a rising tone of incredulity. "I see myself as a feminist, but I still find myself doing it sometimes." He rose to two feet before continuing passionately. "Until men see themselves as caregivers and not just breadwinners, we're not going to lessen the burden our society puts on women," he opined. "It's not just women who need to solve the problem; men need to be on board too.'"

"I'm glad you're not a sexist," praised Jewels.

Our red-bearded driver continued, "Right now I need some help setting up." he coaxed.

"Where are we?" asked the woman in the tan and green scarf.

"Crane Creek State Park in Ohio," he answered.

I laid back down to wiggle out of my sleeping bag.

"Where are we?" I heard English Tessa ask British Sue.

"Sod all if I know," she answered. "All I know is I desperately need to have a slash."

"Oh God, I need a piddle, too," her friend gasped. "Let's get on with it shall we?"

I was at a nine on the pee scale, so I said, "I need to go too."

The girls and I climbed down from our bunks and began rooting through the mountain of sneakers and boots on the floor next to the dinette. Big Dave was sleeping alone in the cave beneath the table below the boy and his mother. We tried to keep quiet, but the girls started to giggle because they had to pee so badly. The giggling interrupted Big Dave's soft snoring, but his massive body remained motionless except when he coughed once.

British Sue could not wait for her friend to find her hiking boots, so we went ahead. "What's this place?" she asked me after we stepped outside.

"Crane Creek," I told her. "Ohio."

On the way to the bathroom, we rushed across a field of fresh-cut grass moist with dew. It was a bit chilly in the early morning air.

"Wait," English Tessa yelled from the bottom step.

"She seems to be having a time finding her Wellies," the blond informed me.

"Did you sleep okay?" I asked.

She blew the hair from over her eyes like she was still tired. "It got pretty bumpy," she answered coyly, but I got to sleep after that."

At the bathroom door she stopped and waited for her friend. She shuddered and rubbed her arms for warmth. So, I put my arm around her back and hugged her close for warmth.

"Oh, that's lovely," she said. "You're so warm."

The Driver's Apprentice

"I run hot," I told her.

She made a purring sound and put her hand on my opposite hip. Her friend stumbled across the field wearing boots that were much too big to be her own. Before she arrived, I turned to face British Sue with the intention of warming her with a hug, but she pushed me away as her friend grew close. "I'll be a bit less narky after I brush my teeth," she faltered.

"Oh shit, I left my toothbrush on the bus." I asked, "Could I borrow some toothpaste?"

"By all means," she said warmly. Her friend came rushing up and she hurriedly rifled through her waist pack until she found a little tube. She pressed a lump of toothpaste on my finger and they rushed into the bathroom together.

I brushed my teeth with my finger on the way inside, but there was no sink in the primitive restroom, so I spit in the toilet and went about my business.

I could hear the girl's voices echoing in the ladies' room. I could not make out everything they were saying, but on their way out I heard English Tessa say, "Tell him you fancy a snog." When she saw me waiting there for them, her friend said, "Well, I'll leave you to it then," and she merrily skipped away.

After a moment of awkward silence, I gave British Sue a puzzled look. "What's a snog?" I inquired coyly.

The adorable blond made a guilty expression with pursed lips like she had been caught red handed with her finger in a pie. "A snog is a kiss," she revealed, pursing her lips again, more romantically this time. "Snogging is what you Yanks call making-out."

"Who's the lucky guy?" I asked feigning ignorance.

"My mate Tessa is just winding me up because I said you were fit," she explained.

"Is that a good thing?" I asked.

"I'd say," she said admiringly, sliding her waist pack around to the rear.

"Why's she winding you up?" I asked.

"I 'ave a lad at home," she revealed.

"A lad?" My shoulders dropped with my chin. "You have a boyfriend?" I asked.

"He's a nice enough chap," she appraised. "He's my brother's best friend. It gets a little too close for comfort sometimes."

"We should head back then," I suggested.

"He doesn't own-me," she stated flatly, "and Tess promised she wouldn't tattle."

"Do you fancy a snog?" I asked smiling.

"You smarmy git," she entreated. "What do you think?"

"Totally," I breathed. "I would like that." I certainly did not expect this at seven o'clock in the morning, but I had just brushed my teeth, so I went for it. I took her hand in mine and hugged her with one arm, lifting her up onto her toes. "Good morning," I said with a smile.

"Good morning," she said with her dimples showing. I looked into her eyes and kissed her gently on the lips. She tilted her head and opened her mouth. I pressed on, moving my hand to the back of her head. She broke off the kiss and looked past my shoulder. I tried to lean in for a second, deeper kiss, but she broke the embrace. "Tessa's watching," she said cutely. Then, she led me by the hand like a little kid, walking back toward the bus as fast as she could drag me. Her friend Tessa was all giddy and smiling.

Along the way we passed the guy with the yellow soccer jersey and the girl with the head scarf. They each gave me a courteous nod and we exchanged hellos.

Jewels and Yülia came back from the bathroom together chatting like old friends catching up after years apart. Perhaps it was Jewels' soulful way that opened the German girl's heart, or maybe they both just had big hearts to begin with. It was hard to tell, but it was quite heartwarming how fast they had become best friends. They looked and acted like sisters despite outward appearances, being from distant parts of the world, speaking with different accents, one being a teacher, the other still a student.

Theirs wasn't the only friendship blossoming. Australian Sheila and Mountain Girl were hitting it off bigtime, chatting nonstop on the way to the restroom. They were both extroverts, athletic and active. The Canadian was a snowboard instructor and the Aussie was a Certified Open Water Dive Instructor. They too shared a sisterhood that defied age and international borders.

The maple-lined lakeside at Crane Creek, Ohio was an idyllic spot to make breakfast. The bus was parked sideways along the grass in an empty lot near the bank of a small, gently flowing creek that feeds into Lake Erie. Chicken Jim was standing on the roof, knee deep in the wooden box where I had stored my extra baggage and the Grandfather Elk skull.

Jewels came down the steps holding hands with Yülia. She joyfully praised her new friend, "You're so awesome. I am so happy we met. I hope you don't regret being my buddy. I can't stand being alone in public places, so I'm going to keep you busy."

****

Driver Chris was directing the meal on the far side of the bus. Three eight-foot-long tables had been set up on the wet grass. Two large black plastic trash bags full of mixing bowls and giant silver pots lay on the ground next to a table. A large red plastic toolbox containing cooking utensils sat open on a table alongside a smaller plastic toolbox full of eating utensils. The sexy Peruvian and her Asian traveling partner each stood before a pair of cutting boards wielding large kitchen knives, chopping fruit. After each apple, pear, or banana or other fruit was chopped they would scrape the pieces into a giant stainless-steel serving bowl.

Berndt Toast was steadying a stainless steel five-gallon cooking pot for Driver Chris who was filling it with water. When the pot was full, the driver told Berndt Toast, "Always be wicked careful when you light this thing." As I approached, he warned, "Stand back!" As he turned the valve on the propane cooker, he held a long-shafted lighter under the pot at arm's length. He grabbed his red beard in one hand and held it off to the side. Click. Poof! The whole stove ignited in a ball of flames that licked all the way up the sides of the pot. Driver Chris pulled his hand back quickly.

"That's why we call it the blaster," he explained, displaying the burnt hair on the back of his hand. He turned it up all the way. The low-profile stove made an incredibly loud jet engine sound, producing a flame under the pot like the business end of a rocket.

The cool bush hat came back from the bathroom with an Irish girl on each arm. The ladies went back inside the bus, but he strolled around checking out the scene. The dignified woman with the fine clothes and Spanish accent came out of the bus, followed closely by her Asian friend. When approached by the young Brazilian she looked him straight in the eye and introduced herself with a slight courtesy. "My name is Ursula. I am from Lima, Peru. May I ask your name?"

His one brow rose as he inspected her with a one-eyed grin. "I am Juliano Pento from Brazil!" He took her hand and kissed her knuckles before adding, "I am so pleased to make your acquaintance." His syllables danced off his tongue marvelously, but she was not impressed.

Without a hint of an accent she asked, "What part of Brazil are you from, Juliano?"

"I am a' from Rio de Janeiro," he said proudly, rolling his r's like a river in spring. The muscular little Brazilian conjured images of Ricky Martin, and she was starting to conjure the Hispanic Fly Girl from In Living Color, Jennifer Lopez. She possessed the quintessential bodacious body to play the part. The two superstars seemed like the perfect couple. Both were extremely good looking and versed in the romantic languages. There was only one foreseeable problem with such a frontpage relationship. Jennifer would never be caught dead playing second fiddle to the hordes of women throwing themselves at Ricky's feet.

She started speaking with him in a language I assumed to be Spanish, but later learned to be Portuguese. She spoke with an inquisitive tone which he responded to in short often one-word answers. They switched back to English and his shoulders relaxed. "I'm so glad you know Portuguese," he told her. "It has been a long time since I have had anyone to speak with in Portuguese."

I got the vibe that he thought himself to be of a lower social class than the Peruvian. "I dated a rich girl in high school," he told her. "She grew up with seven personal servants. Her parents think I am not good enough for her, and they stopped letting her see me, but she sends me letters. Now she's trying to decide which man to marry. She said, 'One drives a BMW and the other drives a Mercedes. I'm leaning toward the Mercedes.'"

"Philistine!" she jabbed, but he did not hear her, and she did not care.

"Are you looking for something to do?" Driver Chris shouted up to me.

"Sure! What needs doing?" I asked.

"Well," he began to explain, "we like to keep the first meal really simple, so the passengers don't have to work too hard on the first day. So, we will not be cooking anything. This way everyone can learn the kitchen scene, where to find stuff and how things work. So, we are just having cereal, granola, yogurt, and easy stuff like that."

"What do you need me to do?"

"We need another roof person. So, why don't you get up on the roof and help Chicken Jim get the fruit for the fruit salad?"

"All right."

"Be careful up there."

"Will do." This was so cool. At the green metal ladder, I said hello to Driver Brian through the driver's window. He was sitting in the driver's seat writing something. "Good morning, Brian."

"Good morning," he replied. He looked up wide-eyed as I lifted myself onto the first rung.

I asked, "Are you keeping a journal?"

"No. It's just my driver's log."

"What's a driver's log?" I asked.

"We have to log every hour and every mile we drive," he explained. "It's the law. Sometimes the park rangers ask us for it, and you can get a ticket if your log entries are not up to the minute. It's a pain in the ass, but I need to fill it out before I go to bed."

The Driver's Apprentice

"So, what you're saying is, there's a lot more to becoming a Green Tortoise driver than learning how to shift without the clutch," I concluded.

"Ha," he huffed. "There sure is." He nodded with a tilted head. "Chris mentioned that you want to learn the ropes."

"I sure do," I told him. "Chris just made me the new roof person."

"Excellent," he said. "If Chris has to leave, we're going to need all the help we can get running the show around here," he told me. "In theory, everyone is supposed to help equally, but we cannot babysit every last passenger, so the work can mount up. Chicken Jim is easily distracted and sometimes he can be hard to find, so it would be great to have another Driver's Apprentice, especially if Chris takes off."

"I'd love that." I marveled. "Just tell me what to do."

"Well, for now, just follow Jim's lead. He'll show you what needs doing."

"What if he's not around?" I asked.

"If Jimbo is not around, watch and listen to everything Chris says and follow his lead. If you pay attention, you'll be able to tell what he needs before he has to ask you for it."

"Thanks for the tip," I said. "I'll do my best."

"Well, don't work too hard," he cautioned me. "You paid to be here, so don't take it too seriously. It should all be in good fun."

"It's all good," I responded with excitement and started up the ladder.

He chased me with his words, "Remember, Jimbo works for us, so don't let him make you do all the work."

"I won't," I told him, then I stopped. "I'm just curious." I asked, "How long has Chicken Jim been an apprentice?"

He contemplated my question for a moment with a look up into the space of thought. "He worked for the owner's son for ride credit before he started driver's training," he revealed, "but I think he's started training in the middle of last season."

"Jeez. How long does it take to become a driver?"

"Usually not that long," he answered with a laugh. "He's taking it slow."

Truth be told, I did not care if Chicken Jim did make me do all the work. I was just psyched to be helping and learning from the Green Tortoise Driver's Apprentice. I checked to be sure my mountain bike was securely fastened to the roof. From up there I could see everything that was happening in the kitchen below, like an Osprey in a high nest.

A short distance from the bus, a long footbridge crossed over to a small island in the middle of Crane Creek. The island was crowded with big-leaf oaks. The sounds of bird life were all around us, and the bushes on the riverbank rustled with life. In the river I could see several white birds walking slowly in the shallows looking for food.

"Johnny Lovebus!" Chicken Jim greeted me with sticky sweet enthusiasm.

"Yes, indeed," I said happily. "Those birds are amazing."

He looked up. "Those are great egrets," he informed me. "There's a ton of them here."

I chose the sign of the day, the great egret of Crane Creek, Ohio.

A foot-and-a-half-deep wooden roof box stretched two thirds the length of the bus, containing an unimaginable array of fresh fruit and vegetables, like the display stands at a farmer's market. There were coolers, bags of groceries, sacks of potatoes, onions, and dozens of milk crates full of smaller items and a variety of canned goods.

Chicken Jim gave me what seemed like a job description. "The first duty of a roof-person is to get the tables off the roof. We already did that, so you don't have to worry about that until the meal is over, then I'll show you how to get them up here, put them on the rack and tie them down." He waved for me to come closer to where he stood in the middle of the roof box. "The second job is opening the roof-tarp in preparation for mealtime when we arrive and fastening it down before we leave."

"Sounds pretty straight forward," I observed.

"Here's the tricky part," he said, picking up a honeydew melon. "You have to learn how to throw the food down without hurting the catchers." He called out, "I need a catcher!" Berndt Toast was standing below us looking up and put his hands up to catch. Chicken Jim leaned over and dropped the melon.

The rugged German caught it against his chest with a thud. "Scheisse!" he exclaimed.

"That's easy enough." I laughed, "What's next? I mean, how do we know what needs to be thrown down?"

"The driver usually tells you what he needs, but we make fruit salad for every breakfast, and the ingredients are always the same. We'll need one more honeydew and three cantaloupes, five bunches of bananas, half-a-dozen kiwi, a couple bags of grapes, and two bins of strawberries."

I grabbed a honeydew and carefully dropped it to Berndt Toast. This time he caught the fruit with both hands and did not have to use his chest. "Nice one," I complimented.

"Nice one!" said Chicken Jim.

After we had passed down the remainder of the fruit, Driver Chris shouted up to us, "We need cereal and granola."

The Driver's Apprentice

"When you pass down the milk crates you need a tall person to catch them," the driver in training explained. "You never drop milk crates. They are too hard to catch." He picked up the first of three milk crates and stepped to the edge of the roof box. He rested the milk crate on the roof outside of the roof box, explaining, "Use the side of the bus to guide it down so it doesn't tip over." Someone took the milk crate from his hand.

He pointed at a crate containing a giant bag of granola. I brought it to the edge of the bus and rested it on the roof outside the roof box, but no one came to get it. I spotted the guy in the yellow soccer jersey standing next to his traveling partner, "Hello," I said, getting his attention. "Do you mind grabbing this?"

"Sure," he said.

Chicken Jim stood on his tiptoes to watch the transfer.

The South African soccer fan reached up for the milk crate, balanced it on his fingertips and successfully lowered it into his hands.

"What's your name?" I asked.

"I'm Gavin," he said in what sounded like a mild British accent.

"Are you from South Africa?" I asked.

"Cape Town," he replied with an affirmative nod.

"Nice to meet you, Gavin. I'm Johnny Lovebus." I introduced myself. "That's my bus name."

"We know all about the bus names," Gavin gave the woman in the head scarf a knowing look.

"We read a bunch of names in the notebook on the dashboard," she confirmed. "Some of them are funny, but I think some are a bit crass. I don't think German girls like to be called Fräulein."

Chicken Jim stepped into sight. "Everybody gets a bus name," he said. He handed me another milk crate. The second one was much lighter than the first, containing only dry cereal.

Gavin walked away with his crate and his friend moved into position below me. "Hello Johnny Lovebus," she greeted me cordially. "I'm Marian, Gavin is my fiancé. We're traveling around the world together."

"Well congratulations," I said warmly.

"Thank you kindly," she said with a slight bow of her head and a bit of a courtesy.

"It's so cool that you get to do that together," I remarked. "Did you get engaged on the road, or did he ask you before?"

"I asked him actually," she put forth.

"Really?" I said both impressed and surprised.

"At Niagara Falls," she said proudly, "on the Maid of the Mist."

Gavin returned and said, "You will always be my fair maiden."

I could feel Chicken Jim's eyes on me. I lowered the milk crate and Marian lifted her hands above her head, waiting for me to pass it down. "If we can travel around the world without killing each other, marriage should be a piece of cake," she concluded. "Isn't it true my love?"

"Tis true my lady," her fiancé responded gallantly.

I lowered the milk crate as far as I could. She was standing on her toes trying to reach the milk crate with her fingertips, but she could not reach it.

"Go ahead and Drop it," she said. "I got it."

"Here it comes," I warned her, and I dropped it.

Marian caught the milk crate on her fingertips and balanced it on her flattened palms, but when she tried to lower it into her arms, she failed to manage the transition and she dropped the milk crate. A bag of Corn Flakes launched out when it hit the ground, but the actual cereal did not spill. Gavin rushed to pick it up.

She was not impressed with him coming to her rescue. "You're my knight in shining armor," she teased him.

"Sir Gavin of the Green Tortoise at your service," he responded dutifully.

"Ha!" Chicken Jim laughed. "Sir Gavin! That sounds like a bus name."

His fiancée chuckled.

"If I have to live with that," he proclaimed, "then I get to choose her name."

"I hereby dub thee Maid Marian," he proclaimed.

"Like hell," she scoffed.

"After the Maid of the Mist," he backpedaled.

"That's so romantic," she marveled. "I can accept that," she acquiesced.

"That's awesome," I said.

Chicken Jim looked so proud of himself. "Hey everybody," he announced. "This is Sir Gavin and Maid Marian!"

Driver Chris shouted, "We need the tea box and the coffee!"

Chicken Jim pointed behind me and said, "The tea box is over there."

I picked up the tea box and looked inside before bringing it over. The crate was full of every kind of tea imaginable, Earl Grey, English Breakfast, Cinnamon Orange Spice, Caravan, Chai, Ginseng, Darjeeling, Jasmine, Ceylon, Orange Pekoe, Herbal Teas, white tea, green tea, you name it. I passed it down to Sir Gavin.

The Driver's Apprentice

Chicken Jim tossed down five pounds of coffee in a huge brown paper bag.

I watched and listened as Driver Chris instructed the passengers on how to make Cowboy Coffee. "On the Green Tortoise we make Cowboy Coffee," he announced. "The recipe is simple." He held an orange, twelve-ounce, plastic mug above his head. "Fill one of these up to the top with coffee," he instructed, scooping coffee out of the brown bag. He removed it carefully and showed the passengers the full mug of ground coffee. In his other hand he held up a gallon-sized stainless-steel coffee pot.

"Pour the coffee in an empty coffee pot," he explained as he poured the coffee into the pot. He turned the orange mug upside down and banged the edge against the side, then he flipped the mug into the air toward the dishwashing station. We all watched the spinning orange blur arc and fall. It landed short of the three buckets of water rebounding off the grass, but the spin he imparted on the mug gave it just enough energy to bounce back into the air. The mug caught the lip of the middle bucket and dropped in with a splash. There was a round of laughter and applause.

Surprisingly, He looked at us with an expression of self-disparagement and said, "Oops!"

"You made it!" cheered Yülia.

"Wrong bucket," he acknowledged.

I stood in awe.

He took a few steps toward the propane burner and went right on with the lesson. "After the water boils, you lift it by the handles like this." He lifted the huge pot off the blaster barehanded using only the small metal handles. "Be careful not to touch the pot itself," he warned. "It can be very hot and if you drop the water that's not good either." He walked bowlegged with the heavy load over to his intended target. "Then you will fill the kettle like this." He expertly pressed his thumbs on the small handles, using his index fingers like an axle to rotate the pot into pouring position.

"Go ahead," said Berndt Toast holding the kettle ready with a firm grip on the handle.

Driver Chris expertly poured boiling water into the coffee pot without spilling so much as a drop. "One mug of grounds makes one gallon of coffee. It's as simple as that," he instructed. He picked up the orange mug off the grass, filled the mug, and proceeded to take a sip. "That's Cowboy Coffee!" he said, licking coffee grounds from his lip. "It's a Tortoise tradition," he decreed, spitting on the ground. "You'll get used to it."

This seemed pretty funny at first, as many of us were laughing. "Don't you need to strain it?" Yülia asked.

"Nope," he said, as he stirred the coffee with a large metal spoon. "Just pour and drink."

My ears perked up when I heard an Irish accent. "Does anyone fancy a cup-o-tea?" The dirty-red-haired girl approached the food table dressed in a green hoodie. Her dirty-blond girlfriend walked up on the opposite side of the table in a flannel button down open at the front like a jacket.

Sir Gavin rushed to her side at the table and offered her the tea box.

"That's a kindness," the redhead thanked him. The new day's light accentuated the colors of her hair and the freckles on her fair skin. She had a light airiness about her that spoke to the heart of my younger self, reminiscent of the first girl I ever kissed. Her cheeks were flushed red in patches, and her low manicured eyebrows rode slightly beneath the rim of her deep eye sockets below a high graceful forehead. A few wispy strands of auburn hair hung on her bangs over her greenish-blue eyes and small straight nose.

Maid Marian stepped up, "I'd love a cup of tea."

"Howya?" asked the Irish girl.

"I'm doing well," she answered. "How are you?"

"Grand," she replied. "I'm Kyrah and that's Joyce," she said with a slight tilt of her head and a smile.

"Nice to meet you both," she said fancifully. "I'm Marian."

"Maid Marian," her fiancé corrected her as he approached.

"Maid Marian is my official bus name," she explained. "This is my fiancé, Sir Gavin," Maid Marian publicized.

He gave them a friendly little wave with a bent wrist and asked, "Where are you lovely ladies from?"

Kyrah laughed. "I'm surprised you have to ask. Can't you tell I'm Irish from my porcelain white skin," he waved her hand in front of her face, "and my green jumper?" She held the garment open by the lapels and added, "Penney's finest." She smiled like she was teasing. "We're definitely not from any country that has any sort of sun in it. I'm as white as paper, as exotic as Brennans' Bread." Her greenish-blue eyes sparkled when she talked.

The two girls exclaimed in one voice together, "We're the Irish Twins!"

"I love it!" grooved Chicken Jim.

"That's what everyone calls us at Uni," Irish Kyrah explained.

"I'm not entirely Irish though. I'm a bit more multicultural than all that. Rumor has it that I'm part Scottish and Welsh. I don't have any English in me whatsoever. Thanks for that."

"I probably should have guessed you were Irish." He turned to include his fiancée. "We're from South Africa."

The Driver's Apprentice

"Isn't that special," said the blond facetiously. "Sometimes it seems like all of us are from divided countries colonized by the UK."

"It's never been a 'United Kingdom' slashed Maid Marian.

"Hopefully, the fighting ends with the rise of Mandela," Sir Gavin commented.

"We've learned not to hold our breath," she added.

Sir Gavin handed them their mugs as the two ladies perused the selection of teas.

"Another kindness," Irish Kyrah thanked him. "Look love!" she called out in a high-pitched voice. "They have Barry's tea." She held up a box of tea to show her dirty-blond twin. She was a true ginger with a teaspoon of sugar.

"I'll 'ave a cuppa," her friend responded in a deep throaty voice with an identical Irish accent. She wore bright-blue sparkly eyeshadow and had an obvious nose piercing that made a statement rather than accentuating beauty.

Irish Joyce was attractive enough to deserve the attention of any man's eye, but her attitude and temperament told you not to fuck with her and that she did not take shit lying down. Her demeanor spoke more to experience than innocence. She seemed older and more jaded than her kindhearted twin. Her voice and confident shoulders would have suggested androgyny had it not been for the gorgeous braided bun at the back of her head. She was a true blond with a pinch of pepper.

Flip-flop walked up and Sir Gavin jumped to it, presenting her with a plastic mug as she arrived.

"Fancy a cup of Barry's tea?" Irish Kyrah offered.

"No," Flip-flop responded looking into her cup with apprehension. "I'll stick to coffee. Thanks though."

As she walked off toward the coffee station Irish Kyrah chased her with her words, "Suit yourself," she said in a beautiful brogue. "You're missing out. Barry's Tea is Ireland's finest."

"I've never heard of that kind of tea. Is it good?" asked Maid Marian.

"Oh, it's deadly," the redhead assured the South African woman. "I'll fix you a cup."

"I'm sure you're better at it than me," she admitted.

"The trick is to let it steep before you add your milk and sugar." She turned to greet her friend, "Top of the mornin' to ya sis." She put two tea bags in each mug and poured the hot water. "How'd you sleep?" she asked.

"I was completely knackered, but getting to sleep was murder. It was fugin' freezing."

"Wasn't it though!" Irish Kyrah agreed wholeheartedly. She hugged her arms around herself and raised the hood of her forest green sweatshirt, pouring milk into her tea. "I'm such an eejit when it comes to waiting," she admitted. "Waiting is brutal when I'm freezing." After adding the sugar, she stated, "You should always stir it seven times anti-clockwise and tap it twice for good luck." She demonstrated and passed the spoon to her sister who proceeded to do the same, tapping twice at the end.

Maid Marian took the spoon, poured her milk, and stirred without adding sugar or tapping twice.

"What brings you two to the states?" Irish Joyce croaked after taking a noisy sip.

"We're traveling around the world," she revealed. "How about yourselves?"

"We're midwives," they said together in one voice. "We just got certified."

"That's awesome!" said Maid Marian. "I'm an RN."

"I just got my NARM certification," said the dirty-blond.

"I'm a CPM," said the dirty redhead.

Maid Marian looked pleased to hear this harmony of excited voices. "That's great," she praised them. "I've always looked up to midwives. That's important work you do." She nodded in approval. "I'm not that brave," she admitted.

Irish Kyrah spoke soulfully. "Having a baby is probably the best day of your life, and I we want to help make it that way for them. It is brilliant to be able to help somebody bring their little baby into the world and be a part of that. That is what I love about it. I will never get tired of it. It's a privilege for anybody to be present and to see a new human being come-into-the-world."

"That's a wonderful sentiment," Maid Marian praised. "I wish you both the best of luck."

"We're on our way to San Francisco to start our practice," Irish Kyrah boasted.

"You know I hate it when you brag like that, sister," Irish Joyce rebuked her. "We'll need to get certified in California and probably volunteer as doulas first," she contended.

"Opening a practice is a big first step," Maid Marian remarked. "Some real-world experience would help you get there for sure."

Flip-flop returned after cleaning her mug and asked, "Can you hook me up with some of that Irish Tea?"

After Irish Kyrah stirred seven times anti-clockwise and tapped the rim of her mug twice, the four girls walked off sipping and discussing the Irish sister's midwife plans.

****

After passing down dozens of more food items, there was a pause in the action. So, I asked Chicken Jim, "Where are you from?"

"Shamokin, Pennsylvania," he told me.

"No way!" I reacted in surprise. "My mother is from Shamokin.

"Ah, right on," he related. "I grew up in Pottsville. That's right near Shamokin."

"Ha," I laughed. "You're from Shamokin-Pottsville?"

"Ha!" He laughed. "I never thought of it like that." He smiled fondly at the thought. His eyes drifted like he was watching smoke rings rise. "I went to Pottsville Highschool."

"How did you end up on the Green Tortoise?" I asked him.

"I took a cross country trip two summers ago," he expounded. "That's how I met Chris." He looked proud. "He encouraged me to apply for a job as a driver, but the owner said they had to get to know me before I could be trusted, so I ended up working for ride credit. Obviously, that didn't pay good."

"Brian told me this is your second season as a Driver's Apprentice," I told him. "Why is it taking you so long?"

"Oh, shit! He told you that?"

"Yes."

Chicken Jim stopped talking, took me by the arm, and looked serious suddenly. "No matter what happens, if you decide to work for the Tortoise, when you meet Gardener or his son, never let them know you saw me on this trip, okay?"

"Why not?" I inquired.

"I'm trying to fly low, like under the radar," he explained. "If they figure out how many free trips I've flown, they might clip my wings."

"Okay," I said. "I won't say a word."

"As far as you're concerned, I don't exist."

"You don't exist," I confirmed my understanding.

He relaxed when he heard this. "Don't get me wrong, I think Gardner is a freaking genius, but his son's methods are a little unsound, if you know what I mean."

"How's that?" I asked.

"His son makes you work like there's no tomorrow."

"What kind of work did you do for him?"

"At first, I worked in a boatyard stripping paint off the hull of the Green Tortoise sailboat."

"No way, the Green Tortoise has a sailboat?"

"Yes, it's a thirty-eight-footer named Felicity. I worked for weeks scraping and repainting."

"Were you paid for that?" I questioned.

"Yeah, I got minimum wage, but they let me live on a bus in the old warehouse on Jerrold Street, and I could eat leftovers from the adventure trips. So, I had almost no expenses. After that, I worked delivering Tortoise brochures to all the coffee houses in San Francisco. After a few months I finally got to do some driver training, but I never actually sat behind the wheel when the bus was moving. I just watched other drivers in training drive up and down the west coast from San Francisco to Seattle, around the Olympic Peninsula."

"I did a bike tour from Seattle to Olympic National Park and down the coast through the Redwood Forest," I told him excitedly.

"Wow, that's cool," he said appreciatively. "I love the Great Northwest."

Driver Brian was resting inside the bus until the food was ready. Driver Chris took off for the men's room, so we had nothing to do for a few minutes until he returned. Chicken Jim stood by my side and whispered, "Now that you're one of us, I can trust you to keep a secret, right?"

"For sure," I said. "What is it?"

"It's top secret," he warned me. "You can never tell a soul."

"Okay," I whispered.

He lowered his voice even more. "You have to promise me you will keep this between us."

"Okay! Okay! I promise," I told him. "You can trust me. I swear."

"Well," he said looking around all cloak and dagger, "that girl, the one who speaks Spanish..."

"Jewels?"

"No, the other one."

"The Peruvian?"

He nodded.

"She's super-hot," I commented.

"Yes, there's more to her than meets the eye," he informed me. He looked around again to check if anyone might be listening. "She's not what she appears to be," he stated enigmatically, "and neither is that guy she's with."

"They seem harmless," I remarked.

His eyes widened. "You best stay away from them," he warned.

"Why?" I demanded.

"She works for the government," he revealed. "I think she's a spy!"

The Driver's Apprentice

"Dude!" I said in a high-pitched voice of disbelief. "Everyone who lives in Washington works for the government. That doesn't make her a spy."

He ducked down, looked around and put a finger to his lips. "Shush!" He leaned in close. "He's some kind of Chinese inspector, or something like that," he told me in a whisper. "He's traveling all incognito and shit."

"Who? PAC-MAN?" I asked.

"I don't know what to call him anymore," he scoffed. "All I know is that's not his real name."

"Of course, it isn't," I scoffed.

"Seriously, dude!" he said. "I heard the drivers talking about it."

"No way," I spat disbelief. My father's words crossed my mind. Believe none of what you hear and half of what you see. "That's ridiculous," I objected. "Why would he lie about his name?"

"He needs to get to San Francisco off the grid," he said mysteriously.

"Why not just take Greyhound?"

"You can't buy a ticket on Greyhound without ID, even if you pay cash," he explained. "The Tortoise never checks ID," he informed me.

"Really?" I marveled.

"Lots of people use fake names when they take the Tortoise," he snorted. "Coo, coo, coo! We get a lot of reservations for people like John Doe, and people use names like Seymour Weed. Harry Ballsack, Phil McCracken, Hue Jardon. You get the picture."

"Ha!" I laughed.

He grumbled a few steps off a whisper. "The way he hangs on her reminds me of that Chinese guy who always jumps out of the closet in the Pink Panther movies."

"His name was Cato," I informed him. He was referring to the Peter Sellers films about a bumbling detective who repeatedly fails to capture an international jewel thief known as the Pink Panther. "Cato was Inspector Clouseau's Chinese manservant," I explained.

"Exactly!" He said pointing at me. "He was always camping out in the closet waiting to pounce on the guy."

"Pink Panther is a perfect bus name for her," I said laughing.

"I'm sticking with Ursula and PAC-MAN for the time being," he told me. "I don't want to piss her off. She means business."

"Here comes Chris," I said. He was on his way back from the men's room. Chicken Jim put his finger to his lips. "Be sure to keep this on the low down," he requested before resuming the business of preparing the morning meal.

After I ate breakfast, the job of roof person worked the opposite way. The milk crates were handed up, the food tables were slid up on the side of the bus, Chicken Jim showed me how to tie them in place, and two heavy trash bags were passed up and tied down on top of the tables.

****

When it came time to swim Driver Chris made the announcement. He pointed in the distance behind him and said, "If anyone wants to go for a swim, there's a beach on the island across that little bridge. You'll be able to see the beach once you're on the bridge. There's sign over there that says no nudity, but the beach is totally private, so you can ignore that sign."

"It doesn't say 'No skinny-dipping,'" goofed Chicken Jim.

Our driver continued unfazed. "You can do whatever you want when you get over there. You'll figure it out. The choice is yours, but we can't have everybody sitting on the seats in wet bathing suits, and there's no place to hang wet shit to dry."

"Why would anyone care?" demanded Fräulein Vera.

"You have to understand," he told us loudly enough for us all to hear. "The eastern half of America can be pretty uptight," he admitted with a tone of embarrassment. "The signs east of the Mississippi always say, NO CAMPING, NO FISHING, NO SWIMMING, NO ALCOHOL, but west of the Mississippi all the signs say, CAMPING, FISHING, SWIMMING, and alcohol is always allowed. In Montana you can drink alcohol in your car while you're driving." He summarized. "We generally have more fun once we cross the Mississippi, but you can have all the fun you want over there. You don't need a bathing suit."

Driver Chris seemed way more relaxed than earlier in the morning, like he had come back to himself. I could tell he clearly enjoyed playing the role of a guide to the great outdoors. It was his natural state of being, like he was in his element. He clearly loved being a Green Tortoise Adventure Bus Driver.

Jewels and Yülia led the charge across the footbridge, leaving me and Chicken Jim to finish cleanup with the help of Berndt Toast. Most of the Tortoise passengers were already swimming by the time Chicken Jim and I got the tarp tied it down. Once again, the hearty German guy refrained from swimming. I had to assume this was due to his prosthetic leg. We crossed the footbridge to the little island and walked to the small sand beach facing out into Lake Erie. Through the morning-fresh air and bright sky, I could see for miles across the placid lake.

The Driver's Apprentice 143

Big Dave stood up to his waist in the water, maintaining a posture with his hands before him probably communing with the fish again.

On the side of a tall white lifeguard chair there was a wooden sign that read, 'NO ALCOHOLIC BEVERAGES,' and 'NO NUDITY ALLOWED,' but someone had hung a towel over part of the sign, so it now read, "NUDITY ALLOWED." Judging from the piles of clothing marking the boat ramp, hardly anyone was following the East Coast rules. Flip-flop was letting it all hang-out, having been reluctant to do so just yesterday. It was like we had joined a cult, like we had found our tribe. The fun was infectious.

"Woohoo!" shouted Chicken Jim over the water with hands cupped to his mouth.

"Woohoo," I followed suit. A few of the passengers in the water called back.

Sir Gavin and Maid Marian came out of the water in bathing suits and sat on a towel while Chicken Jim and I undressed.

"So where are you from, Johnny?" asked the South African guy in cool accented syllables.

I told them, "Rhode Island," as I continued to undress. "How did you find out about the Tortoise?" I asked them.

They smiled at each other fondly like only the recently engaged seem to do and Maid Marian spoke, "We met on a Tortoise trip in Costa Rica."

"Wow, that's out of sight!" said I.

"It happens all the time," Chicken Jim chimed in as he tossed his Ozzy shirt on top of his overalls. He really wasn't naturally endowed, but he seemed perfectly comfortable standing there naked.

Maid Marian continued, "We were friends at first, of course, but when we got back home Gavin convinced me to move to Cape Town. Now, I work as a nurse at the hospital on Cape Point."

"What's it like in Cape Town?" I asked.

"I love it!" Sir Gavin answered with a chuckle. He spoke playfully, "Marian can't seem to adjust to the baboons."

"Damn straight, I can't get on with the baboons. Can you blame me?" She nudged him hard. They made a cute couple.

"There are baboons in Cape Town?" I asked with surprise.

"Crikey!" exclaimed Maid Marian. "Baboons are everywhere on the cape. They block the road, they steal your trash barrels, and we can't even leave our windows unlocked because they'll come in and eat up all the food. People have come home and found baboons sitting on their bed watching the telly."

"Ha!" I laughed.

"It's not that bad," pleaded Sir Gavin.

"It's bad enough," she said. "The farmer's market at the preserve has to escort shoppers to their cars because the baboons jump on them and steal their bundles."

"That's crazy," I said with wide eyes.

The adorable yellow-haired Aussie came running up behind us. "This isn't fair," she huffed. "I was trying to find my togs, but I couldn't locate my rucksack." She looked around quickly. "We're alone?" Before anyone answered she kicked off her sandals, pulled her shirt down over her ass and dropped her drawers. Then she tucked her ponytail inside her shirt collar and lifted her shirt in the air above her head.

Several passengers had been waiting for the Aussie to lead them in water aerobics. About ten girls were standing in two rows with their feet on the bottom and their heads above the water, ready to begin their workout. Without communicating any plan, Chicken Jim and I spontaneously ran into the water side-by-side, yelling and screaming with our arms flailing over our heads, swimming between the rows of girls.

Five minutes after the aerobics class started, we heard tires skidding. Two all-terrain vehicles had stopped short on the footbridge to the island. In their path stood Berndt Toast, still in his street clothes. Two uniformed park rangers gawked at us with wide eyes and mouths agape. The German had purposefully delayed their arrival. He stood there for a few moments talking shit from them, acting dumb, speaking only German before he stepped out of their as commanded. The tires squealed again as the ATVs took off and headed toward us.

This gave Australian Sheila plenty of time to submerge herself, but it was obvious what was happening. We were stone-cold busted. I stayed close to shore while Chicken Jim swam over to Driver Chris to discuss the situation.

The two noisy ATVs arrived on the beach. The park rangers climbed off. They were not wearing guns, but I could see handcuffs on their belts. The ranger in charge was taller and thinner than his overweight partner. He sauntered to the beach with his subordinate one step off his shoulder. He waved for us to come out with his hand in the air. "Everyone out of the water!" he shouted with his hand cupped at his mouth.

"This is unacceptable!" exclaimed Peruvian Ursula from the shallows.

Further out in the water, I heard Driver Chris command, "Everyone stay where you are." Then he started swimming toward shore. The Peruvian threw him a steely-eyed look. With daggers in her eyes she hissed, "I will handle this!" Driver Chris looked bewildered. He stopped swimming. Peruvian Ursula walked up the boat ramp

The Driver's Apprentice

acting as if she was the one in charge, like nothing was out of the ordinary, despite being completely naked.

The ranger's staring eyes made me instantly angry, so without thinking I rushed out of the water to stand by her side. I did not bother to cover my private parts as I ran ashore.

When the short ranger saw that I was naked too, he hastily pocketed his notepad, clicked his radio, and said, "Unit one to base. We've got a two-eighty-eight down at the beach. Please acknowledge."

The tall one talked out of the side of his mouth. "More like a two-point-five incher," he said with a snort of laughter.

Admittedly, it was not my proudest moment. The head of my shriveled penis was peeking out of the bushes like a red-headed woodpecker.

The tall ranger put his hand up to block sight of me and said, "Cover that shit, son." He continued to peer around his raised hand to ogle the Peruvian.

The shorter one licked his lips and waved his hand in the air over his head yelling, "Come on in here! All you people need to come out of the water, right now!"

The tall ranger removed the notepad from his pocket and jotted something down. His radio crackled. "Base to Unit One. Two-eighty-eight in progress, acknowledged."

I cupped my hands over my junk and continued to approach the park rangers alongside the Peruvian woman until the taller ranger put his hand up for us to stop. "That's far enough," he commanded. They both inspected the Peruvian woman's body for hidden weapons, looking her up and down as if she was armed and dangerous. She did have nice guns, but I sneered at the rangers. Their eyes were otherwise criminally engaged. Much to their chagrin, the intelligent woman held one arm across her breasts and spread a tight fingered hand over her pubic region.

"I'm gonna need to see identification miss," said the lead ranger.

"What seems to be the problem officer?" asked the confident young Peruvian woman. "We haven't harmed anyone." She shrugged her bare shoulders with a shimmy of a head shake. "I sincerely hope there's not going to be a problem here."

"There most certainly will be a problem here little lady," the tall officer glowered. He waved the others in from the water, but Driver Chris staved them off.

"What did we do," she asked pretensively.

His partner rode her face with a stern look. "This is a state park," he derided her. "We don't take kindly to a bunch of nudists disturbing the peace. We're gonna need to see your ID right now."

Peruvian Ursula politely disagreed, "We're not nudists, and we're certainly not disturbing the peace. We were just swimming."

"Without your clothes on!" the tall officer snapped.

"We didn't mean any harm," she attested.

The tall senior ranger spoke curtly. "The sign clearly says, 'NO NUDITY ALLOWED.'"

We all looked at the sign at the same time. I could not help but snicker because the sign actually read "NUDITY ALLOWED" with the towel hiding the word "NO." The Peruvian gave me a stern sideways glance. This confused them for an instant. The senior ranger shook his head in frustration.

The junior ranger shouted over our heads. "Everyone out of the God damn water! Right now!" He put two fingers in his mouth and whistled loudly. "I said right now!"

The senior ranger shouted toward the swimmers, "Let's go people! Bring it in!"

Peruvian Ursula remained stoic. "None of them speak English," she informed them. "I will call them in, but you can't stand here watching while they get dressed. That would be ill advised," she warned them. "Those people are foreign diplomats here as guests of the United States on a diplomatic mission."

My eyebrows jumped, but thankfully the rangers were not looking at me with her standing there naked.

"On a what?" the commander snapped.

"They are international diplomats here for conference," she lied.

"That don't look like no diplomat bus," scoffed the junior ranger.

"It's an environmental youth conference," she asserted.

"They don't look like no diplomats," he said.

"I assure you, they are," she attested.

"Aren't they a bit young to be diplomats," the junior ranger said to his superior.

"They are young," she stated flatly. "Many of their parents are high ranking government officials. We have representatives from Europe, Australia, Asia, Africa, and South America. "They were glued to her every word. "As many of you know," she remarked, "nudity is not regarded as a crime in most civilized countries. It is customary in many cultures to bathe in public without garments." She said this with a sideways bow of her head.

This got their attention. I turned my head to follow their gaze as they looked at the people in the lake. No one had left the water, although Driver Chris had positioned himself closer to shore. "I've

The Driver's Apprentice

heard about the nudist beaches over there," snapped the commander. "That don't make it right doing it here."

The junior ranger spoke up. "I've heard the French have tits on their TV commercials." He froze for a second before reanimating. "I'm sorry miss. Pardon my French." He pursed his lips in dismay for a moment. "I meant to say breasts," he fumbled. "Yes, they have breasts on TV in France," he clarified, "on the commercials."

"Shut-up Floyd," snapped the commander. "What's your name, miss?

"Ursula," she answered.

"How are you affiliated with these people?" the commanding officer asked.

"I'm just the interpreter," she said, putting her fingers to her sternum. This gesture exposed her left breast for a moment. It mesmerized them.

"You sound American," he observed with a tone of frustration.

"I am American," she confirmed in a courteous voice. "I am also a citizen of Peru."

"We're going to need to see your ID," demanded tall the ranger.

"I have two passports in my purse back on the bus," she informed him.

"So, you don't have ID," said the short fellow, making a note in his notebook.

"Not at the moment," she said with incredulity. "My outfit doesn't have any pockets."

"What about you?" asked the senior officer, pointing at me.

"I don't have a passport, I told him. "I only have a driver's license."

"Where are you from?" he demanded.

"Rhode Island," I told him.

"I'm gonna need to see your Rhode Island driver's license," he ordered.

"I don't have it on me, sir," I explained.

"Why not?" he demanded.

"I'm naked," I flubbed a laugh.

Peruvian Ursula choked back what would have been a hyena cackle.

Time dragged under the weight of their silent derision. "My wallet is on the bus, sir. I can run and get it right now. It's right on the dashboard, sir."

"Let me ask you this Mr. Rhode Island." He seemed pleased with himself. "Is it customary in Rhode Island to bathe without garments?" he asked me.

I laughed at first, but I realized he was serious. The Junior ranger was jotting in his notepad again. He obviously expected an answer. So, I cleaned up my act and addressed him with a straight face. "No, sir."

"Then why are you standing here naked?" he rebuked me.

"I was just going with the flow, sir," I said. It was the first thing that came to my mind. I couldn't help but laugh. Peruvian Ursula stomped her foot. I dropped my eyes and mumbled, "Sorry."

The tall ranger side-eyed his partner who stood eagerly poised with pen pressed to paper. "Is that your bus?" he inquired.

"I'm not the owner," I told them shaking my head.

"Then who is?" he demanded.

"It's owned by the Green Tortoise," I stammered. "It's a tour bus."

"That's a commercial tour bus?" he marveled.

"Yes."

They both turned and looked at the big green hand-painted Tortoise bus. "Are you shitting me?" the shorter ranger marveled.

"No, sir," I said flatly. "I am not shitting."

"Don't be a Smart Aleck," he advised. "Are you the driver of that bus?"

My body went rigid as a feeling of imminent danger shot up my spine, but my mind failed to register the threat. "There are two drivers," I mumbled.

"We're gonna need to speak to the other driver too," said the ranger. "Where's he at?" He looked over my head and again waved for the swimmers to come to shore.

"He's sleeping inside the bus," I revealed. "He drove all night to get here, and we have a long haul in front of us today."

"Where are you headed?" the younger ranger asked suspiciously.

"San Francisco," I told them.

"Ha! Hippies!" The junior ranger laughed. "That explains it."

"My clients are here for the environmental summit," the Peruvian insisted fastidiously.

The tall thin senior ranger ignored her. "Well son," he told me. "I'm gonna need you to call your passengers in here to shore so we can get to the bottom of this."

"You'd like that wouldn't you," snapped the angry Peruvian. She shook her head in frustration and marched her feet up and down like a pouting child.

The Driver's Apprentice

I calmly reached my hand out toward her and said, "I got this." It was like some sixth sense told me exactly what they needed to hear. "I am deeply sorry," I humbly offered. "If you need to arrest somebody, please arrest me. Our foreign guests should not have to suffer for my stupidity. I should have known better. This was my mistake. I should have stopped them from swimming naked. I take full responsibility."

"Nobody's getting arrested yet," clamored the lead officer, "unless you keep ignoring my orders." He raised his voice, "Now call your people here, or we'll arrest every last one of you."

Peruvian Ursula spoke up. "They won't come out of the water with you standing here ogling them," she insisted. "That won't translate well. Not in any language."

"Call them in here this minute," the leader insisted, "or I'll be forced to put cuffs on you right now." He stepped towards her with his hand on his belt.

"That's not going to happen," decreed the Peruvian. "You can't arrest me," she scoffed. "I have diplomatic immunity." She turned her back on him, took a few steps and bent down to pick-up her clothes.

"Like hell we can't," snapped the junior ranger reaching for his cuffs. He dramatically unbuttoned the button on his leather handcuff pouch.

"You can take me in; but the charges won't stick," she insisted.

"What's that supposed to mean?" asked the junior ranger.

His boss grunted. "That means she has diplomatic immunity, shitstick."

"All foreign diplomats have immunity," she told them flatly.

She was good. She sounded so convincing; it was like she believed it herself. I started to think it might be true. Her confidence delighted me. I was suddenly no longer nervous. It was like my body went on remote control and I knew exactly what to do. We were in deep; might as well go deeper.

I stepped closer to the officers with my wrists held together, knowing full-well that the proximity of my shriveled manhood would make them uncomfortable. "You can arrest me," I pleaded. "I don't have immunity," I told them. "I'll probably lose my job, but I'd hate to see you two get in trouble. You should save yourselves the hassle. You don't want to create an international incident." I paused to let this sink in.

"There will be legal ramifications if you don't allow them their privacy," the Peruvian informed them without cracking a smile. "All foreign diplomats are guaranteed protection from prosecution. You will be held responsible as individuals in the eyes of the international court, without the protection of the local government or law enforcement agency."

The two rangers eyeballed each other with a look of defeat.

I stepped even closer and put my arms out in front of me with my wrists together. They both fell back on their heels.

"Put some God damn clothes on son," the commander bellowed. I walked away to do so, and he addressed the interpreter. "You tell them they've got five minutes to get back to the bus. Then we'll see who's who and what's what."

"Thank you," she said with a sigh.

The two of them exchanged a series of reassuring nods.

"Thank you, sir," I said, as I pulled up my pants hastily.

The rangers mounted their redneck steeds and buzzed away.

****

"They're giving us five minutes to get back to the bus!" Peruvian Ursula shouted over the water to Driver Chris.

The noise of their four-wheelers was drowned out by the sound of rushing water on the boat ramp behind me. Driver Chris stood up so quickly it sounded like Poseidon himself shooting up like a geyser. "Let's go!" commanded the sea god, waving his mighty arm in the air, guiding the skinny-dipping passengers ashore. His massive torso created a magnificent wake, mixing air and water in a frothing torrent. A tempest of rain fell from his arms and a waterfall dripped from the tip of his beard. "To the bus!" he commanded.

He spoke to us as he strode up the incline. "I heard some of what you were saying," he huffed low so that only we could hear. "You told them you're a diplomat?" he asked the Peruvian with a tone of incredulity. "I thought that was a secret." He bent down to pick up his clothes.

"I told them we were all diplomats," she said coyly.

His eyes jumped open.

"We're heading for a youth convention in San Francisco," she informed him succinctly. "I'm the interpreter and nobody speaks English." She made it sound like it was totally real. Like she was simply stating the facts.

"That's genius!" he commended her with open arms, but she refused his wet naked hug. The passengers stumbled ashore like sailors after a shipwreck. There was a roar of conversation in several languages, but Poseidon's voice reigned supreme. "Everyone needs to get back on the bus as quickly as possible and don't let the rangers hear you speaking English."

The Driver's Apprentice

Moments later the entire busload of Tortoise passengers rushed to get dressed on the boat ramp next to us. Evidently, PAC-MAN did not have a bathing suit. He had no towel and nothing to change into. He had been swimming in his pleated dress shorts and a white t-shirt rendered transparent by the water. Through his shirt one could see a light brown Ace Bandage wrapped around his upper ribs below his armpits, covering an area similar to a sports bra. I assumed he had recently suffered a bruised or cracked rib. He didn't tell; I didn't ask. The Pink Panther saw me looking and quickly wrapped Cato's shoulders with her towel.

The passengers had a thousand questions, but one voice jumped out. "Are we getting a ticket? shouted the petite German girl.

"Not if we can help it," answered Driver Chris.

"Are they going to arrest us," Little Josh asked in a tone of hope.

"No, Josh," his mother soothed him, holding a towel around him as he changed out of his swimsuit.

Fräulein Vera spoke heavily accented English while pumping her fist. "American jail is for pussies!" She beat her chest like King Kong. "Bring it on mother fuckers!"

"Shush!" Irish Joyce shushed her new German friend. "You'll get yourself arrested!"

"So, what!" she postured.

"If you get arrested, I may never see you again," scolded Irish Joyce. "Maybe I'd like to get to know you for more than just a day," she revealed.

The German girl blinked her eyes in thought.

Chicken Jim shouted, "They can arrest my dick!"

"You will like to be in handcuffs, ya?" snapped Fräulein Vera.

"Wouldn't you like to know," the rookie shot back at her.

"We've got it under control," pleaded Driver Chris. "Just get dressed and start heading for the bus."

Hilariously, Flip-flop hopped around off balance with one leg in her shorts and one toe caught in the other, revealing her lack of underwear and her unshaven-state-of-affairs. A million years seemed to pass overnight since she swore off skinny-dipping the previous day. Juliano offered her his hand and I heard her introduce herself. "My name's Jen," she told him. "But everyone's been calling me Flip-flop." She released his hand, stepped into her footwear, and added, "for obvious reasons."

He cast a puppy dog look at the Peruvian and said, "You see, I am a gentleman."

"One good deed does not make a night of a nave," she snapped.

Mountain Girl put her hand on Juliano's shoulder to help her balance and said, "Don't listen to her, eh. She doesn't know what she's talking about." Then she turned and asked him to help her with the clasp on her bra.

We got dressed and reconvened. Peruvian Ursula's Chinese friend was now hovering two feet off her right shoulder, shivering in her towel. The actual driver asked. "Is there anything else I should know?"

"They think I'm one of the drivers," I admitted.

"Ahh," he recalled. "I saw you offer up your wrists." He lifted his chin in commendation. "Nice work. That took balls." My shoulders dropped with relief. It felt so good to spill my guts. I had been worried about what he would think of me if I messed things up.

"Anything else?" he asked.

"I told them about Brian," I blurted. "That the other driver's sleeping on the bus."

"Oh shit!" he exclaimed. "That ties my hands. You two will have to see this thing through to the end."

I swallowed hard.

"We got this," Peruvian Ursula reassured me.

The four-wheelers were buzzing again.

"What's the plan?" the real driver asked.

The buzzing stopped and we all looked. They were watching us from the middle of the bridge. The first fully dressed passengers were just starting to walk away.

"They're watching us with binoculars," our redheaded driver announced.

Fräulein Vera shouted, "Jackasses!"

"Watch out for the pigs!" shouted Chicken Jim. "They have binoculars!"

A few of the still-half-naked passengers screamed before turning away to finish dressing. The partially naked passengers calmly turned their backs on the ogling rangers, who were still sitting there on their mopeds in full view of us on the bridge.

"Men are so fucked up!" Jewels lambasted. She shouted, "Fucking jackasses!"

"Ya! Point your asses at the jackasses!" shouted Fräulein Vera. This drew a splash of laughter from Berndt Toast which made all of us laugh even more coming from a fellow German. Her wordplay was hilarious considering the language barrier.

Now, everyone else with clothes on also pointed their asses at the rangers.

Not to be outdone, Chicken Jim shouted, "Point your asses at the jackasses with the spy glasses." There was a crescendo of laughter.

The Driver's Apprentice

Not to be outdone herself, Fräulein Vera bent over and started slapping her ass. She shouted, "You will spank your asses!"

All at once, more than half of the passengers started slapping their asses like a mob of shaking rumps.

"Don't make them angry!" cried Peruvian Ursula.

"You win," conceded Chicken Jim.

I caught a glimpse of Jewels and Yülia dressing side by side. I was stunned by the dramatic difference between their bodies. They were like salt and pepper. The dark-skinned New Yorker's voluptuous curves flowed from the center in stark comparison to the German girl's boyish external frame. The petite untrimmed triangle of platinum-blond was a mere goatee when compared to the full-bodied beard and mustache of the more primal beauty.

Both Jewels and Yülia's spirits were sensational in their own right, but together their energy was a force to be reckoned with. They had just met, but their relationship was already a source of inspiration for others. It was a good feeling just being around them. I could only imagine with wonder how their positive energy might infect us henceforth on our journey.

"Here comes Brian!" shouted Flip-flop.

Sure enough, she was right. Driver Brian was hauling ass, running in his Birkenstocks toward the bridge. He bounded up the ramp and ran right past the rangers without slowing down. The rangers yelled for him to stop, but he thrust a one-second-finger in the air and yelled, "I'll be right back!" We laughed until he ran up to us. He bent over breathing hard with his hands to his knees and said, "Dude! I am so sorry. I fucked up. I did not hear them coming. Otherwise, I would have warned you. Sorry dude! I fell asleep."

"No worries, man," Driver Chris consoled him.

"Are we in trouble? If we are, it's totally my fault," he breathed. "I'd still be asleep if that German guy didn't wake me up."

"It's all good," Driver Chris informed him nonchalantly. "Johnny Lovebus told them he's a Tortoise driver and Ursula explained how all of our passengers are foreign diplomats."

"What?" he quavered. "Are you serious?"

He lifted a finger in the air dramatically, "With diplomatic immunity."

When the blond driver looked at me, I shrugged.

"You told them that?" he drilled the Peruvian woman.

"They expected us to get dressed while they stood there watching," she testified.

Driver Brian's big blond head rose as he shot a look over at the bridge and interjected, "They do seem a bit perverted with the binoculars."

"They started asking for ID," the Peruvian explained in a lower voice. "I had to do something before they started taking names and clicking radios."

The two drivers exchanged knowing looks as she continued to explain in stride. "We can't let a little shitstorm ruin our entire plan, now, can we?" I was looking to them for a reaction, so I followed their gaze. When I saw what they were looking at my eyes jumped open with a rush of insight.

"Really!" jeered Peruvian Ursula. "Come on guys!" She spoke with a sense of familiarity I did not recognize at first. They were co-conspirators.

My eyes locked with hers. At a glance I knew she knew I knew. She had seen my wide-eyed reaction when the drivers looked over her shoulder. The had both looked with concern squarely into the face of Pak Chan, also known as PAC-MAN, the Chinese man Chicken Jim had just finished telling me was not who he seemed to be. It was his ID she did not want checked, and now she knew I knew. Our eyes held focus on one another like steel girders, until I felt a tingle of danger and looked away.

Thankfully, Chicken Jim staggered into our circle with one leg in his shorts and said, "If that cop wants ID I'm fucked. I haven't seen my wallet since we left Boston."

Peruvian Ursula leaned in like a basketball coach to reveal her strategy to the team. Her long jet-black hair swooped over her shoulder when she leaned in to say, "We need to get everyone who speaks a foreign language to sit up front. People who only speak English need to sit in the back. I'll act as interpreter, so all questions and answers pass through me."

I eyeballed the mysterious Chinese man while she coached us. He looked harmless enough. He had a pleasant looking face with an endearing smile. He was a normal looking Asian man as far as I could tell. He did appear slightly effeminate, based solely on his lack of height and slender frame. However, it did appear strange how he doted on his Peruvian traveling companion. He followed her around taking tiny little steps. He hung on her every word like Inspector Clouseau's Chinese manservant, Cato. I still could not tell if that made the Peruvian woman Inspector Clouseau or his nemesis, the jewel thief known as the Pink Panther.

She put her flattened hand out in the center of our circle. The two bearded Green Tortoise drivers put their hands in. I put my hand on the stack. Chicken Jim seemed to wake up at the last second and put his hand in. Then, Pak Chan stepped forward and put his little hand on top. All of us looked over at him at the same time. I could feel the Pink Panther's eyes on me like fur on a cat.

The Driver's Apprentice

"Let's go!" she shouted. Our eyes turned center as she lifted the pile of flattened hands up into the air with a cheer. "Booyah!"

"I'll take care of Pak," said the red bearded driver.

Her mouth suddenly spewed a series of sharp syllables in Cantonese. Cato's master nodded confirmation and Driver Chris joined the conversation. As soon as they hammered out an agreement, the red bearded driver started walking backwards away from us, thumbing over his shoulder. "Let's go Pak," he said.

"Good luck guys," said the Chinese man as he crossed the circle and went on ahead.

Driver Chris kept walking backwards as he spoke to us with a humorous inflection in his voice. "I'm just gonna act like a passenger and blend in... all casual like." Then he winked at me, and I swear on my mother's eyes, when he turned to walk away, he leapt in the air and clicked his heels like a leprechaun that had just found his pot of gold. He clearly loved this life.

Driver Brian spun on his heel to address Berndt Toast who had been getting dressed behind him at arm's length. "Foreign language speakers sit up front," he began. "English is off the menu." Then he moved on to tell someone else. I turned and told Maid Marian, "No more speaking English if you can help it and try not to talk to them unless they ask you questions."

Chicken Jim was slow to understand. The Peruvian woman scowled at him and he asked, "So, we're supposed to hide the Americans and ignore the cops?"

"No, Jimbo," she shook her head in pity and spoke to him like a child. "You just need to lay low and shut up." He stuttered trying to protest, but she made a shush finger and pretended to zip her mouth and throw away the key.

With that he turned and smugly asked Jewels, "How do you say, 'I don't speak English?' in Spanish?"

Driver Chris rushed ahead in time to keep the passengers from crossing paths with the rangers. Six or seven passengers including the petite Chinaman were waiting for the rest of us on the ramp. The rangers encouraged them to cross the bridge with a wave, but Driver Chris held them off, giving the rangers the one-second-finger. The officers started their engines and rolled forward, but the red-bearded guide turned his back on them to gather the growing crowd, successfully blocking the end of the bridge. This led to hilarity when the rangers were forced to back up their ATVs.

With beepers beeping and flashers flashing the senior officer cussed out his fledgling, "Get off my ass, Floyd!" he admonished.

Fräulein Vera pumped her fist and shouted, "Fick die Polizei!"

This gave us ample time to spread the word and gather the stragglers by the bridge.

While Driver Chris coached the Americans to use the side door. The Peruvian woman conspired with the others. "Don't talk unless they ask. I'll answer for you in English."

Chicken Jim was instructed to lead the English only speakers. He kept repeating the instructions, "Follow me and don't speak English." Guitar Johnny lambasted him for talking too loudly. "You'd know to keep your arsehole shut if you'd ever got the black glove treatment from the coppers in the back of a paddy wagon."

"No one's getting a beating," huffed the exhausted Peruvian.

Guitar Johnny still wanted no part of following the trainee. He disparaged him as he darted through the crowd to get away. "Fuck off and keep your distance from me, you loon. I'm not following you."

I told Flip-flop and the British girls, "Just lay low in the back; you'll be fine."

The enormous blond driver shepherded the group across the bridge like a herd of zombies. He looked me over and said, "I assume you don't have a class C license."

"I don't," I told him shaking my head anxiously.

"I'll try to keep you out of jail," he told me with a nod that ensured my understanding. "Go right in and take a seat," he urged. "Leave the talking to me. It would be great if we can get away without a ticket, but if someone has to pull their license, it might as well be me. I've got a clean record, and I'm the one who fell asleep, after all."

Chicken Jim and Mountain Girl were the first to veer off toward the opposite side of the bus. There was no reaction from the park rangers, so the rest of the English only speakers broke off from the herd and followed them. The rest of us kept shuffling. Driver Chris and PAC-MAN were the first two 'passengers' inside the bus. The Chinaman was eager to find a change of clothes, and the red-maned driver leapt like an orangutan over the cooler and cushions to open the side door.

"Keep them moving," directed Driver Brian.

"I'm on it," I said anxiously, rushing toward the bus. He split off from the pack and went to address the park rangers who had parked a few yards off. I followed the rest of the foreign speakers until we were all lined up at the door.

When I got to the bus door, I could see that Peruvian Ursula had taken charge of the situation. Passengers were sitting on the front platform obediently awaiting her commands. She snapped her fingers. "There's a chance the rangers know Spanish. You need to sit further back," she told Jewels before announcing to the group. "If you can

The Driver's Apprentice

speak a language other than Spanish, please sit close to the front." She ushered them back with a guiding hand.

PAC-MAN went to the driver's cabin to change his clothes, although the Europeans would not have cared if he dropped his shorts right there in the aisle. Nudity was nothing new to them.

"Come here," the Peruvian prodded Yülia, waving her forward. I watched the yellow-haired, sparkling, young, German girl work her way against the tide in the aisle. "Don't be shy," she told her. "You look innocent. Sit right up here." She directed her to the first seat near the door.

"Get back there," she admonished Chicken Jim as she shooed him away.

"I want to see how this goes down," he pleaded. "I'm supposed to be training, you know."

I spoke to him through the open window and asked, "Didn't you lose your wallet?"

He was like, "Oh yeah!" He went to sit on the back platform.

Jewels plopped down next to Yülia on the front platform and said, "Yo hablo español."

"You need to go back," the Peruvian prodded Mother Michelle, but the Hippie mama did not move. "I know enough French to play along." She pushed her son away. "Go!" She told him, "Hide under the dinette." Little Josh leapt under the dinette like a lizard into a crag of rock.

The daughter of the Peruvian ambassador coached others on diplomacy. "Remember, you are guests from other nations here on a mission of peace. If they come inside feel free to talk amongst yourselves, just don't speak English and don't talk to them unless they talk to you."

Peruvian Ursula advised Jewels independently of the others. "There's a good chance they know Spanish, so be careful what you say." I walked back along the side of the bus. There was no big hold up. It was just a slow process. I could see Guitar Johnny through the windows on the far side of the bus smoking a cigarette.

Big Dave was the last person in line, so I followed him up the steps and down the aisle. "You should probably sit facing backwards," I advised him at the dinette.

"Good thinking," he intoned in a deep voice. I helped clear a path for him to sit. After the big Hippie sat down, I took a seat on the cooler in the center aisle.

Despite the palpable tension, the Peruvian translator sat calmly on the buddy seat while we all watched Driver Brian talking with the rangers. It was a full house on the front platform. The South Africans were sitting behind the driver next to the South American with the Indiana Jones hat. Then came Mother Michelle, Jewels, and Driver Chris. I had to stand up to let PAC-MAN pass through the aisle. He was carrying his wet clothes with his Ace Bandage slung over one shoulder so it could dry. He was wearing loose fitting sweatpants with a matching sweatshirt that had glittery letters reading, 'SWEATS bi ebe.' It was the type of matching sweat suit popular in Europe, but you wouldn't catch an American wearing a flashy sweat suit like that, at least not people from my neck-of-the-woods. That kind of outfit was far too effeminate for most Americans. He took a seat across the aisle from Fräulein Vera and the Irish Twins.

The rangers did most of the talking, sitting on their ATVs the whole time. When they finally got off their vehicles, each one shamelessly removed a pair of binoculars from around their necks. "I can't believe they were spying on you guys," Berndt Toast complained.

"Kein Englisch bitte!" The Peruvian translator snapped at him in German. "No English!"

****

The mood changed dramatically when the officers started heading toward the bus. Suddenly, the whole bus was a flurry with foreign tongues. For a moment it seemed like I was sitting in a room full of aliens, like the bar scene in the Mos Eisley Cantina. Driver Chris was chucking knives at PAC-MAN in Cantonese, and the Asian man was striking back fast with even sharper blades. The engaged South African couple were chatting up a storm in Afrikaans, the Germans started spaken ze Deutsch. Juliano asked Peruvian Ursula a question in Portuguese and she responded in kind along with Jewels asking questions en Espanol. Then, the Irish Twins' tongues started twirling and my ears were filled with the delightful boroughs of Gaelic.

As Driver Brian came up the steps, he waved for the Peruvian to make room. She let him squeeze past her and he sat sideways in the driver's seat. He watched her conversing with the Brazilian and grimaced knowingly.

Right on que, as the two men reached the top step, the cacophony of foreign tongues reached a crescendo. The two rangers stood side by side in front of the dashboard. The portlier ranger seemed frustrated. "May we have your attention please," he shouted.

As silence fell, Peruvian Ursula's last three audible words were painfully easy to understand. "Pervertidos con binoculares." She looked up at them with a wry smile. Driver Brian's face looked like he just ate a handful of hot peppers.

The ranger asked the reclined driver, "Do any of them speak English?"

The Driver's Apprentice

"Sure," Driver Brian answered merrily. His eyes widened when the Peruvian made a strained face at him. "A little," he added with a desperate shrug.

The fat ranger's shoulders dropped. He turned and addressed the passengers, speaking slowly. "Do you speak English?"

"Eu nao falo ingles," said Juliano.

"Ich spreche kein Englisch," said Berndt Toast.

"Wǒ bù huì shuō yīngyǔ," said PAC-MAN.

"Je ne parle pas anglais," said French Sandrine, followed by Mother Michelle, "No parle anglais."

Everyone was smiling and stifling laughter. It was comical.

Peruvian Ursula spoke up. "I can translate."

"Thank goodness," said the ranger. He tipped his hat to the Peruvian and put his hand out for her to shake. She intentionally looked away and left him hanging. He stood up straight and the hammer came down. "We need you to explain to them how they violated the laws of the United States against public nudity and indecent exposure."

The translator started in Spanish. She said, "Estás violando nuestras leyes contra la desnudez pública y la exposición indecente." She said, "Nimm dich nicht nackt," in German and "Niet naakt worden," in Dutch. Her Germanic words caused some stifled laughter. In what I guessed to be Afrikaans, she said, "Hou jou onderbroek aan." She barked two words in Cantonese at PAC-MAN and Driver Chris.

PAC-MAN asked, "Nà shì shí me yì sī?"

"Wǒ bú zhī dào," said Driver Chris in response.

"I'll explain to them later," she told the rangers.

The taller ranger addressed the translator. "You tell them this is America. These are our laws and they must abide by them."

Now she spoke to Juliano in Portuguese. "Eles acham que a nudez é um incidente internacional." She followed in German, "Und das mir keiner aus der Reihe tanzt!" then Dutch, "De aap is uit de mouw gekomen. Amerika regeert de wereld." She was obviously abbreviating the ranger's message, but the mono-linguistic American park rangers seemed none the wiser.

"En français s'il vous plaît," Mother Michelle demanded.

"En Amérique, vous devez suivre les règles américaines," the Peruvian obliged. Finally, she rolled her eyes at Juliano and said, "Eles são ainda mais pervertidos."

"Coruja," he answered seeming hurt. "Não estou pervertida," he objected. This triggered a heated exchange between the two that went too fast for anyone but a native speaker of Portuguese to understand a single word. He obviously had the hots for her, and she wanted no part of it. The rangers looked at Juliano sympathetically and said, "She's just playing hard to get."

The chief ranger shook his head at them. He gestured to his colleague with a tilt of his head like it was time to leave. We almost got off scot-free, but at the last second Little Josh popped his head out from under the dinette. He just could not resist peeking. The ranger of less stature saw the boy and alerted his boss, "There's a minor on the bus, sir."

"What the heck?" the man in charge blurted. "Send that child up here."

All breath ceased.

"Venez ici! Venez ici!" Mother Michelle coaxed him out.

"Josh! Come out of there, please," requested Driver Brian.

The boy stood up in the aisle, his mother waved for him to come and he rushed to her side. She hugged him, then turned him gently in her arms to face the rangers.

The poor kid's lips were bright red, chapped and puffy. The fat one said, "Awe. What's your name little girl?"

"I'm a boy," Little Josh objected with a shrill voice.

The two men looked rebuked. "You could've fooled me," whispered the thinner man.

The fat ranger studied the boys red lips like he was Sherlock Holmes, shaking his head in confusion. "Are you the mother?" he asked.

She answered with a perfect French accent, "Oui. C'est mon fils."

"You should be ashamed of yourself, exposing your child to this depravity?" judged the ranger incredulously.

The translator snorted a laugh in her throat before she translated, "Vous n'êtes pas inquiet d'exposer votre enfant à cette dépravation?"

To everyone's delight, Mother Michelle answered, "Non! Je pète dans votre direction générale."

"Ha!" French Sandrine spit out a laugh and started speaking French to her very quickly.

Mother Michelle gave her a perturbed look and responded, "Non."

The translator explained to the ranger. "The French have a much more casual attitude about nudity. I assure you. She takes exceptionally diligent care of her son."

Satisfied, the ranger shooed the boy away and said, "You can go back to where you crawled out of."

Mother Michelle said, "Merci."

Then Little Josh said, "Merci."

The Driver's Apprentice

This made her snort laughter. As she tried to control her smiling face, she took her son by the arm and led him toward the dinette. She smiled broadly and made funny faces at the rest of us as soon as her back was turned.

The junior ranger rolled his eyes and said, "That would have been a lot of paperwork."

"No kidding," said his commander. He gave Driver Brian a stern look and said, "I trust you and your clients will abide by state park regulations. If you ever come back this way; we will be watching."

"You bet your ass," said the other one. There was a laugh from everyone on the front platform. The rangers eyed them suspiciously.

"You don't need to worry about us," our driver said convincingly. "This was our first and last time skinny-dipping here, that's for sure."

"Okay then," the chief ranger looked at his deputy still writing on his notepad. "Put that damn thing away, Floyd! We won't be filing any paperwork on this one. This fella agrees to see things our way." He turned and spoke just to Driver Chris and me, "Consider this your once and only warning. If you ever come back here and do this kind of thing again you won't be getting a second chance. I don't care what country you come from. You can't be running around here naked as a jaybird."

"Yes sir, thank you sir," said Driver Brian.

I rose to my feet and said, "Thank you officers." I gave them a respectful nod.

The ranger turned and addressed the entire group. "I hope you all enjoy the rest of your stay in America. This is the greatest country in the world. I hope you enjoy it." Both rangers waved and walked down the steps.

As soon as the rangers started their ATVs there was a big round of applause.

Mountain Girl came forward and sat next to Juliano. He still seemed hurt by Peruvian Ursula's harsh tones and unreciprocated flirtations, but she did not seem to care. When he said something to her in Portuguese, she shot back with a rapid succession of harsh words. Mountain Girl hugged him protectively and said, "Leave him alone. He's mine." She clearly liked him, and she was not going to let the Peruvian get in her way.

Once the whine of the four-wheelers was out of earshot, Driver Chris came forward and exchanged double high-fives with Peruvian Ursula, PAC-MAN and Driver Brian. Then, he shouted, "What do you say, three cheers for Ursula and Johnny Lovebus!" He started them off, "Hip, hip, hooray," and the whole busload of Green

Tortoise passengers finished the cheer together. People thanked me from all directions.

On his way to the driver's cabin Driver Brian gave me a high-five and said, "I need to fucking sleep."

Everyone raised their hands for high-fives as I walked forward down the aisle. When PAC-MAN raised his hand for me to slap, I saw down his shirt. He was fit for the most part, but I couldn't help but notice, he was sporting a set of man-boobs, the kind of little pointy tits one might expect to find on a fat guy. This distracted me for a second, causing me to miss his hand.

Peruvian Ursula caught me looking down her friend's shirt, and she shot me a hateful look. "Mind your manners!" she snapped.

Berndt Toast shook my hand and whistled. "You're one crazy mother licker," he said. "I thought for sure they were going to arrest you."

"They almost did," I laughed.

"It was hilarious how they made you cover your penis," he spat with a laugh.

"What penis," scoffed Peruvian Ursula.

"Hey," I objected. "Speaking of minding your manners..."

I sat next to Driver Chris on the buddy seat. "You've got good driver instincts," he praised me. "We'll make a driver out of you yet, Lovebus."

"I'd love that," I told him.

"Right on!" he agreed. "Consider yourself a Driver's Apprentice." Chicken Jim stood in the door well giving me the evil eye.

I was overjoyed with tears of joy welling up in my eyes. I had somehow become a Green Tortoise Driver's Apprentice, albeit unofficially and without pay. The bus was so much cooler than I could have ever imagined. I would have done anything to become a Green Tortoise driver. My fate and that of Driver Chris' brother were indubitably linked, making the seconds tick by like Ringer's Lactate dripping from an IV bag.

7
Indiana Dunes

While the rest of us used the bathrooms one last time, Driver Brian went to sleep in the driver's cabin and Driver Chris changed into a pair of red lifeguard shorts and a stained grey t-shirt with the words, 'I am Made of Meat' half hidden behind his copious facial hair. The beautiful brown-skinned teacher from New York was sitting on the buddy seat with her back leaning against his shoulder, so I sat on the first seat across the aisle next to Mother Michelle. She was telling the Irish Twins all about her previous cross-country trip.

Apparently, PAC-MAN had only brought one change of clothes with him, so Driver Chris reluctantly allowed him to hang his wet garments on the dashboard handrail. While it seemed odd to bring no clothes on a ten-day adventure trip, I found his tiger-print underwear even more disturbing. I was not the only one who noticed either. Chicken Jim called him out on it as soon as he hung them up to dry. "Are those yours," he questioned with a laugh.

The Chinese man grew defensive. "Why yes," he stammered. "What's your problem?"

"I've just never seen underwear split down the sides like that before," marveled the Pennsylvanian. "They look like something my grandmother would wear."

"They are very comfortable," he defended.

Is that polyester?" asked the rookie.

"It's silk," he explained.

I felt bad for the guy, but I had to admit, his underwear was snazzy. I had never seen anything like them before. Although, this was my first experience seeing an Asian man's underwear.

"Leave him alone, Jimbo!" Driver Chris admonished. Then he shouted, "Buddy check!"

"Buddy check!" I shouted. Several others repeated the call. I spotted my buddies, Guitar Johnny, Big Dave, Mother Michelle, Little Josh, British Sue, and English Tessa. They were all present. I counted twenty-one passengers not including Chicken Jim. The buddy check calls trailed-off and the bus grew quiet. "Everyone's here," I told the red-bearded driver.

"Great," he responded. He attached a pen to his logbook, tossed it onto the dashboard and started the engine.

Jewels asked him, "Where are we headed?"

As he turned the bus around in the parking lot he spoke in a distracted manner. "Our first stop is Toledo, unless there's a good place to stop along the highway. I'd rather not go into the city unless we have to. I need to call for an update on my brother. There's a Greyhound Station there in case I need to go home."

"Goddess forbid," said Jewels.

"Yeah," he breathed. "I'd hate to have to put you guys on a Greyhound. Once you've experienced the Tortoise, you can't go back. Greyhound can be a twisted nightmare of back spasms. Hopefully, the news is good at home."

"You must be beside yourself with worry." Jewels spoke soulfully. "I'm here for you if you need anything; I'm your girl." She was so empathetic and wonderful. Her mere presence made you feel better even if nothing was wrong. "Did you find out how the accident happened?" she asked.

"It may not have been an accident at all." He took on a serious expression. "Our best guess is that he was mugged," he spoke with emotion in his voice.

Jewels' face went blank and her whole body froze.

"Oh my God," that's terrible cried Yülia. "Did they catch the guy?"

"No. It's not like that. It's just a theory," he informed us. "The police were never called." He stroked his beard as if he was anxious and kept hold of the wheel with one hand. "The important thing is he survived."

"How is he doing?" Jewels wanted to know.

Driver Chris reluctantly continued. "Well, he's not out of the woods yet. He fractured his skull twenty-nine times, so he's got a long recovery in front of him, even if he does survive."

The teacher's body remained rigid like she was experiencing pain. "What does your heart tell you?" she asked him.

Indiana Dunes

The driver paused in contemplation as he turned out of the parking area onto the narrow park road. "I think he's gonna pull through," he resolved.

"Right on," Jewels crooned.

"I have a feeling it's gonna be a wonderful day," he surmised.

"I do too," Jewels agreed.

"We'll be driving most of it, but I love to drive, and we'll be stopping at a place called Indiana Dunes for dinner later on. The dunes are awesome. There's miles and miles of sand dunes that overlook Lake Michigan." I marveled at his ever-present enthusiasm for the outdoors.

"Ooh! That sounds nice," enthused the New Yorker. "I've never seen Lake Michigan," Jewels shared her positivity.

"It's huge," observed the red-bearded driver.

"That's what she said," shouted Chicken Jim from somewhere in the back.

"How big is it?" asked the schoolteacher.

He informed her, "It's like three-hundred miles long and a hundred miles wide. It's got something like sixteen-hundred miles of coastline."

"Wow!" She remarked, "It's like an ocean. There must be a ton of fish."

"There are," he told her, "but you can't eat them."

"Is it polluted?"

"Totally."

"Still?" She questioned.

"It's the PCBs," he explained. "They take forever to degrade. Half-a-billion pounds of that shit made it into the environment before they stopped it."

"At least they stopped it," she commented.

"I learned about that in college," I interjected, "There were several rivers flowing into the Great Lakes that were so polluted they actually caught fire."

"No way!" Jewels gasped.

"The Canadians were not happy," he said. "That's what drove our government to pass the Clean Water Act in the early seventies.

"It's really sad," said Driver Chris. "I love fish."

"Do you ever cook fish on the Tortoise?"

"We can't," he explained. "We're not allowed to cook any kind of meat. It would corrupt our cast-iron pans and make the vegans and vegetarians sick."

"What's on the menu for dinner tonight?" she asked.

"It's Brian's turn to cook." He hesitated. "I think he's planning something Mexican, maybe quesadillas."

"Oh, I love quesadillas," Jewels crooned.

"Yeah, me too," the driver concurred. "Brian is a great cook, so whatever he has planned will be awesome. The Dunes are so beautiful. They are utterly amazing. I've been there so many times, but I always love going back. It's like a maze of trails through a thousand dunes. If you get lost, you can always climb to the top of a big dune and see the lake. At the water's edge there is a cliff overhanging a beach with sand like the ocean. We have to pick up one more passenger in Chicago at nine o'clock, so there will be time for you guys to go out on the town and listen to the Chicago Blues."

"That all sounds so wonderful," she marveled. "I'm sure the news will be good with an attitude like that."

"You create your own reality," he quipped.

"It sounds like your head is in a good place," she observed with empathy. "Sometimes, you need to have compassion for yourself," she advised. "You can vent to me. I'm here for you," she offered.

"I go back and forth between serenity and turmoil," he admitted. "Sometimes my heart races and my thoughts run out of control, what with all the possibilities on the horizon. If my brother does not make it, I will have to stay home to help my parents. I might have to live in Connecticut and get a job. I must accept it. This might be my last trip."

"Oh no!" she fretted. "I'd be upset about that too," she empathized. "You clearly love your job."

He laughed. "Who wouldn't?" He sat up straight in his seat, letting the wheel fly through his hands as we came out of a turn. He heaved a sigh. "I feel like I finally found my thing, my role in life. Sharing amazing places with people you love is not a bad gig," he said with cheer. "I'm definitely in my element behind the wheel," he concluded. He shifted into second gear with precision. We were headed out of the state park, moving slowly on the narrow roads. The bus dipped from side to side on the uneven blacktop. "My parents run a bed and breakfast near Hartford," he revealed.

"That's cool," she praised.

"It's a lot of hard work," he said. "They could never do it without my brother helping, and they depend on the income. That's the only way they've managed to retire. I would at least have to stay home until we figure out a solution, so my mother won't have to get a job and go back to work. That would break them. Maybe they could hire someone to make the beds and do the laundry, but that might not be possible. They don't pay my brother a dime. He helps them run the place in exchange for room and board. He works nights as a bartender."

"I'm visualizing you driving forever," she said dreamily.

"I don't want to drive forever," he revealed. "Maybe two or three more years. That's all. I've had a good run as a Tortoise driver. I've seen what I came to see."

"Right on," Jewels grooved.

"I've had some real good times," he said, "but it's the people that have changed my life more than anything. I want to have kids someday, so I can share what I've learned and take my family places I never got to go."

"No doubt," she said. "I think you'd make a great dad."

"I'd certainly make it a point to do a better job than my father," he opined. "He never took us anywhere. All I knew growing up was within one day's driving distance of Hartford."

"I've learned so much sitting in this seat," he restated. "I feel like I know America now."

"That's wonderful." She hummed, "Mmm."

"I've had so many great teachers," he said, looking over at her on the buddy seat. Since I started driving, I've learned more than most people do in a lifetime. I've lived an awesome life in such a short time," he said with wonder, "and I'm only twenty-six."

"You parents will be lucky to have you back if it comes to that," she concluded. "Your enthusiasm will keep them young. Maybe you can travel with them?"

"I don't know about that," he huffed. "My father and I don't get along. He thinks I'm a bum."

"Is it true? Are you a bum?" she asked.

"I feel like one sometimes," he admitted, "when I compare myself to friends I grew up with," he replied. "When I see their houses and hold their babies, I feel like I missed the boat, but it doesn't matter if I'm a bum right now. This is only temporary."

Jewels hugged his arm warmly and said, "First of all you're not a bum, even if you drive the Tortoise for the rest of time. You are doing what few people get to do in life; you get to work doing a job you love." She let his arm go so he could be free to make a turn. "I love my job too," she gushed. "I absolutely love what I do, and I love who I am."

"I'll never be good enough to please him," he glowered.

"He's shaming you," she said matter-of-factly. "You need to let go of that shame."

"I wish it were that simple," he said.

"It is!" she perked. "One of my students taught me a technique. It's worked wonders for me."

"What's that?" he asked.

"You just need to understand the difference between guilt and shame," she informed us.

"What's that?" he inquired.

"Guilt goes, but shame stays," she quipped.

"Okay," he responded.

She explained. "Guilt is a feeling you get when you've done something that you know is bad. It's a personal assessment of your own behavior. You feel remorse for a while, then you get over it. Maybe you vow to never do it again, but the guilty feeling fades away." Jewels checked herself. "Unless you did something really bad, but even then, you get over it."

"In jail," joked the driver.

"Is there something you're not telling me?" she questioned with a laugh before continuing. "Shame is an internalized belief that you yourself are somehow bad or defective," she explained. "Shame comes from other people's assessment of you. Shame is way more insidious because it keeps weighing on you like it is true, even though it's not. Shame is a lot like jail, except you keep yourself there. Shame is a constant cycle of judgement, regret, and failure. It can be hard to get out."

"Interesting," Driver Chris appraised.

"You just need to remember: You put the 'I' in guilt, but others put the 'me' in shame."

"So, what's the solution?" he asked.

"When you have negative thoughts about yourself, just ask, 'Says who?'" Her face lit up with joy. "That's what my student taught me." She was bursting with pride and excitement. "If it's not your own opinion, let it go."

He tilted his head in contemplation.

She paused before concluding, "Once you figure that out, it's easy to give up feeling sorry for yourself and get on with your life."

"I can dig it," he said nodding. "I'll give it a try."

She glowed with warmth. "I'll channel some good vibes your way," she said sympathetically.

"Your student sounds brilliant," he marveled. "Do you teach at a college?"

"No!" she laughed. "I teach at Washington Heights Elementary."

"My gosh!" he gasped. "How old is this kid?"

"Eight," she said nonchalantly. "She's an old soul."

"I guess so," he mumbled.

"Don't let your father get you down," she advised. "You know you still deserve his love even if you are a bum," she said with an obvious wink.

"I guess so," he acquiesced. "I can't help feeling bad for my father though. All he's ever done is work his whole life. He never went on vacation. He never saw America. I hardly talk to him. My sister doesn't talk to him at all. My brother does, but he almost died last night. Without him, my dad will have no one left except my mom, and he can't stand listening to her talk all the time. He tells that to her face."

"I wouldn't exactly describe my parent's lives as awesome either," Jewels related. "They never went on vacation without us, and it's still hard to convince them to do anything good for themselves. It must be hard to put yourself first when other people depend on you. They struggled their whole lives to support us."

"I hear that," said the driver. "My father struggled his whole life too. He grew up dirt poor living in the projects in Hartford, and his father was an abusive alcoholic. Somehow, he managed to start his own company, so we always had a nice house and everything. I'd say he was a success."

"Sadly," Jewels lamented, "your father's achievements won't matter on his deathbed. When his time comes to leave this world, he won't be thinking about his company. He'll be thinking about the relationships in his life."

"Or the ones he failed to repair," added Driver Chris.

"Is your father abusive?"

"He's pretty strict," Driver Chris admitted.

"So, he's authoritarian?"

"Sounds about right," he confirmed. "You might say disciplinarian." He downshifted and let the engine slow the bus down as we approached a stop sign. "He hit us with a belt when we did bad shit," he revealed, "but we deserved it most of the time."

"No child ever deserves to be hit with a belt," Jewels empathized. She put her forefingers and thumbs together in a lotus pose and said, "I'm sending your inner child love through the divine Goddess."

"Which goddess is that?" he inquired.

"Atabey," she answered definitively. "She is the supreme goddess of the Taínos."

"Tell her I said, 'Hello.'" he said with a chuckle.

She closed her eyes for another second and smiled. "She says, 'Hello' back."

"He stopped hitting us when we got older of course," he informed her. "My mother made him. She was always the peacekeeper."

"Mothers rock," Jewels proclaimed.

"She has always loved me no matter what," the driver praised. He stomped the clutch, put it into first, and we started forward as smooth as silk. His left knee rose, and his right toes eased into the fuel.

"I have a wonderful mother too," Jewels related. "She's the best." She paused in contemplation while he shifted and got up to speed in second gear. "Mothers seem more connected to their children. It must be wonderful having a baby living inside your body. It fosters such compassion, but it's not just biology; it's instinct. Fathers miss out on that connection."

"My father really messed up," Driver Chris opined. "He alienated his children." He grew impassioned as he spoke. "My sister didn't talk to him for seven years, because he didn't approve of her marrying a firefighter."

"What's up with that?" Jewels asked.

He shook his head in disbelief despite the years. "He told her husband, 'A firefighter would never be able to support her in the way she is accustomed to living.'"

"That's terrible," Jewels consoled him warmly. "Firefighters rule!"

"The ironic thing is that my brother became a fireman." His limbs flailed as he executed another shift and the bus floated into third gear.

"The one who's in the hospital?" she questioned.

He nodded and said, "Yeah. It's not like we were rich either. We were never spoiled. My father was a tightwad." He lifted his chin with a chuckle. "I once asked him for money on prom night because I was flat broke. I had blown all my money on the tuxedo and flowers, right? So, he asks me, 'How much do you need?' I tell him, 'Fifty bucks.' He says, 'Forty seems like a lot. Here's twenty,' and then he hands me a ten and says, 'Don't blow it all on beer.'"

"Oh no," Jewels cried.

"As I got older it just got worse," Driver Chris expounded. "I haven't had a good relationship with him since college. He found out I was drinking and had me withdrawn from all of my classes. Even though I stopped drinking, I had to go to rehab before he would pay for me to go back to school."

"That seems harsh," she stammered, "really harsh."

"Rehab was good for me actually," he told her. "I got a year's worth of therapy in thirty days. I learned how to identify abuse, to understand that it was not my fault."

"Right on," she said. "It sounds like you still have a lot of resentment."

"I still have some healing to do," he admitted.

"My dad passed recently," the young Dominican woman revealed.

"I'm sorry to hear that," he consoled her.

"Everyone you love is going to die and you never know when," she forewarned. "It made me sad at first, but it helped me realize how important it is to make amends with the past and to re-establish meaningful relationships with the important people in your life. When you die, the only thing that matters is love."

"I've never considered making amends with my dad," he admitted. "He's way too stubborn."

"It takes great resolve," she said with a wry smile. "You have to take care of yourself first before you can take care of others. The responsibility falls on you, right?"

"Right," he agreed.

"Well, if you think it will make you whole, healthy, and happy, you can reclaim your relationship with him. You just need to love him unconditionally like a parent loves a child. Wouldn't you want your own son to do the same for you?"

"I probably would," he admitted. "I never thought of it that way."

"Let me tell you," she expounded. "I have plenty of students that act out and cause problems in my classroom, but I can't just turn my back on them. I must forgive them unconditionally. Sometimes I have to cultivate compassion before I can forgive them, but forgiveness is its own reward. It opens our hearts to love."

"How do you cultivate compassion?" he asked.

"Cultivating compassion is a process," she explained. "It starts with acknowledgement, understanding and acceptance. From there it's a natural progression to forgive."

"That sounds easier said than done," he observed.

"Not necessarily," she contended. "At least, that hasn't been my experience. Compassion is a force of nature, like water seeking its own level. It's there whether we acknowledge it or not."

"That's awesome," he marveled.

"I believe there's compassion in every interaction on earth," she opined. "Whether it's between the people we choose to care about or the processes of Mother Nature." She radiated such positive energy I found myself believing her every word. "When the pebble binds the soil, it allows plants to grow. When you stand in a river you accept, without thought, the natural death and decay suspended in the water from upstream. Each time we inhale life we exhale death. Compassion is in the wind. Stop and listen and you will discover compassion in everything. Even if not noticed at first, compassion is always there."

I sat back to think about it and got lost in thought.

****

We turned onto Route 2, following signs west toward Toledo. A warm breeze blew through the windows and I could tell it was going to be another hot and humid day.

Irish Kyrah came forward and sat with her sister in her lap next to Fräulein Vera on the front platform. She set aside a bottle of conditioner and a comb and began taking out her twin sister's braids. She lovingly applied conditioner to the hair as she painstakingly unwrapped and detangled the braids. She combed through the blond hair gingerly with her fingers before cautiously employing a hairbrush. The lower length of her sister's hair looked a bit dead from peroxide, like it might clump into dreadlocks if left uncombed.

With each stroke of the brush, she held the hair protectively with her opposite hand, starting at the tips and working her way up to the roots. She combed the hair with a mother's love for the longest time, making long sensual full-length strokes. It was pleasurable just to watch. One knew from this display that her empathy was universal, like that of a nurse. Her caring extended outward past her sister to all comers. She would make a wonderful midwife.

In dramatic contrast, Irish Joyce remained emotionally detached from the entire process, despite her sister's loving attention to detail. Her rigid utilitarian demeanor bore a strong resemblance to that of a doctor, maintaining emotional distance without a trace of sentimentality. It was obvious that she held herself in high regard, but she was not likely to say so. She was the kind of woman I had learned to respect as a young man, having grown up in a family of liberated feminist women. One could imagine her strength of character inspiring the same in others, and that she would also make a competent midwife.

As soon as the combing ceased the braiding began anew. The dirty redhead began by weaving smaller locks of hair, so they formed lines over the dirty-blond's ears and across the back of her head. The long-haired Canadian girl with the bright red lipstick sat next to them so she could pay closer attention to the process. The Aussie girl with the golden-blond ponytail joined them next, followed by Peruvian Ursula with her thick jet-black tresses. The lot of them chit-chatted merrily while they watched Irish Kyrah's fingers work their magic.

"We're going to have-a-go at opening a maternity shelter in San Francisco," the motherly hairdresser informed them. "We intend to start our own practice."

"That sounds wonderful," Fräulein Vera praised. "What inspired that decision?"

Yülia was listening now too, so Irish Kyrah began to explain to all of us. "We both just graduated from the National Midwifery Institute." She told us in her sweet rolling brogue. "The NMI is the most respected midwife school in the world. We both received splendid marks."

"There you go wagging your tongue again Kyrah," her twin sister harassed her in a raspy counter. "You actively outright brag. You openly say you are sensational. You have not a shred of humility." She was nonplussed. "You can't go around saying, 'We'll soon be having our own practice,' like it's already a sure thing." Her head moved and her spine straightened as her sister pulled the hair from her temple.

"It's not just a flight of fancy," Irish Kyrah asserted in her velvety Irish voice. "It doesn't hurt to believe in ourselves. We'll have no problem opening a shelter."

"Is a maternity shelter like a homeless shelter?" Fräulein Vera asked.

"The women we hope to take in don't need to be homeless," Irish Kyrah answered, twirling hair between her fingers all the while. "Our shelter will be open to anyone who is pregnant and needs to get away from the place they're currently living."

"We can't take just any old slag off the street," Irish Joyce expelled. "She must least be with child, and hopefully far along enough to not require proof." She turned her head to meet her sister's eye causing the braiding to halt. "I don't want to dampen your enthusiasm, but you can't save the world."

"We can try," huffed her twin. "The number of pregnant women who are victims of violence and abuse is staggering. They need to have somewhere to go so the baby can be safe."

"How will you find these women without an office or a business address?" Fräulein Vera questioned.

"There's no shortage of need," she responded enthusiastically. "We could probably stand on a street corner, hitting up every fat-bellied passerby. There is such a need for it. Scads of women need a safe place to stay while they're with child." Irish Kyrah continued to braid without looking as she turned to make eye contact with the others. "I think we're sensational. I wish you could be as proud of us as I am."

"How can I be proud of something we haven't achieved yet?" the doctorly twin hypothesized.

"We have begun!" the idealistic twin exasperated. "We both have our degrees. We have a plan, and as soon as we get certified in California we can start practicing."

"I'm not saying that I won't give it a lash," conceded the practical twin, "but we don't have the money to go right out and open a shelter. How on earth do you hope to help women when we don't have a place for them to stay?"

"You ought to relax sister," the dirty redhead responded. "We'll find a place, even if they have to sleep on the floor of our apartment for a while. Once we start helping people the funding will straighten itself out." Her words reflected her strong beliefs. "If we can find the women, we can find the money," she added.

"She's got such a kind heart," the dirty-blond scoffed while rolling her eyes. "She's a bit too idealistic at times. She can be so sentimental. Especially when it comes to boys."

"How am I sentimental with boys?" asked Irish Kyrah.

Her twin sister rebuked her, "You kept all the stuff Louie gave you even though he broke up with you over the tele, dear heart." She addressed all those gathered. "Personally, I would have taken all of his filthy shit and burn it in a ritual ceremony in the backyard, like I did my secondary school books."

"I love my teddy bears," Irish Kyrah objected. "I can't believe you want me to burn them. Why would you want to hurt them? They certainly never did anything to harm you."

"You kept the jewelry he gave you," chided her sister.

"This necklace is beautiful," she attested. "Why shouldn't I keep it." She addressed the others holding a gold necklace away from the freckled skin on her neck.

"What about the bracelet?" Irish Joyce teased.

"Louie made it for me," the gilded girl grinned as she displayed her dirty, matted, knit bracelet. While she was busy time-travelling back to her beloved ex-boyfriend, she did not take any notice of her sister grinding her teeth in a smile and throwing daggers out her eyes. "I met him in Vermont," crooned the redhead. "He crochets," she marveled. "After our first date we crocheted together. He did it perfectly, but I crocheted somethin' that looked like a fugin' piece of shite. I can't think of any other adjectives."

"Twas that before you got the ride?" her sister chided. "Because I can't imagine he still kept that lump of shite if you hadn't fleeked 'im."

"Shush you cunt!" she scolded her twin sister. "You'd have them think me feckin' oirish!"

"Did you squitch 'im, or not?"

"He wasn't no holy Joe, but we didn't do nothin' but a bunch of shiftin' that first night."

"This sounds interesting," said Yülia as she walked up unannounced. "You shifted some guy? Is that like a hand job?" she inquired.

We all laughed. Yülia was so young and innocent.

"Feck no!" Irish Kyrah rebuked. "Shiftin' is an Irish flavored term for some tongue-on-tongue action."

Indiana Dunes

"Look she's gone scarlet!" her sister teased.

"I'm not!" She denied the accusation, but her cheeks were clearly flushed.

"I hate PDAs," remarked the dirty-blond.

"What's that?" asked Yülia.

"Public display of affection," she explained. "You'd never catch me smooching my girl in public. Guys get off on it. Why put yourself on display like that."

"Please Joyce," the red-haired sister pleaded. You know I hate that word. Smooching sounds like what a baby does to a cookie when it dissolves in its mouth." She looked around to gain support. "I just prefer the word shifting." Evidently, the language of love is alive and well in Ireland.

Her sister chimed in. "You should also know that, in some parts of Ireland, "fleek" and "shift" can also mean the whole hog, but it depends on how you say it. So, tell us, sis. When did you get the ride?"

"Feck off! I'm not telling you that."

"What does it mean to 'get the ride?'" asked Yülia.

Irish Joyce answered for her embarrassed sister. "When it comes to the full 'how's your father,' there are various ways of announcing the news to your mates. At home you would say you 'flashed' a fella, but that sounds like you showed a bloke your tits if you say it here." She spoke with husky intonations reminiscent of Brenda Vaccaro's famous smoky voice. "As for the Irish's top answer, there's only one way we roll, and that's 'riding.' We'll usually announce that we got 'the ride,' like it was a stand-alone thing, as if we seduced a good-looking genital, we found at the pub – just an easy-going penis, sitting there, enjoying his paper and pint."

Irish Kyrah was trying to look like this was all news to her by keeping her eyes bizarrely wide-open, but her sister kept going and we all loved it. Irish Joyce was a riot. She had everyone in stitches. She continued, "Depending on how much you liked a bloke you would say it was 'a serious line' or a 'casual line.' Ye know, 'a once-off.'"

"Surprising for a country as small as ours, we can be so cinched into our own little boroughs, with each its own accent and varied mating rituals." She continued speaking as her sister changed her focus to the braiding on the other side of her head. "I'm not implying that the country folk make love like whiptail lizards while jackeens swallow each other whole after intercourse but mating rituals do vary between Cork and Dublin. As a result, there is a million ways to say you got physical with someone. We'd say, 'I jagged him,' or 'I got off with him,' or 'I met him,' or 'I wore him.'"

"I wore him?" scoffed Peruvian Ursula. "That's gross."

The Irish girl's accent was standing out more and more as she reverted to slang. "Yes," that one has a nasty cousin. "We'd say 'Did ye smell gas off him?' because if he stank of gas, it meant he'd a car, so you'd go with him for the wheels."

"Ugh!" reacted Flip-flop.

"That's dehumanizing," observed Peruvian Ursula.

We were all happy to let Irish Joyce continue. "It's so funny," she told us. "If you want to know who your Irish mate's been riding you ask, 'who are you wearing?'"

"And that's not meaning the fella's cologne, either ladies," added Irish Joyce. "Irish country boys can bring up a right awful smell."

Jewels from New York joined in from the buddy seat. "The guys in New York call it 'stank on the downlow.'"

"Eww!" reacted Yülia. It was all in-good-fun.

"Like that's something a lady wants to hear," Jewels added.

Irish Kyrah took off where her sister landed. "My favorite ones are for guys you'd never want to score. We'd say, 'I wouldn't ride them if they'd pedals.' That's popular at home right 'bout now." She paused, and then her eyes lit up again. "Oh, and if he'd nothin' much going on in the trouser department you'd say, 'Oh, he's got no ballroom.'" Now, the other twin was tearing up. She had us all rolling with laughter.

"What about when you go to town on yourself?" Irish Kyrah asked us all.

"Masturbation?" Jewels questioned.

"Yeah. You know. Having a sneaky diddle," she answered. This drew laughs.

"I love masturbation," enthused Jewels. "I do it all the time." She smiled broadly with pride. "I believe the Goddess designed our bodies so that, when we lie down, our hands naturally come to rest on our genitals. It's her way of saying, "Go on, touch yourself. Don't be ashamed. You need to figure out how your body works, so that when you grow up, you won't be waiting for a man to come along and have sex with you." She made a motion with both hands working together as one, dexterously demonstrating her favorite masturbation technique. "You'll be having sex with yourself for years before a guy tries that shit on you. By then you'll know better. So, you'll know not to let it happen."

Irish Joyce turned to speak to the Peruvian girl. "How 'bout you Ursula? Do you masturbate?"

The debutante nodded convincingly. "Well, even if you don't have a BMW; you have to buff your beemer." We laughed.

Irish Joyce spoke in a rich brogue, "We say, 'Flicking the little man out the boat.'"

"Feeding the Donkey," countered her twin. It went back and forth between the twins.

"Shinin' and wavin.'"

"A hand shandy."

"Pulling the belly off yourself," laughed Irish Joyce.

"Jerking off," I interjected.

"Guys have a slew of terms for it," revealed Irish Kyrah. "Yanking. Tearing the handle off yourself," she added.

"Beating your meat," interjected Chicken Jim. He had been hovering. I went back and forth with him.

"Jerkin' the gherkin."

"Pocket pool."

"Waxing your carrot."

"Whacking off."

"Shucking the clam." They all went Eww! That was over the top. "Sorry," I said.

"How 'bout you Johnny?" Irish Joyce asked the guitar player. "Is there an English term for masturbation?"

He adjusted his glasses on his nose and said, "Crying on the toilet." Then he added, "I don't do it much myself."

"Does it really make you cry?" Yülia asked innocently. Guitar Johnny just rolled his eyes.

I was dying laughing.

"Do you masturbate Lovebus?" asked Irish Joyce.

I was taken aback for a moment as I wiped tears from my eyes. "Masturbation is especially important in men. If we do not masturbate, we go slowly insane." I made a cocked-up face. "Look at the priests that molest boys."

"You don't seem crazy to me," chided the dirty-blond Irish girl. "So, I take it you masturbate."

"Not too much," I answered.

"Why not," she coaxed.

"It doesn't do much for me. It's not anything like having an orgasm with a woman. When you do it yourself, the orgasms are lame."

"My orgasms are awesome," she raved. "I love giving myself orgasms." She nodded around at the others. They all seemed to agree. "I've got a dildo with me in my rucksack," she revealed.

"That's lovely," added her twin.

"I think maybe masturbation is different for guys," I surmised. "I don't get off on it like when making love. It's nothing but a bodily function. It's very clinical. Masturbation is like brushing your teeth, back-and-forth, back-and-forth, back-and-forth, spit." Everyone laughed.

"Ya!" laughed Fräulein Vera. "It sounds like a blow job!"

Flip-flop spoke up. "Have you guys seen Father Guido Sarduchi from Saturday Night Live?" Most of us had. "Remember what he said about masturbation?" None of us remembered, so she continued. "Sorry, I can't do his accent, but Father Guido said, life is a job, and for every day of your life you get something like fourteen-dollars. When you get to heaven god pays you, but then you must pay for your sins. Murder is like a hundred thousand dollars, but masturbation is only twenty-five cents."

"I take it you're Christian?" asked Irish Kyrah.

"Yes," she confirmed, "Catholic."

"Do you believe masturbation is a sin?" the Irish girl queried.

"If I did, I'd be going straight to hell," she said with a laugh. "Those quarters add up fast, twenty-five, twenty-five, twenty-five, twenty-five." We all nearly died laughing.

When the braiding of Irish Joyce's hair was complete, she looked magnificent and our bellies hurt from laughing. A shoelace-thin tightly wrapped braid crossed the center of her forehead from the top of one ear to the other. Braids intertwined in a simple crisscross pattern falling from her temples down along her cheeks. Similar braids fell from each ear and followed her jawline until they hung together with the two from her temples. One larger braid crossed the top of her head from ear to ear. Finally, a massive thick braid fell past her shoulders between her angel wings.

****

The bus exited Route 90 to stop at the Pilot Travel Center in Perrysburg Ohio, south of Toledo. We were allotted thirty minutes to get lunch and be back at the bus. Driver Chris went inside to call for an update on his brother. Jewels and Yülia went inside with a large group of ladies.

The Peruvian debutante was delighted to see the sign that said, 'PAY SHOWERS.' She came forward with a small Louis Vuitton suitcase and asked Driver Chris, "Do I have time to bathe?"

He said, "No," and explained. "If you take a shower everyone will want one and we'll be here all day. You'll be able to shower at Indiana Dunes before we head to Chicago."

"I don't see why I can't shower here," she insisted. "You said we have thirty minutes. I'll make it back in time."

"If you're not back in time," he told her sternly. "I'll have to leave without you."

"You wouldn't dare," she sneered. She barked orders to PAC-MAN in Cantonese before rushing out. Chicken Jim was standing outside the door. "Don't let my friend Pak out of your sight," she told him. "He needs to stay on the bus."

I went inside to use the men's room, then I explored the truck stop for fifteen minutes before going back to the bus. I stood around outside listening to Flip-flop describe the dozens of earthquakes she experienced in Northridge when she was at Cal State the previous year. She was one of the only exchange students that showed up that semester. She thought about staying home, but as she said with a laugh, "I can't tell you how many times the dishes flew out of my cupboards."

Chicken Jim approached me across the parking lot making a strained face with big eyes. He motioned behind him like he wanted me to check something out. Peruvian Ursula and PAC-MAN were standing outside the door of the truck stop diner. She did not look happy with him at all. He just stood there taking it like a man as she yelled at him.

"Looks like the Pink Panther's pissed at Cato," commented the overall-clad Pennsylvanian.

"What did he do?" I asked.

"He went inside without her," he informed me.

"So what?"

"She told me to make sure he didn't leave the bus," he admitted. "I ain't taking orders from her, dude. A man's gotta eat."

We watched as she handed PAC-MAN a big pair of mirrored sunglasses. He put them on obediently. She gave him a baseball hat. He placed it high on his head sitting on top of his spiked hair. She appeared displeased. She grabbed the hat off his head and folded the rim a few times, breaking-it-in. Then she tugged the hat down on his head, so it fell over his ear-line, East Coast style. Despite this getup, his slight frame left him looking somewhat androgynous, like a little boy who had yet to fill out.

Driver Chris stormed out of the diner exit and rushed past them. Chicken Jim and I followed him to the doorway. When he got to the bus, he threw his daypack on the dashboard in anger. He got into the driver's seat and sat there fuming silently for a few moments with a wrinkled expression of pain on his face. Suddenly, he straightened his arms, locked his hands on the steering wheel and began thrashing about like he was trying to rip it out of the dashboard. I stepped away to give him some space, but the rookie remained in the doorway. Driver Chris kept his arms stiffened throughout the entire ordeal. His shoulders shook violently, and his face screamed in silent anger. When he stopped physically quaking, he put his elbows on the wheel and dropped his head into his hands.

The passengers assumed the worst and whispers of speculation spread. I stood back in the doorway to see if I could help.

Maid Marian stepped forward and gave her condolences with a somber face. "I wish I had the right words; just know I care."

Her fiancé's words trailed behind hers. "I'm so sorry for your loss," he said softly.

Mother Michelle came to the buddy seat at the same time. She was clearly distraught with grief. "My thoughts and prayers are with you and your family," she told him as she moved in for a hug.

"My father is such an asshole," he told her.

She put her hand on his shoulder. "It's hard to endure the loss of a child."

"It's not like that," he snapped. "My brother is still alive."

"He's alive!" Mother Michelle exclaimed. "That's wonderful news."

"That's awesome bro," I told him from the doorway.

"That's great," Sir Gavin cheered.

"'He's alive!" the Irish Twins celebrated simultaneously, and they came outside to spread the good news.

Guitar Johnny sure seemed pleased. He grabbed his guitar and went outside to play.

"Chirp, chirp, chirp!" Driver Brian was calling on the bus phone. "Chirp, chirp, chirp!"

Driver Chris snatched the plastic receiver off the hook and said, "Hey," then turned to look out the window. "Yeah, I'm okay," he spoke quickly with embarrassment. "I was just blowing off steam. My father's being a prick." He huffed a sob and his belly contracted in a series of spasms. "My mother and sister stayed overnight at the hospital. I couldn't reach them, so I had to get the details from him."

"Give him some space," directed Mother Michelle as she came outside. I took position under the side view mirror. The agreed upon time to leave was at hand and a crowd had formed near the door. Lots of passengers had been listening and relaying details to the others in low voices and whispers. Everyone backed off a bit, but Mother Michelle stood on the bottom step, as much to keep the others at bay as to keep an eye on her son in the busy parking lot.

The phone conversation continued. "He survived the surgery," he let his co-driver know. "They removed a chunk of his brain the size of a golf ball above his right eye." He closed his eyes and took a breath as he listened to his co-driver. "Yes, it's a good thing," Driver Chris agreed. "They said it's a miracle that he's survived this long."

There was an elongated pause while his co-driver spoke.

The red-bearded driver began to speak more calmly. "It's the part of the brain that controls inhibition, but he didn't have much of that to begin with." I could see tears in his eyes in the mirror. "I don't know," he replied. "Thanks," he sobbed.

Passengers were returning from the truck stop building, but Mother Michelle kept them from entering out of respect.

"I couldn't get any more information," the driver's tone harshened. "My dad was being such a douchebag. I had to hang up on him." He shook his head while he listened. "He wants me to come home, like today."

"You should go," urged Mother Michelle from the stairwell.

"I know you can brother," our driver said into the receiver, 'but I can't go now. Not yet. My place is here. I refuse to create that reality. As long as I keep on truckin' my brother will be fine." There was another long pause. "Thanks man," said Driver Chris. "There's nothing you can do right now. You need to sleep. I am fine driving. It will take my mind off things. Thanks. You're a good friend."

Driver Chris started speaking quickly before ending the conversation abruptly. "I'll let you know. I have to go now. Everyone is back. Get some sleep. Talk to you later." He slapped the phone on the hook. Two seconds later, I felt the bus list to the side, and I knew instantly that Driver Brian had lifted his massive body out of the roof hatch. He would soon be heading this way across the roof to console his colleague.

Guitar Johnny was strumming away, so I figured I would go stand by him and listen with the others. The gigantic blond Green Tortoise driver looked like the Abominable Snowman striding high atop the bus. Driver Chris came outside to talk with his him, waiting at the bottom of the ladder by the driver's window a few yards off.

The British guitarist strummed the chords to Peter Gunn and wrapped it up with a little solo.

"There's something fishy about that snooty rich bitch and that Asian bloke," he whispered. "She claims they aren't a couple, but she treats him like they're married."

"How's that?" I asked.

"She treats him like a piece of shite," he scoffed. Guitar Johnny was hopelessly dreary at times. I hoped relationships would not leave me feeling so dark. The Englishman often presented a complex web of pessimism that spoke of a rough tortured childhood and many exposed nerves.

When PAC-MAN and the Pink Panther reached the two Drivers, she demanded, "What's the status?"

"We're good to go for now," Driver Chris told her.

"Fantastic!" she responded.

"He survived the surgery, but he's not out of the woods yet," divulged Driver Chris. "I'm getting a lot of pressure to come home," he confessed. "I'm still undecided, so no promises."

"She looked at him with a cold look of disdain. She shook her head in frustration. "You need to shit or get off the pot," she asserted. "Either stay or go. You can't do both."

Guitar Johnny stomped his boot-heel and softly shouted, "Bollocks! Did you hear that bitch? She's bloody awful."

"No kidding," I agreed with his soulful protest.

The Peruvian woman suddenly trained her attention on our group as if she had heard Guitar Johnny's boot-heel hitting the tarmac. She gave the lot of us the hairy eyeball, making eye contact with each of us in a sneer that varied according to her level of disdain. She turned back to Driver Chris and soothed the grieving driver, "I'm glad to hear things are going well for your brother, but you've got to make a decision. Pak needs to arrive in San Francisco on schedule. If you need to go home, go home. We just need to know as soon as possible, so we can make other arrangements."

"Don't worry about me," PAC-MAN told him. "If you need go home, please go home. Family come first."

"Yes. Don't worry about us," the Peruvian rejoined. She corrected her friend's grammar, "Family comes first. If you need to go home, by-all-means go home."

"You'll be the first to know," Driver Chris reassured her.

"Nice hat!" Driver Brian teased PAC-MAN. The blue brimmed hat said Toledo Nation in big black script letters on a field of white.

Despite her lowered voice I heard the Peruvian complain about all the cameras at the truck stop.

"CCTV," acknowledged Driver Brian. "They're cameras all over the place at truck stops."

The Chinese man removed his hat, ran his fingers through his spiked hair and addressed Driver Chris. "I'm sorry to hear about your brother," he said. As the two men talked, I gave PAC-MAN another once over. He was significantly older than most of the other backpackers on the bus, possibly thirty years of age, although it was hard to tell. He had no trace of a beard, and his skin was devoid of blemishes, wrinkles, age lines or crow's feet, making him appear deceptively young. I am sure the ladies were envious of his perfect skin tone.

Chicken Jim walked up with Yülia and Jewels. "Tell him what you just told me," he coaxed.

The young German girl seemed embarrassed at first. She hesitated, worried about who might be listening. She whispered, "She stopped him from making a phone call, and it sounded like she was yelling at him in Chinese."

"She physically stopped him from making a phone call," clarified Jewels with audacity, "and she was definitely yelling at him." She wagged her finger in the air authoritatively. "That's not cool! If she's abusing him, I've got a problem with that," Jewels snapped.

"She seems to have some kind of power over him," whispered the petite German. "She made him go in the bathroom with her."

"She took him in the ladies' room?" I asked with incredulity.

"It was a family bathroom," clarified the New Yorker. "But, she dragged him in there with her. We were standing right there when they came out." She made a face of incredulity before adding, "She clearly has him under her control."

"He could be in trouble," suggested Yülia.

"I'm going to say something," touted Jewels. Her anger was out of character. She was no longer her normal wonderful self. "We can't let her continue to abuse him like that," she declared.

"I knew something was rotten in Denmark," blurted Guitar Johnny. "She probably follows him in when he goes to spend a penny."

"What's that?" Chicken Jim asked.

"Maybe he's a dangerous fugitive and she's a bounty hunter," the Englishman surmised.

"Really?" said the adorable German coed. "Did she tell you that?"

"I'm just talking a bit of rubbish," Guitar Johnny scoffed at her.

"There's no way she's abusing him," I surmised. "She's got class and manners like a lady. She went to the same college as me. She speaks seven languages for crying out loud."

When the four of them started walking toward us, Guitar Johnny said, "I'd hate to be on her whipping post." Then he twisted his foot on the last of his cigarette and headed inside.

"We need to get him alone so we can ask him," Jewels whispered to Yülia. "Let's try to get them apart."

"What are you looking at?" the Peruvian woman demanded upon approach.

"Why are you being mean to me?" asked the New Yorker. "I didn't do anything to you." The Peruvian made a horrid face. "You're mean to your friend too. You can't treat people like shit and expect them not to object."

"It's none of your goddamn business," chided the debutante. "He's still my friend. That should tell you something."

"If that's what you call being friends, I feel bad for the both of you," snubbed Jewels.

"Well don't," was the Peruvian's only response.

I felt like running, lest I be clawed-to-death by the two tigresses, so I went inside and sat across from Guitar Johnny on the front platform. PAC-MAN came in behind me with his chaperone. She pointed at the seat behind the driver and he sat down obediently.

"Fuckin' 'ell!" spat Guitar Johnny. "That's what I've been getting on about." He raised his eyebrows and said, "Maybe we should keep an eye on them." I agreed with a slow nod and he went to put his guitar up on a bunk.

The distraught Irishman got behind the wheel and Peruvian Ursula took the buddy seat.

Four passengers were seated at the dinette. The South African's were playing a card game across the table from the windows and Flip-flop sat across from the German guy with black hair. "Berndt," he said, introducing himself to the South African woman.

"I'm Marian," she said demurely with a bit of an upper-body curtsey. He put his hand out and they shook.

"Maid Marian," her fiancé corrected her.

"That's my bus name," she said fondly.

"Mine is Flip-flop," said Jen.

"That's a good one," said the German. He spoke with a strong Bavarian accent, but his English was great. "Everyone's been calling me Berndt Toast," he informed them both. "Where are you from?" He asked.

"Boston," answered Flip-flop.

"Cape Town," answered the woman with the bandanna in her hair.

"I'm here for college," the German informed them. "So, I have the whole summer to travel. What brings you to the states?"

"We're on a walkabout," her fiancé interjected. "I'm Gavin." They shook hands.

"How do you guys like the trip so far?" Flip-flop asked the couple.

"Ha!" Maid Marian answered after a shared laugh with her partner. "I was just telling Gavin that, 'This is one of the most bizarre experiences I've ever had in my life.'" We all laughed. The South African woman had a lovely accent. She dropped the h's in words like have and honest and truncated the word bizarre with a long vowel sound like she was at the doctor getting her throat checked.

"I totally agree," her fiancé added. "There's nothing like the Green Tortoise where we come from." We all agreed. "What a cool way to see America. Lake Erie was so beautiful," he marveled. He pronounced beautiful like it was three words, butte-e-full. "What do you make of the trip so far?" he asked.

Indiana Dunes

"It's awesome," the German responded with enthusiasm. "Everyone has been great."

Maid Marian shook her head in agreement and gave Berndt Toast a smile and asked, "Are you traveling with anyone?"

"No," he answered, shaking his head. "I was planning on buying a car to drive to California with these guys I met at the youth hostel in Boston, then Sue and Tessa told me about the Green Tortoise," he explained. "I'm so glad they did. The car was going to cost everything I had saved, so it was an easy decision to hang with the British girls."

English Tessa interjected, "I'm English!"

Their conversation went on, but I found it difficult to listen. Peruvian Ursula was sitting on the buddy seat talking to Driver Chris. I was dying to know what they were talking about, so I moved to the closest empty seat. He was telling another driver story. He was full of them.

"I've seen a lot of crazy shit driving for the Tortoise," he told her. "Late one night on Route One in Northern California, a car flew past the bus, hummin' like a bitch at over a hundred-miles an hour. The police were hot on his heels. I counted fifteen police cars all chasing him at high speed."

"Wow!" observed Yülia from the seat by the door.

Driver Chris continued his story. "We got stopped by a roadblock on the hill heading down into Crescent City. The whole place was lit-up like a Christmas tree, so a bunch of us climbed an embankment to get a better look. There were like fifty cop cars surrounding the guy. They were yelling at him with a megaphone, but he refused to get out of the car. Finally, after like ten minutes the guy comes out of his car welding a frying pan, trying to make them think he had a gun."

"Did they spray him with bullets?" Yülia asked like a little kid who had watched too many cop movies.

"No," he explained. "He was trying to commit suicide by cop. He had just broken up with his girlfriend, and he wanted the cops to put him out of his misery."

"Wow! That's intense," observed the young German girl.

"I've heard about people doing that," revealed Peruvian Ursula.

"I met a cop at a fuel station a few towns up, who told me they had been chasing the guy for more than three hundred miles, all the way from San Francisco. They were waiting for him to run out of gas."

"Damn!" she miffed. "What an incredible waste of public resources."

I got a chance to speak with Australian Sheila on the front platform. Besides being drop-dead gorgeous, I found her to be quite interesting. When I asked her if she was on a walkabout, she explained how that term is offensive because it delineates class lines between aboriginals and modern Australians, putting down the ancient people. I listened intently to her stories about travel, earning money in Europe and visiting places in America that I had never heard of before. In turn, I told her about life in Rhode Island and the beautiful places that I had seen on my cycling adventure in the Pacific Northwest.

Midway through our conversation the gorgeous Aussie whipped off her shirt without apprehension, revealing a tight sports bra. Without air conditioning it grew increasingly hot inside the bus. By midday, most of the guys including me were bare-chested and many of the girls had stripped-down to their bras.

****

A drinking game broke out on the back platform midway through the long drive to our next stop at Indiana Dunes National Lakeshore. I figured I would sit at the dinette to watch them play from a safe distance until I learned the rules. I took a seat next to Little Josh who was listening to Fräulein Vera's Walkman. I suspected that he had not asked her permission and that he was using it without her knowledge. Peruvian Ursula took the seat right behind me a few minutes after I sat down at the dinette.

French Sandrine was reading a book, sitting across from us next to Big Dave. The big man kept his eyes on the scenery like he was remembering life on a tour bus back in the day. Little Josh walked by, looked at the French girl and said, "I didn't know sardines could read."

While I watched and learned the drinking game, I overheard South American Juliano trying to impress Peruvian Ursula with his accomplishments in soccer. He was clearly trying to convince her that he was deserving of her affection, but she was like a Teflon pan and his shit did not stick.

The game was like Twenty Questions. The players had to guess the name of the famous person written on a piece of white medical tape stuck to their foreheads. If you ask a question that gets a yes answer, then you may keep asking questions until you guess the name on your forehead. If you get a no answer, you must drink a couple ounces of your beer, you lose your turn and the next person goes.

The piece of tape on Mountain Girl's forehead read Albert Einstein. She had obviously shared her bright red lipstick with the other girls. All the ladies were wearing it except Mother Michelle, who sat to her right. Her tape read Joan of Arc. To her left along the windows, sat

Indiana Dunes

Irish Kyrah, who's tape read George Michael, and Irish Joyce, who's tape read Martina Navratilova. Maid Marian's forehead read Oprah Winfrey. She was reclining comfortably in Sir Gavin's arms. His forehead read Nelson Mandela. Chicken Jim's tape read Ozzy Osbourne. He was sitting across the aisle from the South Africans followed along the windows by Jewels, Yülia and Flip-flop. The white medical tape on their foreheads read Grandmaster Flash, George Bush, and Mark Wahlberg in that order.

I heard Berndt Toast asked, "Am I American?"

"Yes!" blurted Irish Joyce along with several other players. "Totally American!" she added. Her tone provided an additional clue, pointing more toward Americana, glamor, and kitsch.

"Am I male?" he inquired.

"Yes," the players answered.

He asked, "Am I on TV?"

"Yes," they all confirmed again.

"Am I old?"

"Yes!" Irish Joyce proclaimed with authority. Several players laughed.

"He's not old!" Irish Kyrah protested with a tone of sympathy. "I feel bad for him when you say he's old."

"He's terribly old," her twin nodded profusely, clearly intending to lead Berndt Toast on a wild-goose-chase. "Think about it," her dirty-blond sister prodded. "Compared to us he's a dinosaur."

Everyone's eyes bulged, but Berndt did not visibly catch onto this obvious clue.

The dirty redhead replied with a mischievous smile. "He may be old but he's not extinct."

The Player's eyes widened but Berndt Toast's face remained static. He pondered this information and asked, "Do I speak with an accent?" He was beginning to sound more confident.

Irish Joyce responded to her sister's funny look by saying, "Yes, he speaks with an accent."

"He's never going to get it." Irish Kyrah shook her head in consternation, but none of the other players disagreed. "Take another turn Berndt," she urged him.

Berndt Toast's eyes shot open like he was starting to catch on. "Does my accent make me sound stupid?"

The players answered with a resounding, "Yes!"

"He's not stupid. That is his normal voice," protested Irish Kyrah. "That's just mean."

"Is my body huge?" Berndt Toast asked with a tone of growing confidence.

"Yes!" they proclaimed again with a great burst of laughter.

Now he seemed thoroughly sure he knew the name on his forehead. "Am I Arnold Schwarzenegger?" he asked assuredly.

Several players shouted. "No!" over a role of laughter.

"Scheisse!" he cursed in a guttural German accent. He peeled the tape off his forehead looked at it in disgust and said, "Who the fuck is Barney?"

"He's a dinosaur," Flip-flop tried to explain, but the German youth did not want to hear it. He just threw up his hands and crawled toward me to get another beer.

"Play with us," he said as he drew near. "We're trying to drink as much as we can, before the beer gets warm." Four cases of beer were stacked on top of the built-in coolers.

"Why don't you put ice on it?" I suggested.

"We can't fit any more in the cooler," he told me.

"Right on!" I said, appreciating his generosity. "I can help." He passed me a beer. "I'll take a couple more," I suggested, intending to pass them out.

"You're my kind of man," Berndt Toast responded.

Peruvian Ursula giggled. When we turned to look at her, she looked back at us with a facial expression reserved for admiring openly gay people. Then she turned away quickly. This bewildered me. Obviously, she had been watching us.

"She thinks you're gay," I said with a chuckle.

"Correction," he said, "she thinks we're both gay."

Before I could respond the Pink Panther strode past us like a cat and pounced off her hind leg onto the back platform. As she pawed her way across the mattresses on all fours she passed into the center of the circle and leaned-in to whisper in Irish Joyce's ear. The dirty-blond looked us up and down with a shrug as the Peruvian took a seat next to her.

I fed beers to Berndt Toast until he had an armload and we headed back to join them.

Irish Joyce's bright green lace bra was unhooked so that the clasps flapped like wings under her arms. Her snow-white B-cups looked awesome from the side. She caught me looking and smiled with her bright white teeth, then she waved me over and made room for me to sit between her and Mother Michelle.

As I crawled toward her on my hands and knees, I passed a beer to Flip-flop on the far side of the circle and she said, "Thanks." I took a seat.

The tape on Mother Michelle's forehead said, "Joan of Arc." When I sat down, she grabbed my knee and gave me a wide-eyed look. Her body language and facial expression told me she was trying to tell me something secret, but she did not say a word.

The dirty-blond Irish girl with the nose piercing eyed my two beers suggestively and said, "I'm all out." I handed her one. "You're so sweet," she said. "That's a kindness!" She cracked the beer and drank half of it in one swig, then she choked back a burp and smiled.

My eyebrows jumped when she licked her lips suggestively. I cracked my beer. It was not cold, but it was refreshing in the heat.

Berndt Toast passed out his beers and took a seat. "Are you playing or what?" he asked me.

I gamely said, "Yes."

Irish Joyce passed the beer back to me and eagerly grabbed the roll of medical tape. She rose to her knees and proceeded to crawl into the middle of the circle with her bone-white breasts flopping like udders below her unclasped green brassiere. I could not behave my eyes. She spun around to face me and rose to her knees. She pondered for a moment until Peruvian Ursula kneeled-up and whispered something in her ear. Suddenly, she demanded, "Where's my pen?"

Guitar Johnny, whose game name was Elvis Presley, passed her an indelible marker.

The loose-breasted Irish girl painstakingly maintained her balance while writing a mysteriously long name on the tape, twice catching my wandering eyes inspecting her bare breasts.

"You will not look," scolded Fräulein Vera, so I closed my eyes.

Irish Joyce ripped off the piece of tape and dropped the roll and pen. She leaned over my folded legs and pressed the white strip onto my forehead with her thumbs. Just at that moment the bus shifted, and she lost her balance. Her whole body fell on top of me. I moved my head to the side and said, "Woe!" as our chests pressed together.

She caught herself with her arms at my sides, landing with her cheek pressed against mine. She breathed the words, "Aren't you a fine thing." I could smell beer on her breath, and I could feel her warm breasts touching my bare chest. I was temporarily frozen, unable to muster speech. I would have tried to help her up, but my hands were holding two open cans of beer.

Everyone was cracking up as she lingered there.

"Stop actin' the maggot," chastised the dirty-redhead. "Get off of him and get on with the game."

I secured the beers in my lap and moved my hands to her ribs. She seductively slid her cheek against mine until we were eye to eye, then she went to kiss me, so I closed my eyes and puckered up. She pulled me in and started making out with me. There was a whoop of laughter and the circle of women passengers went "Woo!"

"You're a cute hoor," objected Irish Kyrah, sounding jealous. "I thought you didn't like public displays of affection," she quipped.

"You wouldn't be caught dead kissing a girl in public." She looked to us for support and added, "She won't even do me a kindness."

I made out with her for no more than three seconds before she broke off the kiss and said, "He's clearly not gay." She laughed playfully. There was a burst of laughter followed by a moment of silence. With a kiss on the nose, she pressed her hands on my thighs and pushed me away.

"He could still be bi," commented the Peruvian, seeking confirmation from me with a tilt of her head.

"I'm pretty straight," I attested.

"Tis a fret!" said Irish Joyce as she settled next to me. "I was going to ask you to join us." This brought on whoops and catcalls from all present.

When the laughter ebbed, Australian Sheila spoke up and told me, "You've got lippy on his nose."

Everyone laughed when they looked at my face. "What?" I asked. They all laughed again. Evidently, there was lipstick on my nose. I wiped it off the best I could.

"What about you?" Irish Joyce addressed the hearty German guy. "Are you gay?"

He said, "No," as he shook his head.

"You could have fooled me," teased the Peruvian.

Again, the laughter came from all sides. During the melee Mother Michelle gestured to me holding a Kleenex pinched between her fingers. "Come here," she said, "there's still some lipstick on your nose." I leaned in and as she wiped my nose. She gave me a pointed look, gesturing toward the Irish girls. "Those girls are not your type," she advised in a whisper. "They are too worldly for you."

My eyes grew wide with astonishment. "Excuse me!" I sputtered.

"I can tell you're a one-woman-kind-of-guy," she surmised.

"That I am," I told her.

She could not say anything more because it came to be her turn in the name game. Her tape read Joan of Arc. She asked the group, "Am I a woman?"

"Yes."

"Am I old?"

"Yes."

"Was I born before the eighteen-hundreds?" Yes. "Am I Joan of Arc?" She asked. Yes! And many of us felt, for a few minutes, that she just might be Joan of Arc.

Fräulein Vera, on the other hand, asked a million questions and never would have guessed the name on her forehead because, as she complained to Chicken Jim, "Who the hell is Timothy Leary?"

Indiana Dunes

When the Brazin kid named Juliano came to sit down, Mountain Girl pushed Mother Michelle out of the way to make room for him. Before he sat down, I grabbed the tape and wrote, "Indiana Jones." I passed the tape to Mountain Girl. As she stuck it to his forehead, he read the name on her tape and commented, "You're a genius!"

"Thank you, eh," she responded with flushed cheeks. This brought a few chuckles, but the sexy Canadian failed to see the humor in his comment, not knowing she was Albert Einstein. It was obvious she took his comment at face value, as a sign that he liked her.

The laughter came in droves when everyone read the white tape on Juliano's forehead. His resemblance to the famous explorer was uncanny. Even after he guessed the name, no one called him Indy except me. Juliano was such a fitting name because of how he pronounced it with his accent. The rest of the passengers never called him anything else.

When my turn came to ask a question, I asked, "Am I a man?"

Irish Joyce said, "Most definitely."

"Am I on TV?" I asked.

"A wee bit," said Irish Joyce, before the others had a chance to respond.

This caused British Sue to eye the Irish girl suspiciously. She seemed puzzled by her answer, so she clarified. "On MTV."

"Don't give it away," Irish Joyce chastised.

"Am I a singer?"

"Well, yes."

"Am I Gay?"

"Yes!" Peruvian Ursula laughed loudly.

"Am I still alive?" They all looked at me cross-eyed, shaking their heads and said, "No." So, I had to drink. "I was thinking Liberace," I told them. Several beers later I was still no closer to guessing the name on my forehead. When the game ended, I took off the tape. It read, "Freddie Mercury."

We drove through the hottest part of the day. Even with all the windows open, the temperature inside the bus was brutal without air conditioning. Mother Michelle complained about the heat a couple of times, but she knew from experience on the Sunny Southern Route that there was nothing that could be done. Driver Chris kept prodding us to drink water. I could see why. I was already starting to feel the drain of energy that comes from being dehydrated.

****

By the time we made it to Indiana Dunes National Lakeshore the passengers seemed tighter and more unified, having survived the sweltering journey together. We were getting to know one another better, if not by conversation, then by perspiration. We were promised a chance to swim at a beach on Lake Michigan after dinner if we helped cook. We would have less time to take a shower before going out for nightlife in Chicago, but the passengers who agreed to help clean-up and shower first would not be able to swim.

Indiana Dunes National Lakeshore features an amazing labyrinth of windswept dunes giving the area an otherworldly quality that sets it apart from any other place in America. The unlikely combination of high sand dunes and tall pine trees creates an environment both protected from the wind and cooled under the shade of evergreens, while the fresh seaside air enlivens the senses.

The bus stopped beside a small field with picnic tables and a cookout grill reserved for large groups. The area was large enough for several busloads of people to hang-out and prepare a meal. Flip-flop's suggestion to play soccer was well-received, but when she tried to find her soccer ball, she came up empty handed. The field was flat and perfect for soccer, so several passengers started helping her look.

Flip-flop and the other searchers became convinced the ball was no longer on the bus, and they were about to give up when, almost as an afterthought, she thought to ask the little kid if he had seen the ball.

When Little Josh found out they wanted to play soccer he ran inside the bus and produced the ball in under a minute. When asked where he found it Little Josh told them it was in the driver's cabin. Flip-flop was flabbergasted. "I looked in there," she said in disbelief. "It wasn't there when I looked. I don't see how that's possible. Oh well. I'm glad you found it," she said. The game began and we thought nothing more of it.

More than half of the passengers played soccer with Flip-flop while the rest of us helped prepare dinner. The Bostonian was clearly the best player, despite the efforts of the European guys to show her up. Guitar Johnny donned his soccer jersey and did his best not to embarrass himself by passing the ball before she had a chance to steal it from him. It turned out she had played soccer competitively in college. She scored more goals than anyone else and ran circles around the other women. Juliano may have been a better player, but his legs went limp whenever he went toe to toe with a female competitor. It was cute, but the girls didn't appreciate being patronized.

While the game was being played, Chicken Jim sat on a picnic table plucking away at his guitar, singing bits of popular songs but never playing a whole song from start to finish. This left me alone on the roof to do all the work, just like Driver Brian had warned me. My plan was to leave Chicken Jim and the soccer players to deal with the cleanup. There were plenty of them to help him wash dishes and pack up.

It was make-your-own quesadilla night. As solo roof-person, I saw firsthand everything that goes into making a Green Tortoise dinner. First, I passed down the three food tables, and they were quickly set up. One of the tables was populated with four propane stoves. A cast-iron fry pan was placed on each of the eight burners. A second table was equipped with knives and cutting boards, while the third held our plates, mugs and eating utensils.

Driver Brian called for thirty-six avocados. That seemed like a lot, but who was I to argue with the chef. I tossed them down to the catchers one by one without incident. The chef showed the crew how to remove the pit from an avocado by embedding the blade in the pit and giving it a twist. He called for a bag of onions, sprigs of cilantro, and a sack of garlic bulbs. All these ingredients were chopped and mashed into the avocado. Two cups of salsa and a whole container of sour cream were folded in with the juice of six limes. He tasted the giant vat of guacamole with his finger. He called up to me for the salt. I tossed it down to him. He salted the mixture, gave it a stir, and tested it again with the same unwashed finger. "Success!" he announced, and the guacamole was served at once with two five-pound bags of tortilla chips.

Mountain Girl and Juliano managed to gain credit for cooking by helping at the last minute after returning from the showers. They were starting to hit it off despite his affinity for the Peruvian. Chicken Jim did not think it was fair that they should be able to swim after dinner. "They can't do that!" he complained to Driver Chris.

"There are no rules on the Tortoise," responded the red-haired Irish driver without a second thought.

Despite being told the non-rule, Chicken Jim still chastised Juliano. I am sure he was jealous of the South American's good looks and fortune. He told me later that he decided to let them off the hook because, as he said, "He needed to shower cuz he had the 'funk on the downlow.' He was up in the bunk all day with Mountain Girl."

"I call him Indiana," I told him. "His hat reminds me of a young Indy." Everyone admired Juliano for his good looks and charm. Everyone that is, except Peruvian Ursula, who kept him at arm's length with her snappy answers despite his desperate pleas for her attention. She told the Irish girls, "Boys like him are a dime a dozen in Peru."

Mountain Girl's response was hilarious. She said, "I have a dollar! I'll take ten, eh!"

"Don't sell yourself short," the Peruvian advised. "El es un hombre puta."

"No charge for you my love," responded Juliano having overheard.

When the food was ready, more than a dozen stainless steel serving bowls were laid-out with a different ingredient in each one. The ingredients were shredded cheese, non-dairy vegan cheese, black beans, refried beans, diced tomatoes, shredded lettuce, chopped onions, diced green peppers, hand sliced olives, sour cream, multiple choices of salsa, and the rest of the guacamole. The colorful spread was a feast for the eyes. The entire meal took a little over an hour to prepare, but with so many people helping, it seemed easy.

Each passenger was given a turn at the stove to cook themselves a quesadilla with ingredients of their own choosing. We all ate to our heart's content. Once done eating Driver Brian bagged-up the leftover guacamole. "This is for midnight munchies after your night out in Chicago," he explained.

Driver Chris put his dish and cup in the wash bucket and made an announcement. "If you helped cook dinner, you're welcome to follow me down to the beach for a swim in Lake Michigan. The rest of you need to help do the dishes and clean up." The boy complained audibly. "Don't worry, Josh," he told him. "There'll be plenty of time for the clean-up crew to swim later. Chicken Jim will bring you down to the beach when it's time."

Then he shouted, "Jimbo! Get this place cleaned up." The driver-in-training nodded. "I want it spotless," he directed him, "better than we found it." He gave the passengers a few minutes to gather their gear and we gathered by an opening at the edge of the woods.

Guitar Johnny walked over near us and started rolling a smoke.

"Weren't you just playing soccer?" I asked him flat out. "You're on the clean-up crew."

"Indeed, I was," he admitted, "but I'd rather be buggered sideways than take orders from Chicken Jim." He scoffed. "He's a duffer."

Juliano showed up at the last second. I gave him a what's up look, and he said, "I sweat a lot during the game. No one will stand the smell of me." I heard what he was saying, but I knew he was just trying to get close to Peruvian Ursula.

The bunch of us followed Driver Chris on a hike through a thin forest of wispy pines growing on the slopes of white sand dunes. The ladies fell back in a clump walking slowing, gossiping about the guys. Irish Kyrah's delightful laughter and Irish Joyce's loud gruff brogue. Guitar Johnny kept turning around self-consciously every time the girls laughed.

Indiana Dunes

We trudged through the sand up and down slopes until we came to the top of a massive dune overlooking a sandy beach. The infinity of Lake Michigan stretched out before us for over four hundred miles, and the shoreline stretched as far as the eye could see in both directions. The sun hung low in the sky just a few hours before sunset, creating an eerie orange-red glow on the western horizon. We could see the outline of Chicago through the haze of air pollution. The water in the lake looked crystal clear and inviting.

Guitar Johnny and I paused for a moment on top of the dune and watched the other guys glissade down the steep slope, creating avalanches of sand beneath their feet. We glissaded down behind them and stood by the edge of Lake Michigan while the guitar player casually rolled another cigarette. Driver Chris encouraged Berndt Toast to swim, but he declined.

There were catcalls from on top of the sand dune when Juliano removed his shirt. The ladies were standing together on top of the dune watching the men undress. He flexed for Peruvian Ursula. I could not understand what was so wrong with Mountain Girl that he would risk losing her. I thought he was out of his mind.

Guitar Johnny took his shirt off slowly. I noticed a tattooed name obscured beneath his chest hair. "What's that?"

"That's my ex, Gloria," he responded sheepishly. "My life is full of such regrets."

I hoped that my life would not be filled with such regrets. Just when I dropped my shorts, the girls came glissading down the dune, running together in one big clump of feminine hysteria. They were mostly naked except for the bikini-clad Peruvian and the topless Aussie. They screamed and yahooed in exotic accents all the way down the hill into the water, running right past the stunned Englishman. I soon found myself surrounded by a gaggle of beautiful foreign women in the crystal clear water of Lake Michigan.

Australian Sheila looked out of place with her bright red bathing suit, but I could not keep my eyes off her newly braided ponytail. The Irish girls had done an amazing job, making her look totally gorgeous. British Sue was there, and I made it a point to try to swim near her and to flirt with her.

When Chicken Jim arrived, Driver Chris grilled him. "You couldn't have possibly finished the clean-up that fast."

"Brian woke up and started telling people what to do, so I left him to it," the rookie said smugly. "Berndt Toast promised me he'd close up the roof."

"That's not what I told you to do," Driver Chris chastised him.

"Do you want me to go back?" the driver-in-training asked.

"It will be done by the time you get there," the lead driver spat.

"Oh good," spouted the trainee mindlessly.

The water in the lake was shallow for a long distance from shore, and Irish Joyce suggested that we have a chicken fight.

Juliano squatted down for the clean-shaven Mountain Girl, and she slipped smoothly into position on his shoulders. She was so much fun compared to the Peruvian who wanted no part of our escapades. Chicken Jim picked up Australian Sheila in her tiny-weenie-red-bikini. More teams formed. I quickly asked British Sue, "Will you be my partner?" She nodded, so I crouched down for her to get on my shoulders. With my head sandwiched between her bare thighs, I stood up and struggled to keep my balance. She extended her legs out before us to help steady us. Driver Chris crouched down to accommodate Fräulein Vera on his shoulders, and we all laughed hysterically when she complained about his beard tickling her thighs. It was great to see him in such a good mood.

Chicken Jim and Australian Sheila were the first to attack. She shouted, "Get them!" as he ran toward Driver Chris and Fräulein Vera. He quoted Pink Floyd, "Look mummy, there's a little plane up in the sky." Then he made the sound of a diving aircraft and swooped in for the attack. Australian Sheila leaned back at the moment of impact and braced her legs like battering rams.

Fräulein Vera put her hands out to push her, but the Aussie's long legs jousted her right off Driver Chris' shoulders, sending her screaming backwards into the lake. She cursed in German when she came up for air, but she got right back on her mount. Chicken Jim then strutted around with the Aussie on top, counting coup. He sang the rest of his Pink Floyd tribute to her, "Vera! Vera! What has become of you?"

That was when British Sue yelled, "Get him!" I began chasing the driver-in-training around, but Fräulein Vera beat me to it. She came up from behind them and pushed them right over. We laughed and laughed as the war went on.

The whole time Guitar Johnny watched from the sidelines immersed up to his midsection chain smoking. Judging from his reactions, we must have looked hilarious slam-dancing naked, playing chicken in Lake Michigan. "That was g... g... g... great fun!" he stuttered while we were getting dressed.

The sun was on its way to setting and we would need its light to find our way back to the bus. We dressed in a hurry and Driver Chris led the group back toward the bus. On the walk back he told us all about the great music and nightlife in the university district of Chicago. A short walk through the woods from the bus brought us to the shower rooms where we prepared for a night out in the city with blues music and cheap beer.

8
The Chicago Blues

At some point on the two-hour drive into Chicago I had drank enough beer to necessitate the use of the pee funnel for the first time. After the laughter ebbed, I stood up in the stairwell and scowled at the Chicago skyline to the west. It all seemed grey to me, the sky, the buildings, the fate of millions of souls bound together in such proximity. When the bus pulled off the highway at the exit for the University of Illinois at Chicago, the abundance of neon lights made things much more colorful, and all the hype about the Chicago Blues started to make more sense. The sidewalks were crowded with young people headed in all directions. Big groups, small groups, pretty girls, hot guys, black people, white people, Asian people, crazy people, you name it. This was clearly a multicultural hub with an amazing nightlife.

Driver Chris parked in the designated spot near the Chicago Greyhound station on South Halsted Street a few minutes after nine o'clock. Big Dave claimed to know the owner of the best blues club in the area. He had worked there as a bouncer back in the day, so we agreed to go with him to check it out.

Several of the girls tried to convince Flip-flop to come with us, but she insisted on staying behind because she could not afford it. A few of us guys offered to buy her drinks, but she said she did not want to owe us any favors. So, we said our goodbyes to Flip-flop.

Before we left Peruvian Ursula spoke to her traveling companion in Cantonese. Driver Chris assured her that he would be fine. She handed him the baseball cap, and we headed out as a group to the clubs on the campus of UIC. The short Chinese man walked behind me in front of Peruvian Ursula. Jewels and Yülia walked and talked with him the entire time. They asked him the standard questions,

The Chicago Blues

if he liked America. Of course, he did. How long he had been here? Three weeks. Have you been to Chicago before? He had performed at the Chicago Symphony Orchestra.

They talked about the places he visited around the world, of which there were many. When they asked about his family, he revealed that his wife and two sons were waiting for him in San Francisco. His English was fair at best, so they ended up doing the majority of the talking. He was friendly enough with hello how are kind of interactions, but I could tell much of the details of American English were lost on him, not to mention Yülia's English with a German accent. He asked Yülia a few questions about Germany, like where she was from. She was from Dusseldorf. He asked her what she was studying in college. She was going for biotechnology.

Juliano strutted like a rock star walking with a hot Irish twin on each arm. Mountain Girl was not talking to him anymore, because he was such a flirt and he seemed otherwise enthralled with the Peruvian girl.

We stopped to listen to a trio of street performers playing the blues for tips at the entrance to a schoolyard. The leader fingered his way through the three-bar blues with amazing skill on an electric guitar plugged into a small battery-operated PA. The other front man played a harmonica with both hands wrapped around a mic amplified on the same PA. This created a heavily distorted mix of old-school blues. Behind them sat the one-man rhythm section banging on a pair of five-gallon bucket drums. Our group dropped some change and a few dollars into the open guitar case and moved on with Big Dave in the lead.

We walked past several bars with live music, occasionally stopping to listen from the sidewalk. Some of our passengers wanted to go inside one of the clubs. The place was hopping with a line out the door. A bouncer was checking IDs behind a velvet rope. We found out there was a show, but the cover was outrageous, so we kept moving. Big Dave reassured us that there would be no cover at his friend's bar where he was leading us.

When we arrived at the House of Blues, a bouncer stood outside checking IDs and collecting a ten-dollar cover. Most of us were too poor to be interested in paying a cover just to enter a club no matter how good the music promised to be. The bouncer agreed to let Big Dave go inside to find his friend. Yülia did not have a fake ID, so that dampened our spirits too. The Old-Growth-Hippie came back outside with the club owner wearing a big smile. He remembered his former bouncer on sight. Admittedly, Big Dave was hard to forget.

The appearance of the club owner filled us with hope and excitement that we might get in for free. So, we greeted Big Dave's friend warmly. The guys all shook his hand and several of the girls greeted him with a hug and a kiss on the cheek. This warm welcome did the trick. The velvet rope was raised, and we all filed inside. Yülia was admitted under the promise that she was the designated driver.

The club was dark and homey, like no bar I had ever seen. The whole place was furnished like a wealthy person's living room with couches and lounge chairs set up around coffee tables with Oriental carpets on the floor. Candles burned in decorative sconces on the side walls, where artwork and paintings hung over antique end tables. I felt like I was in a bordello or a place where men in robes smoked cigars. This was a high-end place. The music was rocking, and it was exciting just to be there.

The owner led us past the bar through a pair of dark red velvet curtains into the main music hall where a small stage stood over a recessed dancefloor. The area was corralled on three sides by railings lined with tall tables. The fifteen of us stationed ourselves around three high-tops along the railing to the right of the stage. The bar behind us had tall leather armchairs with tassels dangling off the arms. Across the room a row of five reserved alcoves sat unoccupied with ice buckets on each table. Most of us had never been to a place with bottle service.

The owner reminisced with Big Dave briefly, then a waiter arrived. "I'd like to introduce you to my old friend Dave," he said, throwing his arm around the big man. "He bounced for me in the early eighties." The young man shook hands with the big man.

"What can I get you to drink sir?"

The owner of the club spoke up for him, "Dave says his friends like cheap beer." We all cheered. He was all smiles. "Give them dollar draft beers until midnight," he instructed. Now there was a huge cheer. At a dollar apiece we could all afford to get drunk.

"That gives us two and a half hours to drink as much as possible," said Mother Michelle. She stepped forward with a twenty-dollar bill held between her crossed fingers and said, "I got the first round."

Big Dave was not having it. "Put your money away, he told her. "I've got it."

"How many would you like?" asked the waiter.

The big man looked around at the fifteen of us and answered, "As many as we can get!"

The waiter took the bill and said, "Twenty beers coming right up!" This brought on the biggest cheer yet. Big Dave was the hero of the moment in Chicago.

It was still early, but we brought such a large group of rowdy people into the club that we were the center of attention. A zydeco band was jamming when we arrived, but they cleared the stage after

The Chicago Blues

only a few songs, making way for the headlining blues band. We move the three tables together and sucked down the first twenty beers. As soon as Mother Michelle's beer was gone, she held twenty dollars over her head and ordered another round. A few beers remained unclaimed and she sucked another one down while she waited.

As soon as the blues band took the stage the Green Tortoise passengers started cutting loose on the dancefloor. The foreign girls were so much fun. They did not need to be intoxicated to let it all hangout. It was amazing. I had never experienced live blues. The band opened with Muddy Waters, "I'm Your Hoochie Coochie Man."

> The gypsy woman told my mother
> Before I was born
> I got a boy-child's comin'
> He's gonna be a son-of-a-gun
> He's gonna make pretty women's
> Jump and shout
> Then the world gonna know
> What this all about
>
> Don't you know I'm here
> Everybody knows I'm here
> Well, you know I'm the hoochie-coochie man
> Everybody knows I'm here
>
> I got a black cat bone
> I got a mojo too
> I got John the Conqueror
> I'm gonna mess with you
> I'm gonna make you girls
> Lead me by my hand
> Then the world'll know
> The hoochie-coochie man

Chicken Jim kept trying to dance with Fräulein Vera, but she kept stomping on his feet with her hiking boot every time he tried to shimmy up to her. He smirked fondly each time her heel landed on its mark. It was hilarious and painful to watch. If toe pain was her way of expressing her true love for him, they were destined to be together.

Big Dave did not drink, but the bar served food like a restaurant until midnight, so he sat with Berndt Toast, Yülia and Jewels at a regular dinner table in the adjacent room. They devoured burgers and fries while the rest of us danced and drank.

Mother Michelle pounded her third beer and ordered a shot of tequila. "This is the first time in weeks I've been able to cut loose without having to worry about Josh," she quipped, knocking back the shot. "I promised Josh a really fun trip after his father died," she revealed, "but the trip turned out to be way too expensive. She sipped her fourth beer every few words, leaving behind lipstick stains. "We ended up coming east on the southern trip with Chicken Jim, Chris and Brian," she explained. She became increasingly popular after revealing this to the other passengers, and they listened intently to her tell wild stories about the previous trip.

Evidently, the passengers on her first trip liked to get naked. They went skinny-dipping every single day except the day they went to New Orleans. To rectify this the passengers found a public fountain to swim in, right in downtown New Orleans. She proudly displayed a photograph of about thirty Tortoise passengers posing naked in the fountain in the middle of Spanish Plaza. A second picture showed them swimming and lounging like it was a Roman bath.

Michelle looked disconcerted for a moment. "Sometimes I'm afraid that Josh is seeing too much too fast." I could sense a trifle of frustration in her voice and a slight slur in her speech. She smiled at us all, "He sure has a lot of stories." She seemed lost in thought for a moment, as she looked for a cigarette. "I usually don't smoke," she said, as she lit up. She blew a smoke ring and took another drink of her beer. "Josh knows I smoke weed, but if he saw me smoking cigarettes, he would be so angry. He really cares about me. Especially since his father died."

Maid Marian empathized with her, "I think Josh is a really right-on kid. He seems smart enough to handle the truth. I'm sure he knows he can come to you with questions, right?"

"Questions," Mother Michelle exclaimed, "fuck, he has a lot of questions!" She exhaled a blue funnel cloud of smoke above her head. I ordered the next round of beer. I was psyched that it only cost me ten dollars. Mother Michelle gave me a sexy look when I handed her a fresh beer. I must not have been the only one she eye-fucked for a drink. This middle-aged black man came over and offered to buy her a cocktail. She showed him her beer and said, "I'll take a shot." She followed him over to the bar and spoke with him for a few minutes.

"She's going to get herself in trouble if she's not careful," Guitar Johnny predicted.

"Leave her alone," chastised British Sue. "She's having fun."

"She's clinging to that unsuspecting punter like a limpet on a rock," he argued. His instincts were right. I shadowed him while he went over to break it up in case there was an issue. He had to pry her off the man and reel her back to our table. She told us that he asked

The Chicago Blues

her back to his place, so we formed a circle around her to keep him and his free cocktails at arm's length.

Guitar Johnny and I went on a walk to explore the rest of the bar. Much to our delight, we discovered a second stage behind one of the black curtains in a room furnished with couches. The room was gorgeous, like a parlor in a mansion. Our ears drew our eyes to the amazing woman on stage. She was of grand proportion, buxom, in a blue dress, belting out the Chicago Blues. These were sounds I had never heard nor could ever have imagined. We decided to get the others and come back, maybe we could get a couch or an alcove.

Back in the other room, Johnny enthusiastically informed the group. "Right in the next room," he told them, "there's a middle-aged ball breaking Mama belting out 100% filth in front of a seriously kicking little outfit."

See what I've been saying," I whispered to British Sue. "I told you he was cool."

"Who," she asked.

Guitar Johnny!" I spat with a laugh. "Did you hear what he just said?"

She gave me a look like I was dumb for asking and said, "He was going on about some filthy woman in a nice outfit breaking his bullocks in the other room."

****

Suddenly, there was a commotion by the curtain to the barroom. The bouncer was leading an obtusely convex pregnant woman by the arm. "Can one of you help her into the bathroom please," he called out to the waitresses. "I have to stay on the door." The waitresses just stood there looking dumb like this was not in their job description and they did not know what to do. A few female customers stirred in conversation, but no one stepped up.

The Irish Twins eyed each other and rushed over to help. Fräulein Vera followed them with Maid Marian close behind. The twins took the woman by the arms and headed toward the ladies' room.

The black woman in her mid-thirties suddenly stopped and doubled over in pain. "Oh lord Jesus!" she cried. "The baby's comin.'" She held the Irish girls' arms like railings as she contended with the deep contraction.

I moved closer to see if I could help.

"What's your name?" asked Irish Kyrah.

"Leena," said the woman in a huff of painful breath.

"Nice to meet you Leena," she said. "I'm Kyrah. We can help you if you let us."

"I'll take all the helps I can get right about now," she floundered.

"We're midwives they said in one voice together. "We can help you."

"Praise the lord Jesus," she proclaimed. "What you on girl?" she asked them.

"Do you think you need an ambulance?" asked the dirty redhead.

"I am not folding," Leena assured them. "I don't need no ambulance. I just needs to catch my breath and rest up a bit, then I'll be on my way."

"How far along are you?" asked Irish Joyce, taking command of the situation.

She struggled through the rest of the contraction and informed her, "I'm 39 weeks and one day today." They continued to hold her arms as she shuffled her feet toward the back of the bar, panting out of breath.

"When did the contractions start?" she asked her.

"They's been goin' on for some time now," she revealed. "I knew I 'ad to get out the jam, so I started walking to the hospital, so I'd be close when the time comes."

"You were walking to the hospital?!" asked Irish Kyrah sympathetically.

"It ain't far now. Only 'bout a couple blocks. I thoughts I could get there," she said, "but the contractions came on quick."

"How close are the contractions?" asked the dirty-blond sister.

"They've been coming back to back for the last couple of blocks," revealed the woman.

There was a jog in the wall inside the ladies' room but there was no outer door.

Before they entered Fräulein Vera told the twins, "You will tell me what to do."

"Go get a chair," Irish Joyce directed her.

I jumped to get one. She came out, I passed it to her, and she brought it inside.

Maid Marian asked the bouncer, "Is there a telephone close by? We may need to call for an ambulance."

"There's a phone in the back," the muscular man told her. "Just let me know and I'll have the bartender make the call."

"Thank you," she said. "I'll let you know in just a second." She followed Fräulein Vera into the bathroom. A few moments later she came out and calmly shouted to the bouncer, "We need an ambulance. Her water broke."

The bouncer left his post and called to the bartender across the room, "We need an ambulance," he shouted. "We've got a pregnant woman ready to pop. Call the Boys in Blue!" The bartender rushed through the kitchen door behind the bar. Lots of curious people were moving toward the ladies' room, so I took position by the door before the crowd gathered.

When he returned Maid Marian asked the bouncer, "Do you have an emergency blanket so we can wrap her up?"

"I don't think so," the bouncer admitted with a furrowed brow.

"How 'bout a tablecloth?" she suggested.

"I can do that," he said, turning on his heels.

She went inside and I heard her say, "The ambulance is on the way."

Irish Joyce's commanding voice echoed in the tiled bathroom. "Vera love, would you turn off the tap for me. I don't want to touch it now that my hands are clean?"

When the woman contracted in pain again, she started crying.

"Don't be worried Leena," I heard Irish Kyrah tell her. "We're going to get you to the hospital. We'll stay with you until help arrives."

"I'm not worried," the woman said. "I've been through this before. I'm just coppin' a personal. Ah! I told my man I didn't want any more babies, but he kept ridin' me. Woo wap da bam." She wailed in pain with another contraction. "It's happening!" she trilled. "I think I needs to lie down. This baby seems determined to come out right now."

"We need you to sit down for a minute while we have a look," Irish Joyce let her know the plan.

Maid Marian came out and said, "They seem to have it under control."

The bar owner came out of the back and rush toward us with a fat stack of white bar rags and black folded tablecloths. "They've been freshly laundered," he told us.

He handed them to Maid Marian, and she bolted inside the bathroom.

"I needs to lay down girl," Leena insisted. "I can't have a baby in no chair."

"Let's have a look see first, love. We'll be able to tell how far along you are. May I have a look?" There was silence. "She's super anterior," Irish Joyce informed them, "I'd call it a good eight centimeters."

"Oh God!" Leena shrieked with a contraction. "It's coming soon! It's coming soon!" I could hear her moaning and sucking for breath. "I feel pressure in my hips."

"She might not make it to the hospital," Joyce prognosticated. "She's closer to ten centimeters. Maybe we should get her into position on the floor. Let her get comfortable until they arrive."

"I'm with you on that," Leena agreed.

"Help me spread this out," said Maid Marian.

"Put some of those towels under her head," Instructed Irish Joyce.

"Oh Lord," cried the woman again. "I wants to push," she informed them.

"She's already presenting," said Irish Joyce.

"Scheisse," gasped Fräulein Vera.

"Help will be here soon if you can hold on," Irish Kyrah prodded.

"I don't think I can wait. I'm gonna push," she announced.

"Go ahead and push," instructed Irish Joyce. There was silence. "Just like that keep going! Keep going! Good! Good! Good!"

The woman gasped and howled in pain.

"That's it darling, well done," she spoke in a strong Irish brogue. "The baby's crowning. You're gonna feel that. Lots of pressure. Lots of pressure."

"I feels like I'm on fire!" Leena screamed like a train whistle.

"Good job Leena! Good job! We're making progress!" Irish Kyrah coached. "You're gonna feel lots of pressure. That tissue's got to stretch. It's gonna hurt as long as the head sits right there, okay?"

The woman was blowing out and sucking wind hard between contractions.

"You can do this," coached the redhead. "You're doing great."

The woman breathed audibly while she rested.

"Why don't you go ahead and try pushing again just like we did before, okay?"

"Deep breath now. Here it comes," said the redhead.

"Grab hold of your legs," her partner instructed.

"Are you ready?"

"Here we go!"

"Push really hard Leena!"

"Come on Leena!" prodded her partner.

"There you go. There you go," Irish Kyrah coached her.

"Push! Push! Push! One! Two! Three! Four! Push! Push! Push!" Irish Kyrah coerced.

"Five! Six! Seven! More! More! More! Eight! Nine! Ten!"

The woman gasped for breath and shrieked in pain.

"Deep breath, now! Long and hard! Breathe! Let's do it again. Deep breath. Long and hard. Breathe!"

"Where the hell's that ambulance?" shouted Maid Marian.

Fräulein Vera came out to see.

"The bouncer's waiting on the curb," I told her, and she went back inside.

"Ready? One! Two! Three! Push! Push! Push! Breathe! Breathe! Breathe! Push! Push! Push!"

"Good job!" the redhead cheered her on.

"Come on Leena! That-a-girl! Five! Six! Seven! Breathe! Breathe! You can do it! Eight! Nine! Ten!"

"Ah!" she screamed.

"Come on Leena. You can do it!" Irish Kyrah coached her. "Give it everything you've got this time. Breathe! Breathe! One! Two! Three! Four! Breathe! Breathe!"

"Push with everything you have," coached Irish Joyce.

"Five! Six! Seven! Eight! Nine! Ten! Breathe! Breathe!"

"Try not to dig your elbows into the floor?" Joyce's lovely brogue recommended.

"Okay," the patient gasped in a forced breath.

"Pass me more towels Vera. Help me pad her elbows."

"Use your bottom Leena," Joyce's voice encouraged. "Push from your bottom. Breathe! Breathe!"

"You're doing so good. It's right there."

She was clearly in agony trying to breathe through the pain. "Should I push again?" asked Leena.

"You're a strong one," Irish Kyrah praised. "If you can push, yes. If you have the energy, that would be smashing. Do you feel like you can?"

She must have borne down because Irish Kyrah coached, "Push! Push! Push!"

Irish Joyce advised, "Grab behind your legs. Use your butt. Lots of pressure. One! Two! Three! Four! Five! Six!"

A high piercing scream resounded in the tiled room.

"Yes! Here it comes! Yes! Push Leena push!" Irish Kyrah's voice titillated with joy. Yes! Push! Push! Here it comes. Give me one more tiny little push, Leena."

"Oh Leena. It was brilliant," Irish Joyce praised.

"Is the baby out?" Leena wondered.

"Yeah, the head is out," Irish Joyce informed her. "Just wait for the next contraction. That was brilliant."

Irish Kyrah was overjoyed. "Good job Leena. It's coming now! Push! Push!"

"Get that baby out! Ready? One! Two! Three! Four! Five! Six! Breathe! Breathe!"

"Oh Leena, there he is!" The redhead's voice was giddy with joy and light that could bring hope to all of humanity. The sounds of a baby squawking echoed from within. This was followed by a series of sweet joyful sighs. When we heard the baby crying all those gathered cheered outside the ladies' room door.

"Oh, Leena congratulations!" Irish Kyrah laughed with bubbling joy. "It's a boy!" She sniffled and laughed again joyously. "Ahh! He's so beautiful," she gushed. She kept laughing with blissful sobs and a sniffle. "Breath now. Just keep breathing," she coached. "Oh, ho, ho Leena! Oh, ho, ho, ho! You did so good Leena."

Are you okay darling?" asked Irish Joyce.

"I'll be fine. How's my baby?" asked the woman.

"Oh! He's a darlin,'" Irish Joyce told her. "He's beautiful! Do you want to see him, Leena? He's so beautiful! I'm going to put him on your chest, okay?"

I was crying so hard in the doorway that I could hardly see. A feeling of elation swept over the small crowd listening outside the door.

When the new mother met her baby for the first time. She said breathing out of breath, "Oh, my little man. Aren't you somethin' else? My my oh my! Would you look at him. I am so sorry. That must have been so hard for you. Oh, my lord, you're so beautiful! Thank you God. Thank God you ain't popped. You're so beautiful!" She spoke with the joy only a mother can know. "Oh, my goodness," she told the baby as they must have been wiping him down with bar rags. "Yes, we'll get all of that goop off of your face, off your eyes, yes, yes." The baby squawked but was not crying. It was such a wonderful moment.

"Does he have a name yet?" asked Irish Kyrah.

"Junior," Leena announced.

"Welcome to the World Junior," proclaimed Irish Kyrah. "That was a rough time for you little guy. We know. That was rough," she soothed the baby. "I bet you're wonderin' what the heck just happened?" She spoke to the baby in a sticky sweet high-pitched voice reserved for newborn babies. "Welcome to the world."

There was a titillation of pure joy in the restroom of the blues bar as the baby began to softly cry. "He's tiny," Leena observed. The baby squawked again. "Why is he so tiny? My belly was much bigger this time, bigger than when I had my first two."

"He is a bit small for 39 weeks," assessed Irish Joyce. "What did your doctor say?"

Leena responded flatly, "I don't have no insurance. I can't afford no fancy doctor. Last time I saw one was when I got tested for pregn't."

Maid Marian comforted the new mother. "He looks perfectly healthy to me," she observed.

"Who dat?" asked Leena.

"My name's Marian," she told her. "I'm a nurse."

"You gots a funny accent," said the belabored woman. "Where you from Maria?"

"I'm from South Africa dear."

"You hears that Junior? My lord! Mama found you two midwives and an African nurse in a barroom bathroom. That's a miracle, baby Junior. It's gonna be a good life for you. I promise. It's gonna be a good life. You's a miracle baby, Junior! You's a miracle baby!"

"Awe, he's so beautiful," marveled Irish Kyrah. "He's got nice big hands and such long fingers."

"His hair ain't lackin,'" Leena marveled with a laugh. "That's your daddy showing up there that is."

Maid Marian said, "I'll be right back." She came out and made the announcement, "She just delivered a baby boy." There was another cheer among the bystanders. "Where's that damn ambulance," she glowered.

"The bouncer is waiting out front," I reassured her.

"Ahh!" Leena screamed for dear life again. "Lord Jesus!" she proclaimed.

Maid Marian turned quickly to go back inside the ladies' room.

Irish Joyce tried to comfort Leena. "That's just afterbirth pain. It's your body's way of shedding the placenta and shrinking the uterus down to its original size."

"Ah!" Leena screamed for dear life again. "Listen girl. I've had two babies before this one and that ain't no afterbirth pain. I'm still having contractions."

Just then the bouncer pushed the door open with a bang and held it for the EMTs. "She's in the ladies' room," he informed them. "Straight ahead in the back."

A paramedic holding a medical box led the way, followed by two young men on either end of a rolling stretcher. "Clear a path, please!" the leader shouted. The crowd of Green Tortoise passengers and bar patrons staggered like penguins out of the way, stepping to either side of the door. I put my back against the wall at the opening.

"We'll have to leave the stretcher out here," he informed his men. The stretcher would not fit around the jog in the wall inside the ladies' room door, so they had to go inside without it. "Get a few more guys in here," he commanded before entering the bathroom with the first stretcher bearer. The other EMT paused outside and pressed the button on his collar radio. "All hands on deck!" he shouted.

"We've got a baby in here!" shouted the leader. "We're going to need everyone to clear the room, please."

Irish Joyce spoke up. "When the baby was delivered, he had a lot of mucus in his mouth and' down in his throat. He didn't really start cryin' at first, so I think the best course of action is to suction out his little airways."

"Thank you, Miss," the leader said. "We'll take it from here. We need suction!" he told his men.

Leena screamed again, "Ah!"

"Hello ma'am. I'm Lieutenant Murphy and this is Private Hendrix and that guy right there, he's called Rocket." He pointed at a young bronzed Italian fireman. "How are you feeling ma'am?"

"What's it matter how I feel? How's my baby?"

"Let's have a look then," he reassured her. "If you don't mind, I'm just going to examine your baby here for a minute."

Irish Kyrah came out of the ladies' room flushed in the face, wet in the eyes and gushing emotion. "The baby's here. I'm so excited. It's always so emotional. I cry every time. It's a miracle every time I see a baby being born. It's so neat. I'm so excited that he's here. That was so amazing. He's just so awesome."

I high fived her and hugged her. "You're amazing," I told her. Everyone rushed in for hugs and high-fives. Even some of the strangers reached out and touched her lovingly.

"Ah!" the new mother screamed again.

Irish Joyce came out as happy as if she had the baby herself. Her gruff exterior was gone. It had been replaced with a pure energy and revitalized spirit. She high-fived us all. We all cringed when Leena cried out in pain again. Irish Joyce cupped her hands around her mouth and yelled into the bathroom, "Breathe, Leena! Breathe!"

Two more EMTs entered the bathroom, so we all tuned in to listen.

"We're going to cut the cord so we can move you out of here and onto a stretcher," said the lieutenant. "Rocket will hold your baby until we get you in the ambulance."

"I promise I'll take good care of him ma'am," Rocket told her. A moment later Rocket came through the door holding the swaddled baby boy. We all got a quick look, but he moved toward the exit without stopping.

"Ah!" screamed Leena.

Irish Joyce cupped her hands around her mouth again and yelled, "Remember to breathe, Leena! Breathe!"

"Hold my hand," said Private Hendrix.

"I'm going to examine your belly now," Lieutenant Murphy forewarned her. "You'll feel a bit of pressure." There was a pause. "Stethoscope," he demanded. Another pause. "I've got a second heartbeat here. There's another baby."

"What you talkin' 'bout?" gasped Leena. "Are you frontin' your moves?"

"You're having twins," Lieutenant Murphy told her.

"Are you fuckin' treatin' me?" she exclaimed! "Another baby! For realz? How's that even possible?"

"We're going to lift you now, Leena," he informed her. "We'll have you outta here in no time."

"Ah!" she screamed again. We could hear her sucking wind, and breathing hard.

"One, two, three, lift!" instructed the lieutenant.

Two EMTs came backing out the bathroom door each holding a leg, followed by two more firefighters supporting Leena's back under each arm. Lieutenant Murphy cradled her head in his hands from behind. They put her gently on the stretcher and covered her with a sheet.

As they prepared to leave, Leena reached her hand out to Irish Kyrah. "Can you come with me," she asked her. "Will both of you come?" She asked Irish Joyce as she stepped up and took her hand.

"I'd love to, but we have a bus to catch," she responded.

"Ah!" She seethed in pain from another contraction.

Private Hendrix held her other hand during the contraction and said, "I'm sorry but they can't come in the ambulance ma'am. Only relatives can ride along." He addressed the twins. "You aren't relatives, are you?"

"We're her midwives." Irish Joyce displayed contempt.

Private Hendrix made eye contact with Lieutenant Murphy and said, "It's only a couple blocks." He looked at Irish Kyrah with puppy dog eyes. She sure looked pretty in the barroom light. The commander gave the nod of approval.

"Is it close enough to walk back here?" Irish Kyrah asked.

"It's only three or four blocks," Private Hendrix told her.

Irish Joyce spoke directly to Maid Marian. "Don't let Brian leave without us," she instructed.

"I wouldn't dare," she responded supportively.

"Let's go Leena," said Irish Kyrah. "Breathe for me, Leena! breathe!"

The stretcher rolled, and they all left together. We were stunned. In a moment they were gone.

****

The remaining Tortoise passengers returned to our tables were Maid Marian offered to buy the next round. She handed the waitress a twenty-dollar-bill and ordered, "Beers for everyone!" The waitress came back with a helper and delivered twenty more beers. At one point the zydeco band gave a shout out to the Green Tortoise. As if possessed by B.B. King himself, the bandleader summed it up. "Lord have mercy, you Green Tortoise people sure can dance."

Peruvian Ursula was the hottest ticket on the dancefloor. She shook her voluptuous rump with a vivacious Latin-spirit. All of us guys tried to dance with her, but it was more like we were swaying beside her and around her because her moves were so exotic. The Brazilian guy tried his best to keep up, but even he could not do justice to her swiveling hips. PAC-MAN remained seated at the table where she could see him the entire time. He had changed into a flannel shirt and he was still wearing his new baseball hat, despite the heat in the sweltering bar.

I danced to the Chicago Blues with British Sue until I was soaking wet. As we left the dance floor, she backed me up against the railing for a sloppy kiss out of sight of her friend. We hit it off conversationally, as far as I could tell from her shouting. Even though I had just met her yesterday, I felt a connection developing.

"You don't smoke do you?" she asked.

"No," I answered.

"I only smoke when I drink," she told me. "Do you want to step outside while I pull a fag?" Having lived in London, I knew that this meant she intended to smoke a cigarette. I had recently quit smoking menthols again, so I let he go outside alone. I took a seat at the table where I shouted conversation back and forth with Mother Michelle. English Tessa stood close to us struggling to listen without saying a word.

Guitar Johnny took the opportunity to chat with PAC-MAN. The Chinese man's English was fair, but his little voice was hard to hear in the noisy bar. I leaned in to listen after I heard him shout, "I'm a classical musician."

"Oh! You're a professional musician," retorted the Englishman. "Doesn't that take the biscuit."

PAC-MAN nodded and said, "I travel around the world with the Hong Kong Chinese Orchestra."

He was impressed. "What do you play?" he asked.

The Chicago Blues

"My proficiency is with the flute."

"Oh, I love to listen to the flute," he revealed, "but I'm gormless when it comes to playing the woodwinds."

"My spouse plays a number of traditional Chinese instruments, like the Erhu."

"The Erhu?" questioned the Englishman.

"It's a bowed instrument!" he shouted over the din.

"I didn't realize your wife is in the orchestra. That must be nice," commented the Guitar Player. He peered around the room and on the dancefloor. "Where's your friend?" he asked. Peruvian Ursula was nowhere to be seen.

"She's dancing," Pak informed him.

"I'm very interested in hearing more about your music career, but it's really hard to hear in here," he told the Chinese man in the Toledo hat. He shouted, "I'm going out to have a smoke. Would you like to join me outside?" Guitar Johnny gave Jewels and Yülia a wide-eyed look and the three of them led PAC-MAN away.

Two minutes later Peruvian Ursula returned to the table and asked, "Where's Mr. Chan?"

"Who?" asked Mother Michelle.

"You know who," she answered curtly. "My friend, where is he?"

"Maybe he's cutting loose on the dancefloor," suggested Mother Michelle.

The Peruvian looked around the bar in a panic. "Did anyone see where he went?" She looked at me suspiciously. I shook my head. "Will somebody check to see if Pak is in the bathroom?"

Berndt Toast said, "I have to go. I'll check when I'm in there."

When he returned empty-handed, she really started to panic. She frantically walked around doing a circuit of the whole bar. She came back furious. "I find it hard to believe, nobody saw where my friend went," she said, scowling at me.

"He'll do fine," consoled Mother Michelle.

"You don't understand," she told her. "Pak knows not to walk off like this. I'm afraid something bad has happened to him." I walked around pretending to search, but of course I knew he was outside talking with the girls. I needed to buy them more time.

British Sue came back to the table smelling like smoke. I tried to stop her with a wide-eyed look of concern, but she did not realize what was going on, and she spilled-the-beans. "Pak outside with the black girl and the little German lass, catching a breath of fresh air, love."

"Damn it!" exclaimed the Peruvian. "When was this?"

"Just now," responded the Brit.

"I knew they were up to something," spat the debutant.

"Who?" I asked, playing dumb.

"The two Julies," she snapped. "I'm going out to find Pak. If he shows up back here will you tell him to stay put?"

"Sure," I said.

She grabbed her purse and went outside to search the streets. A few remarks were exchanged between the British girls and Mother Michelle about how this was strange, but no one had a clue what was going on, so I started explaining what the two Julies had seen at the rest stop east of Toledo.

"It's rather lovely out," British Sue said to me. "We should step outside for a snog."

"Let's wait till she comes back," I told her. "I don't want to miss this."

A few minutes later British Sue pulled me onto the dancefloor for a slow song. Her feet followed mine around in a tight circle as I held her close. When the song ended, she pulled my sweaty hand and led me off the dancefloor.

English Tessa had gone to the ladies' room with a few of the other ladies.

"We can't wait all night," she pressed me.

"Do you Fancy a snog?" I teased.

"I thought you'd never ask," she said with a huff.

I locked eyes with her romantically. "Do you want to go back to the bus?" I asked her coyly.

"Do you promise to be a nice bloke," she shouted, squeezing my fingers. I nodded. "Let's go before Tessa gets back." She slung her purse over her shoulder and headed for the door. I lifted my chin to Guitar Johnny on my way out. He looked surprised to see me leaving. British Sue and I stepped outside into the Chicago night. Peruvian Ursula and the others were gone.

The mood on the street on the campus of UIC was exceptionally lively, like Greenwich Village, New York. The abundance of neon, streetlights and traffic signals obscured the stars and moon, but it was still romantic. The artificial light brought the city to life, like the bouncing blue light of a heart monitor in a dark room. We held hands and talked intimately on our journey back to the bus.

While we waited in a crowd at a crosswalk, I held British Sue in my arms from behind to keep her warm in the brisk wind. She asked me, "What's your deepest darkest secret?"

I felt I could trust her, so I quietly whispered my story in her ear. "I was touched inappropriately by my friends' older brother when I was twelve," I revealed. "He got us drunk, showed us porn and I woke up with him touching me."

"Crikey!" she spit. "That must 'ave been a sideways pill." She stepped away from me and turned around fast to look me in the eyes. "You're not a poof, are you?" she asked.

"No!' I shook my head incredulously.

"Well good," she smiled. "I wouldn't want to be budging up the wrong tree."

"Don't worry about that," I reassured her with a crooked smile. I was starting to regret trusting her so readily.

"So, did you twat him over the head?" she asked.

"What?" I said dumbly.

"Did you haul off and whack the bloke?" she wanted to know.

"No." I shook my head thoughtfully. "I'm not sure that would have made things any better or different."

"What'd you tell your parents?" she pressed.

"I never told anyone until I was in therapy in college," I revealed. "I was so ashamed. I repressed it for years."

The light turned and we started walking. She turned her head to make sure I could hear her. "You're obviously not repressing it anymore," she observed, "but I'm not sure that's the kind of thing you ought to be spreading around town."

"So, what's your deepest darkest secret?" I asked her with incredulity.

She stopped on the opposite curb where we needed to cross again and said, "I was just going to tell you that I've never cheated on my boyfriend before, so I'm feeling a bit off."

"Okay," I said. "I can dig that."

"Ta," she said in a whisper. "Just don't tell Tess. She's dating my brother. If she spies us for sure it will get back to him."

Back at the bus British Sue said, "I need to scrub my chicklets," and she went in to get her toothbrush.

I found my toothbrush and waited for her outside while I brushed.

I found PAC-MAN sitting on the curb alone. "Ursula was looking for you I told him.

"I figured as much," he said solemnly.

"Good luck with that," I consoled him.

Driver Brian was awake talking with Driver Chris by the front bumper.

I overheard the grieving driver say, "If my sister didn't take the phone away from my dad, I would have hung up on him again."

"Fuck dude," said the big blond co-driver.

I approached them with a lift of my chin.

Driver Chris acknowledged me with his eyes. "My father is such a fucking prick," he lamented. "He's always thought my job is meaningless, but now he's insisting that I should walk away from it, like I can just do that willy-nilly whenever I want."

"I'm sure the Tortoise will understand if you have to leave," the Californian told him. "If you need to go you should go."

"I told you man." He shook his head as he spoke. "I'm not going anywhere near my father when he's being like this, unless I absolutely have to."

"I understand man," his friend related.

"My sister wants me to come home too. She thinks I should say goodbye before my brother dies. If my father knew she agreed with him, it would send him over the top thinking that he's right."

"Is that the sister that thinks you're gay because you live in San Francisco?"

"Yup! That's her. I call her the Church Lady," he laughed. "She told me I should never be alone with her kids because I smoke pot and she wouldn't want to have to explain me to them."

"You don't even smoke weed," his partner observed with a shake of his head.

"I have smoked weed in the past," he confessed.

"As if you don't have enough going on right now, right?"

"Well, she may be holier than thou, but if it wasn't for her, I'd already be home by now, on account of my mother."

"If you end up going home, you're going to have to deal with your father either way." His co-driver shrugged. "Maybe it's best to patch things up over the phone now, so the rest of your family doesn't have to deal with it later. Especially your mother. You kind of owe it to her right?"

"I owe her the world," he confirmed. "She's always protected me from him."

"Maybe it's your turn to return the favor," Driver Brian suggested.

Driver Chris has a look of consternation. "Maybe so," he responded finally.

"How is she managing through all of this?" Driver Brian asked.

"She hasn't left the hospital since they brought him in," he told his friend. "The other firemen are doing four-hour shifts, looking out for her twenty-four hours a day."

"That's amazing," his partner cheered.

"I feel a lot better knowing there's a fireman by her side twenty-four-seven, when I can't be there myself."

"Firemen look out for their own, that's for sure," he remarked.

"Fuck they do," he said flatly. "Every one of them has pledged to cover a shift for my brother, so he doesn't miss a paycheck while he's laid-up."

"That's amazing," his partner reiterated.

British Sue came outside and started brushing her teeth. The way she scrubbed them with her toothbrush made her look like a rabid animal with foam spewing in a rim around her mouth. She came to my side when she was ready to go. She looked at Driver Chris standing there and asked, "How's your brother?"

"I'll be making an announcement," the Irishman informed her. "Suffice to say, I'm sticking around."

"Spot on," she said.

When Peruvian Ursula arrived back at the bus, she tore into her Asian friend like a Cantonese banshee. Her outburst made a scene on the sidewalk, causing both passengers and passersby to take exception.

Jewels stepped up and shouted, "Leave him the fuck alone!"

"Ya!" joined Yülia. "You have no right to yell at him like that."

"What gives you the right to run off with him?! You have no idea how worried I was!"

"He was with us the entire time," Jewels defended.

"We weren't going to let anything bad happen to him," added Yülia.

"We care about him," spat Jewels.

To which the Peruvian responded, "We don't need your help. Pak's safety is my responsibility. Leave us alone!" She went on and on. The two Julies were both such nice girls it was hard to listen to the authoritative woman berate and belittle them.

They tried to ignore her and walk away, but she chased them down with more angry words. The girls offered no more excuses and they hardly defended themselves. Whatever the Chinese man had said to them rendered them non-confrontational. Everyone was gossiping, but Jewels told them not to worry, everything was fine, and it was let go for the time-being. "If Pak doesn't want our help there's nothing we can do about it," she concluded.

****

British Sue went inside and climbed into the last bunk over the back platform. There was barely enough room for the two of us to fit up there, but it forced us close together, so that was cool. It was too hot to keep the covers over us, and Little Josh was sleeping under the dinette, so we had to be very discreet and keep quiet.

We lay there holding one another in an intimate way, whispering conversation in the relative privacy of the dark bus. The music was playing, and the sound of Chicago traffic was loud enough so that no one could really see us or hear us. After a few minutes of relaxing there, side by side, it seemed very natural to hold her in my arms.

British Sue turned over on her side and held me for a while. She seemed to be studying me. I could feel her sexual energy building and emerging through her body language. Her petite frame seemed even smaller in my arms. Her right arm found its way under my neck, and we were both perfectly comfortable with our faces inches apart.

Our conversation flowed on and on, without much effort like a canoe on a river. I could feel the heat and moisture of her breathing. I wanted to kiss her so badly, but I did not. I was waiting. I did not want the space between us to close just yet. I had a burning desire to throw myself into her fire, her breath had grown so hot, and the cool air of the night kindled the flames even higher.

In that moment we seemed as comfortable as two lovers who had known each other their entire lives. Our bodies had already worked their own magic, becoming an artwork of flirtation and infatuation, intertwined in such intricate comfort as to give the feeling of one body. Her face did not disappear as I closed my eyes and met her lips with mine. It only seemed to grow brighter in the moonlight of my mind.

But hold back we did the tidal wave of deeper passion. In doing so, we heightened the enjoyment of our long lovemaking kisses. Even the kisses became too much at times, leaving us breathless. Her blond hair felt like raindrops against my cheeks, as our lips crashed like soft cymbals of luxuriant sensation. The slow grindings of her hips solicited ancient rhythms from the skin of my drum, drumming her pelvic cadence against the taut flesh of my thigh. My one hand held her shoulder softly across the back, while the other traced the curve of her hip into the valley of bare skin beneath her blouse. Her body moved closer still, and the kissing became more intense and my hand made its way up her rib line.

My heart beat so strongly that I felt nervous from the pounding in my limbs. British Sue's breathing grew stronger, until her quiet, moaning breath broke the seal of our lips, escaping the circle of our solitude. We both broke off the kiss in the same instant and looked around the dark bus to see if anyone had heard her confession. The only passenger visible was Big Dave, lying on the converted dinette table bed. He winked at me and closed his eyes again, pretending to sleep.

The Chicago Blues

British Sue and I grabbed the top edge of the blanket with one hand and pulled it up over our heads, laughing softly like happy children. We embraced for a long time with happy smiles reflecting in each other's eyes. Looking into her face, I could see the soul of a child inside her heart; I wondered if she could see the same.

This time we kissed without restraint or fear of being discovered. British Sue rolled over on her back, pulling half my weight on top of her, and I ran my fingers through her hair and held her head with both hands while we kissed.

Again, the waves began to lap at the shores of her radiant beach. I could feel the moist heat through her shorts, and I reached down and traced up her inner thigh with my finger, not touching her shorts at first, but feeling her leg muscles tighten and her hips begin to rise. I liked her legs a lot and traced this trail several times as our tongues explored the source of each other's kiss.

Her breathing quickened again, and she took her mouth away from mine to draw a full breath of air, still breathing so close to my face that I could feel her panting softly between words. "It just feels so good." She looked around again nervously. "I don't think I can keep my voice down. I hope you don't misunderstand," she said.

I sat up on my elbow, pulling the blanket down from over our heads; the air was much cooler than under the covers. Nothing had changed. No one was looking.

We kissed again for a long time and I could feel her breathing quickened once again. This time, I felt her hand reach out to mine and she pulled my long fingers down to her crotch. When I tried to work her panties aside, she unbuttoned her shorts to help me.

We continued to kiss until she broke off the kiss and drew in a deep breath as she had a quiet shuddering orgasm. So, after another long sensual kiss, I asked her, "Would you like to make love?"

She gasped, "I can't be caught dogging with all these people about. Not that I'm opposed to a little rumpy pumpy. Besides, how do you know I'm not all fur coat and no knickers?"

Suddenly, all sorts of voices could be heard outside the bus. All the lights came on inside the cabin. The group was returning from the Blues Club. I pulled the covers over us again. British Sue buttoned her shorts and curled up with her head on my stomach. Juliano flopped down on the back platform, surrounded by rowdy drunk chatting ladies. He was in his glory. Mountain Girl sat off on the fringe looking disdainful. His affection for her was fickle at best.

When British Sue's friend came back, she saw us on the bunk together and gave her a knowing look. She whispered something in her ear before climbing up into her bunk.

While the passengers all piled onto the back platform, I heard a new voice among them that said, "Party on dudes!" A guy I had never seen before was hanging all over English Tessa. He wore intelligent-looking glasses and had hair like Woodstock from Peanuts. He caught me looking at him. He gestured toward British Sue and gave me a wink. "Party on dude!" he said again.

I gave him a dude wave and said, "Hey bro."

At first, I thought that this guy was some stowaway that English Tessa had picked up at the bar, but now I figured it out. He was the new passenger that was getting on in Chicago.

He asked English Tessa, "Where do you want to sleep?"

"I'll be kipping in this bunk with my mate," she answered with her hand on the bed rail.

"Is there room up there for me?" he asked her in an honest voice.

Both British Sue and English Tessa cracked up laughing.

"Get stuffed!" spat British Sue. "She's got a lad waiting for her at home. Tis me brother."

The new guy looked right at me in a very greathearted way and said, "It was worth a shot."

"I love it," I cheered. "It's like my mother always said, "It's better to ask than assume otherwise." He spoke with Tessa for a while as she prepared for bed. His English was great, and he had a cool Dutch accent. He spoke using lots of Americanisms like he was trying to be hip.

I said, "Hello."

The young curly-haired guy looked at me curled up with British Sue. He smiled knowingly and introduced himself. "I'm Mark from the Netherlands," he told me. I offered Mark my now vacant spot on the top bunk by my feet. He passed me my sleeping bag. "Everyone on the bus has a bus name," I told him. "Mine is Johnny Lovebus."

"My American friends call me Deutsche Mark," he told me.

"That's a great bus name," I offered. "Nice to meet you Deutsche Mark."

He seemed pleased. "Party on dude," he said with a laugh.

Before retiring for the night, Driver Chris called for our attention, standing next to the buddy seat. "Hey everybody," he shouted. "Listen up! It sounds like everyone had an enjoyable time tonight," he shouted. There was a bunch of hoots, hollers, and cheers. "I hope you all got a chance to listen to the Chicago Blues."

"It was super," shouted Jewels.

"Wunderbar," gushed Yülia.

"Spot on," agreed Guitar Johnny.

"I'm glad you liked it," he said. He waited for quiet.

I had to pee anyway, and I did not want to miss any part of this update, so I got down out of the bunk. The fortunate Brazilian tucked in for the night between Mountain Girl and Australian Sheila. I headed up the aisle to listen to Driver Chris' speech. The Miracle Conversion had already turned the front platform into a giant bed, so I had to tiptoe between reclined passengers.

"I got some grave news about my brother," Driver Chris continued solemnly. "Not to belabor the point, he slipped into a coma this afternoon."

"Oh shit!" blurted Peruvian Ursula from the seat behind the driver. A lot of consolations followed, so her outburst went unnoticed. She made big eyes, took a deep breath through her nose, and spoke with PAC-MAN in Cantonese.

Driver Chris continued in a loud voice. "The good news is that the trip goes on!" There was a muted cheer and a few high-fives. Due to the alcohol, the possibility of the trip ending had completely slipped my mind. British Sue and I shared a happy look.

"I told you so, mom." Little Josh's voice could be heard under the dinette.

"Don't want you to get your hopes up too much," Driver Chris warned us. He had to shout over the chatter. "Anything could happen at this point." There was near silence. "As for right now, Brian will be driving through the night. Tomorrow morning, we will be having breakfast on the Mississippi River."

The new Dutch passenger Mark had not been listening. He had no idea what was going on. "Are you sure you don't want to sleep with me, Tessa?" he asked in the gap of silence. There was a big laugh exaggerated by alcohol, but it got quiet again quickly.

"Like I was saying," he reiterated. "Things are not going well with my brother, so I'd like to share what I know about his condition, just to set expectations."

Maid Marian was seated in the first seat by the door and she reached out and squeezed sentiment into his fingers.

"He has what's called a traumatic brain injury. The surgery to remove pressure on his brain was successful, but now he's in a coma."

There was a gasp of sorrowful reactions and condolences as one would expect.

"Thank you," he said to those around him, making eye contact as he nodded and touched hands with passengers who leaned forward.

Yülia came forward and hugged him, then to a seat up close with Jewels. This type of thing went on until people started shushing each other because he was waiting to talk.

Maid Marian spoke up as it grew quiet. "Just so you know," she informed the grieving driver, "as far as brain injuries are concerned, a coma isn't the worst thing in the world."

Sir Gavin spoke up reassuringly, "A coma is the body's way of dealing with a brain injury."

Driver Chris asked him, "Are you doctors or something?"

"Not a medical doctor," he clarified. "I know just enough medicine to get me in trouble. I have a PHD in physical therapy," he explained, "but I see a lot of brain injury victims in my practice.

"I'm a nurse," responded Maid Marian. "Hopefully, the coma won't last long. If you'd like, we can talk about it later. Maybe Gavin can shed some light, at least lend an ear."

"Thanks," he said.

"You're welcome," she told him.

He began again. "The doctors said that this is not the kind of coma that can last forever like you see on TV. They expect him to wake up eventually. The doctors want to see how he does tonight, and they will make an assessment in the morning, but that does not mean that he's out of the woods yet. They told my family to prepare for the worst. They keep warning us that he could still die any minute. The next twenty-four hours are critical. Now you know as much as I do. I will call again in the morning and give you another update after breakfast. If you have any questions, please ask Brian. I'd rather not talk about it anymore. I need to get some sleep, so goodnight, everyone." He waved to us, patted his co-driver on the shoulder, squeezed Maid Marian's hand and started moving toward the back platform.

More condolences and hugs were shared on his way toward the driver's cabin. I was the last one he passed on this way into the driver's cabin. We made eye contact and I grimaced without a word. French Sandrine opened the driver's cabin door as he approached, he slipped inside and closed the door.

Flip-flop returned from the mean streets of Chicago with a hilarious story about her escapades. "I finally found my ID," she told the other girls. "I figured I could get one of the guys to buy me a drink or two, so I went out to find everyone, but I got horribly lost and I had no idea where I was going." She sighed with a big breath. "I was so upset I started crying," she reported.

The ladies sympathized with her with a series of coos and love sounds.

"I was standing in a crosswalk literally in tears and this vanload of guys pulled up and offered me a ride. So, I jumped in."

We all laughed. "Are you out of your mind taking a ride from strangers!" Mother Michelle admonished.

The Chicago Blues

"Hell no. It was lost and cold and they were so nice," she told us.

"Right on, eh," praised Mountain Girl.

"They asked me why I was crying and if I was okay, so I laid down my whole sob story about how I couldn't find my friends and that I didn't have any money to buy beer, and when they dropped me off just now, one of the guys gave me twenty bucks."

There were cheers and lots of laughter. Everyone then told her about the baby being born in the bathroom of the bar and how the Irish girls and Fräulein Vera had acted like heroes. Fräulein Vera shirked off the attention like it was no big deal, but everyone was still proud of her. She was worried sick that her birth coach girlfriends would make it back in time before the bus had to leave.

Everyone was present and accounted for except the Irish Twins. Driver Brian resolved to wait for one extra hour, but as time drew near Maid Marian and Fräulein Vera started pacing up and down the sidewalk, discussing contingency plans. I overheard Maid Marian ask the driver if he would let them take a cab to the hospital to find their friends.

Just then a fire engine pulled up and double parked alongside the bus with its lights flashing. The driver jumped out and started directing traffic around the vehicle on the narrow two-lane street. The massive red and white side door of the pump truck opened. Irish Kyrah was sitting in the high seat wearing a fireman's turnout coat.

Fräulein Vera screamed, "Hurrah!"

Maid Marian shouted, "They're back!"

People inside the bus rushed to the windows and a round of applause and cheers resounded. The red-headed Irish girl unbuckled herself and Private Hendrix took her by the hand and helped her down to the street. He climbed down beside her and turned back toward the door. Irish Joyce came forth next wearing her own fireman coat. She was graciously ushered out of the spacious cab by the Italian fireman known as Rocket. Like perfect gentlemen, the Boys in Blue helped the ladies take off the heavy jackets, and they tossed them into the truck.

The girls urged the firemen into the bus to have a look around. When they came up the steps they were greeted with another round of applause. They waved like rock stars and answered a barrage of questions. Both of Leena's babies were doing fine. The second baby was also a boy she named Buddy. The firemen did not stay long but they were a big hit with the ladies, and it was sad to see them go.

I lingered on the sidewalk as they said their goodbyes. Private Hendrix said, "We'll be sure to lose the paperwork on Leena's trip to the hospital, so she never gets charged."

"She'll never see a bill," added Rocket.

On cue the Irish girls each hugged their boy in blue. It was a picturesque and romantic moment despite the traffic noise, the obnoxiously bright city lights, and a busload of passengers watching out the bus windows a mere five feet away. The Irish Twins simultaneously looked up at the boys in a way that invited a kiss. Rocket bent over and pecked Irish Joyce on the lips. She flashed approval with her brilliant baby blues, and he closed his eyes on the blinding lights.

Irish Kyrah's blue-green eyes lit up like Hugh Hefner's Hot Tub, and Rocket's dark Italian eyes popped open like a fish, ready to jump in. Like a kid in a swimming pool, I had to avert my eyes lest they get wet from the splash.

Irish Kyrah went inside the bus and took the buddy seat where Driver Brian proceeded to chat her up. He was clearly impressed with the twin's heroic delivery. "Someone said you're planning to open some kind of shelter for pregnant women?" he asked her.

"Yes," she answered. "That's the plan, when we get to San Francisco."

"That's wonderful," he praised. "Obviously, your good at it. I have friends in the city who do a lot of volunteer work," he offered. "I can put you in touch with them, if you like."

"That's a kindness," she gushed. "I'm akin to people who donate their time. It does so much more than money. Don't get me wrong. We need all the money we can get. Joyce thinks it's the most important thing, but I think giving precious time is even better. It opens your mind to the real issues and changes your perception. It creates a memory for you and everyone you help that lasts forever."

"You have a beautiful spirit," he praised her.

She glowed with light. "Chicago was fierce. Where are we off to next?"

"Right now, we drive through the night. Chris will be making crepes on an island in the middle of the Mississippi River tomorrow morning."

"Oh, I love crepes," she gushed. "What kind of crepes?"

"Every kind," he answered. "You'll have lots of choices. You make your own."

With that thought in mind, I headed for bed. Like so many Americans I had never seen the Mississippi River. When I climbed up into the bunk to cuddled-up with British Sue, I felt something moving by my feet, so I hung my head outside the bunk and strained to look. My new friend, the Dutchman, was climbing up into the bunk beside English Tessa. She caught me looking and put a finger to her lips. I made a face that said I would never tell. I nodded good luck to my friend and laid back next to British Sue. "We get to see the Mississippi River in the morning," I told her.

"Luvvly-jubbly," she said, as she closed her eyes and our lips met.

9
Breakfast on the Mississippi

I woke up a few minutes after sunrise. Little Josh had gotten up nice and early, making sure that his mother paid heavily for her night out drinking. She held her head as if it were a drippy eggshell. "Wake up mom, we're crossing the Mississippi River!" Mother Michelle tried to rise from her bed to see the water, but the yolk was dripping off the shell. She lowered her broken head with care; she was down for the count. Thanks to British Sue's premature evacuation from the Blues club, our eggs were intact.

I looked down the length of my body when someone touched my foot. English Tessa had one leg hanging off the bunk and she slipped down onto the back platform out of sight.

I watched British Sue lying there breathing softly, cuddled up with her head on my shoulder and her hand against my cheek. She opened her eyes and caught me looking. I brushed her hair from her brow with two fingers and kissed her softly on the forehead. She closed her eyes to go back to sleep and I left her with a sigh.

I felt surprisingly well-rested, so I went up to sit on the buddy seat next to Driver Brian. We had traveled across the entire state of Wisconsin in the middle of the night. Claiming to be "Experienced in 'matters of the bladder,'" the big blond driver pulled off I-90, near La Crescent Minnesota. "Hangovers prefer porcelain," he taught me. Many of the passengers were suffering from the Chicago Blues, and the Minnesota Welcome Center had running water and flushable toilets. It was encouraging the way he was always trying to help me learn how to

Breakfast on the Mississippi

be a good Green Tortoise Driver, even though I knew the chances of that happening were slim to none.

Deutsche Mark and I met up in the men's room in front of the mirror while brushing our teeth. He addressed me with a good-natured wink and a foamy smile. He stopped brushing to say, "I'm so psyched. Chris just told me that we're going to Wounded Knee." He continued brushing.

"What's Wounded Knee?" I asked after I spit.

The Dutchman stopped brushing abruptly and stared at me in the glass. "I can't believe you've never heard of Wounded Knee," he marveled. "I thought everyone knew about Wounded Knee." He had an incredulous look on his face. "It's where the US troops massacred the Indians." He went on with a tone, trying to spark my memory. "One-hundred-fifty women and children were murdered with Gatling guns and cannon fire. They were torn to shreds with fifty caliber bullets."

"I remember now," I said in astonishment. "That's in the Badlands, right?"

"Right!" he confirmed.

"That's how Crazy Horse got famous," I postulated.

"So, you do know about it," he rejoiced. He took a swig of water, gargled and spit. "Chris gave me this cool book to read."

"*Black Elk Speaks*," I broke in, finishing his thought.

"Yes!" he confirmed. "You know it?"

"Not really," I confessed. "Chris was telling me about it the other day."

Deutsche Mark spoke with enthusiasm. "It tells the story of the fall of the Red Man from the eyes of one of the holy people. Pretty cool stuff. You should read it, man."

"I'll take it after you," I suggested.

"Absolutely," he enthused.

My interest was piqued. "My cousin wrote a children's book about Crazy Horse," I told him. "It's the story of the sculptor, the guy who is carving the mountain into the giant sculpture of Crazy Horse. The sculpture won't be finished in our lifetimes, or our children's lifetimes. It's already the largest sculpture in human history."

"Dude! We're going there on this trip. I'm so psyched we get to see it."

"I know," I agreed. "Driver Chris told me. We're camping on Cuny Plateau, too. It's awesome!"

"The sculpture of Crazy Horse is pointing at Wounded Knee by the way," he informed me.

"How do you know all of this?" I asked him.

"I learned about it in Secondary school," he said matter-of-factly.

"They don't teach us any Indian history in school here in the states," I complained.

"I'm psyched we're going to Wounded Knee," he gushed. "If you don't know the history you should read the first chapter," he recommended. "It's really tragic and heartbreaking. I'll give it to you as soon as I'm done."

"Yeah, definitely. I'd like that," I said with enthusiasm. "You're not going to believe this, but I found an elk skull in California and I have it with me on top of the bus."

"What?" he marveled. "An elk skull?"

"It's true," I told him.

"That's really weird dude," he commented.

"It's got antlers and everything," I divulged. "It's up there right now. I'll show you sometime."

He laughed. "What the heck do you have that for?" He asked incredulously, "Are you taking it on tour?"

"No," I said with a laugh. "I'm bringing it back to the forest where I found it. I am tempted to say it has some kind of power over me, like a totem, but I don't believe in that sort of thing. Just in case, I want to put it back."

"I believe in that stuff," he said nodding persuasively. "That skull sounds like a power object. In that case I see why you would be weirded out. I'm a bit spooked myself just hearing about it." He was adamant. "How would a power object find its way to you of all people?"

"I'm not sure," I said, "but I've got a little Indian blood in me, or so I'm told. One of my distant ancestors was a Nova Scotian Indian."

"That's interesting," he grooved.

"My mother says that's why there's no hair on our chests." I pulled up my shirt in the mirror and exposed my baldness.

He laughed at this display and flashed his blond bushy chest hair in the mirror. "I wish I had Indian blood," he bemoaned jealously.

I sat on the buddy seat watching Driver Brian update his driver's log. As we got up to speed, I silently watched him shifting, studying each movement, studying how he turned the wheel hand over hand. I noticed how he kept checking the mirrors, and how he kept checking repeatedly whenever he changed lanes. I took the plastic-coated road atlas off the dashboard, tracing the Mississippi River North to its headwaters at the Cut Foot Sioux Lake. "The Mississippi starts on an Indian Reservation?" I questioned.

Breakfast on the Mississippi

Driver Brian nodded knowingly. "The word Mississippi is an Indian word; it means 'broad river.' It's the biggest, but not the longest in America."

"What's the longest?"

"The Missouri."

"How much longer is the Missouri?"

"It's hard to say," he admitted. "The Mississippi keeps getting shorter."

"What's that?"

"Man keeps shortening it," he informed me. 'The Mississippi lost a hundred miles since the turn of the century."

"Yeah right," I scoffed in disbelief. My father's advice about believing anything you hear came to mind.

"I'm just telling you like it is," he said mildly. "The Army Corps of Engineers has eliminated most of the bends in the river where it curved back on itself."

"Why would they do that?"

"Shipping," he said flatly. "Making the Mississippi straight means bigger profits."

"That's insane," I remarked.

"They don't do it as much anymore," he expounded, "but the cutoffs in the thirties and forties increased the slope of the river, just enough to cause a slew of problems. There's a ton of evidence that suggests those cutoffs are the cause of much of the flooding in the lower Mississippi you see on the news all the time."

"It's hard to believe man caused all those natural disasters," I remarked. "You'd think they were smarter than that. We put a man on the Moon for crying out loud. How could mere mortals dare tell Mother Nature to obey their commands? Go this way not that. Don't bend go straight."

"Mark Twain joked about it, actually," Driver Brian informed me. "He said, 'The Mississippi would only be a mile long in less than a thousand years if the cutoffs continued at the same rate.'"

"Well," I nodded in approval. "There you have it."

For a moment he seemed lost in lucid thought. Then he spoke. "We can build walls and trenches to stave off the inevitable, but there is no man-made shoreline that can stay the axe once the sentence has been wrought. Nothing man-made will ever exist that Mother Nature can't destroy with a laugh."

We drove south into La Crescent, Minnesota and then back east toward La Crosse Wisconsin. We were headed toward an island situated between the east and west channels of the Mississippi River. We passed through miles of gorgeous wetlands before crossing a low bridge with a sign that read, "Welcome to Wisconsin." Driver Brian gracefully maneuvered the big green bus down the narrow tree-enshrouded streets of Barron Island into Pettibone State Park. The road curved around the rim of the small island and then broke out of the trees at the river's edge.

Before me flowed the mighty Mississippi, Ol' Man River, the Big Muddy, America's greatest flow. The Algonquin called her Misiziibi, but to an English major like me this was Tom Sawyer's playground, the Huckleberry Highway, the Aorta of the American Heartland. I felt a lump in my throat, and I swallowed hard as tears welled up in my eyes, like my heart had been wrung dry on a washboard.

I had no preconceived notions or expectations about seeing the Mississippi River for the first time. I had no way of knowing that it would become a quintessential life experience. The visceral reaction took me by complete surprise. Seeing the Gathering of Waters made me feel wonderfully happy to be alive. It connected for me a missing piece of my identity as an American.

When my eyes first set upon Old Blue, I was struck not by her beauty, but by her breadth. She was not just scenic; she was epic. The Mississippi made the Colorado look like a mere trickle. Had I not known I gazed upon a river I would have assumed the enormous body of water to be a bay, like parts of Narragansett Bay where I grew up in Rhode Island.

An enormous barge chugged along slowly a quarter mile offshore. Two massive steamboats with red paddlewheels churned the water close to the far bank near La Crosse. Sailboats dotted the blue waterway, tilting with the wind and coming about with plenty of open water on all sides. Dozens more vessels moved about on the half-mile wide section of river, yet there was room enough for a thousand more.

The bus pulled over near a huge, round, ornate gazebo big enough to house a merry-go-round, fifty feet from the bank of the Mississippi. Verdant fields of grass shone with dew in the early morning sun to the left and rear of the gazebo. Low hanging boughs of trees with small leaves sprouted in clumps next to the bus and on the other side of the domed structure.

Driver Brian seemed totally fresh, even after the long drive, obviously excited about the rest of the trip. We had rushed through the eastern part of America so that we could now slow down and enjoy, what according to him, was, "the real trip." He wanted to start the western half of our journey with a fabulous meal by making his favorite Tortoise breakfast, beer batter crepes.

From up on the roof, I could see the city of La Crosse, Wisconsin, less than a mile away, across the stretch of dark greenish blue that is the Mississippi River. Old-fashioned riverboats chugged

Breakfast on the Mississippi

along, whistling, with their graceful steam stacks and paddlewheels painted red. Some of the passengers walked down to the edge of the river to get their feet wet in the early morning sunshine, marveling at the power of the massive river that most of them had only read about in books.

The morning sun was still in the eastern sky, and I could feel the powerful spirit of the Mississippi River flowing through my world. Standing up there on the roof beside Chicken Jim, I imagined we were Lewis and Clark, trading foodstuffs with the local tribe. I looked up and down the river in both directions at the perilous currents, and I wondered if those currents could rip a canoe to shreds. How the native people crossed this powerful river in a wooden canoe, I could not fathom.

In a huge mixing bowl, Driver Brian whipped up two bottles of dark beer.

Up on the roof Chicken Jim told me that, "Brian and I had to buy that beer out of our own pocket-money."

After the foam had been whipped out of the beer, Brian added one egg per person and a shot of oil. Next, he mixed in half a bag of buckwheat flour. He let the beer, eggs, and oil and flour sit for a few minutes, then he added milk until the batter was the consistency of eggnog.

The rest of the ingredients were as follows: a large bowl of sliced strawberries, four pints of fresh blueberries, a bowl of fresh raspberries, sliced mango, cut kiwi fruit, and a large bowl of fresh, hand-whipped cream. We made applesauce, cooked right there that morning. Alongside the bowls of crepe fillings were about ten jars of jellies and jams of all flavors. Right next to the bowl of strawberries, alongside the peanut butter, was the best ingredient of all, hazelnut chocolate spread called Nutella. It was so delicious that it made my eyes roll back in my head.

The idea was to cook about a hundred crepes in all, before anyone ate, so that the entire group could enjoy the meal together. The enormity of the task did not seem to faze Driver Brian at all. The crepe chefs gathered 'round him for their lesson. He closed his eyes for a moment, as if he had forgotten where to begin, but when he opened them, there was an infinite clarity.

Driver Brian held the spatula as if he were the conductor of a great symphony. He splashed a little oil into one of the sizzling-hot pans and like a clash of cymbals, his concerto began. With his spatula hand he picked up the pan and began swirling the oil around. With his other hand, he simultaneously stirred the giant bowl of crepe batter. The sizzling faded and the rhythmic clanking of the ladle ceased, as the ladle rose from the bowl, pouring out just the right amount of batter. Batter met pan with another sizzling swirl, spreading a harmonious layer of airy crepe.

All eyes were on the spatula, as we prepared to witness the profound art of crepe making. He smiled a bit and looked around in a cheery way, and he did nothing but whistle and hum for several minutes. Looking around in the air at us up on top of the bus and smiling, he tapped the spatula rhythmically on the edge of the cast iron pan. Driver Brian was the King.

The crowd of people watching shifted around restlessly like peasants. Driver Brian nodded his head in reassurance and said, "Never fondle the crepes." Then, with a flick of his wrist, he exposed the perfectly golden-brown underside. He flipped it and the delightful crepe landed perfectly in the center of the pan. When the crepe was finished cooking, he brought it over to a large, covered serving bowl, which rested on a huge pot of boiling water.

British Sue returned from the riverside and weaved through the crowd as Driver Brian was finishing his demonstration. We could see her from the top of the bus. Driver Brian looked around for a volunteer just as British Sue arrived. She stepped up as confident as a little schoolgirl, plucking the spatula out of the chef's hand. "I'll be the first crepe chef," she said with a distinctive English mannerism.

Everyone watched British Sue like a hawk, anxiously examining her every move to see how closely to the lesson she could perform the art of crepe making. Of course, Chicken Jim and I knew that she had just walked up, and she did not seem to have the rhythm.

British Sue haphazardly dipped the ladle into the bowl with a clank. She picked up the hot, cast-iron pan with her bare hand and promptly threw it back on the stove with a clash. Driver Brian handed her the hot pad.

Without any oil, she sloshed a little too much batter into the pan and chucked the ladle back in the bowl with an audible 'bloop.' Driver Brian looked offended. Before the crepe finished cooking, she moved the spatula like she was going to fondle the crepe, but Driver Brian looked at her sideways and she withdrew.

With a cacophony of spatula sounds, she tried to flip the crepe, but she could not seem to pull it off alone. It had burned a little. After Driver Brian helped her with the all-important flip, he looked away for half a minute and said, "I'll need a bunch of people to start cooking. Once you're done with your share, you should explain to someone else how the cooking is really supposed to be done."

At that moment, the cool Dutch guy named Mark came strolling over to the gazebo. He had been sitting on the riverbank getting twisted, smoking weed with Jewels. He had not heard a word of

Breakfast on the Mississippi

Driver Brian's cooking lesson either. He stepped through the crowd and asked British Sue, "Do you need me to take over for you?"

British Sue said, "Sure." She slapped the crepe onto the big silver bowl and began teaching the Dutch guy how to cook crepes. Driver Brian looked perplexed. Per his instructions, he was expecting her to cook for a long time before giving up her post. He remained quiet however, longing to see how this madness would unfold.

We all bent our ears to hear her explanation of the cooking process. British Sue dunked the ladle in the huge bowl of batter, poured it in the pan, and instructed, "First you get your juice, then you whack it in, and twiddle it about!" Everyone within earshot laughed and laughed. The driver's intricate explanation of the fine art of crepe making had been reduced to one sentence, straight out of Monty Python. She rotated the batter evenly in the pan, tossed it back on the burner, and handed him the spatula. "Don't fondle it," she advised. "It's not wise to upset a Wookie.

Amidst the laughter, British Sue picked up her finished crepe and walked over to the fixing tables, making like she was going to eat her crepe right in front of us. We all thought it was funny, especially Driver Brian, who had tears in his eyes from laughter. British Sue was a holy immaculate riot.

Deutsche Mark laughed with us, despite not knowing exactly why people were laughing. Then he said, "Party on dudes!"

Driver Chris came to breakfast wrapped in a sleeping bag. French Sandrine made him a crepe and they ate together on the bank of the Mississippi. When they finished, they went back inside to sleep. On their way inside they must have woken Irish Kyrah because she came out, made a crepe, and sat down with her sister and Fräulein Vera. The German girl had taken a liking to Irish Joyce, and for the first time her sister Kyrah seemed like the third wheel.

Mother Michelle bumped elbows with me by the crepe bowl when I went up to eat. "I'm not asking you to kiss and tell or anything, but I've noticed you've been hanging around with that British girl."

"We fooled around a bit," I admitted with a laugh as I put a crepe on my plate. "What's it to ya?"

"Call it motherly instinct," she shrugged with a tilted head. "You're a nice guy, and I don't want you to get hurt." She put a crepe on her plate.

"I'll be all right," I told her. We moved to the table with the toppings.

"She has a boyfriend back in England," Mother Michelle informed me.

"She told me that," I said flatly. I dumped a scoop of thinly sliced strawberries on my crepe.

"Do you think she plans on telling him?" she asked, choosing bananas for her own crepe instead.

"Probably not," I admitted. We kept moving down the line. "I'm fine with that. What happens on the road stays on the road."

"You seem nicer than all that," she assessed.

"I don't think she's trying to pull the wool over my eyes if that's what you're thinking." I worked the knife in the Nutella jar.

"I don't think she's capable of that," she scoffed.

I filled a big silver spoon with hand-whipped cream from the big silver bowl, and asked, "What do you mean?"

She nodded with a hungry smile and scoffed, "She's not exactly your intellectual equal."

"Ha!" I laughed as I plopped the whipped cream onto her banana crepe. I took a step back to give her a look. "I'll be fine," I huffed. I filled the spoon with whipped cream for myself.

"I'm just saying," she smirked, shaking her chin. "It's a long way to England to visit someone who isn't being honest with her boyfriend." She folded her crepe in half and took a bite.

"I'll keep that in mind," I said as I folded my crepe.

"You're welcome," she said chewing. Then she took another bite and said, "These are delicious," before she walked away.

I took a seat next to Jewels and Yülia at one of the picnic tables in the gazebo. It was truly an idyllic setting for a morning meal, with the mighty Mississippi flowing past just twenty yards away. A golden-brown crepe stuffed with fresh strawberries, a thin bed of Nutella and fresh whipped cream tastes purely divine in the mouth. Food had never been this good. After a few tasty bites I asked Jewels, "What did you and PAC-MAN talk about last night? You sure took the bull by the horns."

Jewels looked around anxiously searching for Peruvian Ursula. She was sitting far away on the grassy bank of the Mississippi with PAC-MAN, so it was safe. She leaned in and said, "I have a hard time believing it, but Pak doesn't want our help. He's got no problem with her."

"We asked him if he was in danger and he said, 'No,'" Yülia interjected.

"Wow!" I reacted.

"There's nothing we can do if he doesn't want our help," the soulful New Yorker reiterated.

"All he cares about is being reunited with his family in San Francisco," added Yülia.

"He doesn't think she's mistreating him, but we're not buying it," revealed Jewels. "Victims of abuse often protect their abusers. I have a sense for these things. I feel the tension. Something is up with

Breakfast on the Mississippi

those two. They're hiding something," she speculated. "He's full of fear, but he's helping her hide something."

"She pushes him around and she's so mean to him," observed Yülia.

"Why would he be afraid?" I questioned.

"I don't think it's a physical threat," Jewels deduced. "When I offered to call the police, he said that might prevent him from ever seeing his family again."

"What's up with that?" I questioned.

"We think she's holding his family hostage," Jewels revealed.

"No way," I objected. "That's ridiculous. He told me himself. The Chinese government is keeping his family away from him until he shows up in San Francisco. It's part of the deal when they let him travel alone without a chaperone."

"He seems to have a chaperone," Jewels observed.

"She's no criminal," I remarked. "I'm sure she has his best interest at heart."

Peruvian Ursula saw us sitting there together when she came to the wash station to do her dishes, so we stopped talking and focused on eating the wonderful crepes.

****

After breakfast, we packed up the bus and walked to a nearby beach. Little Josh ran. A few of the passengers had crashed hard after breakfast and were sleeping in the bus.

The Pink Panther gave me the hairy eyeball when I walked past her and Cato on the walk over to the beach. "Misery acquaints a man with strange bedfellows," she commented as I passed. This left me puzzled, but I remembered the nasty look she gave me earlier when I was talking with the two Julies at breakfast. She could tell we were gossiping about her. She probably thought I was siding with them. I did not want her to think I had chosen sides, so I figured I should say something to that effect. Maybe she would share more details about her relationship with her friend if I remained her ally.

A park ranger drove up when we arrived at the beach. Driver Chris went to the window of his truck to greet him with his sleeping bag draped over his shoulders. The officer had a list of park rules for us to follow. Once the ranger was gone Driver Chris called us together to make a general announcement.

"Clothing is not optional here," he informed us. The park ranger said they've had a problem with Green Tortoise passengers getting naked here before, and he warned me that he'll be back to check on us later. He also made me promise to read this list of rules in front of everyone." He ran his finger down the list and shook his head as he read. "There you go!" he remarked. "I read it in front of everyone. Now, go have fun!" There was a lot of laughter.

"Hold on! Hold on!" he checked himself as we started walking away. "A couple of these rules sound important." He held up a finger for silence. Silence was not happening now that he had been goofing around, but he continued anyway. "Rule number one." He held up a finger. "All pets must be under physical restraint at all times."

"Does that include Chicken Jim?" shouted Vera. People laughed.

Driver Chris continued, "Rule number two." He read, holding up two fingers. "A leash of no more than 6 feet shall be used by all." Even more people laughed.

"That's d... d... d... downright k... k... k... kinky," commented Guitar Johnny.

Driver Chris stopped reading. "The rest of these rules don't apply to us. Just keep your clothes on. Have a good time." He waved us off.

Big Dave waved me over to a path that led away from the small beach, telling me that he had something to show me. Down the little path, we found a comfortable log to sit on while Big Dave packed his pipe, reminiscing about all the times he had crossed the Mississippi. He even sang me a little song about sloshing your feet in the Mississippi mud.

While Big Dave sang, Australian Sheila bopped down the trail, humming her own Mississippi song. She blushed and tittered embarrassment, as she was looking for a place to squat. Her golden blond ponytail boomeranged happily back the way it came.

Big Dave took a drag from his pipe. He confided in me. "The boy saw his mother smoking with me this morning," he intoned deeply as always. "I tried to tell him that we smoke to kill pain and that pain comes in many forms, but he's too mad to listen to reason right now. Understandably, he's angry at both of us."

I was feeling great, so I stood up and asked, "Want to go for a swim?" He remained seated and waved me off in a manner that told me he could care less to swim if he had to wear a bathing suit.

The beach was fantastic. The water was perfect. Riverboats chugged across the river. Little Josh played Frisbee with Deutsche Mark, English Tessa, and British Sue on the beach and in the shallows.

Another chicken fight erupted after Fräulein Vera taunted Australian Sheila, seeking vengeance for their loss at Indiana Dunes. This time Berndt Toast shouldered Fräulein Vera and they reigned supreme, knocking over or chasing away all would be challengers.

Breakfast on the Mississippi

Despite the ranger's warning Guitar Johnny went skinny-dipping. To keep from being seen he entered the water upstream. We soon realized that he was trying to swim across the river to the nearby island. It soon became clear that the strong current was getting the better of him. Driver Chris stood up and yelled, "Come back! Come back!" He was seriously concerned.

"Do you think he knows that's a shipping lane?" asked Driver Brian.

Suddenly, out of nowhere a paddle-steamer was heading right towards him, aiming to chew him to shreds in the giant spinning waterwheel. Everyone started yelling. We all thought he was crazy. He waved his arms for the boat pilot to see him, but it was too late. We held our breath as his head disappeared in the wake of a passing speedboat. He must have been very frightened. Luckily, neither boat struck him. He swam back to shore as quickly as possible.

"The bloody boat, almost r... r... r... ran me over!" he exclaimed when he was close to shore. If it had been a speedboat, I'd be a dead git from Grimsby." After a sigh of relief, we all enjoyed some heartfelt laughter with Guitar Johnny.

Chicken Jim sat by the water's edge playing Blackbird. The Pennsylvanian's choice of songs annoyed the British guitar player because, as he said, "My voice would ruin that song." He refused to play it or sing it. Even when he played songs he did know, he constantly disparaged himself and apologized repeatedly for every missed note.

The Brit brought his guitar over so they could play together, and they strummed Merle Haggard's, Mama Tried. As he struggled through the song, Driver Chris told him to stop apologizing and he seemed to take it to heart.

When the song ended Guitar Johnny remarked, "I can't believe I'm bloody alive, sitting here right on the banks of the Mississippi singing country songs. A week ago, I was in Birmingham. Lawd have mercy!"

Swimming in the Mississippi was cool. I swam graceful, dramatic strokes, kicking like a frog and enjoying the feeling of the Mississippi river on my skin. I was feeling exceptionally happy that morning, like I was young again. I loved all the new places I was getting to see; I loved all the new people I was getting to meet; and as a result I was able to love myself for the first time in a while.

Jen from Boston came swimming over to me and said, "Check this out. It's wicked cool." She dug into the sand with her foot, dipped her face into the Mississippi River and produced in her hand a small white clam with brown striations.

"There are clams in here?" I marveled. "Shellfish in fresh water?" I puzzled. "On the banks of a river?" Most of the clams she found were alive and well. We both kept half of an empty shell to take home as a souvenir. I chose the sign of the day: the Mississippi River Freshwater Clam.

****

After a leisurely morning swim in the Mississippi River, Driver Chris took the wheel and his partner, the gigantic blond master-crepe-chef, took the buddy seat. The lead driver opened the trucker's map on the steering wheel, studied it for a few moments, then spoke to his co-driver under his breath. "There's a Greyhound Station in La Crosse, but the next nearest bus station is in Sioux Falls," he told him.

"Ouch," his partner reacted with his eyes popping. "How far is Sioux Falls?"

"Dude, it's like three-hundred miles west," he exasperated, "all the way across Minnesota and twenty miles into South Dakota."

"Come on," his co-driver begged to differ. "There has to be someplace to catch a Greyhound between here and South Dakota."

His partner told him. "According to the map, there are bus stops every fifty miles the entire way, but there's nothing out there but corn, dude. We can't make people wait for a bus on the side of the road in the middle of Minnesota. We need a place they can wait inside."

"Good point," his co-driver conceded. "You'd better call home from here. The sooner the better."

"I agree, but I don't want to fight with my father again. I'm gonna call the hospital directly. There are no phones in the intensive care unit, but my sister said they were trying to get him a room."

"Good luck getting through," the blond-bearded Californian wished him well. "I hope he's doing all right."

"You'll be the first to know otherwise," he told him.

"I guess so," he acquiesced.

"If I do have to leave, I'll have no choice but to stay at home with my father," he mused. "I wish things could be different."

"He's a stubborn old curmudgeon," his colleague commented.

"I've given up trying to fix him," said the redhead. "I have to distance myself emotionally."

Driver Brian breathed heavily through his nose and held his breath contemplatively as we waited for him to speak. "Not for nothing brother," he addressed his partner diminutively. "You're the one who's always saying, 'You create your own reality.'" He shrugged with a tilt of his head. "Well, maybe you should listen to your own advice."

"When it comes to what?" questioned the big red beard.

"When it comes to this whole thing with your dad," answered the big-blond beard. "You can't give up so easy. I've learned that we need to invest in our relationships to have lasting happiness. Relationships have a greater effect on our wellbeing than our jobs or our money."

His superior eyeballed him with a lowered brow and a squinted eye. "I'm listening," he said.

"Maybe you need to give your relationship with your dad the attention and work it deserves before you give up on it. Do it for yourself, screw him."

"That sounds a bit selfish, don't you think?"

"Investing in yourself isn't selfish. It's the most important thing you can do. You have to put on your own oxygen mask before you can save the person sitting next to you."

Driver Chris nodded in confirmation. "It just sounds like a big investment without much hope of return."

Driver Brian spoke kindheartedly. "You've told me repeatedly that I need to visualize what I want out of life, plot a course, and take one step at a time. What's keeping you from doing that?"

"I'm not sure."

"What's the best-case scenario with your old man?"

"His DNA would have to be altered for him to love me the way he did when I was a kid," he related.

"And for you to love him?"

"Yes," he acquiesced.

"Ha!" Driver Brian laughed. "Don't you see it?"

"See what?"

"It's as clear as day from where I'm sitting."

"What is?"

"You need to visualize that shit."

"Visualize his DNA changing?"

"No!" The big blond smiled candidly. "You need to visualize and manifest your love for him, regardless of his lame ass curmudgeon bullshit."

Driver Chris bobbed his head in agreement with a thoughtful grimace.

"How did you feel about him back then?"

"I loved him with my whole heart. He meant the world to me."

"So, visualize that shit," Driver Brian advised.

"I hear you brother, but I've tried to love him despite himself and he hasn't changed at all. Creating your own reality doesn't work on other people. Besides, he doesn't believe in that forgiveness." The

Irishman shook his head from side to side in frustration. "He disapproves of every step I take."

"He can disapprove of you all he wants, that's his prerogative, but he can't control you, just like you can't control him. The only thing you can control is yourself." The young man behind the wheel stroked his red beard contemplatively as his partner advised him, "Visualize a healthy relationship with your dad, the way it used to be, with you loving him and him loving you. You know you cannot control him, but you still have the power to create your own reality. You tell me that all the time. Plot a course, take the required steps one at a time, and you'll get there, eventually."

"What would you have me do?"

"If your best-case scenario is to love each other like when you were a kid, you can at least get halfway there by loving him the same way you did when you were a kid."

"That would take a lot of work," he scoffed.

"What would be your first step?"

He remained silent for a few seconds. "Forgiving him?"

"That sounds like a good first step. Plot the course brother. Plot the course."

"I hear what you're saying," he conceded. "Thanks."

"No problem," said the Californian. "I hope it helps."

Driver Chris had said the buddy seat was a platform for wisdom. This seemed to prove his words true. He stood up and said, "I need to get some sleep." He stepped aside and I took his seat.

The enormous man headed back, took off his shoes and walked over the back platform toward the driver's cabin. The co-driver was obliged to kick French Sandrine out because, as the man behind the wheel told me, "Drivers always trump girlfriends. It's part of the Tortoise Driver's Code," he explained.

"There's a Tortoise Driver's Code?" I questioned.

"Yup," he said, "but the code only works if everybody plays."

"I thought you said Sandrine was just a friend?" I inquired.

"She's a groupie," he remarked casually.

"More like a grouper," interjected Little Josh from the seat behind him.

"A groupie?" I inquired.

"Yes. If you're going to be a driver, you need to watch out for that shit. Chicks will follow you from trip to trip, hoping to be your girlfriend. She's only my girlfriend for the sake of appearances."

"Appearances?"

"Yeah," he answered. "Driver's girlfriends can ride for free as long as the office knows in advance," he confirmed. "It's totally at their discretion." He wrinkled his lips beneath his red mustache. "If word

Breakfast on the Mississippi 241

leaked out that she's not my real girlfriend, I'd be in serious trouble, so keep your mouth shut if you ever work for the Tortoise. You can't have a new girlfriend every trip and expect her to ride for free, but I haven't been in an official relationship for a while, so we should be all set. Besides, she was a paying customer first. The office prefers it that way." He nodded understanding. "They get a lot of freeloaders. I'm letting her ride back to San Francisco on the house. She would have paid either way, so I figured I'd help-her-out just this one time, before she takes off."

"Where's she going?"

"She claims to be continuing her trip around the world after this, but I'll believe that when I see it. I've been trying to shake her loose for a while."

"Shake her loose? Why?"

He cast me an are-you-for-real look. "I need my space. She's been cramping my style."

"How so?"

"She was all jealous when I hooked up on the last trip," he said nonchalantly.

"No way!" I gasped. "You hooked up on the last trip? While she was here?"

"Sure," he said with a shrug.

"How did that go over?"

"She was upset for a couple of days." He eyeballed me with a smirk. "She should have seen it coming," he said with a shrug. "I told her how it was going to be before we left, that I'm not interested in being tied down. Not while I'm on the bus anyway."

"Wow! That's crazy," I observed.

He shot me a look in the mirror then glanced over at my eyes before returning his attention to the road. "Take my advice," he said, nodding his chin and stroking his beard. "Don't tie yourself down when you're on the road. Newbies always make that mistake. They think getting laid on the bus means you're in a relationship."

"I've never had that kind of luck yet," I confessed.

"Don't get me wrong," he advised with a shrug. "I never enjoyed this kind of sex life off the bus. I'm not the best-looking guy in the world, even under this big-old beard." He stroked his long red mane affectionately. "Back in Connecticut I had to fight for every phone number I ever got, and half of 'em were fake."

"Awe man!" I laughed. "I hate that."

"It's not just me," he added. "There's something totally magical about this old bus."

"Absolutely!" I cheered.

"It's like a youth hostel on wheels, only better." He smirked. "The trips are always full of European backpackers. We sleep in the same room for weeks at a time; we go on adventures together; we eat together; we get naked together. So, there's ample opportunity to make friends with your fellow travelers, if you know what I mean."

"It's a love bus," I observed.

"Basically," he agreed. "The bus is one big bed. It just depends where you choose to sleep."

"I'll say," I interjected.

His eyes wandered off as he contemplated fond memories.

"I love this bus!" I exclaimed a little too loudly.

He put his finger to his lips. "It's even easier when you're a driver." He nodded. "We have our own private bedroom." He motioned his head back toward the rear. "The driver's cabin is like icing on the cake," he surmised.

"I love this bus!" I whispered. "I can see why people would want to stay indefinitely."

"Dude!" he exclaimed. "Talk about groupies, I drove this cross-country trip one time with this guy named Raoul Hafwirth. That was his bus name anyway." He reflected in thought momentarily. "Come to think of it, I don't even remember his real name. Anyway, when we got to Boston a whole group of passengers refused to leave the bus."

"Hmmm?" I questioned. "They refused to leave?"

"We told them it was time to go, but they wouldn't get off," he clarified.

"Why?"

"Well," he said with a chuckle, "word had spread that we were headed to Cape Cod for a nine-day layover, and they insisted we let them hang-out with us."

"No way!" I marveled.

"Yeah dude!" He chuckled. "It worked out great in the end, too. We had to collect money for food to keep them fed, but they did the shopping and the cooking. They helped clean the bus. They did the laundry. They helped with everything. There was even a diesel mechanic who helped us with the bus maintenance."

"That sounds awesome," I reveled.

"It was so cool," he remarked. "We took them to Newport."

"No way!" I exclaimed. "I'm from Rhode Island. Isn't Newport great?"

"It sure is," he agreed. "We dropped them off at the ferry so they could go to Block Island."

"That's amazing!" I marveled.

Breakfast on the Mississippi 243

As we drove out of Pettibone Park, I watched Driver Chris shift up and down, methodically following each movement, mapping out the steps in my mind. "You're only ever gonna shift when your land speed syncs up with your engine speed," he instructed me. "It's a pretty small window considering it's a moving target," he informed me. "If you're in the zone shifts happen; if you're not shifts will hit the fan."

"Ha! I'll have to remember that," I said. "It sounds like a metaphor for life." I snorted a laugh.

"You always need to remain vigilant," he advised. "You have to be ready to shift at any moment."

"Why can't you just use the clutch?" I asked.

"The clutch gives you a little more wiggle room. It opens the window a bit wider, but you can still fuck up a shift if your calculations are off, even by a little."

"What calculations?" I questioned. "I thought you always downshift into the top of the next gear."

"That's the theory," he said, "but the proof of the pudding is in the eating, or in this case the shifting. It's easy to slow down in one gear and go straight past the top of the next, especially in traffic."

"What happens then?" I inquired.

"Watch," he said. He backed off the fuel in third gear until the engine was quiet and we were going slowly. "I'm still in third gear but we're going slower than the top of second gear. So now what do you do?"

"Catch the top of first?" I suggested.

"You could, but what if you're on the highway and it isn't safe to slow down that much? What if you need to speed up to get safely through an intersection?" He looked at me sideways.

"Catch the middle of second?" I guessed.

"Yup." He stomped the clutch and jiggled the stick into neutral. His foot eased into the fuel. The engine revved. He pointed to a piece of red tape on the tachometer. "The top of second is right there and we're going slower than that, so you know the shift point must be somewhere down here." He pointed half an inch below the tape.

"The top of second is twenty-seven, right?"

"Yup." He adjusted the fuel until the tachometer aligned to where he had pointed. He pulled back ever so gently on the shifter. His hand shook immediately, and he pulled back with hardly any force at all. He applied fuel and we zoomed into the top of second gear, then he shifted back into third. "Simple," he said with a smirk.

"That's so cool," I marveled in reverence. "I still don't understand why you don't use the clutch just to be safe."

"Using the clutch makes shifting easier, but it doesn't make it any safer. A lot of Tortoise drivers see it as a weakness, like a crutch, and they refuse to use it. They see it as a last resort."

I had to ask. "Why would they think that?"

"Don't get me wrong. A lot of good drivers use the clutch, but the consensus among drivers is that it can make you lazy. It keeps you from remaining focused. You have to understand the culture. There's a lot of different philosophies around shifting and driving in general. Some of us see driving the Tortoise as a transcendental experience. Experienced drivers don't have to think about shifting anymore. It's become second nature to them."

"Shifting is a transcendental experience? Come on," I scoffed. "I know it's hard, but come on, seriously?" I could feel my father's pessimism weighing me down like an anchor, keeping me from believing the extraordinary, acting like a blockage at the base of my spine, like a glacier had formed in the crack of my ass. I wanted to believe driving the Green Tortoise was a transcendental experience. I just couldn't rush in blind, lest I get tricked into believing something that would later make me look stupid.

"Seriously," the red-bearded driver maintained. "I once heard the owner say something like, 'Your eyes focus on what's coming down the road; your mind plans your next move; but when it comes to shifting, your spirit needs to transcend the physical plane."

"It's like Caddyshack," I commented. "Stop thinking, let things happen, and be the ball."

"Yeah. Kind of like that," he said. "There's a force in the universe that makes things happen. All you have to do is get in touch with it."

"Be the ball, Danny; be the ball," I said jokingly. "You're not being the ball, Danny." We laughed together.

Little Josh was kneeling up on the bench at the dinette with his head hanging out the window. "Watch this!" he yelled inside. An elderly woman was walking towards us on the opposite sidewalk struggling to holdback a dog on a leash. As the bus roared past, just for fun he yelled, "Watch out!" The poor old lady nearly jumped out of her skin.

Josh was cracking up, but no one else was laughing. We all looked out the window to see if she was okay. The grey-haired woman stopped and turned around to look as the bus rolled away, but the dog kept pulling her backwards. When she turned back around, she slammed face-first into a phone pole. There was a collective gasp of horror.

"Stop the bus!" commanded the big man in the overalls. "Stop the bus right now!"

"That was so mean, Josh," slammed Yülia.

"That lad's a bloody monster," observed Guitar Johnny. Many more unfavorable comments were leveled at the boy. Josh hid his laughter. To make matters worse the dog ran around in circles, trapping the old lady's legs against the pole with the leash.

"You have to stop," Yülia shrieked.

"We need to help her," shouted Jewels.

Driver Chris checked his mirrors, engaged the blinker, and pulled over on the empty curb.

"Jesus God!" Grumbled the enormous Hippie. "The kid has no respect for anything!"

Mother Michelle had not been watching, but she knew something serious was afoot. She rushed forward and asked her son, "What did you do?"

"I did not!" he denied, holding back snorts of laughter.

She repeated, "What did you do!?"

"He accosted that poor woman across the street back there," Big Dave informed her.

"I did not!" insisted the boy.

"You scared her half to death!" the Old-Growth-Hippie insisted. The boy scowled at him and gave him the finger. His mother surveyed the onlookers.

"He yelled at her!" confirmed Yülia.

"You could have given her a heart attack," warned the big man.

"I hate you," shot the boy.

Mother Michelle looked out the window, saw what was happening, took her son by the neck of his shirt and dragged him outside. She yelled at him as they crossed the street. She was outraged. She freed the old woman and made her son apologize. Little Josh was still crying when they returned to the bus. "Get in there and don't come out," she impelled him. He went to the driver's cabin, closed the door, and that was the last we saw of him for a while.

****

In silence Driver Chris drove over the Barron Island Bridge onto the mainland in La Crescent Minnesota where we parked against the curb at a gas station. As he got up to leave, he said, "I'll have to remember to keep my cool if I'm ever going to make amends with my old man."

"Be the ball, Danny," I coached him supportively. "Be the ball."

Before he left, he shouted to the passengers, "We'll be here for about ten minutes. You can go inside if you need a bathroom, but if you don't have to go, please stay on the bus." He jumped down the steps and ran to the payphone on the side of the convenience store.

Guitar Johnny lit up a smoke on the curb. I was standing with him chatting casually when Peruvian Ursula came out of the bus with PAC-MAN. She spoke to him briefly in Cantonese before going inside alone. A few minutes later after checking the place out, she waved for him to come inside.

"Is she afraid of the frigging Paparazzi?" the Englishman remarked.

A bunch of female passengers were standing around in a circle listening to Juliano tell stories about life in Brazil. I stood close by listening. He went on about the great food, the perfect wine, beautiful women, and the amazing nightlife in San Paulo. I stepped closer when he began telling a story about a friend's brother in the military.

"I have a friend whose brother was in the Brazilian Army," he told us. "He got drunk on patrol in the jungle and fell asleep with his arm hanging out of his tent."

"Did the mosquitoes drink all of his blood?" asked Little Josh.

"No!" proclaimed the Brazilian. "Much worse!" He made a horrible strained face. "He woke up with no feeling in his arm. A twenty-foot-long boa had swallowed his whole arm, all the way up to his shoulder."

Several girls reacted squeamishly which he seemed to enjoy.

I said, "Get the fuck out!"

"No way! No how!" reacted Irish Kyrah.

Flip-flop was like, "That's crazy."

"It's true," the Brazilian said in a tone that made me believe. "He woke up with the snake's nose pushing on his neck." He tilted his head and gestured with his hand like it was a snake head, with his fingers bumping into his neck. "It was trying to eat him whole."

"That's freaking awesome!" I commented.

"Oh my god stop," cried Mother Michelle. "Enough of that story, Josh." She walked away but he refused to budge, so she kept going without him.

"What if he didn't wake up?" Maid Marian asked desperately.

"He'd be gone I suppose," he answered candidly before continuing his gruesome tale. "He screamed for his friends to help and come bring a machete. The soldier went to cut the snakes head off, but my friend's brother yelled, 'No! My arm is in there."

There were more squeamish cries and disbelief.

Little Josh kept shouting, "Awesome!" the entire time.

Breakfast on the Mississippi

"So, they measured an arm's length from the snake's head, and he made a fist. Then they cut the snake in half, so his fingers were sticking out." Everyone was either grossed out or refusing to believe. "He couldn't feel his arm, so they decided to take him to the hospital with the snake still on his arm. He wore it like a sleeve until they got him off the mountain."

A heavy breath left my lungs. "No fucking way," I objected with my father's voice in my head.

"That's not the worst of it," he told us with an expression of incredulity. "If you've ever killed a snake you know; when you chop off its head, it still lives for a while after."

We all went, "No way!"

"Awesome," shouted Little Josh.

"The snake kept trying to swallow the rest of him all the way to the hospital. He said it was breathing in his ear the entire time."

"Bullshit!" objected Peruvian Ursula.

"It's true," Juliano attested. "I saw his arm at my friend's house. It was disgusting. The snake's digestive juices dissolved the skin on his whole arm and hand. It looked like oil on water. The whole thing, all the way from his shoulder looked iridescent. It shimmered in the light, and he had no hair at all on his entire arm."

British Sue wretched and covered her mouth like she was holding back vomit.

Little Josh kept shouting "Awesome! Awesome! That shit's awesome!"

Driver Chris returned ten minutes later. He went up the steps looking a bit melancholy, but it appeared that his brother was still among the living. French Sandrine was sitting on the buddy seat and she moved her legs out of his way so he could sit down. He turned his shoulders quickly and snatched the white plastic phone off the wall. It was a strange kind of phone that did not require dialing. You simply picked it up and it beeped on the other end.

Mother Michelle came forward to listen. Driver Chris made eye contact with her in the mirror, then turned sideways to continue speaking. Under normal circumstances, one might think eavesdropping on someone's personal phone conversation was totally rude, but he understood at a glance that she was now responsible for spreading the news, so she was intent on gathering as much detail as she could from the secondhand conversation.

"Hey man," he addressed his co-driver congenially. "Yes, I did," he said. "They got a recliner for my mother, so she's more comfortable now." He turned to look toward the back of the bus. "She says he's sleeping peacefully," he informed his partner, "but it was touch and go last night." He went quiet for a moment. "He started to wake up in the middle of the night," our driver spoke somberly, "but something went wrong." He paused to listen before responding. "From what I could gather, it sounds like his vitals spiked and then his heart stopped." He paused again.

Mother Michelle gasped in astonishment and touched his shoulder.

"I know brother," he thanked his colleague. "They made my mother leave the room when they brought in the crash cart, so the details are blurry after that point." He hung on the line for a moment. "It's all good brother," he said. "They were able to bring him back. He's sleeping peacefully now."

There was a collective sigh of relief among those listening.

"Thanks man," he said to his partner. There was a pause before he answered, "No. My sister wasn't there, and I didn't get a chance to speak to the doctors or anything like that." The suffering young man's brow furrowed as he listened. "Well, that part didn't go so well." He turned back around and lowered his voice. Driver Chris described the scene graphically, "I went in loaded for bear, but I shot-myself-in-the-foot." He paused to listen to a question. "I was visualizing forgiveness for everything he's ever done, but he started fucking with me again. My mother tried to hand him the phone, but he asked if I was coming home. When she said no, my father said, 'As long as he puts those people before his family, I don't want any part of that god forsaken Hippie.'"

He paused to listen again. "No. He wouldn't take the phone. I never got a chance. I got so pissed off. I couldn't even talk to my mother after that. You should have heard the way he said, 'Those people.'" He paused. "Yeah, he called me a Hippie." He paused again. "So what? If I am a Hippie, he wouldn't love me?" A moment of silence passed. "I'm not being unreasonable, am I?" He shot me a look. "Am I?"

I shook my head. "No way!"

"He's just a fucking prick and that's all there is to it. Now, get some rest bro. Please don't worry about me." He said, "Goodnight!" He hung up the phone.

Mother Michelle took that as her cue to start spreading the word. "Good news people," she began.

****

Flip-flop waved for me to come to the back platform. I was happy to give Driver Chris some much needed space, so I excused myself and headed back. I found her lounging on the back platform with Fräulein Vera and the Irish Twins. Each girl's head rested on their

Breakfast on the Mississippi

neighbor's lap forming a square with their legs pinwheeled out in four directions. Irish Kyrah patted the empty seat in the center between them. "There's room for you here love," she said invitingly. "We've some questions for ye."

I made eyes with the Bostonian and nodded to say thanks. As I got into position to take a seat, I realized the space in the center of the girls was too small. The others attempted to widen the formation, but it quickly became obvious that the solution was to make a circle out of the square. Irish Kyrah graciously invited me to rest my head on her lap. That meant that East Coast Jen's head would be resting on me. This was great. It took some doing, but they managed to sprawl out in a circle wide enough for me to lie down.

The short-haired German au pair seemed gloriously content having Irish Joyce's head resting on her pubic region. She had been hanging all over the doctorly Irish midwife ever since witnessing her heroic delivery of the baby in the Chicago blues bar bathroom. It had become obvious and widely accepted that they were lesbians. Not that it mattered. It went unsaid without the batting of an eye.

However, I now understood Mother Michelle's advice about Irish Joyce being too worldly for me and how I was more of a one-woman guy.

Once we were settled in, I asked Flip-flop, "What's on your mind?"

"We don't really have so many questions as we want your opinion," she revealed.

"Opinions," corrected the blond twins.

"Okay opinions," the Bostonian acquiesced.

Irish Joyce addressed me directly. "How's your gaydar?"

"Be nice!" Her sister scolded her with a backhanded swat, but then she asked, "What do you make of Juliano?"

I paused in thought like a deer in the headlights, feeling slightly self-conscious. "I don't know?" I answered. "He seems like a nice guy." I paused. "He's obviously good looking."

"Damn straight!" agreed Irish Kyrah emphatically. "He's a real looker."

"If you're attracted to him, you should tell him," I advised her. "I'm sure he'll be flattered, even if he doesn't like you. You should give it a shot."

"No, no, no," Irish Kyrah laughed along with the others. "We don't want your opinion of him." She had to lower her voice as she became increasingly animated. "We think he might be gay!"

"All the pretty boys always are," Joyce added. She seemed convinced.

"No way," I objected. "That guy's a stud."

"It takes one to know one," snickered Flip-flop with a snort of laughter.

I gave her the hairy eyeball. "I'm not gay," I complained.

"That's not what I meant," she said with a chuckle. "You said he's a stud."

"I can't be sure he's straight," I huffed. "I don't judge dudes like that."

"So, your gaydar sucks," Irish Joyce surmised.

"I guess it does," I agreed, "but..." I looked around trying to spot Juliano, then turned back to the group. "I can tell you one thing." I lowered my voice and projected into the center of the circle. "Mountain Girl totally has the hots for him," I opined.

"We all think he's hot," revealed Fräulein Vera. "That does not make him not gay."

"Maybe you should ask him," I defended. "Like my mother always says: 'Stop guessing; just ask.'"

I heard a female voice that sounded like it came from inside a cave. "Juliano is definitely not gay, eh," the voice said with a clearly Canadian accent.

"Ya!" shouted Fräulein Vera, suddenly thrusting her hips upward. Irish Joyce rose to a seated position, and we all looked up at the same time.

Mountain Girl's head suddenly appeared right above us hanging over the edge of the bunk. Then Juliano's head popped out next to hers, and all our hips bucked with laughter. Mountain Girl and Juliano had been laying together in the bunk directly above us making out. "Would you please stop talking about us?" snapped Mountain Girl. "I can't focus, eh."

"I also find it very distracting," pleaded Juliano. At this there was an explosion of laughter.

"Clearly not gay," surmised Irish Joyce. There was more laughter. The couple went back to doing whatever they had been doing. A moment later Mountain Girl squealed with delight and there was another cackle.

"How 'bout the guitar player?" queried Irish Joyce.

"Alter!" snapped Fräulein Vera. "Der Typ is Irre!"

"In English please," directed the blond Irish girl.

"The Chicken boy?" she stabbed. "He's crazy!"

"I was referring to the other Guitar player," Irish Joyce informed her.

"Er ist ein geiles," she said flatly. "Musiker er ist ein prima Kerl!"

"English," the midwives prodded sternly.

"He will be a great musician," she translated. "But I will not share his taste in music."

"He's brilliant, but he seems a bit damaged," surmised Irish Kyrah. "I overheard him talking about his ex-girlfriend. He has a bit of a broken heart."

"There you go earwigging again," chastised her sister.

"It's not like that," she denied. "He knew I was listening. He hardly talks."

"He's horribly bashful," assessed English Tessa from her seat close by against the window. "He's a smart guy. Cheeky fella really. He stutters horribly at times, but he sings like a bird."

"Would you do him?" asked Irish Joyce bluntly.

"He's a gentleman and a rocker," English Tessa whispered, "but I find him a bit Gammy. He's as thin as a rail."

"He needs to suck a lime to ward off the scurvy," jabbed British Sue.

"I'd fuck 'im," announced Fräulein Vera.

"I would do him," confided Irish Kyrah.

"Have at him," her twin said jealously. "Just leave me clear out of it."

"You dare not tell him I like him that way," Irish Kyrah threatened.

"How about you Flip-flop," Irish Joyce asked the Bostonian.

"He wouldn't be my first choice, but I'd put him in my bus five," she reported. "I like how he's always snapping his fingers, gathering up a tune."

"You will tell me about this five," demanded Fräulein Vera.

"It's a list of the top five people you would be with, if you could without consequences," she explained. "People on the bus anyway," she clarified.

"There's hardly five blokes on the bus," scoffed English Tessa.

"It's just an expression," she contended.

"Leave her alone," snapped Irish Joyce. Then, she asked the soccer player, "Who's on the top of your list?"

"I'd rather not say," stammered the Bostonian. She was choked-up.

"Who would you feck?" Irish Joyce pressed English Tessa.

"It seems a bit shabby to reserve people on a list," she commented. "I have a boyfriend at home."

"She's dating my brother," British Sue informed them.

"I said without consequences," reasserted Flip-flop.

"She likes the Dutch bloke," her friend exposed.

"You prat!' exclaimed English Tessa.

"Don't get your knickers in a twist mate," she responded. "I haven't been an angel either." The two of them exchanged a fist bump.

"I like Johnny," spouted Maid Marian. She and her fiancé had been sitting quietly, listening the entire time. "Only if there were no consequences in or out of wedlock, of course."

"Thanks," I responded with a laugh. "You're not so bad yourself."

"I was talking about British Johnny," she clarified.

Everyone laughed.

"Not that I don't like you too Johnny," Maid Marian backpedaled.

I was so embarrassed, but Sir Gavin lifted his chin at me and said, "It's all good."

"We need to keep the two Johnny's straight," declared Irish Joyce. "He's Johnny Lovebus," she said pointing at me. "The fella with the guitar, we call him Guitar Johnny, because he wears that thing like a badge."

Maid Marian reached out, touched my shoulder, and said, "You can be in my five too." She tossed her hair in a way that made my heart flutter. Sir Gavin just shrugged.

I felt the need to fan myself, so I took a deep breath and said, "Likewise."

"I'm flattered," she said.

"You'd be in my five," Irish Joyce told Maid Marian. The Irish blond lifted her hips under Fräulein Vera's head and suggested, "How about it?" The German girl came to attention and said, "Ya!"

"That's so sweet," responded the South African woman. "If only I were gay."

"Don't let me stop you," interjected her fiancé. Then he added, "Please." We all laughed. Maid Marian was extremely attractive. I'm pretty sure we were all having improper thoughts. Her husband moved closer to her like he was aroused by the talk. He put his arm around her and asked, "Aren't you curious who's in my five?"

"By all means," she lilted. "Do tell."

He coughed into his hand and said, "Let's just say, it would be more than five." We laughed again.

"What about Brian?" Irish Joyce asked. "What do you guys think of him?"

"He's really not my type," joked Sir Gavin.

"He was totally hitting on me last night," revealed Flip-flop.

"He tried chatting me up too," added English Tessa from outside the circle.

"Scheisse!" Fräulein Vera joined in. "He's a fucking pig, just like that Chicken fucker."

"Brian is so nice," Jewels defended him from the fringe. She had been trying to read a book. "He can hit on me anytime he wants."

"He has a fiancée!" English Tessa objected.

"That doesn't mean anything," scoffed Irish Kyrah.

"He told me he was in love with her," she argued. "He told me all about her. He seems to love her."

"He told me too," Jewels testified. "You've gotta respect honesty. We all know how hard it is to find an honest man. Just because you love someone doesn't mean you have to stop loving other people."

"You think so," mumbled the Bostonian.

I gave her an inquisitive look. She shrugged. "He told us he's in a polyamorous relationship with his fiancé," I disclosed.

"That's brilliant!" blurted the Irish Twins in unison. "We're poly too!"

"You will tell me what that means," Fräulein Vera demanded.

"It's a free and open kind of relationship where you can love as many people as you want," explained Irish Joyce. "It's called polyamory. You don't have to stop loving other people when you find the one you love the most."

"Good for him," cheered Irish Kyrah.

"Good for me," rejoiced the schoolteacher. "I would totally do him."

"Me too," agreed the red-haired Irish girl.

"That's not fair," I complained. "When I love more than one girl, they all end up hating me."

"That's right," chided Flip-flop. "Not on my watch."

"See!" I exclaimed.

Juliano hung his head over the rail once again to address us. "If you love all women equally, they will love you in return."

I mumbled, "Easy for you to say."

With that Mountain Girl said, "Not so fast lover boy." She grabbed his shoulder and said, "Get over here, eh." She pulled him back on top of her and said, "You're all mine, eh."

The girls all laughed.

"You will tell me more about this polyamory," pressed Fräulein Vera.

Irish Kyrah revealed her thoughts wholeheartedly. "Most relationships end with cheatin.' That's just another form of being polyamorous, in my opinion. People need to stop living in denial. It is not human nature to be with only one person your whole life. People are just too uptight about being faithful to one person. They're scared of being alone, but half of them end up alone anyway. It makes me want to start a club when I get back home to teach people about it."

"What are you getting on about?" Irish Joyce objected. "Back home that would go over like a fart in church."

"I think the world would be a better place if everyone embraced polyamory. There's clearly nothing wrong with it." We went on and on about the virtues of loving as many people as possible until we finally came to the conclusion that, as Irish Kyrah summarized it, "It makes no sense to limit yourself to loving one person. We should all be free to love whoever we want whenever we want and as many people as we want without having to hide our love from one another."

"Alas it be true," Irish Joyce conceded with a sigh. "The sexual mores in Ireland are behind the times."

It was determined that the Peruvian was too strait laced and uptight to be with another woman, and I dispelled any conjecture that she was romantically involved with the Chinaman. "There's something up with that guy," suggested Irish Kyrah in a hushed tone. "I can't quite put my finger on it, but there's something cocked-up with him for sure."

"That hairdo makes him look like a dyke," assessed Irish Joyce without turning down the volume of her voice.

"It takes one to know one," teased her sister.

The conversation went on and on like this until they had talked about every eligible person on the bus. The girls spoke openly and loud enough for prying ears to listen and hear without much effort, but they spoke unreservedly. However, they never mentioned Yülia. She was just too pure, young, and innocent to be deflowered publicly. Australian Sheila was deemed questionable because Irish Joyce openly wanted her, but truthfully all evidence pointed to her being straight too. At some point I nodded off with Flip-flops head in my lap.

10
Party Across the Great Plains

When I woke up, we were in the parking lot of a liquor store somewhere in the middle of the Great Plains. Other than the grocery store across the street, there really wasn't anything else around for miles. Driver Chris stood up, holding the safety bar by the door with one knee on the buddy seat. "Listen up guys. We are in Albert Lea, Minnesota. We're stopping here for one hour to stock up on supplies. There's a grocery store across the street where we'll be doing a little food shopping. They have a snack bar, but don't eat too much because we'll be stopping for dinner in a couple hours at a gorgeous lake." He waited for some chatter to subside. "The lake is super beautiful. So, you'll have a chance to swim there. After dinner we'll be driving through the night to Badlands National Park in South Dakota.

Tomorrow night we will be camping on an Indian reservation. Alcohol is hard to find in Indian country. The Indians do not allow liquor stores on the reservation, so we will be buying supplies for the party here. This will be our last chance to stock up on alcohol for the next few days, so everybody might want to contribute. Chicken Jim will be collecting money and taking orders, although you are welcome to do your own shopping if you prefer."

There was more chatter before he continued. "The eastbound Green Tortoise cross country bus will be meeting us in the Badlands tomorrow night for a camp-out party. It's a Tortoise tradition to compete to see which bus has the most fun. Ever since I first teamed up with Brian our bus has won every time, so I'd like to keep our winning streak alive."

"What do we win?" Little Josh cried out.

Driver Chris contemplated this over the din. "You get to have a wonderful time," he answered. "I know you guys won't let me down, but I want to encourage you to be as wild and crazy as you can possibly be, so we're guaranteed to win. So, get psyched and get whatever you need to show the other bus what it means to have a good time."

The passengers cheered with a bunch of yips and yahoos. Berndt Toast made an Indian war whoop by patting his mouth repeatedly. Judging from how many of the Green Tortoise passengers made the same sound, people all over the world must have made Native American war whoops as children. We were simply excited to be heading into Native American country that's all. Our white-man war whoops were performed in ignorance for sure, but not with any intentional disrespect or malice toward Native Americans.

The popularization of this patting of the mouth phenomenon is a product of television, historical fear mongering and the inability of most white people to make ululating mouth sounds. It should come as no surprise that Native American warriors never made such sounds in battle. Rather, this was our failed attempt at mimicking the ululating sound rare Native American women make in celebration when warriors return from battle. Our excitement for Native American culture would culminate in a celebration on sacred land in the days to come.

A small rectangle of bright green manicured grass graced the otherwise featureless parking lot just outside the bus door. This seemed completely out of place amidst the fallow fields of Minnesota. The sprinklers at the liquor store had recently run, leaving the long blades of grass ashimmer with dew. The Irish girls ran out first, followed closely by Fräulein Vera. Their squeals of joy made obvious the pleasurable feeling of hot bare feet on wet grass. All the passengers piled off the bus in similar fashion.

There was a strip mall across the street with a supermarket. Several people were craving meat, so they planned to find food together. Peruvian Ursula asked Driver Chris, "Is there any where around here to buy a bathing suit?"

"You could try that store across the street," he recommended. So, the Peruvian escorted PAC-MAN to the department store; Driver Chris led a small crew across the street to shop for groceries; and Chicken Jim collected money for the party fund. I gave him a twenty and rested on the grass with a few of the other passengers.

Driver Brian knew exactly what to do. He gave me some instructions and I set out to do as he asked. As I climbed the ladder, I saw Chicken Jim through the driver's window counting the money he had gathered. Driver Brian passed him two fifty-dollar bills and the rookie had to start counting again. I quickly peeled back the tarp at the front corner of the roof box. I found the two wooden boxes Driver Brian had described. I removed the expensive-looking outdoor speakers and set them up on the roof. I dangled the wires in front of the Driver's window and Driver Brian plugged them into the stereo. With a click of the switch, the driving, rhythmic masterpiece of South American funk, called "Umbabarauma," pulsed to life, thumping provocatively in our chests.

Everyone went berserk, dancing like mad hatters at a psychedelic mushroom tea party. I had never seen people dancing with such wild, frolicking movements. We were laughing because of how wonderful it felt to dance that way, laughing unrestrained and free. We were dancing like the children in our hearts.

Driver Chris had inspired us to be as wild as we could be, and Driver Brian supplied the musical stimulation. Chicken Jim rushed into the liquor store with the Irish Twins. I was dancing wildly on the roof, rocking the bus back and forth with my weight. Passengers inside the bus began swinging back and forth visibly rocking the bus left and right. The Tortoise bus had come to life again, swaying to the tribal rhythms of South American funk. Everyone seemed to be experiencing the same joyful release. It was such a great feeling, people from such varied backgrounds and diverse cultures, sharing such a wonderful moment together, dancing like freaks in a postage-stamp sized square of freshly watered grass in a liquor store parking lot in Minnesota.

The meat-eaters came back with delicious smelling takeout, and PAC-MAN arrived in a bathing suit with a Billabong rash guard, the kind of shirt intended to be worn while swimming. Judging by the number of shopping bags his Peruvian friend had taken him on a shopping spree.

Chicken Jim and the Irish Twins raced toward the bus in a train of three shopping carts with wheels click-clacking across the parking lot. It was hilarious. The two girls were out of their minds laughing in brogues reminiscent of Irish children I had once seen running on the green fields atop the cliffs of Galway. Chicken Jim pulled up alongside the bus with a shopping cart overloaded with alcohol. We gave each other a knowing look as he passed up the first of two cases of Brut Champagne for storage on the roof.

I heard more laughter coming from the direction of the supermarket. Driver Chris pushed the first of three overflowing food carriages. I beamed a huge smile at him, quickly opening the rest of the roof box to make ready for the new supplies. The fresh fruit and vegetables looked magnificent. The dancing passengers tossed up a dozen beautiful eggplants, three kinds of lettuce, eight small boxes of mushrooms, two flats of tomatoes, four bags of onions and all varieties of fruits and melons. The food just kept coming until the fixings for a week's worth of meals packed all the coolers on the roof. Driver Brian went inside with bricks of butter, followed by a line of passengers carrying blocks of cheese, tubs of yogurt and vats of sour cream. Milk, eggs, and shredded cheese were passed into the bus through the windows. The music of the Talking Heads triggered another seizure of dance. Everyone knew the words to The Talking Heads "Life During Wartime."

> I got some groceries, some peanut butter,
> To last a couple of days
> But I ain't got no speakers, ain't got no headphones,
> Ain't got no records to play
>
> Why stay in college? Why go to night school?
> Gonna be different this time
> Can't write a letter, can't send no postcard,
> I ain't got time for that now

A conga line formed, and the party marched up the steps of the bus without missing a beat. Before closing the roof box, I grabbed one of the five-gallon wash buckets and a gallon jug of wine. Driver Brian went back to sleep in the driver's cabin. The bus rolled away from the liquor store with music blaring out the open windows.

> And you may find yourself
> Living in a shotgun shack
> And you may find yourself
> In another part of the world
>
> And you may find yourself
> Behind the wheel of a large automobile
> And you may find yourself in a beautiful house
> With a beautiful wife

As the bus roared away from Albert Lea, Minnesota. The cushions on the front platform were sent to the rear of the bus, and the whole front platform was converted into a dance floor. We were off again, parading down the highway in Minnesota on our way across the Great Plains, with nothing to look at outside but cornfields and farmlands. As the bus passed through this fertile breadbasket, we had a rolling dance party with a wild assortment of half-naked international dancers.

Party Across the Great Plains

And you may ask yourself, well
How did I get here?
Letting the days go by, let the water hold me down
Letting the days go by, water flowing underground
Into the blue again after the money's gone
Once in a lifetime, water flowing underground

I took to drumming on the wash bucket drum, standing in the door-well, adding a tribal feeling to the music. Deutsche Mark gave me a knowing look and said, "Party on dude!" In that moment, the zany Dutchman was my best buddy in the whole wide world. We drummed together like two brothers who had shared a lifetime of joy. We were living in the moment, cherishing the experience. The past was irrelevant. I cast off my former life like a pair of hockey gloves before a fistfight. Life was good. I was digging it. It was happening. I felt a profound sense of joy, like I had felt earlier that day while swimming in the Mississippi River.

The front platform was absolutely packed with sweating passengers, cavorting like lunatics. Five or six people danced on each bench and eight or nine more undulated to the throbbing beat in the aisle. People started drinking beer and passing a bottle of wine. Girls were hanging out the windows, trying to get truckers to blow their air horns.

We danced with wild abandon in a swirling maelstrom of undulating madness. All the ladies loved watching Juliano dance. He had a certain Ricky Martin swagger when he took his shirt off. Flip-flop danced with him, rubbing up against him provocatively. When the song was over, he grabbed her around the waist and dipped her body horizontal. When he lifted her back to a standing position, she appeared dizzy. He pulled her close and started making out with her.

I danced until I was completely exhausted by the heat. I was dripping sweat and needed to rest, so I went back to rear platform to chill out. One by one, the other overheated dancers came back to join me. The back platform soon became crowded with reclined bodies. This caused the evacuation of the non-sweaty passengers, so a second wave of spastically dancing Tortoise passengers filled the dance floor.

The back platform soon became overcrowded so that we were all touching each other, despite efforts to keep cool. When Flip-flop and Juliano came back, there was no space left, so they crawled up into a bunk together. I suspected they were fooling around.

****

I woke when Driver Brian stepped over me on his way forward from the driver's cabin. I had passed out from exhaustion and was sleeping in a twisted pile of bodies on the back platform. We had all grown much more comfortable and loving with each other since Chicago. Driver Brian had slept through the entire party. I sat up as the bus pulled into a parking lot alongside a beautiful lake surrounded by a thick forest of trees.

There was a sign at the edge of the parking lot, unlike any other I had ever seen in the east. Below the words Loon Lake, the sign featured a row of symbols: a picnic table, a swimmer, a boat, a fish, a tent, a hiker, and a dog. Sure enough, we had crossed the Mississippi. This was no uptight eastern signpost; this was the beginning of the Great American West! This was the beginning of the great adventure.

Driver Chris parked the bus facing the lake overlooking a lush field of grass that sloped down to the water's edge. There was only one other car in the parking lot. A couple was sitting on a picnic blanket close to the water's edge watching their children swim. The brakes hissed and the engine died. Driver Brian surveyed the landscape, turned, and made an announcement. "This is Loon Lake, Minnesota. We're stopping here to make dinner."

"What's for dinner?" shouted Little Josh.

"We'll be making my mother's eggplant parmesan!" shouted Driver Brian. "Everything is fresh from the market, so it should be amazing."

"Goodie! Goodie! Goodie!" the boy expressed joy. "I love your eggplant." He told everyone, "We had it on the last trip. It's awesome."

The blond-bearded driver continued, "I know it's hot, and all of you will probably want to go swimming, but we need some people to hang back to start the meal. If you cook, you can swim after dinner and you don't have to help with the clean-up."

There was a lot of talking as passengers made plans to either swim or cook. Australian Sheila offered to lead water aerobics, which persuaded a bunch of girls to swim before the meal. While the others were talking, Driver Chris got up and said, "I don't know about you, but I'm starving. I'll get things started for you." He left the bus.

Driver Brian held up a finger. "This is a public place, so you will need swimsuits." There was a moan of displeasure followed by a laugh. We all preferred to skinny-dip now, having done it several times together. Keeping our clothes on was boring. Even with a twelve-year-old kid on the bus, swimming nude had become the new norm. However, that way of being did not extend past us. Our guide bent down and looked at the family sitting by the water. "There are people down there, and I don't think they would take kindly to a bunch of naked backpackers crashing their afternoon with their kids. So, please keep your clothes on. There's plenty of lake to swim in, so please give them space."

Passengers were already milling about getting ready. "Everyone off the back platform, so people can get their suits!" It was so hot. Saying anything more would be a lost cause. The bus swayed to the side as Driver Chris passed outside the driver's window on his way up to the roof. His colleague motioned for Chicken Jim to follow and stepped off the bus. I followed close behind him.

"Why don't you guys swim first?" Driver Brian suggested. "We got this. Be back soon though," he requested. "This meal is labor intensive." So, I swam with Chicken Jim for about fifteen minutes, just enough time to cool off, or at least take the edge off the intense heat.

The aerobics class was in full swing. It was mostly ladies, but PAC-MAN was out there bare chested, sporting his ever-present Ace Bandage. It was funny because he fit right in with the ladies. The way his bandage crossed his chest under his arms made it look like he was wearing a sports bra and he was as short or shorter than most of the ladies.

A speed boat with a water skier came whizzing by. It was a bunch of college guys having fun in an overpowered boat with dual outboards. The boat took an obvious second pass coming closer to the girls doing water aerobics. The skier tried to jump a wave generated by the earlier pass and ended up losing control. He dropped the line and skimmed even closer to our girls.

"I want to try, eh," shouted Mountain Girl.

"Give it a shot," offered the boy. So, the Canadian started swimming out to the boat.

"Someone go with her!" demanded Jewels from the water's edge.

"So much for the water aerobics class, eh," said the equally athletic Australian girl. She dove in behind her friend and swam to the boat. The boy helped Mountain Girl with the skis while the other boys pulled the Aussie into the boat. The boat took off and Mountain Girl stood up on the skis on the very first try. The boat whisked them away, traveling so far across the lake that we soon lost track of them.

"She's good on skis," appraised the New Yorker.

"She bloody well ought to be," commented Guitar Johnny. "She's a professional ski instructor."

By the time Chicken Jim and I returned to the bus after swimming, an assembly line of cooks was already preparing the feast, dipping the eggplant into Driver Brian's special batter. We fried up two massive bowls of hot food while the other half of the passengers swam in Loon Lake.

At one-point, Little Josh came running into the kitchen area to find his mother. He was afraid of what he had seen. "Dave's talking to the fish!" he exclaimed. "He waved his hand and made the fish jump. I swear I saw him do it." Of course, nobody believed the kid except me, although this did draw our eyes to the lake.

Jewels pointed at the water and screamed, "Look! It's Mountain Girl."

"Wunderbar!" shouted Yülia, chopping tomatoes by her friend's side.

Her skiing skills really were top notch. She carved like a pro with perfect form and consistently landed jumps off the swells in the wake of the boat. Naturally, as the boat grew closer all of the spectators started waving.

"Do you think she can see us?" asked the petite German, waving frantically. Just then, Mountain Girl gave us all a big wave. "Wunderbar!" shouted Yülia. However, when she grabbed the rope again, Mountain Girl's legs wobbled, creating slack in the line. When the line came taught, she sped up suddenly and launched off a wave out of control. Her legs were thrown apart in the air like an Olympic ski jumper. She had no choice but to release the rope and lay back and relax. Her skis came off with her legs up in the air. Her hard body hit the water, making a splash like an asteroid.

The boat turned around to pick her up and we went about the business of cooking the eggplant Parisian, without a second thought. A few minutes later we heard the boat motor buzzing again and Jewels announced, "She's skinny-skiing!"

Despite the driver's warning about nudity, Mountain Girl was now skiing without any clothes.

"She's naked?" inquired Driver Chris with a tone of concern, standing on the far side of the kitchen.

"Naked as a jaybird," confirmed Chicken Jim.

"Keep it down," he scolded. "Maybe no one will notice if we keep it quiet." All the while, the family picnicking on the waterfront remained unaware.

Driver Brian was crafting a fresh-made red sauce, in a huge cooking pot, made from fresh tomatoes, garlic, onions, and mushrooms. He offered Jewels a taste.

"It's like a four-star restaurant," she raved. She rewarded him with a soulful hug for his efforts. The dinner was topped-off with a huge bowl of garden-fresh salad, and freshly shredded Parmesan cheese.

We were all so hungry; we couldn't wait to start eating.

Party Across the Great Plains

As mealtime approached, the drivers started worrying about the girls on the ski boat, so they sent a few passengers down to the water to wave them in. Both girls came ashore fully dressed. Australian Sheila soon had us all in stitches, as she coerced the Canadian into sharing the intimate details as to exactly how she ended up water skiing naked.

The conversation first caught my ear when I heard Mountain Girl exclaim, "My bikini came off when I went down, eh!"

"Atta girl," praised Juliano.

"Close your ears, Josh," advised his mother.

Mountain Girl gave Juliano the finger and said, "In your dreams."

"Close your eyes too, Josh," the boy's mother muttered weakly. She stood behind her son with her hands cupped over his ears as he struggled to listen. He eventually escaped her grasp and went to stand by Chicken Jim.

"You should have seen it," Australian Sheila enthused. "She caught some big air off a giant wave."

"We saw her crash," Yülia informed her gleefully. "It was wunderbar."

"Did you happen to notice how I landed crotch first?" asked the Canadian. "My legs were spread like a Barbie doll."

"That's what she said," shouted Little Josh.

Chicken Jim gave him a high-five.

"Seriously Jim?" Mother Michelle chastised the rookie. "I'm holding you responsible." She muttered to the side, "I'm so glad he never played with dolls."

Mountain Girl addressed the throng of ladies, "It wasn't funny, eh. I broke the lace on my top, and I couldn't find my bottoms." She displayed the knot she had tied to repair her shoulder strap. The girls listening groaned sympathetically. "I looked everywhere, eh," she bemoaned dramatically. She put the back of her hand to her forehead feigning frustration. "I figured they'd sunk to the bottom."

"You didn't give the blokes a chance to search," teased the Aussie with a snicker. "You swam right over to the boat."

"I was in shock, eh," contested the Canadian.

"They lads were more than happy to pluck you out of the water nude," she chided. She turned to the group and explained, "The lads just wanted to 'ave a Captain Cook of her fanny."

"I had so much water in my nose, I couldn't even talk, eh," pleaded the Canadian.

"It was hilarious," laughed the Aussie. "You should have seen what she did when she got on the boat." She pressed her finger to the side of her nose and pretended to blow with one eye closed.

"What's that," begged the innocent blond German girl.

"A Bushman's handkerchief," clarified the Aussie.

"We call that a snot rocket!" Chicken Jim stepped forward. Much to the dislike of all present, the driver-in-training blew boogers onto the ground with a finger to his nose.

"Don't you dare, Josh," shouted his mother.

"You did that in front of the lads," tittered British Sue.

"Fuckin-a," boasted Mountain Girl.

"You're disgusting!" observed Maid Marian.

"Hey now! That's my girlfriend," objected Juliano.

"I'm not your girlfriend, eh," Mountain Girl snapped at him.

"You're not?" questioned Flip-flop.

"No!" she confirmed with a sneer.

"I'll take him if you don't want him," said the Bostonian.

Juliano gave Flip-flop a sexy look, making a purring sound straight out of grade school.

"You can have him, eh," huffed Mountain Girl. "He's in love with that Peruvian girl, anyway."

The Australian laughed suddenly, remembering something hilarious. "Tell them what happened when you put on your suit?" she urged her friend to tell. The two girls locked eyes. When things grew quiet the Aussie obliged her friend, "You don't have to tell them if you don't want to." She pretended to zipper her lips. "I won't say a word."

"You will tell us what happened," demanded Fräulein Vera.

"Please tell us," begged Yülia.

Mountain Girl looked around with a Cheshire smile to make sure Little Josh was not listening. She said, "One of the fucktards handed me a towel, but he dropped it on the deck, trying to get me to bend over. I'm sure." She made like she was bending over. "Water was still leaking out of me," she said with a snort. "But I didn't expect there to be so much air."

"Crikey what a blunder," quipped the Australian.

"Oh no!" went the Irish Twins in unison.

"When I bent over to pick up the towel, it all came out of me at once." She snorted again. "It was like a moose call."

We all cracked up laughing. I had to hold my belly.

English Tessa arrived out of nowhere just as she said these words. "What did I miss?" she complained.

Overcome with hilarity, British Sue shouted, "Her front-bottom farted!"

Deutsche Mark followed behind English Tessa. His facial expression was priceless when he heard these words, then at the peak of laughter he said, "Party on dudes!" This brought the house down.

****

Party Across the Great Plains

With my empty plate and cup in hand, I approached the Peruvian Pink Panther at the dishwashing station. Upon sensing me behind her she snarled and tossed her plate into the wash bucket and stormed off in a huff, leaving me to wash her dishes.

There was a children's soccer field with the miniature nets set up on the manicured grass alongside the lake. Little Josh and Guitar Johnny went around encouraging people to play, conscripting anyone and everyone who was not swimming or cleaning up. Driver Brian gave me a nod of approval and I joined the game. Berndt Toast encouraged the Europeans to form a team and they challenged everyone else.

The game was fantastic, judging from the cheers and jeers, but the Europeans got upset because Little Josh played so selfishly. He hardly ever passed the ball, and he tried to score every time. When he did score, he would celebrate, rubbing it in their faces and taunting them. There wasn't supposed to be a goalie because the net was so small, but Little Josh made it a point to stand right in front of our net. Then he spent a lot of time hovering in front of the visiting team's goal, waiting for the perfect pass. Then he would scream, "GOAL!"

As a result, the European players started ganging up on the poor kid. They kept the ball just out of his reach, burning him with fancy moves. They scored on him repeatedly despite his goaltending, and their celebrations were over the top. Little Josh grew very frustrated as he made his way up and down the field repeatedly charging for the ball, but he never gave up.

Flip-flop and I felt sorry for him, so we came to his rescue. I should say, Flip-flop came to his rescue. She kicked ass; I just played along. The Europeans stepped-up their game and started taking the score more seriously. In the end, Flip-flop fed Little Josh a pass that led to him scoring the winning goal. The Europeans may have been put-off by the boy's boasting about how great he played, but they had to congratulate Flip-flop on her exceptional soccer skills.

"You're amazing," I told her as we waited at the water cooler.

"You're not so bad yourself," she responded, then she added, "And you play soccer good too." We laughed together. She was super cute. Deutsche Mark mopped his sweat with his shirt in front of her in line. She took a step back when he raised his arms to wipe his pits. She made a face like he smelled bad, then she sniffed me. "You don't smell," she observed.

"I'm sure you smell better than me," I self-deprecated.

"I don't smell a thing," she attested. "I have a good nose," she assured me. "Maybe it's pheromones." She looked into my eyes and said, "We seem to be genetically designed to be together." My hopes rose when she added, "We've got good chemistry."

British Sue must have overheard because she stepped between us and said, "No one likes chemistry, love." She rose up on her toes begging a kiss, and said, "I hear congratulations are in order." I kissed her, but it felt more like I was rewarding her.

Before she walked away, she sniffed me and said, "You smell like a bog."

After dinner Driver Chris suggested that we collect some firewood for the campout the following night. Chicken Jim responded where he was lying, "Can't we just buy some wood."

Driver Chris chuckled and said, "There's no wood in the Badlands, Jimbo." He laughed and said, "There are no trees." I marveled at the thought of a place completely devoid of trees. No wonder it was called the Badlands. Before they marched off to gather firewood, I asked them, "Is there anything else I can do?"

"Sure!" Driver Chris directed me, "It smells like rain. Make sure everyone gets their luggage back on the bus before the shit hits the fan."

"Will do," I said. I walked around telling the passengers that rain was on the horizon, but only a couple of them packed up and put their luggage away. I wanted to impress the drivers but getting people to do stuff in one hundred percent humidity was harder than I expected.

When they came back with the first load of wood, Driver Chris made a general announcement, "Rain's coming!" he shouted. "You don't want to get caught out in the rain!" He looked at me and asked, "Did you tell them?"

"They didn't listen," I explained.

"Be creative," he told me. "I hear thunder."

"While they passed the wood up to the roof, I went around again, alerting people to the thunder. A few more passengers packed up and loaded their luggage, but there were still at least ten stragglers dragging their feet when the drivers took off for more wood.

Driver Chris said to be creative, so when Juliano walked up, still wet from swimming in the lake, an idea popped into my head. "Juliano Pento!" I called him by his full name for dramatic effect. "I need your help with something."

"I am at your service," he offered.

I explained the situation, "You know I'm training to be a driver, right?"

"Yes, I know this," he responded. "I would love to be a Green Tortoise driver. I picture myself someday meeting you in Panama. You with your Green Tortoise adventure bus and me with my own South American adventure bus." This guy was great.

Party Across the Great Plains

"That sounds awesome," I gushed. "I pray that happens, but right now, I could use your help. Driver Chris asked me to gather everyone inside the bus because it's gonna rain any minute."

"You want me to spread the word?" he asked.

"No. I tried that. They won't listen," I informed him. "We need to be more creative. It needs to be something that will get the stranglers moving, something provocative."

He eyeballed me suspiciously and asked, "What do you have in mind?"

"I want to tell them that you and I have a surprise waiting for them inside the bus."

"What surprise?"

"I want you to do a sexy dance for the ladies," I told him. "You know, like you did this afternoon on the way here."

He responded without batting an eye. "I can do that." He eyed me again. "Only if you dance with me."

I fell back on my feet and said, "No way!"

"Come on," he said. "You can't expect me to dance alone. That would be weird." He pretended to be me speaking, "Please come inside. Juliano has a surprise for you." He shook his head adamantly. "Then I just do a little dance. No way! That would be so weird."

"I see what you mean," I agreed.

"We need something spectacular," he suggested.

"We do?" I questioned.

"We need to be showmen." This sounded hilarious coming from a kid who was barely eighteen.

"We do?"

"Yes!" he proclaimed. "We should do a striptease."

"What? No way!" I fell back on my heels again.

"That would get them inside," he said with a tilt of his head.

"Yes, it would," I agreed. "But we wouldn't go all the way, right?"

"No! Of course not."

"They wouldn't want to see that," I suggested.

"The girls like you," he informed me.

"They do?"

He laughed confirmation. "If we are going to strip, first we need to put a bunch of clothes on."

"The more the better," I said. "Let's meet back here."

I put on a fresh pair of underwear, dry shorts, and I brought with me a pair of socks, a fresh shirt, and a pair of sweatpants. Juliano came back fully dressed. "It's way too hot. You should have waited to get dressed until we were ready," I told him, gesturing to my pile of clothes.

"Good thinking," he agreed. He took off his shirt and his nylon Adidas workout pants. "I should get a coat and a pair of socks," he said. "I'll be right back."

"Shorts too," I reminded him.

"Right!"

"I'm going to start telling people," I chased him with my words. "That thunder is getting closer and the sky is getting dark." He agreed with a waved hand as he ran off.

I proceeded to go from passenger to passenger saying, "We need everyone on the bus. Juliano has a surprise for you. There's going to be a floor show. You don't want to miss it! Think Chippendales!"

Mother Michelle's eyes lit up. "What on Earth?"

"It's gonna be epic," I told her.

When the drivers came back with more wood many of the stragglers were packing up. "I've got it under control," I told Driver Chris. "There's gonna be a floor show."

He said "Nice!"

Juliano returned with his socks on top of a bundle of clothes. A group of girls approached him and asked, "What's going on?"

"What have you told them?" he asked me.

"I told them there will be a floor show, once everyone is inside the bus."

"Did you tell them YOU will be in the show, also?"

"Not exactly," I backpedaled. "I wanted to entice them, not make them throw up."

"John will be in the show also," he told the girls. "Now, you better get inside. It's going to rain." There was a boom of distant thunder.

"One more load of wood and we need to be ready to go!" Driver Chris shouted on his way back into the forest.

Juliano accompanied me as we spread the word. Much to my delight, everyone seemed intrigued and excited except for Sir Gavin. However, he was curious. When he asked us what was up, we made him swear to secrecy before we told him the plan.

He loved the idea. "My fiancée will love it," he proclaimed. "Have you picked out the music?"

"Oh shit!" I had not thought of the music. "How about La Vida Loca?" It was the only song I could think of, only because of Juliano's resemblance to Ricky Martin.

"I don't know that song," revealed Juliano.

I was shocked. "Do we even have that song?" I asked Sir Gavin.

"Probably not," he guessed. "I'll go see what I can do," he told us.

Party Across the Great Plains

"It just a'needs to have a'good a'rhythm," Juliano advised.

"Got it!" said Sir Gavin.

We spent the rest of the time before the wood crew returned making sure that every last person and thing was onboard and ready to go. Juliano kept promising, "You're not going to believe your eyes!" The family having the picnic took off in a rush to avoid the rain.

When the wood crew returned, the bus was packed and ready to go. We explained our plan to the drivers and Driver Brian offered, "I'll control the lights."

While they loaded the wood, Juliano and I got dressed by the front bumper. That is when Juliano revealed his secret. He had been hiding something in his stack of clothes. Now we had to be extra careful not to let anyone see us getting dressed.

Everyone was ready. Driver Chris took a seat in the back. Sir Gavin greeted Driver Brian as he entered the bus. "I have the music all cued-up. Just press play," he instructed.

It was so hot and humid; I was already dripping sweat. It was such a relief when the rain started. It was just a few drops at first. I put out my tongue and faced the sky, but the clouds opened after that and it started to pour. Juliano and I stepped into the door-well and closed the door. The passengers were all scrambling to close the windows. It had grown dark, so Driver Brian turned on the cabin lights. The sound of the rain roared until the last window was closed. It was incredibly humid and hot inside the bus and we had several layers of clothes on.

"Here goes nothing," I said.

Mother Michelle was in the first seat by the door. "Break a leg," she offered, all giddy.

Driver Brian turned off the cabin lights to get people to settle down, but a flashlight came on, then another and another.

"I have an idea," I told Juliano. I put my head over the support bar at the top of the door-well and shouted, "No flashlights!" People booed. "Pass them up," I commanded. Mother Michelle began to pass flashlights over the rail. "We only need four," I told her.

I gave Driver Brian a look and told him, "Keep the lights off for a bit."

Juliano and I stood side by side in the dim light in the wide area between the top step and the driver's seat. Upon seeing Juliano take the stage Peruvian Ursula opened her book and started to read. I gave the blond-bearded DJ a nod. He nodded back and pressed play. Sure enough, the trumpets blared as Ricky Martin's Livin' La Vida Loca blasted on the stereo. On cue Juliano and I lit our flashlights and began spinning them one in each hand as we danced. The passengers went wild cheering and shouting, hooting, and hollering.

> She's into superstitions
> Black cats and voodoo dolls
> I feel a premonition
> That girl's gonna make me fall

We were dripping wet from the rain and Juliano was gorgeous. It gave me confidence standing next to him because I knew people would not be looking at me. I must admit, it was very provocative being up there on stage.

> She'll make you take your clothes off and go
> dancing in the rain
> She'll make you live her crazy life, but she'll take
> away your pain
> Like a bullet to your brain
> Come on!

I let the energy of the crowd take possession until I was no longer in control of my own body.

When it came time to take off our coats, we passed the flashlights back to the eager women seated up front. They shone flashlights on us like spotlights as we took off our coats. I shot a look at Driver Chris in the back. He had a look on his face like a proud father. I gave Driver Brian a nod and he turned in his seat to control the lights. We spun our coats around in the air over our heads as the cabin lights strobed as fast as the driver could flip the switches. The amber aisle lights made it look remarkably similar to a strip club.

> Woke up in New York City
> In a funky cheap hotel

We tossed our coats into the crowd and they went wild. It was so hot. Juliano smiled at me and grabbed a hold of his shirt. It was time for the big surprise. Juliano had found two unclaimed articles of clothing on the dashboard. We ripped off our shirts and revealed that we were both wearing bras. The crowd exploded in laughter and cheers.

Jen from Boston rushed forward and screamed, "That's my bra!"

Mother Michelle shouted, "Take it off!" So, we did. I unclasped his bra and he did mine. The ladies were going wild. We twirled the bras above our heads and cast them into the sea of diving bridesmaids. Flip-flop secured her bra, ripped off her shirt, put her arms through the armholes, and shimmied up to Juliano, pressing herself against his bare chest. He bent down and tried to kiss her, but she spun around, allowing him to secure the clasp. When the job was done, she rewarded him with a kiss that caused the ladies to scream. Mountain Girl gave them a nasty look.

I gave Juliano a nudge and gestured with my hands on my waistband. He knew what to do. He teased them with a dip of his nylon pants. I did the same with my sweatpants. We flashed our shorts to more clapping, cheering and laughter. We both took off our pants and twirled them into the crowd. Then we dropped our shorts, still in our underwear, of course. This would be no full monte. God forbid. We took off our socks and tossed them into the crowd one by one. This was very funny indeed. We were knocking them dead. Maid Marian feigned passing out when a sock hit her in the face.

The song would be over soon. We had given them our best. Our job was done. Or so we thought. The women were insatiable! All of them were still shouting, "Take it off! Take it off!"

Juliano and I gave each other a knowing look and dropped our underwear to the floor. Yes, in the heat of the moment we delivered the Full Monte.

> Come on!
> Livin' la vida loca
> Come on!
> She's livin' la vida loca

When the screams reached a crescendo, I caught Peruvian Ursula's eye as she glanced up from her book. She was checking out my goods. Juliano looked at me jealously and flicked his underwear in her direction with a pointed toe. Flip-flop and Peruvian Ursula both grabbed hold of his black boxers, resulting in a brief tug-of-war where the Bostonian had to overpower the debutante to keep her from throwing them out the window.

For these last few tense seconds, we danced naked with our cocks swinging.

When the song ended, I was laughing so hard I had to reel myself in and take control. Suddenly, I came to my senses, standing stark naked in front of a cheering crowd of horny women. I dove for the wheel-well. Juliano joined me two seconds later. We had to beg for our clothes, but we eventually got dressed.

Mountain Girl came forward to have words with Flip-flop. She was mad at her for hooking up with Juliano. Australian Sheila came to her side for moral support. "I thought you said you're not together," pleaded the Bostonian. "If that's how it is, I'll tell him to get lost."

"Yeah! Tell him to get on a bike," injected the Aussie.

"Don't you mean 'take a hike,' eh?" corrected the disgruntled Canadian.

"I guess it's kind of the same," explained the Aussie. "If we want a bloke to leave us alone, we tell him to get onya bike."

"I love it!" cheered Mountain Girl, and the three of them were best friends again.

Driver Brian turned the engine over, put it into gear and the bus rolled away from Loon Lake. Juliano went back to greet his adoring fans and I took the buddy seat. "You're the fucking man!" said Driver Brian.

"You liked it?"

"It had the makings of a Tortoise legend," he marveled. When Jewels came forward, I offered her the buddy seat and sat behind the driver.

****

The big blond Californian kept us entertained telling Baja stories for a long time as we drove into the night. He spoke passionately with unrivaled excitement, at times gulping for breath between sentences. One story led to the next. "They used to call me Baja," he told Jewels in a voice loud enough to be heard by the half-dozen passengers leaning in to listen behind him. "I worked for the Green Tortoise at their isolated beach camp called Playa Escondido, in Baja Mexico. A lot of crazy shit happened down there."

"Like what?" Jewels entreated.

His face lit up like an amusement park. "It's amazing," he told us. "The beach is surrounded by hills with a fifteen-hundred-foot mountain behind. The Sea of Cortez is jumping with fish and dolphins and orca whales. Sometimes the water is like glass and the waves glow with phosphorescent phytoplankton. When people skinny-dip at night their kicking makes the water light-up like fireflies."

"What does a Baja caretaker do?" Jewels wanted to know.

"My duties were to sell beer and weed to the passengers."

"Really?" I spat.

"It's true," he revealed. "I wasn't allowed to make any money, but I could drink and smoke as much as I wanted."

"That's crazy," I marveled.

"It's a crazy place," he revealed.

"Is it dangerous?" asked Jewels.

"Not so much," he said. "The people are nice, but the desert can be rough. I once saw a group of eight hikers step right over a rattlesnake. It was so camouflaged they could not even see it. It blended right into the rock. If someone had stepped on it, that might have been the end. We were so far out and halfway up a mountain. Not to mention Playa Escondido is at least three hours from the nearest hospital."

"So, the locals are nice," prodded the New Yorker.

"Oh yeah," he told us. "The Mexican men have a reputation for being macho, but they are really softhearted when it comes down to it. They wouldn't be caught dead on a beach without their boots on because of scorpions."

"That sounds intelligent," the New Yorker observed.

"Maybe so," he said, "but I tell you, they are soft hearted when it comes to drowning kittens."

"Who wouldn't be?" she objected.

"You don't understand," he said. "They don't have animal hospitals down there, so there's no way to get a cat fixed, and they need cats to keep the mice and rats away. Sometimes a cat will have babies and there's no one to take care of them, so they have to do the right thing and put them down."

"I see," Jewels said.

"Normally, in their culture it's the man's role to do the right thing and dispose of the cats. So, they give the cats to the fishermen, so they can put them in a sack with a bunch of rocks and throw them overboard. That just doesn't happen because most Mexican men are really kindhearted. They end up letting the cats go on an island they call La Isla del los Gatos Ferales." He said this with a tone of mystery.

"The Island of Feral Cats," gasped the New York schoolteacher.

"Yes, he said. "We call it Wildcat Island. There are thousands of feral cats on Wildcat Island. It's this island out in the middle of the Sea of Cortez."

Jewels made a horrible face and asked, "How do the cats survive?"

"You'd be surprised," he said with a smile. "Once they go feral for a few generations they go back to being truly wild, and they learn to hunt again. I've even heard they can pull fish out of the sea."

"No way!" I objected. He had so many stories it was hard to believe anything he said, but he swore on his mother's eyes it was all true.

His eyebrows told us he was for real. "I once knew this guy who got shipwrecked out there on Wildcat Island. They were trapped there by a storm for three days before the Mexican Navy rescued them. The military guys wouldn't step foot on Wildcat Island, even to help them get their skiff back in the water. They just watched them struggle from the boat. It was not a good scene. He told me the yowling kept them awake all night, and in the daytime the cats would approach you like you were something to eat."

"Oh, my Goddess!" Jewels erupted.

"Yeah. Tell me about it. These were not the kind of cats you pet."

"Are the cats still there?" she begged.

"As far as I know," he revealed. "I don't foresee any Mexicans ever stepping foot on that Wildcat Island." He pulled back on the blinker to change lanes as we merged onto the highway. In one smooth movement he shifted into fourth gear. I loved to watch him shift. He did it with such grace, giving it no thought whatsoever.

"Tell us another story," Yülia encouraged him.

He was more than happy to oblige. "One morning I decided to ride my mountain bike to the top of the fifteen-hundred-foot mountain," he told us. "So, I put on my neon blue race jersey with my matching neon blue bike shorts. You do not wear underwear with bike shorts like that, so I headed up the mountain without giving it a second thought. The road to Playa Escondido is carved out of the face of a cliff with crazy blind curves hanging over huge drop-offs, like eight-hundred or a thousand feet. The road is washed out in places and full of ruts. There are boulders blocking the road that fell from the cliffs high above. It is rough going up or down. So, when I finally got back to the bottom, I was totally exhausted and out of breath."

He was equally out of breath just telling the tale. "I coasted past the farmhouse where the property owner lives." he told us. "Then, I hear 'Clip-clop, clip-clop.' I look behind me and there's a twenty-five-hundred-pound brahma bull chasing me down the road. You know the kind of bull with the big ol' hump on its back with big long sharp horns. That mother fucker broke into a full-paced gallop, chasing down my ass."

We all agreed with our eyes and a chorus of, "No way!"

"I figured the bull was attracted by my neon blue riding clothes, like a matador's red cape, you know. So, I stood up and started pedaling faster. Clip-clop, clip-clop. The bull was picking up speed, so I shifted gears and pedaled faster. Clip-clop, clip-clop. He started gaining on me, so I pedaled as fast as I could, but it was no use. The brahma bull kept gaining on me. Clip-clop, clip-clop. He was closing in."

"He had the hots for you," suggested Yülia. We all laughed.

"Exactly what I was thinking!" spat the big blond guide. "I thought that big old bastard wanted to fuck me."

We all laughed again.

"Who could blame him?" laughed the raven-haired schoolteacher.

He was like, "What?"

"The brahma bull obviously wanted you," she contended.

"I thought he wanted to run me into the ground and tear me to shreds," he breathed.

We all agreed.

"What did you do," begged Yülia.

"I hammered the pedals one last time in a final burst of speed. I jumped off the bike and threw it in front of me," he scoffed at himself, "as if that was going to stop him."

"What were you thinking?" Jewels quavered.

"I don't know what I was thinking," he confessed. "I jumped out of the way and the brahma bull lifted my bike on the run with his horns and flung it off to the side of the road like a rodeo barrel. It landed seat first against a pipe organ cactus. I'll never forget it. It hung there for a second before it fell over."

"What did you do?" Jewels wanted to know.

"I stripped off my shirt, dropped my shorts, and ran screaming into the desert faster than the Road Runner gettin' chased by the coyote." We laughed.

"Remember I wasn't wearing any underwear like I told you before."

"Ha! You were naked!" Jewels screeched.

"The brahma bull turned on a dime and came right for me, despite my lack of clothes. I jumped over some sagebrush, but he tore it up and stomped right after me. I was screaming the whole time, running through the desert in my birthday suit. Brahma bull! Brahma bull!"

Amidst a collective gasp, I said, "Holy shit!" Our ears were glued to his every word.

"I thought that damn bull must have been in love with me or something, because he wouldn't give up. He followed me every step of the way, hot on my heels, prancing left and right as I started switching directions moving from side to side through the cactus, running as fast as I could, changing directions repeatedly." He pawed the air lifting his limp wrists from side to side like he was playing piano. "That shit they say about a bull in a china shop is horseshit."

"More like bullshit," interjected Jewels. We laughed.

"I couldn't believe it. That mother-licking bull started dancing like Baryshnikov, dodging saguaros and pipe organs like a ballerina." He kept playing the piano with his hands.

"What did you do?" cried Jewels.

"I started throwing rocks and cow patties," he told her straight out, "but he ducked and dodged everything I threw at him. I ran around trees in tight circles hoping to tire him out, but he stayed on me like stink on shit. He followed me every step of the way. He stayed on my back no matter what I did."

"Finally, he tired out and I got a little bit of a lead on him, so I got back on my bike and rode like the wind, but then I sat down! When my bike hit the cactus, it had left barbs in my seat."

"Oh no!" howled Jewels with the rest of us.

"Yes!" he proclaimed. "It fucking killed. I was going nuts trying to pick cactus barbs out of my ass, riding as fast as I could toward the Green Tortoise Beach Camp. The whole way I heard, 'Clip-clop, clip-clop.' So, at the last second right before he got me, I veered off-road onto a mountain bike trail. I thought I was home free taking the shortcut back to camp, but my plan backfired. Low and behold, the bull was smarter than me. He stayed on the road while I had to jump over a bunch of downed trees and shit. The bull ran just fast enough to catch up with me where the two paths merged. I swear to god the brahma bull would have got me if I didn't launch into the air off the jump at the end of the trail where it met up with the road. This whole time I'm screaming, 'Brahma Bull! Brahma Bull!' I didn't want to endanger all the passengers back at camp, so I had to warn them, right?"

"Sure!" spat Jewels, and we all agreed.

"So, I kept yelling, 'Brahma Bull! Brahma Bull!' and all of the passengers in camp came out to see what was happening.

"No way!" I said.

"So, I blaze into camp. At the last second, I jumped off my bike. I leapt over the cooler pit and I climbed an ironwood tree, screaming, 'Brahma Bull! Brahma Bull!' Just then, Michael the kayak guide steps right into the bulls' path. It skids to a halt at his feet and he smacks it right between its horns with the whiffle ball bat. So, Michael says to me, 'You just need to let him know who's boss.'"

There was a gasp for air and a lot of laughter before he continued the story.

"To make matters worse there was a group of about twenty Tortoise women laughing at me," he revealed. "It's not every day you see a giant naked guy clinging to the branches of an ironwood tree."

We all had a good long laugh, made comments, and jeered him about it, but his stories folded fluidly from one to the next like the hips of a cowboy on an eight second ride. "That brahma bull turned out to be a real pest, but I did get my revenge," he reflected.

"Do tell," said Jewels with eyes full of admiration.

He seemed eager to continue to cover his embarrassment. "He wouldn't leave me alone after the bike incident," Driver Brian told us. "He kept showing up in camp. It was unnerving."

"You broke his heart," suggested Yülia.

"You may be right," he admitted. "I tried to shoo him off, but he wouldn't leave," he said with a shrug, then he shook his head. "The next morning, we found the food pantry had been knocked over and a bunch of our corn had been eaten." He shook his head again. "I knew it was the brahma bull, but there were mountain lions in the area, and the drivers wanted to play it safe. So, we secured the pantry to a tree and wrapped the whole thing in a tarp, but I was right. In the middle of the night that mother-lickin' brahma bull tore the tarp to shreds with his horns and made off with a fifty-pound sack of onions."

"Ha!" I laughed.

"That's a lot of onions," Jewels marveled.

"A ton," he agreed. "They come in a big gunny sack," he informed us.

"Did the bull eat the whole fifty pounds?" I had to ask.

"Yeah! Just about," answered Driver Brian. "I followed a trail of onions into the desert to his hideout in the arroyo. No one believed it was him until they saw the burlap sack hooked on his horn."

"Ha!" I laughed with the others.

"That's funny," said Yülia.

"It was hilarious, actually," he recounted. "He had eaten a hole right through burlap, but there were still a few onions he couldn't reach in the center of the bag. He kept trying to fling the sack off his horn, but the onions at the bottom kept smacking him in the face and in the side of the head, depending on which way he threw his head." We were all laughing and smiling now. He was throwing his head around pretending to be a brahma bull. "It was driving him mad." He sounded joyful.

"Poor bull," sighed Yülia.

"Are you serious?" he demanded.

"What?" she asked.

"Everyone always sides with the bull," he complained.

"He was lonely," pleaded Yülia.

"He stole our onions!" he contested.

"Did you help him get the sack off his head?"

"I didn't," our driver insisted. "Some of the passengers felt bad for him so they got Michael to help. You know the guy with the whiffle ball bat?"

"Did the bull stop bothering you after that," asked Jewels.

"No!" he said. "The drivers led him away again and again, but he kept coming back, so I plotted my revenge."

"That poor bull," sobbed Yülia.

"What did you do?" Jewels wanted to know.

"I made a gut bomb," he said proudly.

"A what?"

"A gut bomb," he explained. "I filled a five-gallon bucket with the remaining onions and the half-eaten corn and all the kitchen scraps from dinner that night and laced it all with a shitload of cayenne pepper. I mean a shitload."

"Ha!" I laughed.

"You did not?" protested Jewels.

"That's so mean," cried Yülia.

"It was for his own good," reasoned Driver Brian. "If he kept eating people food, the farmer would have had to put him down. We didn't have a choice. We had to send him on his way." He seemed almost giddy with excitement.

"How did you get him to eat it?" I questioned, feeling giddy myself.

Driver Brian smiled. "I didn't have to do nothin,'" he told us. "I just left the bucket near the pantry and went to sleep. In the morning we found the empty bucket, but the bull was gone. Several of our passengers said they heard him leaving camp in the middle of the night, burping, and belching all the way up the arroyo."

"Ha!"

"What happened to him?" asked Jewels.

"I hope he will be okay," sobbed Yülia.

"He was fine," Driver Brian told us. "A few days later after everyone was gone the farmer rode up on a horse." Driver Brian assumed a Mexican accent as he spoke. "He asked, 'What happened to that brahma bull? He didn't come home for a couple days and one of my sons said he saw him down this way.'" His eyes jumped open with an 'Oh no!' expression before he continued. "For a second I was worried that the bull might have gotten sick, or died or something, but after I told him the story he was like, 'I knew that bull must have eaten something hot, because he drank the whole water-trough.'" We all laughed and laughed.

After telling all of these stories Driver Brian took a deep breath and exhaled slowly. He checked the mirrors a few times as he changed lanes on the pitch-black highway. "I have to remember to shut up sometimes." He breathed again.

"Why would you say that?" asked Jewels.

"My cup runneth over and so does my mouth." He struck a meditative pose with his index fingers touching his thumbs, with his hands hovering above the steering wheel. "I've been lucky in my life; I have had so many wonderful experiences. I should be thankful and let other people share their stories." He breathed again.

Jewels struck a similar pose and began to breathe with Driver Brian. Yülia did the same. I followed next.

Party Across the Great Plains

Jewels started telling a story about her own life, growing up in Washington Heights. I laid down between British Sue and Flip-flop on the front platform. I focused on my breathing and began falling asleep.

Brian was right. That I need to start creating my own reality. I decided to be thankful. I was snuggled between two Spice Girls, a blond British babe and a sporty badass from Boston. I had a lot to be thankful for.

11
Badlands National Park

In the darkness before dawn, the Green Tortoise Adventure Bus crawled to a halt along the curb of a dark empty parking lot in Badlands National Park. With the last breath of the engine came a profound silence. I arose from the back platform where British Sue and I had been sleeping. I gingerly tiptoed over the people on the front platform. Driver Brian was asleep with his arms resting on the steering wheel. Jewels had fallen asleep on the Buddy Seat leaning against his shoulder. He stirred briefly as I cranked the noisy swing-arm to open the door. I embraced the cool night.

The atmosphere of this strange new world stood perfectly still. Neither cricket chirps nor cicada songs desecrated this altar of silence. It was an alien environment entirely devoid of sound, like the ticking hands of time had paused mid stroke. I felt like I had fallen into the space between the notes on the sheet music of natural history, listening instead to a symphony of silence in the vast amphitheater of vapid space.

No light of human populations polluted the perfect pitch. No headlights haunted the horizon, no streetlights lit the landscape, no bulbs burned on buildings, no towns twinkled in tungsten, there was no synthetic light anywhere. I felt alone in the universe, like I was bearing witness to the primordial Earth at the dawn of time before the first random event started evolution.

The stars lit up the sky like the glow of a celestial city that stretched from horizon to horizon. With wide-eyed wonder, I followed the path of the Milky Way across the moonless night. The brilliant starlight illuminated a menagerie of giant white formations, peaking a hundred feet above me against a silhouette of stars. A short walk away at the edge of the parking lot, a metal handrail blocked the edge of a huge canyon of similar formations, stretching out below like a kingdom of white sandcastles.

There was so much light from the stars, that I easily found my way to a clump of desert bushes. My imagination explored the parapets one castle at a time. The mountain shaped fortresses in this strange old world appeared soft at the edges as if formed by a child's playful finger. I happily imagined myself on a foreign planet and that the Green Tortoise bus was my moon buggy. I returned to the comfort of my sleeping bag and snuggled up next to British Sue. In my dreams I ascended towers of sand in an alien world.

A vision softly-creeping left its seeds while I was sleeping. On a lonely hilltop I stood face to face with my child-self. I had been trying desperately to recapture my youth and here I was face to face with a vision of my younger self. A combination of abuse and growing up too quickly had left me feeling empty inside. I felt disconnected from who I knew myself to be when I was young. In the yawning hours of my gentle child's dream, everything seemed clear in the light of this astral vision.

As the sun began to rise, I lingered in bed, relaxing. I felt young and not at fault. I knew my eyes would open with a new world for me to explore. I thought, the sun will rise tomorrow, but I might not. I got up slowly as not to wake British Sue. I walked outside into the dawn and let the landscape flow through me.

The long angles of sunlight I witnessed that morning had the power to change my life and inspire me forever. The vast array of delicately colored layers that had built up over the eons, layer upon layer, color on top of color, were waking up from their slumber of shadowy night. The rays of sunlight illuminated the pinkish reds, purples, browns, yellows, oranges, tans, and grays like the layers of a geological layer cake. I was waking up too. I imagined myself returning to this place throughout my life. How could I not.

The massive pinnacles and peaks changed their colors like chameleons, gyrating with vivid colors, and the play of the sunlight brought them to life from the wasteland, creating a living organism out of barren earth. The countless miniature peaks and valleys were bathed in varying shades of taupe and tan, beige and blond, ivory and vanilla. The colors shifted in the shadows and danced in the direct sunlight, creating a visually orgasmic symphony of fantasmic hues. It was like watching the entire process of color changing in the fall foliage in New England, condensed on film over the course of a few minutes.

I stared in amazement at the formations below me on the floor of the canyon for a long time before I noticed that most of the people had gotten off the bus, and now made their way to the edge of the canyon, standing at the handrail behind me. They had been woken up by the splendid array of desert colors shining through the windows of the bus, and they too felt compelled to bear witness to this marvel.

Having borne witness to the long angles of dawn's sunlight illuminating the sandstone formations of the Badlands, the Bostonian's heart was so full of joy that it was as if the sunrise had occurred within her. Overcome with emotion her voice quavered, "It's unbelievable! How could this have been here my whole life and I didn't know about it? No one ever showed me a picture. Why don't they teach us this stuff in school? I've never imagined anything so beautiful. I had no idea this was even possible." Her reaction was both endearing and it served to vicariously amplify my enjoyment of the spectacle of dawn over the Badlands.

Driver Chris was sitting on the rim of the canyon with French Sandrine, swaddled together in his sleeping bag. He was kicking his legs like an overjoyed little kid having the time of his life. He was clearly in his element again. Driver Brian's face was visible in the driver's window with Jewels' eyes lurking in the shadows above his head. He had turned to face the horizon with his chin on his folded arms resting on the window ledge. Jewels leaned up on his back with her arms folded across his shoulders.

Among all the wonderful women present, Jewels stood out as a delightfully holistic and soulful beacon of constant joy. She was wonderful for a thousand reasons before any mention of gender or physical beauty. Her effervescent spirit was paramount. She was full of energy and light. Her words rang true and her voice was always proud. She was dignified, decent, and just.

Her skin was a delicious shade of Dominican Mocha reminiscent of Halle Berry. Her body was voluptuously proportioned, like a living breathing incarnation of the Fertility Goddess that rested in her cleavage. Jewels turned me on body and soul, but she was never on my sexual radar. She was more than all that. She was the heart and soul of our tribe. She was a sacred woman to be treated with respect, like a tribe elder or shaman. She was as rare as an albino buffalo. I would like to think all women are sacred to me, but Jewels stood out as a special being, akin to a Goddess.

In all manners of speaking Jewels had the grace of a true woman. She was the benefactor, the mother of us all. I could feel it when she held my hand. It made me happy to think she was a part of my world and that I was part of hers, however insignificant I may be to her. I was happy to see her bonding with Driver Brian. She deserved to be happy.

I felt a rush of unbounded joy. It was a really cool scene, all these people from around the world, all silently awestruck in harmony

Badlands National Park

with these sublime natural wonders. I had never experienced such condensed human beauty. The colors of the formations changed as the sun rose, creating ever fresh entertainment for the eye. Eventually, the discernable colors would become muted by daylight, but for now the long angles of dawn painted the Badlands with exquisite light.

While I was still rapt in amazement, Driver Chris stood up and folded his blanket. The passengers started putting on their hiking boots and getting ready. Evidently, we would be going on a hike before breakfast. By the time I left the rim of the canyon and returned to the bus, Driver Brian had pointed the way and many passengers had already started walking.

Driver Brian informed me, "It's a five-mile hike, so best to get going now. It will be getting hot sooner than later. Breakfast will be waiting for you at the other end of the trail." Jewels and a few others stayed on the bus with Driver Brian to help with breakfast.

Little Josh shouted to his mother from the trailhead across the road, "Come on, Mom! Let's go already!" She was filling their water bottles.

Peruvian Ursula hiked off with a large group of passengers, but I could not help but notice how closely PAC-MAN kept following her. He even stopped with her when she bent down to tie her boot. I joined Deutsche Mark, British Sue, and English Tessa, who were all among the last group of stragglers to leave the bus.

The prairies of the Northern Great Plains rise to form the Black Hills of South Dakota. The fields of endless grass drop off into the Badlands suddenly, and without warning. In places, one can see the wispy grass of the Great Plains growing right up to the edge of deep canyons. The Dakota Indians call these lands "Mokosica," meaning "bad land," because traveling through this land is not associated with anything good. We were all good though, with high-tech hiking boots, nothing heavy to carry and a clearly marked trail for us to follow. We would be having it easy compared to the first people.

I hiked alongside Deutsche Mark, letting British Sue and her friend get far enough in front of us so that we could talk. "Tessa seems to like you," I commented.

"Yeah. She's into me," he agreed. "It's a shame she has a boyfriend," he said. "Tessa is dating Sue's brother. That's a little too close for comfort."

"That's exactly what she said," I scoffed. We hiked on in silence.

The layers of sediment that form the banded colors of the Badlands are the result of a series of volcanic eruptions that occurred during the same geological period as the formation of the Rocky Mountains. The easily eroded ash deposits from volcanoes, make this one of the most delicate places on earth. The erosion continues rapidly every time it rains, snows or even when the wind blows. Precipitation is rare, but when it does rain the water carries away a huge volume of sediment, washing it into the White River, which flows into the Missouri, and on to the Mississippi. Even though the surface erosion was brand new, we still understood that we were looking at over a million years of erosion.

Later on our hike, we climbed an offshoot of the trail up a ravine into a small cave. Several dozen cliff swallow nests hung from the ceiling of the cave like cement condominiums. The cliff swallow makes its nests by mixing its precious saliva with dirt to form a mortar, which it spits into the shape of a nest with a round cave-like door at the front. The protruding baby bird beaks made the nests look like mounted gun turrets.

Without disturbing any birds, our group found seats within the small cave, and we rested for a while. Deutsche Mark casually lit up a joint and offered it to the girls. They both declined with a quick shake of the head. Deutsche Mark took a couple of drags and passed it to me.

I took a puff, held it, and exhaled. "It's strange," I said. "The first time I've ever been hiking in the Great Plains, I ended up in the smallest most enclosed place imaginable." I passed the joint to much agreement.

Deutsche Mark followed a cave swallow into its nest with his eyes. "You know what would be really awesome to do," he asked plainly. He took a hit and dragooned the word, "Mushrooms!" He blew out a shaft of smoke, making his mouth look like a cave swallow's home. The three of us laughed at the thought, but he was serious. "Mushrooms are good for you, bro," he attested. I snorted and coughed a fit of laughter at hearing this.

"Honestly," he testified. "Mushrooms are not like other drugs. They do not act on your brain; they act as a catalyst to get your body to get itself high. Sometimes you just need to blow out the pipes."

"So, it's a natural high?" I commented facetiously.

"Exactly dude!" He was adamant. "It's the most natural high there is."

"You're starting to sound like a nutter," remarked English Tessa. "Isn't he Sue?" She looked to her friend for support.

"He is sounding like a bit of a loon," British Sue agreed.

He looked at them with incredulity. He defended his position. "You ladies need to do the breathing, feel the feelings, and start believing," he coached them. "Psychedelics are non-addictive, psychologically safe, and self-regulating, so you can't O.D.," he argued. "I'd eat a handful right now if I had them."

"I already feel like I'm off-world," observed English Tessa. "If things get any wonkier, I'd lose the plot."

"It's true?" the Dutchman questioned me, seeking support. "I'm not crazy. Am I?"

"My father always told me, 'Believe half of what you see and none of what you hear.' Sometimes, I can still hear his voice in my head."

"What does that mean?" he asked.

"If it sounds crazy; it's probably crazy," I concluded with a laugh.

"Spot on," British Sue agreed with a titter. All four of us laughed.

"Well, I've done my research," Deutsche Mark said knowingly. "Psychedelics can open our minds to Universal Truth." He said this with conviction. "They can't guarantee enlightenment, but they can float your boat right up next to it."

"How close are you to Universal Truth right now?" I asked.

Deutsche Mark looked down in his hand. He had let the joint go out. "I just pulled out of the harbor, bro!" We all laughed a little and started hiking again.

The delicately banded colors of Badlands National Park are testament to the abundance of minerals in the Black Hills, one of the most variously mineralized areas in the world. Although the land might seem barren and inhospitable to life at first glance, we came to find out that this desolate look was just a facade. Like most deserts the wild land was full of life. Gumbo lilies and evening primrose thrived. The waxy red and yellow blossoms of prickly pear cactus were visible all around us. Cactus was something that I thought only grew in the deserts of the southwest. Green patches of juniper bushes sprouted up in the folds of the terrain. Yucca trees grew on the slopes of every valley. The land was full of life, indeed. We passed an island of green cottonwood and wild rose filled with birds and other small animals, where jackrabbit and cottontail bunnies danced around, as if on stage for us.

We hiked across open fields of sunbaked grass with Badlands formations on both sides of the trail. A series of formations on our left rose a hundred feet while the ground at our feet dropped away into a flat-bottomed pit with delicate formations etched in the tan colored sidewalls. We traversed a narrow slot canyon with exceptionally beautiful water-shaped curves and bends. The morning sun created brilliant pink colors and amazing complex shadows in the surreal passage.

Near the end of the trail, we could hear the sweet melodies of classical music playing in the Badlands. The trail ended across the street from a parking lot where the outdoor speakers were playing

Beethoven on the roof of the Green Tortoise bus. Jewels stood among the cooks lined up at the stoves cooking pancakes. A stack of blueberry, strawberry, chocolate chip, and plain pancakes was visible over the rim of the giant silver bowl. An array of flavored syrups sat on the table next to a bowl of hand-whipped cream. There were many more toppings, a bottle of chocolate syrup, toffee sauce, Nutella, lemon and sugar, an assortment of jams and several bricks of butter.

Fräulein Vera could not stand classical music, so she kept her Walkman blaring German punk music the entire meal. The music of Johann Sebastian Bach serenaded the rest of us as we ate our pancakes among the timeless formations of stone and sand, in a land strewn with ancient fossils.

Big Dave was the last one to return from the hike. From on top of the bus I could see him walking slowly with his thick, cherry walking cane. He had hiked the entire five miles through the Badlands alone. Breakfast was over, but he managed to secure one of the last cups of Cowboy Coffee and a short stack of pancakes. Although, the toppings were almost gone.

While Chicken Jim and I packed the roof box, I could see a family of Amish people getting out of their car. These conservative Pennsylvanians hardly seemed shocked at the sight of our funky green bus blaring Beethoven from Bose speakers. They came right over and spoke with Driver Chris who shared orange juice with their children.

After our meal, several people wandered across the parking lot to visit a geological site. A wooden pathway looped around a geological studies exhibit, winding through an area abundant with fossils and the remains of prehistoric animals embedded in sandstone. The fossils had been covered by millions of years of sediment, only to be uncovered by the forces of erosion. The unique thing about this exhibit was that the bones remain there for people to see, right where the paleontologists had found them, still embedded in stone.

The park is home to a splendid array of extinct swamp animals, including the three-toed horse, the camel, the rhinoceros, the saber-toothed cat, and some scary looking boars. The Badlands was also once home to the huge Titanothere, king of the grass-eating animals. Part elephant part rhinoceros, this huge beast was starved out of existence with the desertification that created the Badlands.

After everyone returned from the fossil exhibit, Jewels and Driver Brian went back together to sleep in the driver's cabin. They had stayed up all night together. Everyone watched them climb into the sleeper berth and close the door.

Driver Chris took the wheel. French Sandrine sat by his side. She made appearances on the buddy seat when he was behind the wheel, but she also spent a lot of time in the driver's cabin alone, pretty much whenever the co-driver was not sleeping. This made her seem aloof, like she could not be bothered making friends with us. She said it hurt too much to keep parting company with people she had come to love. To her credit, she did her best to uplift Driver Chris' spirits, and she sometimes had surprising eloquent flares of wisdom. She spent most of her time with Mother Michelle, helping take care of her son. She may have been just a groupie to Driver Chris, but she was a good person. I am sure he would agree.

As we drove through a menagerie of intricately formed sand formations, I sat next to Flip-flop on the front platform listening to Driver Chris pontificate about the virtues of the national parks. "Every American should visit the big national parks at least once," he opined. "I don't think you can really comprehend what it means to be American without visiting Yosemite and Arches, Yellowstone, and Zion. People have no idea what's out here, how powerful these experiences can be. The national parks may be borne in stone, but they also display ten thousand years of indigenous history. The pioneers must have been stoked when they discovered that shit."

He was driving through such a place as we listened. "Raw unadulterated natural wonders have a way of healing us," he explained. "I see it all the time. Nature heals people. It resets us. It undoes the damage done by our self-centered society. Natural grandeur makes our problems seem insignificant. Five-hundred-foot waterfalls have a way of washing the stress away. It makes your problems seem small."

French Sandrine gasped in awe. "You're so inspired. It makes me want to see them all."

"I can't praise the parks enough," he told her. "I never stop thinking about them, planning trips. I can walk through them in my mind."

"Your words express your thoughts well," she told him. "You could be an inspirational speaker."

For the next several hours we visited park headquarters, bought postcards, and toured the northern section of Badlands National Park. We stopped at several scenic vistas and drove several miles of unpaved gravel road to a place called Roberts Prairie Dog Town. The red-bearded Irishman drove with determination in his eyebrows on the rough and tumble road. He never took his steely gaze off the gravel or his powerful hands off the wheel, as it jerked back and forth on the bumpy washboard.

****

As Driver Chris drove the challenging stretch of road, he recounted a sordid tale for his girlfriend. Flip-flop and I sat up on our seats leaning in behind him eager to catch his every word. His account began innocently enough. "I was here in the Badlands on my birthday a few years back," he told her. "Dude! It was the most unforgettable twenty-four hours of my life."

"Stop calling me dude," his girlfriend complained tiredly.

"How old were you?" Flip-flop asked demurely.

The French girl rolled her eyes and said, "Don't encourage him." She gave Flip-flop a you're-crazy-look.

"I'll never forget. I was twenty-four. The lead driver buzzed me awake at five AM. He says, 'Happy birthday! We got you a present.' They gave me the bus for the day to do whatever I wanted."

"Awesome!" Flip-flop gasped.

"When I asked him what he thought I should do he said, 'You can go back to sleep for all I care, just get the fuck out of the driver's cabin.'" We laughed together. "He needed to sleep of course."

"Sweet!" I intoned.

"It was off the hook dude," the Irishman beamed. "I was just a co-driver back then. I had never had that kind of freedom or power before."

"What'd you do?" Flip-flop wanted to know.

"Well, I tell you one thing," he said. "I wasn't gonna fucking sleep. That's for sure. I had full control of a Green Tortoise bus all to myself. I could do anything I wanted." He sat up and adjusted himself in the seat. "I was so psyched. I wanted to do something no one had done before, blaze a new trail, you know?"

"Sure," I said.

"The Tortoise encourages drivers to explore uncharted places. I just never had the opportunity to do it," he admitted. "I was a greenhorn."

"A greenhorn?"

"A rookie," he explained. "I couldn't think of anything off the top of my head at first, so I just drove."

"Where to?"

"We were in Yellowstone the night before," his memory sparked, "so we must have been heading east." He suddenly remembered aloud, "That's right! I remember watching the sunrise with that tight little brunette from Amherst."

"Here he goes again," his girlfriend mewled.

"What?" he defended. "She was just being nice. She helped me search the map for something to do."

"Did you fuck her?" she demanded.

"I was driving," he scoffed.

"Did you hook up with her?" she pressed.

He smiled coyly. "It was my birthday and we were driving into the sunrise. She lit a candle in a Suzy-Q and offered me a wish. She said it was a blow job," he told her.

"You did not," his girlfriend protested.

"Ha!" I laughed.

"That's not what I meant!" he objected. "She literally had me blow out a candle in a cupcake. The roadhead came later."

Flip-flop and I started cracking up.

He looked at me with a mock-guilty expression like he was a school kid. "Where's the harm in a little roadhead?" surmised Driver Chris.

"Oh my God!" Sandrine exclaimed. "You could have crashed and killed everyone!"

"I slowed down for the good part," he reassured her.

"No harm no foul!" I was dying laughing.

French Sandrine huffed dramatically, turned to me, and faltered, "See what I mean?" She huffed another breath and derided, "You men are all the same."

"Where did you end up going?" I asked, trying to reel in convulsions of laughter.

"Devils Tower," he revealed. "Then we went spelunking in Jewel Cave."

"Wicked," gasped the Bostonian. "Good choice," she praised him.

"Were you the first to take a Tortoise bus to Devils Tower?" I inquired.

"Hell no," he informed me. "Lots of trips have gone to Devils Tower, and Jewel Cave for that matter."

"So, you didn't get to blaze a new trail?"

"I blazed a new trail," he stated proudly. "We were the first bus to serve breakfast while the bus was moving. To make it to Jewel Cave in time for the Candlelight Tour we had to eat breakfast on the road inside the bus before we got to Devils Tower."

Flip-flop crooned, "That's cool."

"Yeah, it was," he commended himself. "Nobody had done breakfast like that before," he expounded, "at least not in recent history. We stopped to boil water for tea and coffee, but everything after that happened right on the bus. Everyone took turns eating at the dinette. It was fabulous."

"Sweet," I praised.

"It was a no brainer really," he commented. "We had cereal, yogurt, bagels, OJ. Everything we needed was right there in the cooler, milk, butter, cream cheese. It was rad." He nodded convincingly.

"How was Devils Tower?" I asked.

"Rockin' dude!" he exclaimed. "When we reached the top of the climb, the girl from Amherst made out with me for at least an hour."

"Is that when she jumped you?" French Sandrine pressed him.

"She was a nice girl," he defended her softly. "It was a long time ago."

"That's a riot," I said laughing.

"How was Jewel Cave?" asked Flip-flop.

"Jewel Cave was totally sick, dude," he enthused. "We went spelunking with hard hats and gloves. It was awesome. We didn't have a single flashlight, only candles in lard buckets."

"That's fantastic," I said.

"The other driver planned it so that there were exactly twenty-four people on our tour, and they sang me happy birthday and had me blow out the candles a quarter mile underground in total darkness. It was the highlight of the morning."

"This is still only the morning?" French Sandrine reacted dramatically. "How long is this story?"

"Oh, that's just the beginning dude," he told her with burgeoning excitement.

"Stop calling me dude," she chastised him again. "I'm not a dude."

He continued. "After dinner with the Indians at Cuny Cafe, we threw a wild rave in the Badlands. It lasted all night. This guy from New York invited me and these three gorgeous girls to eat a bunch of mushrooms. We ended up having a naked massage fest on a communal mattress out in the tall grass. It was off the hook."

"You're impossible," French Sandrine reacted in astonishment. Did you have sex with all of them?" She commented directly to me, "Nothing would surprise me at this point."

He made a face with one raised cheek and a shimmer of his head that said, "No." Then he verbally added, "It wasn't about sex. That would have muddied the waters. It was all about the love, dude."

"Speaking of dudes. Did you make love with the guy from New York?" she teased.

"All five of us made-out together a couple of times. That was a trip," he said, secure in his sexuality. "We were operating on a higher plane." He wiggled his eyebrows at me suggestively and said, "I could tell his legs were the hairy ones because all the Tortoise girls shaved before the cowboy bar at Chico Hot Springs, otherwise it would have been touch and go."

I was laughing so hard. He was off his rocker and their banter was hilarious.

His girlfriend grilled him. "I find it hard to believe you didn't have sex with three naked women in your bed, dude."

"Don't get me wrong," he explained with an elevated tone. "The ladies had fun, but there was no singling anyone out, if that's what you're asking." He addressed me directly. "Suffice to say, the five of us had this group grope thing go on all night, and a whole bunch of other passengers came by out of curiosity, just to see what was going on. You know what I mean?" He nodded in certainty.

"Curious onlookers," I suggested.

"And some innocent bystanders." He completed the picture. "Most of the guys were too shy. They just watched from a distance like it was all part of the tour, but several of the lovely ladies joined us." He reminisced in his mind's eye.

French Sandrine had been shaking her head in disbelief since her last outburst. Now her head dropped into her hand. "I don't know what I'm going to do with you," she said. "You're unbelievable."

"So, you never had sex with any of them?" I asked.

"Well, I did later," he admitted. "Australian Kate led me by the hand to the top of the hill where we made love 'til dawn."

French Sandrine smacked her lips and said, "Of course she did."

"How do you become a driver, again?" I asked in earnest. "My birthday is coming up."

****

As we approached Roberts Prairie Dog Town, Driver Chris explained the difference between a Buffalo and a bison. "The terms are interchangeable," he told us, "but calling them bison seems anti-American as far as I'm concerned." He spoke authoritatively. "I think we should capitalize Buffalo to identify it as uniquely American. Yes, purists will tell you the correct word is bison, but Americans have been calling them Buffalo since the day we got here. Changing the word now is like trying to erase history. That ain't cool. The white man didn't kill all the bison; it was the Buffalo that they nearly drove to extinction."

"You've gotta love American English," I commented. "Our language is a history in so many ways."

"That's what I'm talking about," our driver concurred. "Language is our heritage, both good and bad." He continued passionately. "Obviously, I don't agree with the killing part, but the word bison just doesn't have the same frontier flavor, like the words cowboy and Indian."

"Right on," Flip-flop grooved. "I love cowboys."

"I've heard people complain that the word cowboy connotes heterosexual white males," he scoffed.

"It sure does," Flip-flop crooned. "Cowboys are hot!"

"Believe it or not there's a movement to call them 'People of Cattle.'" He smirked disbelief.

"How is cowgirl offensive?" I questioned. "Cowgirls are hot, too!"

After a long pause, he added, "If you ask the Indians, Native American is no less offensive than the label American Indian."

"That's messed up," I remarked. "I thought Native American was the politically correct term."

"Everyone did, at first," he spat. "It turns out, no one ever asked the actual Indians what they would prefer to be called."

"No way!" I shook my head.

"What do Native Americans prefer to be called?" Flip-flop questioned.

"Does anyone even know?" I questioned.

Driver Chris informed us, "The respectful thing is to call them by their tribal names, Lakota, Dakota, Apache, or whatever nation they identify as part of. The Indians we're going to have dinner with tonight call themselves Lakota. They're like family to me."

It blew my mind that our driver knew real Indians and that we would be meeting them and have dinner with them.

He continued his diatribe. "No one can speak for them all. That's part of the problem. The politically correct majority wanted a term to encompass all Indians, but that's not how they roll. Most Indians do not mind being called American Indian, but that's troubling too because American Indian is the only term for an ethnic group where the word American comes before their heritage. Everyone else is Italian-American or Irish-American, not American-Irish or American-Italian."

"Wow! I never thought of it that way," I admitted.

"Most people don't give it any thought," he opined. "If I need a word to group all the tribes together, I call them 'The Indigenous Prisoners of the United States.'"

"That's awesome," Flip-flop laughed.

"Sad but true," he commented.

"So, you have friends that are Indians?"

"I do," he answered. "You'll get to meet some of them tonight at dinner, Nellie and Frieda Cuny. They are Lakota Sioux. We are having Indian tacos at the Cuny Cafe. It is a place they run out of their home south of the park. They've been friends of the Tortoise for more than forty years."

"No way," I marveled. "I've never even seen an Indian outside of TV." Everyone else was excited too.

The bus created a huge dust trail behind us as we rolled along the dirt road through the treeless plains of South Dakota. From a distance the Prairie Dog Town looked like nothing more than a big wooden sign in an empty field, that said, "PRAIRIE DOG TOWN." As we grew closer, we could see two humongous free-range American Buffalo in the distance. No cage, no fence, nothing between us and them. A sign depicting a man being gored by a Buffalo warned that bison can run up to thirty miles an hour. This was intense.

The Buffalo did not seem threatened at all by the presence of two dozen backpackers piling out of a big green bus at Prairie Dog Town. The brave among us left the proximity of the bus to get closer to the Buffalo, letting the prairie dogs stand between us and the enormous beast. All the while at Prairie Dog Town, I could not keep my eyes off the hairy shanks and mighty bulk of the Buffalo. Even sitting down, each one looked as big as a Volkswagen.

I chose the sign of the day, the free-range American Buffalo.

I spent most of my time there hanging-out with Deutsche Mark and the two British girls. The Dutchman and I were getting on famously and things were going well with the girls. We took pictures of them with their cameras posing with Buffalo. We could not be in any of the shots because their boyfriends might see the evidence. That part was getting old, but they were fine being in our photos, so at least we got pictures of them and the four of us together.

From the first moment we set foot in Prairie Dog Town, Big Dave had remained motionless, staring solemnly into the distance at the Buffalo, not even bothering to look at the prairie dogs. It was as if he had fallen into some sort of a trance. Big Dave had graduated from fish, and now he was communing with the Buffalo.

Australian Sheila walked toward the Buffalo with her camera pressed to her face. As she got closer, the larger of the two Buffalo suddenly stood up and faced her. The huge beast snorted and pawed at the dusty ground staring her down. She immediately ran back and stood on the steps of the bus. She was visibly shaken. "He didn't look real through the camera until I heard him breathing," she said.

She was shocked when Driver Chris told her, "Disturbing the Buffalo is against the law." He was leaning against the bus in the shade. "It's something like a five-hundred dollar fine."

"Oh my God I'm so sorry. I had no idea," she told him.

"You don't need to apologize to me. It's the Buffalo you should ask forgiveness. If the park rangers see you do it, they can give you a fine," he told her. "If the Buffalo sees you as a threat, he just runs you into the earth. It's ironic that the people who protect the Buffalo work for the same government that once paid top dollar for their tongues. They slaughtered Buffalo by the millions to starve the Indians."

"I knew they drove the Buffalo to the brink of extinction," the Aussie told him, "but I didn't know they killed them to starve the Indians. That's just criminal." She remained flustered, having felt the power of a Buffalo moments earlier. "They just killed them and let them rot?"

"Yeah. Pretty much," he informed her. "The Indians saw this as the ultimate disrespect for the spirit of the animal. They traditionally used every single part of the Buffalo, right down to the hooves. The pioneers were such pigs they only ate the choice cuts of meat and left the rest of the Buffalo to rot. Ironically, just eating the choice cuts made them terribly sick because it was such an unbalanced diet, while the Indians thrived because they ate all of the different parts." Driver Chris was an excellent guide. He always spoke with great passion.

Australian Sheila's eyes widened. "It's interesting how their respect for the animal brought balance."

Scattered across the field, between the Buffalo and the bus, were hundreds of prairie dog burrows. The prairie grass grew right up to the circles of gray earth where they made their homes. Their burrows stuck out prominently on the yellow fields of short dried grass. The sign informed us that Prairie Dogs communicate over the 160-acre town with a language of barks and yelps to alert the community about approaching predators. Prairie dogs live and raise their young in an interconnected web of tunnels, where the young are raised communally in highly developed social communities.

If approached slowly, and in a crouched-down position, the prairie dogs were not afraid of people. Some passengers got as close as ten feet away to take pictures of the prairie dogs. When we got too close, they would drop out of sight and come up in a hole a little farther away. Against adamant motherly advice, Little Josh ran from hole to hole, chasing the prairie dogs back underground like he was playing Whack-a-Mole.

The midday sun beat down on Prairie Dog Town, causing sweat to drip off my nose and soak the brim of my hat. French Sandrine pretended to be overcome by the heat and fainted like Scarlett O'Hara into Driver Chris' arms.

"She's like a fish out of water," shouted Little Josh. "Poor little sardine!"

Driver Chris stood French Sandrine back onto her feet and said, "All right, all right!" He announced, "I know this really cool swimming hole on Indian land, if you guys want to go for a swim we should get going now."

We all cheered and rushed to the bus in a mob. French Sandrine took the buddy seat. She only had a moment to take-in the scene before the bus rolled away and left the wild Buffalo and Prairie Dogs behind. The wind through the open windows was a great relief to the motionless hot air of the prairie. After driving a good distance out of the park on the dirt roads, we entered the Lakota Sioux Indian Reservation. Nothing at all could be seen in any direction, except for the flowing ocean of golden prairie grass.

The bus stopped in the middle of the dirt road and the driver exclaimed, "Let's go swimming!" Down a slight hill on the right-hand side of the bus a beautiful kidney-shaped sky-blue pond reflected puffy clouds like a mirage in the vast dryness of the Badlands. "You'll need to wear shoes, or the cactus will fuck-up your feet," our guide warned us. He opened the door for French Sandrine and followed her down the steps. She leisurely watched him strip naked just outside the door. He stepped into his sandals and ran as fast as he could to the water's edge, removed his footwear and dove in.

I followed Chicken Jim outside with my boots in hand. He dropped his pants in front of the disrobing French girl. "Merde!" she exclaimed, covering her eyes, and turning away. "I've seen enough of your little yellow penis for a thousand lifetimes," she chastised him.

"It's the mighty oak that becomes the acorn," he said as he pulled off his shirt.

Although this was hilarious, she was not amused. "It's the acorn that becomes the mighty oak," she corrected him.

"That's what I'm talkin' about," Chicken Jim said coyly. "I'm glad you dig it." She was nonplussed. Once naked he took off running barefoot at full speed down the hill toward the alluring pond. There was no visible cactus in the short flaxen grass between the bus and the water, but he started screaming suddenly. "Ahh!" His momentum carried him another five yards before he could stop completely. He kept howling in pain. "Ahh!" He dropped to the ground on his backside and shouted, "Fuck!"

"Serves you right for not wearing shoes," French Sandrine yelled after him. She shouted into the window over her shoulder with a cupped hand, "You need to wear shoes everyone!"

"Can someone get me some tweezers?" shouted Chicken Jim in desperation.

"We're gonna need the med kit," I called into the bus.

French Sandrine brought the red toolbox to the suffering fool. I undressed and put my boots on. When she squatted down on her haunches to open the medical kit her feminine curves resembled the fenders of an exotic sports car. "You are your own worst enemy," she chastised the rookie.

"How was I supposed to know the ground was covered in cactus?"

"Driver Chris warned everyone," she spat.

"He did?" questioned the rookie.

"You will never learn if you don't listen," she snapped. "It is better to prevent than to heal," she advised before walking off.

He began pulling out cactus barbs from his feet with the tweezers. Hundreds of tiny little colorless harpoons were stuck into the soles of his feet. I felt bad for him. Feeling kindred as the new Driver's Apprentice, Berndt Toast and I carried him back to the relative safety of the bus. We folded his shirt and shorts for him to sit on and left him to his business, now picking spines out of his ass.

When Big Dave dove in, an ear-splitting scream came from the group of passengers already in the water. A school of fish had darted from one end of the pond to the other, swimming around and between everyone's legs. People were freaking out. The big man raised his palms above the surface of the water and the school of fish bolted through the crowd again, eliciting another primal scream. It was driving the girls mad. He waved his hands again and the school of fish darted back across the pond making the girls scream again.

Little Josh exhausted himself rushing around trying to scare the school of fish. It made for one rowdy, wacky, extravaganza of nudity. The cool water felt so good in the intense heat. No one gave a second thought about being seen naked by each other. It was no big deal anymore. We had grown so much closer over the past three days. We were starting to care about one another like we were part of a really hip family.

As Driver Chris explained, we had to get going, lest we be late for dinner on the Indian reservation. We carried Chicken Jim inside the bus where he laid face down on the front platform. Mother Michelle, Maid Marian, and Fräulein Vera all took turns doctoring his backside. The German punk rocker obviously liked to see Chicken Jim suffer because she kept laughing, "Ha!" every time he cried out in pain. The driver-in-training called for his notebook so he could write something down. He read his chicken scratch aloud with pride. "Into a cactus patch I flew, Stuck in the ass for lack of shoe. A pain no one understands, They call it the Badlands."

12
Scenic, South Dakota; Population:12

The passengers on the front platform were sitting with their heads close to the open windows trying to get some relief from the heat. Guitar Johnny strummed and sang softly, putting in the least amount of effort possible. After a while he started taking requests and reluctantly increased both his volume and effort. He had to wipe the beads of sweat off his nose to keep his guitar dry.

British Sue reached her arm out the window and rested it against the dark green skin of the Tortoise. "Ouch!" she winced. "The bloody thing's as hot as a tea keddy!" Her English friend took her by the hand and inspected the red mark on her forearm. "Let's get some cream for that," she recommended.

I took a seat next to Mountain Girl at the dinette. She was playing rummy with Big Dave using the big man's deck of naked lady playing cards. Mountain Girl took a break from the game to recoat her lips with her bright red lipstick. She looked simply delightful in the afternoon light. She certainly did not need makeup. She must have known I was looking because out of nowhere she said, "Everyone's been complaining about dry lips, but mine are perfect, eh." She asked me, "Are your lips chapped?"

"Yes," I told her nodding. "It's awful. I've been using Chapstick, but it's not getting any better."

She jokingly offered me her lipstick and said, "This stuff works wonders, eh."

I declined with a smile and a wave of my hand.

Across from her Little Josh hung his head out the window panting like a dog with his tongue out.

Mountain Girl warned him, "That hot wind just gonna make your lips worse. Then you'll be miserable, eh. Now, get your head in here, please."

Josh yelled into the wind. "It's fun!"

"Trust me, eh. If you keep your head out there long enough, you'll wish you hadn't," advised the Canadian. Having realized it was useless, under her breath she said, "Don't blame me, eh."

To rub her nose in it and make things worse, the boy knelt on the seat so he could get his shoulders through the window and stuck half his body out.

Little Josh was often disrespectful to his mother and he frequently disregarded her advice, so many of the passengers tried to help her reel him in. After she tried once, it was understandable that Mountain Girl could not be bothered to keep trying. She turned in her seat so that her legs were in the aisle and whistled a tune.

Ten minutes later, Little Josh removed his head from the window and sat back in his seat looking distraught. I nudged Mountain Girl and motioned toward the boy so she would look. "Is something wrong?" she asked the boy with concern.

He was holding his hands over his face, "Nothing's wrong." He removed his hands and winced in pain as he touched his lips with his fingers. His lips looked seriously chapped and his cheeks were bright red.

"How are your lips, eh?" the Canadian asked.

"My lips hurt," he said quietly. "How could they get chapped so fast?"

"It appears that you-know-who was right," I commented.

He sneered and touched his lips again and squeaked in pain.

Like the evil Nurse Ratched in the Cuckoo's Nest, Mountain Girl offered help to the wounded boy. "I have something that will help you moisturize your lips, eh. If you want to try it, eh?"

"Yes please."

"Here, let me put it on for you. I'll be gentle, eh."

"Sure," he said.

When I saw her pull the red lipstick out of her pocket I gasped, breathing in quickly through my nose. I closed my eyes and held my breath for a second.

Little Josh wrinkled his brow at me, but then he puckered up and the evil nurse began her treatment. When she finished applying lipstick on his lips, she said, "Now, whatever you do don't touch it, eh." She put the lipstick back in her pocket and kindly said, "That should make things better, eh."

Scenic, South Dakota; Population:12

"I hope so," he said, "but it tastes funny." He put his finger up to wipe it in.

"No, no, no," she warned him. "Don't touch it!" She smiled. "It tastes funny because it has medicine in it. Try not to lick your lips, eh. You'll get used to it."

I nudged her with my elbow. "I've gotta go," I said with wide eyes, motioning with a tilt of my head.

"I'll come with you," she said. We got up quickly and crawled onto the back platform where we hid out of sight. The guitar playing and singing was great, but we could not keep our eyes off Little Josh's bright red lips.

It was only a matter of seconds before Irish Kyrah asked, "What's so funny?" Then she followed our gaze and busted out laughing. "Oh my God!" she held her forehead. "He doesn't have a clue." She put her finger to her lips and nudged her twin, so she knew to keep it quiet.

Irish Joyce stifled her giggles and asked, "Who did it?"

I thumbed toward the guilty Canadian.

She shrugged. "His lips were chapped, eh." She smiled broadly. "He thinks it's Chapstick, eh."

Irish Kyrah warned her, "He's gonna hate you."

"Fuckin-a," she said in agreement.

I agreed with a series of quick nods.

Word spread and the tension of stifled laughter mounted. The guitar playing and singing stopped abruptly as everyone turned for a look, but Little Josh just kept playing solitaire.

Big Dave turned around in his seat and looked at all of us inquisitively. "What happened to the music?" he grumbled.

I caught his eye and he scrutinized my face. I motioned with my head toward Little Josh. At that point no one was laughing because I think we were all holding our breath. Big Dave turned and looked at the boy and his eyes grew as wide as saucers. The big man caught a short laugh in his fist like a cough. "He." His voice was so deep it went unnoticed. Then there were two. "He, He." Then three. "He, He, He."

Little Josh looked confused. "What's so funny?" he demanded.

Big Dave looked at him holding back his laughter. "Your lips are red," he told him.

"I know!" the boy complained loudly.

"Are you wearing lipstick?" the big man asked.

The boy touched his lips and looked at his finger. "Ahh!" he screamed, making a Home Alone face. The back platform exploded with laughter. People were howling. Little Josh wiped his lips on his t-shirt, but his lips were still bright red. "This is bullshit," he shouted.

Then, the most wonderful thing happened. Big Dave lowered his hand from his mouth and let go of all restraint. His deep laughter rolled with his belly in a long series of guffaws. He was beside himself with laughter as jolly and joyful as Santa Claus himself. He pounded his fist on the table until Little Josh looked scared. This only made him laugh harder. He had never laughed like that before, at least not in front of us.

People from the front platform were coming back to have a look and have a laugh. "I feel so violated," shouted the boy. This made everyone laugh again. He was mad but at the same time he was clearly enjoying the attention of the smiling girls.

Mother Michelle heard this and came to his rescue. "Oh, how cute," she remarked.

"It's not cute. It's gross," he said, fighting back tears.

"Where did you get the lipstick?"

"Sarah put it on me!"

His mother looked confused, "Who's Sarah?"

"Mountain Girl!" he shouted. "She did it!" He searched the back of the bus and then the front. We kept our heads down but we were still dying with laughter.

Mother Michelle looked puzzled. "Come on out of there," she directed him. "I'll get you cleaned up." After Big Dave moved his legs, the boy climbed under the dinette table to get out. Then his mother took him by the hand and led him forward. Big Dave's belly was still rolling, although he was trying to contain himself for the boy's sake.

Mountain Girl was holding her belly trying to control snorts of laughter. "I should probably go say I'm sorry, eh?" She composed herself and went to the front platform. When she came back, she told us, "His lips are so sore; Michelle could hardly wipe it off; so she tried covering it up with Chapstick. It's freaking hilarious, eh."

****

Berndt Toast came forward to speak to Drivers. He looked distraught. "I think I might have heat exhaustion," he told them. "I have a headache and I'm not feeling well."

Driver Chris jumped off the buddy seat and shouted, "Can we get some water up here?" He offered his seat with an open palm. "Sit down, please."

Maid Marian took his pulse. "His heart rate is fast, but it's not out of control," she informed us. She put her hand on his sweaty forehead. "He's really hot," she observed. "I'll get a thermometer."

Driver Chris questioned the panting, German. "Have you been drinking water?"

"Ja. As much as I can stomach," he said, "since I started feeling tired."

"Are you dizzy?" he asked. Jewels passed him a water bottle.

"I'm a little lightheaded," he reported. He sipped.

"When was the last time you took a piss?"

"I went a few hours ago."

"What color was it?"

"Yellow."

"Was it dark yellow?"

"Not so much."

"That's good," the red-haired adventure guide responded. "That means you're probably just dehydrated."

Maid Marian returned with the thermometer, said, "I'm a nurse," and stuck it under his tongue. "You should have gone swimming," she grimaced. "The water was perfect."

"I know," he mumbled with the thermometer in his mouth. "It's a little tricky with my leg," he said, gesturing with a hand on his prosthetic knee.

"We would have helped you into the water," Maid Marian insisted.

"All you need to do is ask," offered the blond driver.

Berndt Toast breathed a sigh and said, "Thank you guys."

"You should wet your head," she recommended.

"Dude, your leg comes off, right?" inquired Driver Chris.

"Of course," interjected Maid Marian before turning back to him. "You probably can't get it wet, right?"

He took the thermometer out of his mouth to say. "It comes off easy, but I'm not supposed to get it wet."

"You can take a cold shower in Scenic," Driver Chris told him. "We'll be stopping there in a few minutes."

This came as a relief to the hearty German. "Oh, thank God," he gasped. "I haven't showered since Boston."

"You haven't showered since Boston?" Maid Marian reacted in shock. "And you didn't swim?"

The German just shook his head.

"You should have told us, dude," remarked the blond driver. "We'll make sure you're first in line at the showers."

"You should have said something, bro," reiterated Driver Chris.

"You don't understand," confided the German. "People get freaked out when they see my leg." He put the thermometer back under his tongue.

"You're among friends here, dude," our red-haired driver assured him. "We don't care about shit like that."

"That's the last thing you should worry about," the man behind the wheel comforted him.

"You don't get it," the German guy told them. "It makes people super uncomfortable."

"You don't need to hide anything," insisted the nurse. She removed the thermometer. She read it and said, "Oh, good! It looks fine."

"What happened to your leg?" asked Driver Brian.

"I had bone cancer in my tibia that spread to my knee," he told us in a faint voice. "I was never going to walk again, but my ankle was cancer free, so they repurposed my ankle as my new knee."

"Rotationplasty," gasped Maid Marian. "That's incredible!"

"Ja! That's it!" he confirmed. "I'm surprised you've heard of it."

"I've heard about the procedure, but I've never seen one." She marveled, "From what I gather, it's like a miracle of modern medicine."

"Your ankle is where your knee used to be?" Driver Chris questioned.

"Ja," he confirmed.

"That's awesome!" exclaimed the Irishman. "No big deal. We can handle that."

"You haven't seen it yet," responded the sweaty German. He leaned in to whisper in the driver's freckled ear.

Now, Driver Chris was unable to contain himself. His eyebrows jumped as he said, "No way! That's sick!"

"Chris!" chastised Maid Marian.

"Yes way," confirmed the German. "Think about it," he suggested. "Mechanically, that's the only way it would work. It has to be like that so I can bend my ankle like a knee."

"That's intense," the Irishman gasped. "Can I see it?" he beckoned.

The hearty German nodded, then he crossed his legs with his prosthesis on top and began rolling down his sock. For once Driver Chris kept his eyes on the road.

"You don't have to show him if you don't want to," consoled Maid Marian.

"It's okay," he said happily. He unstrapped the Velcro holding the device in position.

When he took it off Maid Marian gasped, "Jislaaik!" She was unable to contain herself. "It's a miracle," she marveled.

"Wow!" I said in dismay. "That's intense." I could not help myself. His foot was where his knee should have been, but it was facing

Scenic, South Dakota; Population:12

backwards. In every other way it was a perfectly normal foot, with manicured toenails and hair growing on the knuckles.

Jewels peaked over the lead driver's shoulder and said, "Far out!"

Driver Brian took one look and went, "Woe dude!"

Driver Chris contemplated what he was seeing for a moment before saying, "I still don't think you need to hide it from anyone, especially us. You're among friends here, bro."

"I know," he conceded.

"It's all good," I affirmed. Everyone present was super supportive.

"I need to get over it," he determined. "Maybe I'll swim next time. I'd like to try skinny-dipping."

****

While Driver Brian drove through the seemingly endless fields of yellow grass, Driver Chris stood up to inform the group of our impending destination. "We will be stopping for showers in a town called Scenic, South Dakota," he announced. A cheer went up and a murmur ensued as word spread about the showers. It was amazing how excited everybody was about hot showers.

Maid Marian interjected loudly, "Make sure you let Berndt shower first. He's having a bit of heat stroke!"

Our guide continued with a mischievous smile. "We'll be in Scenic shortly, but here's the thing," he said mysteriously. "Scenic isn't very scenic at all. It's a ghost town."

Little Josh let out a squeal of joy. "Ghost Town! Awesome!"

Driver Chris paused to wait for silence and added. "You might see a few Indians with ghosts in their eyes, if you know what I mean. It's a town that isn't quite dead yet."

Little Josh rushed forward to get closer to the action. "Will there really be ghosts?"

Driver Chris put his fingers to his lips and went, "Shh! You'll scare them away."

"This is gonna be great!" spouted Little Josh. Mother Michelle put her hand on his shoulder and he snuggled in against her folded legs.

"Sorry about the lipstick," I said trying to make eye contact with him. When Little Josh looked up at me, I smiled, but he did not respond to me. I felt like I deserved it. He had really been a good sport about the whole thing.

Driver Chris bent down and looked around in an arc to get his bearings, "Keep an eye out for the sign on the way into town. It says, 'Population 12' and that's no joke. Scenic is a ridiculously small town. It's not even on the map."

"Woohoo!" cheered Little Josh.

Chicken Jim was leaning up on his elbows surveying the map to find a drugstore to buy some better tweezers. "Scenic," he shouted. "It's on the map right here." He pressed his finger on the laminated map.

"That's no ordinary map," Driver Chris informed him. "It's made for truckers so they can deliver packages almost anywhere." This prompted the driver-in-training to close the map and to look at the cover. Upon seeing him do this Driver Chris exclaimed, "Quick! There's a turn coming up." He pressed him for an answer. "Which way should I turn?"

"Oh shit, I lost my place!" cried Chicken Jim. He fumbled with the map trying to find the page.

"Hurry up!" exclaimed the driver. "The turn is coming up fast."

The trainee looked out the windshield to see how much time he had before the turn, but we were on a long straight road with no turns in sight. Driver Chris let out a deep guffaw.

As the laughter spread, Fräulein Vera could not hold herself back and blurted out the words, "Jimmy Dummkopf." This caused the rookie to drop the map. As he stood up to pick it up Fräulein Vera pushed his ass with her extended foot, making him kick the map which sent him on a map-chasing trip down into the stairwell. There was laughter from all sides now, and people were craning their necks to see what was happening.

When Chicken Jim emerged from the stairwell, he blew a kiss to Fräulein Vera and fanned himself with the map. "She obviously wants me," he told Driver Chris.

"Anyway!" Driver Chris began announcing again. "The general store has hot showers for seventy-five cents, but please make sure Berndt Toast gets first dibs on the shower. He needs to cool down because he's not feeling very well in the heat. The store has food and a restaurant so you can get something to eat. You can get ice water from the soda fountain, so drink up and fill up. They have postcards and a post office, so you get them postmarked from Scenic. That's pretty cool."

Driver Chris held up a finger to hold off questions. "We don't want to linger too long in Scenic because there isn't really too much to see, but we will stick around until everyone has showered. Feel free to explore the town, use the telephone, and have a drink at the old saloon, but try to stay out of jail," he added. Everyone had a good laugh. Driver Chris explained further, "Hey, I'm serious now. There are jail cells

Scenic, South Dakota; Population:12

right on Main Street, and if you close the door behind you, you just might find yourself spending the night."

"Awesome, yea!" Little Josh kicked his legs with excitement.

We all heard Mother Michelle's tired plea, "Josh, you stay away from those jail cells, you hear!" Little Josh did not hear. He remained focused on the road ahead.

In the middle of the open prairies, north of the Badlands, under the gigantic expanse of South Dakota sky, the Green Tortoise turned slowly at an unsigned fork in the dusty road and headed toward the twelve-person town of Scenic. We could see from a distance that the buildings on the main drag were all made of the same ancient, knotty, sun bleached, grey wooden boards, making it look like the set of an old western. This place had the bones of a ghost town, from the tumbleweeds tumbling down Main Street, to the horses drawn up at the water trough in front of the saloon. This place was authentic cowboy western cool.

"Oh my God," Little Josh spoke for us all in a high-pitched voice. "This place is so cool!" he said, ending with a girlish squeal. He got to his feet and held onto the dashboard handrail in the stairwell with eyes as wide as water barrels.

The bus roared slowly into the quiet town, creating the extraordinary effect of engine sounds echoing off the fragile wooden buildings, magnifying the noise like an amphitheater as we passed each structure. "Welcome to Scenic, South Dakota," shouted Driver Brian for all to hear, "home of the Longhorn Saloon and Trading Post."

The whole town consisted of six buildings laid out on two dirty roads that made a T-junction in the center. One road went straight through town back out into nowhere and the other road was just a short dead end. The Green Tortoise drove past the post office and the small school and stopped at the old-fashioned gas pump in front of the general store. Across the road we could see a sign festooned with dozens of sunbaked cattle skulls that read "Longhorn Saloon." After my eyes adjusted to the sunlight, I noticed the words "No Indians Allowed," painted over with whitewash on the sign above the saloon. This was a ghost town without a soul.

Little Josh ran into his mother's arms, "That place is scary, Mom. Why do they have cow heads up there? Do they kill cows here?"

Mother Michelle looked out the window and comforted Little Josh, but she seemed at a loss for words. "I don't understand any of this," she huffed.

The town of Scenic felt, smelled, and looked like a historical time machine had played a cruel trick on the town and the people there. Next to the Longhorn Saloon there were two wrought iron jail cells baking in the sun on the sidewalk. A crude wooden roof capped the square iron cages, but the doors were wide open. I imagined that the sheriff's office had rotted away into dust, leaving the jail cells behind on the bare ground.

The engine died, but no one moved. It was like we were all waiting for the dust from the dirt road to settle. Driver Chris said, "Berndt Toast has first dibs on the shower, so back off and let him grab his gear so he can be first in line." The passengers scrambled to get into their suitcases, and off to the showers.

****

By the time I got my towel and change of clothes, the line to the showers stretched out the door. It was unclear what Chicken Jim did to deserve it, but Fräulein Vera chased him screaming inside the general store, snapping at his backside with a bath towel. I took my time and decided to explore the town.

Next to the Longhorn Saloon, on the opposite side of the jail cells stood the Longhorn Trading Post. I entered the saloon-style doors and was greeted by a dignified Indian man dressed in traditional clothing with a feather tucked in his hair. "Hello," he said, standing to shake my hand.

"Hello," I replied as we shook. I was mesmerized by the Indian man's incredible outfit and powerful aura. He wore a fantastic turquoise, quilted jacket that was as thick as a carpet, with two winged horses kissing on the back. Fringes were hanging down the sleeves and along the back. "Please take your time and look around. If you have any questions, feel free to ask."

An Indian woman waved to me from the back of the store. I waved to her and said, "Thank you. I will."

The walls of the Longhorn Trading Post were covered with taxidermy, the lifelike heads of Buffalo, cattle, deer, elk, fox, jackrabbit and wolf. As I looked around, I could hardly find a single thing that I had ever seen in a store before. Sure, there were a few simple things, like bubblegum and postcards, but for the most part, the stuff in the display cases was far more exotic and interesting: Moccasins, dream catchers, South Dakota jackalopes, Black Hills gold and silver jewelry, holsters and spurs, Indian artifacts, rain sticks, western clothing, Indian blankets, beaded purses, pottery, Shady Brady hats, Indian crafted tomahawks, and painted cattle skulls.

In the display cases, surrounded by jewelry and other valuable merchandise, were the bones of animals I could not identify. The woman approached me slowly while I lingered over one such display case with a particularly strange skull inside. "If you have any questions,

I would be happy to answer." She spoke in a soothing tone, like a river flowing over rocks.

She must have seen the way I was looking at her dress, because she came out from behind the counter and held her arms out for me to see. "That dress is stunning," I complimented her, shaking my head a little. "It is so beautiful. I've never seen anything like that before."

"Thank you," she said. "This is a Lakota dress made by Nancy Deer-with-Horns." She pointed to the decorations at the neck and continued, "It is a special tanned deer hide adorned with ivory Elk teeth," pointing lower, "porcupine quills, medicine wheels," and lower still, "deer dew-claws and toes."

"It's amazing," I marveled.

She seemed pleased that I liked the dress so much. "Did you have a question about something?" she asked.

"Yes," I answered looking into the large display case. "This skull in here doesn't look familiar." I pointed at the strange fossil. "What is that?"

"That's a very special artifact, over 100,000 years old," she informed me. "It is the skull of a Brontothere, a prehistoric animal that lived here in the Badlands."

"Whoa," I reacted. "Did you find it yourself?"

"No," she said. "Decades ago, a lone Indian rider came into town on horseback and traded it for beer."

"Whoa," I laughed. "I hope you gave him a lot of beer."

"Not too much," the man said. "I didn't want him to drink himself to death."

"How do you know how old it is?" I asked.

She approached the case to explain. "Scientists from the university often come to study the artifacts in our collection. They take them away to study them one by one." She added, "We're raising money to open a museum."

I returned my eyes to the Brontothere. "It looks like a rhino. Is it related?"

She answered, "The Brontothere is in the family of rhinos, but it more closely resembles a horse."

"There were horses living here in ancient times?"

"Yes," she informed me. "We have a Mesohippus fossil right over here." She walked down to show me. The Lakota woman smiled and said, "Your enthusiasm is refreshing. Most tourists are shy around us Indians. They are afraid to ask questions, but you have many. This is good."

I tilted my head and looked at her again, and she tilted her head back inquisitively. "Do you mind if I ask you a personal question?" I asked.

The stunningly dressed woman answered, "You may ask any questions you like, as long I reserve the right not to answer if I am not comfortable sharing."

I formulated my thoughts and asked, "Do you find the word Indian offensive?"

She shook her head, "No. Not at all. Why?"

"Doesn't the word Indian come from Columbus thinking he had landed in India?" I inquired.

The Indian man spoke up. "I'd like to answer this one. If I may." His wife bowed her head slightly and smiled without saying a word. "The referral of Native people as Indians is not from the white man thinking he was in India," he informed me. "Actually, there was no such country as India when Columbus encountered the First People. India was called Hindustan back then." The Indian man expounded, "The Indians Columbus first encountered were peaceful people without war, theft, or possessions. Columbus wrote that the people of the New World were "una gentre en dio" meaning "a people of God" in Latin. The pronunciation of "en dio" got changed to Indian over the years."

"Wow," I said, "That's amazing. You learn something new every day. Thank you so much."

"Don't mention it, my friend," the Lakota man said with a smile.

Thinking I had some knowledge on the subject, I asked with a rising tone, "Are Lakotas part of the Sioux Nation?"

"Yes and no," he said flatly. "Sioux refers to the various Lakota and Dakota tribes, but the word 'Sioux' is also an exonym."

"A what?"

"Sioux is someone else's name for us. It means 'little rattlesnake.' It can also mean 'speaks a foreign language.' In any case, it is not our own word for ourselves. It is a name given to us by an enemy people. Some take offence by it; others wear it with pride."

"I had no idea," I admitted. "No offense intended."

"No problem," he responded. "I see it as part of our heritage. Some tribes have Sioux as their official name. Others do not. Some have both. The Rosebud Sioux Tribe is also known as the Sičháŋǧu Oyáte, Brulé Nation."

"That's very interesting," I remarked.

"Anyhow," he continued, "we call ourselves Lakota, which means 'feeling affection, friendly, united, allied.' Dakota has a similar meaning."

"That's awesome," I marveled.

He went on to explain that there are Seven Nations he referred to as the Seven Fires: the Mdewakanton, the Yankton,

Scenic, South Dakota; Population:12

Yanktonai, Sisseton, Teton, Lakota, Wahpekute, and the Wahpeton. There are eight First Nations reserves in Manitoba, and Saskatchewan and sixteen tribes in Montana, Minnesota, Nebraska and North and South Dakota.

I bought a Coca-Cola and a few postcards, leaving the balance of ten dollars as a donation to the museum. They were very thankful. We said our goodbyes and I stepped outside.

****

Chicken Jim and Little Josh were playing Cowboys and Indians in the cast iron jail cells next to the saloon. They held the bars and stuck their faces out pretending to be criminals. They shouted at the passengers waiting across the street at the payphone. "Let us out! We promise we won't scalp you! It's just a case of mistaken identity!"

Jewels and Yülia were in the adjacent cell. Yülia feigned a swoon and exclaimed, "Oh Lord! Release me!" Jewels stuck her face between the bars with her long thick hair hanging over her face so that she looked like Thing from the Addams Family. This drew a ton of laughs because she looked like someone that we should lock-up-and-throw-away-the-key.

A bunch of passengers crossed the street to snap pictures. Interestingly, Chicken Jim hid his face whenever anyone pointed a camera at him. Either that or he would lift his shirt over his nose like a bank robber. Fräulein Vera used this to her advantage. She pointed her camera at him through the bars, causing him to turn around with his back to her. She took this opportunity to remove the cinder block holding the cell door open. "You will rot in jail," she proclaimed as she slammed the door shut.

Seeing this, Little Josh rushed over to the door of the adjoining cell, kicked the block out of the way and slammed the iron barred door closed on Jewels and Yülia. The girls both screamed when the door clanked shut. Much to their relief it did not lock behind them. We all got a kick out of their reactions, but it shook Jewels to the core. She was visibly upset. She came out of the jail cell in tears.

Yülia consoled her. "It's okay. What's wrong?" But she kept sobbing. We had not seen this side of her before. She was always upbeat, so this was disconcerting. Fräulein Vera and Yülia continued to comfort her, so I kept my distance. I followed them into the restaurant to make sure she was okay.

Tortoise people sporting wet hair and fresh clothes occupied several booths in the restaurant, downing cheeseburgers and soft drinks. The girls took seats at a dinette table where they continued to comfort Jewels. Several other girls gathered around out of concern.

Once Jewels had steadied herself, she began to tell a terrifying tale. "I was attacked and left for dead after being held captive overnight," she revealed. "When the cell door slammed shut it all came rushing back."

"Oh, my Goddess," gasped Irish Joyce.

I softly mumbled, "Holy shit!"

"I'm so sorry to hear that," consoled Yülia.

"When did this happen?" asked Irish Kyrah.

"It was two years ago last fall," Jewels informed them. "I was walking home from a party alone late at night in Harlem River Park. I grew up near there, and I never had a problem with anybody before."

"Why would he do that?" asked Yülia. "Did he rob you?"

"You don't need to share the details if it's too hard for you," consoled Maid Marian.

"It's taken a lot of time to heal," Jewels contended, "but I think I'm ready to put it out there. I'm in a good place here with you guys and I feel strong enough to share without breaking down or worrying that you're going to judge me." The Irish sisters each took one of her hands and Yülia stroked her hair while she spoke. "I want to get it out because women need to know they can't walk around by themselves at night. I hate to say it, but it's the truth. What I went through, I would never wish on anyone," she added.

She began to recount the details matter-of-factly to avoid breaking down. She stayed strong outside, but I could tell she was crumbling inside with fear, disappointment, and weakness. "I heard heavy footsteps coming behind me," she told us. "Then the footsteps sped up, but before I could react, he plowed into me from behind. I was immobilized with his arms wrapped around me."

"Dear Lord," gasped the Irish girls in unison.

She continued to describe the assault. "He dragged me around a corner into a hole in the bushes. I call it a hole because that's what it felt like when I was in there. I couldn't get out." she explained. "He strangled me a bunch of times, kicked me in the head, and beat me with a club."

"Oh God," gasped Flip-flop. We were all in shock and there were many verbal reactions.

"It's a miracle you survived," concluded Maid Marian.

Jewels went on, "I couldn't stand up. I couldn't see because my eyes were swollen shut and I had blood in my ears. So, I couldn't tell if he was still there. My survival instincts kicked in. So, I just laid there in horrific pain for the next eight hours until I heard other people passing by. That's when I yelled for help."

"Did he rape you?" lilted Yülia.

"I have to assume so, the inside of my mouth and throat were ripped apart, but I'm not entirely sure. I was fading in and out of consciousness from a concussion."

"That's horrific," commented Mother Michelle.

"It is possible I was sexually assaulted because there was damage down there too. I didn't wake-up for three days, and by the time they did the rape kit in the hospital it was inconclusive." Everyone was in disbelief.

"How are you doing now?" asked Maid Marian.

"I'm okay now," she assessed. "I have a lot of scar tissue," she informed us. "I had a broken nose, a fractured hand, and I still have partial hearing loss in my left ear."

Everyone was super sympathetic.

"For a long time, my head was always on-a-swivel, and I couldn't walk down the street without having panic attacks," she told us. "I was hypervigilant whenever anyone approached me. Even now, I still have issues reacting to men coming at me, even in a friendly manner... I'm always looking out of the corner of my eye, turning around, checking who's coming up behind me."

We could all understand, and people expressed their sympathies. The consensus was, "We love you."

"I want to stress the importance of not blaming yourself," Jewels advised them. "I internalized it for a long time like it was my fault, like I was to blame because I got myself into that situation. I felt horrendous that I put my family and my friends through that situation. All of our lives changed forever."

"It's not your fault," pleaded Yülia.

"Because I internalized everything and blamed myself for a long time, I want to make sure that others who have gone through similar situations don't blame themselves." She proclaimed, "Women don't ask for this, we don't cause this. This was somebody else deciding to do this and we have to find ourselves blameless in this whole situation."

"You're a survivor," praised Fräulein Vera. "It's inspiring." The rest of us concurred.

"I didn't heal overnight," she emphasized. "I couldn't go back to work for a long time. I mean, how do you explain to children that some random psychopath almost killed me? I'm coming back, but I don't look like myself. I couldn't look at the children with my battered face and lie to them, 'I'm okay, I'll be okay.' I would have broken down in tears as soon as they looked at me."

"You look beautiful now," urged Yülia stroking her hair again.

Jewels went on in depth about her current state of being. "For a long time, I couldn't smile and that just killed me. The best thing I love about myself is my smile," she shared. "I always have a smile for everybody, I love that about myself. I wasn't going to let him steal that from me."

"You do have a great smile," confirmed Mother Michelle.

"You really do," agreed Maid Marian.

"You're the coolest person ever," gushed Yülia.

"As long as men hold us down, we need to keep fighting to get up," Jewels proclaimed. "We need to seek out our sisters at the grassroots level and get the word out woman by woman. We must all stand together until we are all on our feet." Jewels continued. "We need to show our rage. This is not a time to pull punches. The gloves are off."

"You're so strong. I love it," praised the petite German.

"I'm not that strong," Jewels deprecated. "I haven't had sex since the incident," she admitted. "I'm not going to let him take that from me either. I'm just taking my time getting back in the saddle."

"I thought you slept with Brian the other night?" Yülia inquired.

"We were just sleeping," she responded.

"You're such a wonderful person," commented Irish Joyce. "You'll get your groove back, eventually. You'll see. It takes a while." She spoke for all to hear. "I was raped when I was at Uni in Dublin," she revealed. "That's why I had to drop out. It took me years to figure things out, but in the end, I found my calling in life. I became a midwife and a lesbian. You should try it. Girls are yummy."

Jewels responded candidly, "If it comes to that you'll be the first to know, girlfriend."

The Irish midwife spoke with passion and belief. "When a man violates a woman's rights, she has two options. Suck it up or get the fuck out. Neither is pleasant. So, she stays. She does not display her anger. Women are supposed to smooth things over, not to complain or seek vengeance. If we do, we're bitches. They call us the C word or names that start with a W."

The other girls looked at her seeking further explanation.

"Wretched, wicked, witch whore." She spoke with a gravely brogue. "There are more words than snow for an angry Woman. When a man gets mad, we call him a bastard or a son-of-a-bitch. Notice how both of those labels shift the blame on women." This opened some eyes. She continued, "Our society shuns angry Women. It makes some men's skin crawl just to hear an angry woman speak, like Hillary Clinton. To them we're just ranting and raving, and they disregard our anger and write us off as psychos."

Scenic, South Dakota; Population:12

Joyce's sister also had a horror story to tell, as did Fräulein Vera. It started making me sick to my stomach to hear how many of our female passengers had been sexually assaulted. I felt dirty just being male. After the ladies finished speaking, they all hugged, but I kept my distance despite having been sexually assaulted myself, as a child. I was not ready to share my own truth with the world. I wondered if such a time would ever come.

Fräulein Vera surprised her girlfriends by revealing her plans for the immediate future. Having seen more of the United States she had decided to leave New York and travel more. She would be quitting her job as an au pair. The Irish girls offered her a room in San Francisco if she ever needed a place to stay. In a power move the German punk rocker stood right up and went to use the phone to call her soon to be former employer. The Irish Twins offered their support and left with her to stand by her while she made the call. This all made Jewels incredibly happy.

****

Berndt Toast had been singing Bruce Springsteen songs in the shower and received a round of applause when he exited the changing room. The bathroom was free, so I went to wash up. The seventy-five-cent lukewarm shower was far too short. I put on fresh clothes and went outside to check the line at the payphone.

Driver Chris was engaged in an intense argument with his father on the phone. "How could you even think that?" he objected to something his father said. "How could it be my fault? I was a hundred miles away; you were right down the street. Why didn't you do something?" he demanded.

Driver Brian was trying to help him remain calm. "Take it easy man. You're only making it worse," the big blond pleaded with him.

Driver Chris' eyes were watering. "How can I respect you if you don't respect me?" he questioned. "You've been saying the same shit to me for years and I'm sick of it, dad." He took the phone away from his ear so we could hear his father yelling. He made a horrible face. "I might just do that," he fired back. "While I'm at it, I might as well change my name too," he yelled. He held the phone away from his face again as we heard more loud yelling then he shouted into the mouthpiece. "Fuck you!" With that he hung up the phone. The passengers around him tried to console him, but he was not himself.

"That was harsh," commented the co-driver. He put a hand on Driver Chris' shoulder and lead him back to the bus. I followed alongside for support. "Where was your sister through all of that?" Driver Brian asked him.

"She was right there in the room," he revealed.

"She should have pulled the plug."

"He wouldn't give up the phone."

"It's too bad your mother had to hear that shit."

"Yeah. I could hear her wailing in the background. She was begging him to stop."

"So much for your master plan," Driver Brian chided.

"I gave it my best shot, but it seems hopeless. We had a few minutes of plain talk, civil conversation. We exchanged pleasantries like normal people."

"Yeah?"

Driver Chris went on. "He asked me if I would come home, just to visit, even if things turned out all right. I told him I would come home if I could get time off. Then he started in again, blaming me for putting work before family. Then he started blaming me for not being there when my brother fell, and I just lost my mind. How can I forgive him when he keeps doing it all the time?"

"Maybe you just need to be more patient bro," his co-driver offered advice. "Have you tried waiting a few seconds before responding? Sometimes that little bit of time can help you get your emotions under control. There's a substantial difference between acting and reacting."

The drivers went inside the bus. So, I circled back to the line of passengers waiting for the phone. Fräulein Vera and her friends were ecstatic. As soon as the German Punk rocking au pair gave her obligatory two weeks' notice, her employer told her not to come back, and they agreed to ship her things to San Francisco when her host family returned from abroad.

PAC-MAN was on the phone, standing cheek-to-cheek with Peruvian Ursula so she could listen-in. Judging from his facial expression and the tone of his rapid-fire Cantonese, he was full of joy and near to tears, no doubt talking to his family.

Jewels and Yülia appeared content knowing Peruvian Ursula was letting him call his family. They may have dropped their guard, but I remained suspicious. She was monitoring the call. I tried to listen in with a hand cupped to my ear. When I got close to the phone, she gave me the hairy eyeball like I had done something wrong. I made a face but did not say anything.

I lifted my chin to Deutsche Mark. He was hiding from the oppressive sun in the shadow of the building, sitting on a cinderblock near the phone. He was visibly upset.

"Are you waiting for the phone?" I asked him.

"No," he said somberly.

"You look bummed out," I observed.

"Dude!" he exclaimed. "Tessa broke up with me," he groaned.

"No way!" I exclaimed.

"Seriously," he bemoaned. "She had been telling me she wanted to dump her boyfriend, so I was hoping things would work out between us, but now the whole thing is in the shitter."

"That sucks," I surmised.

"It sucks for you too," he warned.

"Why?"

"She said Sue is going to tell you the same thing," he revealed.

"No way!"

"You should have heard Sue and Tessa talking to their boyfriends. They were together at Sue's house in England," he agonized.

"Oh right. Tessa's boyfriend is Sue's brother," I recalled. "So, they were both there?"

"Yeah," he confirmed. "I heard the whole conversation. I was sitting right there, bro." He spoke with contempt in his voice. "They grilled them about seeing other girls," Deutsche Mark remonstrated. "Then they both denied hooking up with us, then they both said, 'I love you' at the end of the call."

The one-sided conversation in Cantonese ended abruptly when the Peruvian coerced PAC-MAN to end the call. "That's enough for now," she decided. "Other people need to use the phone." She barked at him in Cantonese and he handed her the receiver. She began to talk on the phone looking directly at me, then she turned to face the opposite way. I heard her ask, "May I speak to the person in charge?" Then she lowered her voice and cupped her hand over her mouth to talk privately.

I gave Deutsche Mark a knowing look and said, "Something's rotten in Denmark."

"How do you mean?" he asked.

"I think she's lying," I revealed.

"About what?"

"I'm not exactly sure, but I think they are not telling us everything," I answered. "You know, his family is being held captive by the Chinese until he gets to his next concert in San Francisco?" I asked.

"Woe!" he reacted. "I did not know that." He shot me a look to see that I was being serious. He asked, "How do you know that?"

"I heard her talking about it in New York," I told him.

"That must be hard," he concluded.

"Truth be told," I said.

Just then British Sue exited the restaurant and headed right toward me. My instinct was to flee, but there was nowhere to run. We were in a town with six buildings and twelve people, surrounded by non-arable desert.

She walked right up to me and said, "Tessa and I have been feeling a bit manky about cheating on our fellas back at home."

"I'm sorry to hear that," I said.

"We just had a bit of a chinwag on the telly." Her shoulders dropped like a weight was pressing on her. "To be perfectly honest, I wish we'd never rang them up. It's only served to throw a spanner in the works." She straightened her posture with new resolve. "Suffice to say, it's only fair. They're valiantly waiting for us to return, so we've both decided to give it a fresh start and remain faithful to the lads."

"That makes me sad," I lamented with a sigh.

"I'm sad to see you off as well," she said with a note of lingering fondness. "The long-of-the-short is, there can be no more rumpy pumpy between us, love. This has to end."

"I don't know what to say," I muttered.

"Don't feel bad, love. There's plenty of fish in the sea, and there's no shortage of talent in this lot." She put her hand out for me to shake and said, "Friends?"

"Sure," I replied, recalling our first hug on the street in Boston.

She tugged my hand with her soft fingers and said, "Ta." Then she turned and walked coldly away into the heat broiling above the dusty streets in Scenic South Dakota.

"That sucks," commented Deutsche Mark.

"I need a beer," I told him.

"I'm with you," he responded, getting to his feet.

As I walked away Mother Michelle stepped out of the line for the phone and blocked my path. She smiled and said, "I'm sorry you got dumped."

"Thanks," I responded.

"Look on the bright side," she said. "There are a million fish in the sea." Then she stepped back into line.

"What's up with that?" wondered Deutsche Mark.

"She's trying to be a matchmaker," I huffed.

"Cool!" he said. "Do you think she can hook me up?"

****

The Dutchman and I took seats on the front platform and commenced drinking our sorrows away. Driver Chris, Chicken Jim,

Scenic, South Dakota; Population:12

Guitar Johnny, and Australian Sheila were all on board. I offered them each a beer, but they were all set.

The boys were playing their guitars again, while we talked and waited for the rest of the group to return, when an incredibly old Indian man appeared at the door of the bus. He very humbly waved at Driver Chris and gestured like he wanted to come in and look around. The Indian man looked to be about eighty years old, or older. He had a silver ponytail and wore a plaid shirt with blue jeans and tattered boots.

Driver Chris was more than happy to invite the lively and charismatic Indian into our bus, and he shook the man's hand with a smile as he came up the steps. "Come on in and have a seat," he said, "My name's Chris."

The Indian held Chris' hand for longer than normal and peered deeply into his eyes and revealed a gap-toothed smile. "Thank you, my friend," the Indian spoke slowly, "It is hot today. It will be good to sit for a while."

I cleared a seat on the front platform for the Indian, gesturing for him to sit down. I introduced myself, "My name is John, Sir."

He gripped my hand tightly pulling on my arm firmly, looking right into my eyes for several seconds. Dark channels of anguish painted his face with lines and shadows, and his eyes told a story of anguish and struggle. "I am pleased to meet you, my friend," he said, releasing his grip. He nodded respectfully to the women who introduced themselves, but he only shook hands with the men. When he finally sat down his eyes fell on Big Dave, who was sitting across from Little Josh, reading a newspaper at the dinette table. He stared at Big Dave until Australian Sheila spoke. "And what's your name?" she asked, seeming a little miffed. This drew strange looks from the others.

The Lakota man spoke slowly with strength in his voice that made you want to listen carefully to every word he spoke. He was not easily distracted. Several passengers were busy getting new clothes from underneath the back platform. He patiently waited for the right moment to speak so that he never needed to speak loudly or repeat himself.

He tapped his breastbone with two fingers and told us, "I am Strong Shoulders." He clenched his right fist and grabbed his left shoulder, "Strong Shoulders," he said again. He then made two fists and outstretched his arms to show us his tattooed knuckles, so that when he put two fists together, we could read the name. "My Christian name is Seymour," he revealed.

Driver Chris asked, "Which tribe are you from, Strong Shoulders?"

Strong Shoulders spoke again, "I am a Lakota of the Sioux Nation." When he said this, his eyes lit up and a rekindled spiritual energy seemed to glow within him.

Guitar Johnny spoke next, stuttering for an age before he blurted out the question, "Is that sign on the saloon serious? Did those cheeky bastards really have the audacity to ban Indians on Indian land?"

His presence drew a small crowd as he explained the saloon and the history of Scenic. "In my youth, the owners of the saloon refused to serve my people alcohol, because there was too much wrestling and fighting among the braves. Then, about fifteen years ago, the rules were changed, and they started using those old jail cells to corral the troublemakers." I had a feeling that Strong Shoulders had seen these things firsthand, and that he had been locked-up in the public cages himself.

Berndt Toast came back from the general store to put a box of beer in the cooler. He looked much better since suffering from heat exhaustion. It was only mid-day, but it was hot. He took a beer for himself and offered, "Does anyone want a beer?" There was silence.

Strong Shoulders looked to Driver Chris for approval with his soul-rending eyes. Driver Chris nodded his blessing before the Indian took the beer. Most of us now better understood why it might not be a good thing to give Indians beer, but we also knew that he was a Lakota, and that his tribe was on the list of Indians that were allowed in the Longhorn Saloon. If he wanted to, he could have gone across the street and gotten a beer in the bar for himself, if he had enough money, which he probably did not. Pine Ridge is one of the poorest counties in the United States.

Guitar Johnny had been leaning back against the window of the front platform holding his guitar between his knees as he sat listening. Strong Shoulders looked into the British man's eyes and asked, "Would you play a song for my heart?"

Guitar Johnny sat up with a start. "Bloody hell. Play what?" With some prodding from the rest of us, Guitar Johnny agreed to play a song, "Well, I reckon I can muster up a tune," he said, "as long as Chicken Jim plays along."

Soon they were both playing guitar and Strong Shoulders started chanting along with the music, slapping his hands on his legs, and adding his own rhythmic chanting. The guitar playing seemed to evolve naturally into a freestyle jam of improvisational music, centered on the chanting of Strong Shoulders. It sounded as though they were playing his song. Strong Shoulders' chanting was deeply passionate, and many eyes were wet with emotion before the drumming and chanting had stopped.

Scenic, South Dakota; Population:12

After Strong Shoulders finished drinking his beer, he lifted the can and gestured like it was empty. Without a word Driver Chris took the can and tossed it in the recycling. We each said our warm goodbyes to Strong Shoulders, and he walked away down the dusty dirt road. The hidden tragedy of the Indian was starting to unfold before us. The message was clear: Our nation's hoop is broken and scattered. The tree of life is withering. Just before five o'clock, the Green Tortoise Adventure bus left Scenic, South Dakota heading north across the land of the free and the home of the Brave.

13
Cuny Cafe

Part of the magic and intensity of the Green Tortoise adventure travel experience in the Badlands involves eating dinner prepared by a pair of gregarious Lakota Sioux women at a place called Cuny Cafe. The cafe building doubles as their home on land that bears their family name. Cuny Table is located near Buffalo Gap on the Pine Ridge Indian Reservation. After eating dinner, the Green Tortoise is permitted to camp on this gorgeous piece of private land under special agreement with the Cuny family. The Green Tortoise has enjoyed a decades-long friendship with the Cuny family fostered by the owner of the Green Tortoise, Gardner Kent since 1972.

From Scenic we drove south and then west toward Buffalo Gap into the Pine Ridge Indian Reservation. On the vast treeless wilderness south of Badlands National Park, a small group of farm buildings sits at the end of a long dirt driveway. The word "CAFE" was painted in big white letters on the side of a simple square house, painted red with white trim. Two picnic tables sat under a shingled awning jutting out from the building, providing shelter from the sun. A doublewide trailer was attached to one end of the building. A stockade fence corralled the area between the house and a matching red barn. A pair of junk cars and some dilapidated farm equipment sat baking in the sun. Two wooden outhouses, one red and one blue, stood off to the side of the driveway some fifty feet from the house.

Two Indian children were running around in the dirt parking lot. Driver Chris slowed the bus down to a crawl as he pulled over to park on the side of the driveway. The white screen door on the side of the house opened with a bang. A grandmother Indian emerged, wearing a checkered apron, wiping her hands on a dishcloth.

Cuny Cafe

The two Indian children ran to her sides as she walked happily toward the bus. Driver Chris pushed the air brake button and opened the door to greet her. "Hello, Mrs. Cuny," he said smiling. She was clearly a dignified lady.

"Hello Chris," she said as she grabbed the handrail and pulled herself up the first step of the bus into the stairwell. "You don't need to be calling me Mrs. Cuny young man. Just because you haven't been around for a while doesn't mean you're not part of the family." She struggled up another step and waved to everyone inside. Where she lacked in fine motor skill, she more than made up for in spirit and determination. "Where have you been?" she questioned. "It's been months since you came through."

"This is my first trip north this season." He nodded. "I see you're still as sharp as ever Nellie. How've you been?"

"I'm trying to take it all in stride," she said. "How's this old bus holding up?" she asked gregariously.

"Four million miles and going strong," Driver Chris spoke the legend.

"That's how I feel myself some days," she said with a smile. "Thanks for letting us know it's a smaller group than normal. I just need a count of vegetarians."

"Only six vegetarians," he told her.

"Only six," she questioned. "It's such a small group," she remarked.

"I've got some sad news," he told her to the side. "My brother is in the hospital with a severe head injury."

"My heart goes out to you," she told him. "I'm sure Freida will say the same."

"I'll tell you more later inside. I would like to use your phone to make a collect call home if you would be so kind," he requested.

"You're welcome to it," she told him. "Some of your friends passed through last week, but they didn't stop for dinner," she informed him. "Kevin and David, if I remember right."

"Quick and Palmore," he confirmed the other driver's identities. "They probably forgot to call."

"No worries," she said. "We weren't put out none. We just do not want to lose your business. We depend on it."

"I don't know. Maybe they were running behind schedule or something," the red-bearded Irish driver suggested. "Did they get here late?"

"They were here early enough to eat," she reported.

"Did they stop to pay for camping?" he wanted to know.

"Why, yes they did," she informed him.

"They must have had a special dinner planned," he surmised. "Sometimes they do that."

"You should let those young fellers know they can stop for dinner anytime even if they forget to call ahead. Just as long as they expect to wait a bit for us to get food on the table."

"I'll be sure to tell 'em, Nellie," he agreed.

"I should probably say a few words to your passengers," she suggested. He nodded and she struggled up the last two steps. Mrs. Cuny looked past me at the group when she spoke. "Good evening, everyone, I'm Nellie Cuny." We all said hello to the robust Lakota woman. She locked eyes with me and proceeded to speak as if she was addressing me directly. "My sister, Frieda, and I have been making dinner for Green Tortoise groups like yours for near on twenty years. We're always happy to have you as our guest because the Tortoise folks always arrive with open hearts and big smiles, singing joyful songs. Everyone cheered and her eyes drifted from mine. "I hope you all are hungry for dinner," she shouted.

At that moment we all heard a car horn honking. Driver Chris looked in the side mirror and said, "There's a white car behind us, Ma'am." The two children ran up to the bus door.

Nellie Cuny answered him, "Oh, that's just Lisa Marie, come to get the kids." She turned around and urged the children, "Go to your momma, now! Go to your momma!"

"Babysitting the grandkids?" Driver Chris asked.

She turned back and answered, "No. They're not my grandkids. I take care of lots of children, but these kids are Lisa Marie's. Lakota all take a part in raising our children. I was just helping-out a friend today," she said. "Lisa Marie spent the day protesting NAFTA."

"What's that all about?" he asked.

"It's become a genuine emergency for our people," she emoted. "The Sioux have been facing-off against a Canadian gold mining company that wants to mine our sacred areas. They claim to have permission, but we don't have a say in it because the native nations don't have any rights under NAFTA."

"That's ridiculous!" gasped Driver Chris.

"It is ridiculous," she sighed. "As if the government hasn't taken enough from my people, now they've given permission to Canada and Mexico to take whatever they want too."

"I'm sorry to hear that Nellie," our driver stood up and gave her a hug. "Sometimes I am embarrassed to be an American when our government is so ignorant. It's hard to believe that they're still messing with your people."

Mrs. Cuny expounded, "Laws can't govern how the world exists. There are as many ways to look at life as there are eyes to do the looking," Nellie Cuny told Driver Chris. "The white man fails to see that native people live in the land not on it. Our minds are connected to the land, our spirits live here, and our consciousness is planted in it like a seed. The focus of our experience is what we put into the land; the white man's focus is on what they can take out of it."

"I wish there was more I could do," he offered.

"We know your heart is in the right place," she told him. "That's enough for this world. We count you as one of our own."

"Thank you," Driver Chris told her with a squeeze of the hand, and she was off to start preparing tacos with her sister Frieda. Before leaving the bus, he stood up and shouted, "The other Green Tortoise bus will be coming in from the west at any minute, and I'd like you all to show them how much fun you're having by giving them a really warm welcome. Feel free to go crazy when they get here. Don't worry about being loud. The Indians expect us to be rowdy, and they'll probably think something is wrong if we aren't."

Frieda Cuny greeted him with a hug at the door.

Australian Sheila sat with Jewels and a few other girls at a lone picnic table, having a serious conversation. The Aussie was telling them about a sexual assault she had suffered in high school. Guitar Johnny was smoking nearby. When she finished talking, he commented, "Bloody hell! Is there a girl left on earth who hasn't had trouble with a bloke harassing them?"

"Fuckin-a!" shouted Mountain Girl.

"Men should be ashamed of themselves," I surmised.

"Men are dogs," chided the Canadian. "They think with their dicks. Even when they're in a relationship, they can't help but check out every woman who enters the room. It's like they forget about being in love every time the door swings open, like they have attention deficit disorder of the dick."

"A-D-D-D," laughed Chicken Jim.

To lighten the mood, Guitar Johnny, and Chicken Jim fired-up their guitars and led the group in song. I played the wash-bucket drum alongside Deutsche Mark. As the Dutchman and I pounded the rhythms, Guitar Johnny sang, "Bye, Bye, Miss American Pie." Passengers began to dance around the picnic tables outside the cafe. Even Berndt Toast did a little jig, showing off his moves despite his artificial leg.

Flip-flop really got into it, shaking her ass the way only a free-spirited American girl can. She grinded hips with Juliano and twirled circles with Mother Michelle. She even danced with the Cuny's farm dog, holding his paws as he jumped up on his hind legs.

We sang and danced until we heard an air-horn honking in the distance. On the horizon, a trail of dust blazed in from Buffalo Gap.

Driver Brian blew the air horn on our bus and we heard the call returned. A cry erupted from our entire group. All manner of yips and yahoos could be heard echoing across the prairie, growing to a crescendo as the other bus pulled in the end of the long driveway.

Little Josh shouted, "Let's moon the bus!" A mob formed instantly, and we ran to the driveway behind our bus where we blocked the road with more than ten bare asses. Little Josh held his belly, laughing his guts out, rolling in the dirt.

The eastbound bus came to a halt before the row of international moons, and the driver set the air brake. Some people were trying to get pictures of the moon squadron, but it was too late. People from the other bus were climbing out the bus windows, trying to get out of the bus to join the party.

Making big strides, Guitar Johnny came strumming up the side of the bus, singing out "My, my, Miss American Pie." Passengers from both groups sang along. Deutsche Mark and I followed the guitar with the wash-bucket drums.

The driver of the other bus eventually pressed the air brake again and started rolling the bus slowly through the rowdy crowd, tapping the air horn softly to clear the way. Little Josh was now hanging on to the rear bumper, Chicken Jim was swinging from the ladder by the driver's window, and Jewels was running alongside the bus holding hands with the people leaning out the windows. This comradery continued until the bus crawled the last few feet to its final resting spot next to our bus in the parking lot of Cuny Cafe.

The two dark-lime and evergreen buses from the fifties looked like twin sisters. Passengers piled out and integrated into one homogenous rowdy group.

Yülia asked Mrs. Cuny, "Are the groups always this wild?"

Nellie Cuny's face said yes with a nod. She put her hands on her hips. "Most of my people think the Tortoise folks are absolutely crazy, but we're all used to the excitement after twenty years. We've seen it all."

Soon everyone joined in singing and dancing, with more than a dozen countries now represented, Guitar Johnny played "Twist and Shout." When Guitar Johnny finished the song, the entire audience broke out in applause to which he responded with a resounding, "Thank y... y... y... you very m... m... m... much!"

As soon as the other bus arrived, Juliano introduced himself to all the new girls. Mountain Girl seemed snubbed, but nobody else seemed to care. It did not take long before Mountain Girl was off dancing with her new best friend, Australian Sheila. The passengers on both buses were indistinguishable from us in dress and appearance, except for the fact that we were being rowdier and more boisterous, having been spurred-on by Driver Chris. For the moment, we seemed to be winning the Wildest Bus Competition, despite their bus having way more passengers.

****

When dinner was ready, Nelly Cuny stood in the kitchen door ringing a triangular dinner bell like one I had seen in a wild west movie. The two groups mixed in a line stretching out the door.

While in line inside the building, I overheard some of Driver Chris' phone conversation. He was speaking on the phone with his sister. "How long do they think it will take?" I heard him ask her. "That sounds terrible," he responded. "How do they know that? Does the insurance cover that kind of rehabilitation?" he inquired.

It seemed wrong to keep listening, so I had a look around inside the Cafe. It was a normal kitchen like you would expect to find in a modest person's home, featuring a classic old-school chrome handled Frigidaire refrigerator, a similarly dated freezer, and a stainless-steel double sink. The walls were a bit yellowed from decades of serving fried foods. A red checkered tablecloth covered the serving table. Two small dinette tables and one round family style table stood close to the door.

The twelve-foot-square room was clearly the kitchen they used for everyday life, except today it had become a production line of grand proportion, ready to feed sixty-five green Tortoise passengers. Taco fixings lined the green Formica counters. The standard meal consisted of fried Indian bread, topped with meat and or beans for the vegetarians, tomatoes, lettuce, and cheese.

When Frieda Cuny handed me my Indian taco I said, "Thank you so much!" I went outside to eat with the others. The three picnic tables were already full, so I took a seat on one of the long benches surrounding the fire pit. The guitar players were strumming and passengers from both buses were dancing and singing.

Deutsche Mark added logs to the fire. It was a warm evening, but the fire entertained our eyes. My Indian taco was crazy good, and I thoroughly enjoyed the delicious meal, despite how quickly I ate. Other passengers were discarding their paper plates in the fire, so I gave up my seat and added mine to the flames.

Driver Chris came out of the cafe looking upset, so I followed him over to the bus where Driver Brian spoke with him on the bottom step.

"How did it go?" he asked his partner. "Did you reach your dad?"

"I did," he confirmed. "I got straight through to the room," he told his co-driver. "My mother couldn't even talk to me other than to just say hello. Thankfully, my sister was there to help calm her down."

"Did you tell her I said hello?"

"As promised," he confirmed. "She said to thank you for being such a good friend."

"Awe," he squeaked, "I love your mom. What did your sister say?"

"We talked about contingency plans for a number of possible scenarios," he revealed. "None of them are good. The doctors keep warning us to be prepared for the worst. They don't think he's ever going to be the same again, although they still haven't ruled that out. Personally, I don't think they would be warning us if there wasn't something to be prepared for."

I had not seen him look that serious since he got the news that first night in New York.

"It sounds like they just want you to be prepared for whatever comes next," his partner told him. "Did they tell you what to expect?"

"They're fairly certain he's going to have cognitive issues when he wakes up. He may not be able to speak. They say that's quite common." A look of concern came to his face before he added, "Dude, they said he may not recognize anyone. That's normal for this type of injury, but we won't know how bad-off he is until he comes around."

"That's pretty scary," I commented. "Sorry to hear that bro."

"Yeah," he sighed. "If he doesn't recognize my mother that would rock her world. We're worried she'll have a stroke or something. My sister's going to ask the doctor to have a sedative ready for the morning when she finds out. We're trying to get my father to take her home for a while, so she's not there when he wakes up, just in case. We won't know until he wakes up."

"It sounds like they're fairly certain he will come around. Wouldn't you say?" Driver Brian offered.

"Pretty much."

"Well, that's a good sign," his co-driver told him.

"That is a good sign," the Irishman agreed.

"Did they say how long it might be before he wakes up?" said Driver Brian.

"Sort of," he told us. "They're planning to back off on the pain medication starting tomorrow morning to see if he wakes up on his own."

"More good news," his co-driver commented. "What happened with your father?"

"He was as stubborn as ever," Driver Chris revealed. "I must admit. I didn't handle myself as well as I had hoped, but I did manage to exchange a few pleasantries with him before I melted down."

"That sounds like progress," said his co-driver.

"Yeah right!" he scoffed. "We spoke for five minutes before I lost my shit." He shook his head in frustration. "Then he started going off on me, how I was hurting my mother and neglecting my family."

"Wow! He knows how to push your buttons."

"All too well," the red-bearded driver agreed. "I promise you. I was trying to keep an open mind, trying to let his anger flow around me, I was trying to breathe like Jewels taught me, but then he starts blaming me for what happened to my brother, like I could have stopped it if I was there, like I'm to blame for being so far away."

"I hope you didn't take that to heart," said his partner. "It's clearly not your fault that your brother fell off a building."

"I know. I know." He waved him off. "But he was like, 'None of this would have happened if you hadn't left home. If you had only been with your brother that night instead of being on the other side of the country, running around with a bunch of Hippie freaks."

"He said that?"

"Yes! I swear," testified the grief-stricken driver with a tone of disbelief. He made a stark-raving-mad expression, feigning outrage. "He called us Hippies?!"

"Now them's fightin' words," Driver Brian quipped humorously.

He sighed like pride had been hurt. "I can't believe he called us Hippies," he reflected with a hand on his breastbone. "I know we're freaks," he admitted. "We're totally freaks, but not Hippies; no way."

"Yeah, man, I can totally see why you lost your shit," his co-driver acknowledged.

"Almost lost my shit," he corrected him.

"That's a start," his partner praised. "What did you say to that?"

"Dude, I wanted to reach through the phone and strangle him," admitted the red-bearded easterner, "but I couldn't yell inside the Cuny's house. Nellie was sittin' right there. It was like my mind was exploding, but I actually remained calm on the phone."

"Well, dude, hey, That's an improvement," he recognized his partner's achievement. "How did it end?"

"My sister took the phone away from him before I could fire a shot," he huffed. "Yeah, dude, I heard my mother crying afterwards. I'm not sure what he said to her, but I can only assume it wasn't very nice."

"You never fought back," Driver Brian praised. "That's great!"

"You think?"

"Sure. If you don't fight back, you always come out smelling like a rose," he explained. "Now, he has no one else to blame for his anger."

"Well, I wouldn't go that far," he cautioned.

"It's a start brother. It's a start," his partner responded with a righteous series of nods. "Dude, have you eaten?" he asked.

The lead driver said, "No. I'm not hungry now."

"Dude, Go get yourself a taco, and forget about this shit for a while," his friend recommended. "You need a break." They went off to eat together. I felt so bad for Driver Chris, but there was nothing I could do. There was nothing I could say.

Everyone else was having a blast, so I went over to join them. The music and dancing was all around us. One of the drivers from the other bus, a guy named Hal, was dancing with Flip-flop. Berndt Toast was showing off his moves again. PAC-MAN was dancing and singing around the fire pit with his traveling companion. He had a decent singing voice, although high pitched for a dude. I do not know if it is common among Chinese people, but he knew the words to all the American songs. Even Peruvian Ursula was singing. The pair seemed relatively normal for once.

Guitar Johnny stood with me by the fire. After watching the Pink Panther dance with Cato, he said, "The Peruvian lass is actually quite attractive when she's not bossing that poor Chinese bloke about."

The guitar playing stopped only when all the musicians were eating at the same time. Everyone loved the food and we all clapped for Nellie and Frieda when they sat down together.

One of the Cuny family dogs hid under the bench in-between Chicken Jim's legs and ate off his plate several times while he wasn't looking. The rookie driver looked so confused each time he looked back at his plate more food was gone. This alone made everyone laugh to the point of tears. In fact, Little Josh laughed so hard, he spit food out of his mouth. His mother had to scold him when he kept repeating the process for fun. It was not cool to waste food.

What really brought the house down was when the dog came out of the shadows with big red lips from the meat juice. The Indian ladies whooped with laughter. Someone said it looks like the dog is smiling, and that just pushed it over the top. We were in full attack of the giggles, heartfelt joyful laughter.

The fit farm dog just sat there looking innocent until Chicken Jim realized why we were laughing. "Awe, shit! The dog ate half my taco!" he complained. He had to push the dog away while he ate the rest. It became clear that it had become a challenge for British Sue to retain her pee, they were laughing so hard. In the end Chicken Jim gave the dog the last bite and he was justifiably vindicated when Nellie brought him a second Indian taco.

About then a white pickup truck came blazing up the hill from the east. "That'd be Owen," said Nellie Cuny as she rose to her feet. "I best turn the heat back on the taco meat. He'll be wanting to eat."

Her husband pulled up and parked close to the house in a beat-up Ford F250. The old farm truck had seen its share of hard labor. It had clearly been used as a workhorse for decades. The man behind the wheel looked no less careworn. The slender old Indian stepped out of the cab wearing blue jeans and a pearl-buttoned shirt. His face was worn like the washboard ruts in a dirt road after rain. He appeared to be both hard and soft at the same time, like the hands of time had softened him as much as experience had done its hardening. He tipped his straw cowboy hat in our direction before going inside.

Moments later he came out with an Indian taco. Our red-bearded driver approached him offering his hand. "Owen," he said happily. "It's so good to see you."

"Htayétu wašté, my friend Chris. Welcome! I am glad to see you here." The ancient Lakota man walked slowly toward the firepit where he took a seat next to his sister-in-law Frieda.

"I'll let you eat, but there's something I need to ask you later."

"Okay my friend," he said. The Indian man had a quiet peaceful way about him. He ate slowly and surely, chewing each bite like he was savoring the flavor.

"Is it good?" asked Frieda.

He smiled and said, "The Earth has given us all these fine ingredients, but the energy you put into cooking has made them even more delicious." His grandkids rushed at him midway through his meal. They clearly loved him. He put down his plate to hug them and asked them about their day.

"Leave him while he eats," chastised Frieda.

After Owen Cuny finished eating, he rose and put his paper plate in the fire. Driver Chris went over to stand by his side directly across from me and the British guitar player. "Owen," he began, "I recently finished reading *Black Elk Speaks*."

"Ah yes. Black Elk," related the Indian. "He was a Lakota medicine man, a great healer."

"The book talks about a place called Sheep Mountain Table," the driver told him.

"That is a sacred spot," Owen acknowledged. "The mountain top stands on the southern edge of the Badlands, overlooking the National Park. It's not too far from here."

"Is that your land?" Driver Chris asked.

"Yes," the Indian informed him.

"Is there any chance we might be able to camp up there tonight instead of our normal spot? It would be a great honor."

"I don't see why not," Owen mused. "I'd have to unlock the gate, but that shouldn't be a problem. I can have my nephew drive up there with you."

"Yeah, I don't want to put anyone out," our guide spoke with concern.

"No trouble at all, Owen said. "I haven't been out there for the longest time. I might drive up there with him. The view goes on for miles. Someone will have to go with you. I would hate to see you get the bus stuck in the mud. It would be a long walk back."

"Are you sure?"

"No problem at all. I will enjoy it myself. My nephew is on his way here to pick up the kids. I will ask him to drive out with us. I am not sure he has ever been up there. He'll probably love it too."

After dinner with our new Indian friends, we all said a warm goodbye to Nelly and Frieda Cuny, and the party moved back onto the two buses. Driver Hal invited Flip-flop to ride to camp on the other bus, so we made it a point to kidnap a bunch of their passengers for the ride to camp. In the process many of our passengers rode the other bus. We had not been drinking any alcohol in front of the Indians, out of respect for their customs, but once inside the bus it was like Oktoberfest. It did not matter which bus you were on either. The two groups had become one. The groups were all mixed up now, and the dance party was as equally great on both buses.

Owen Cuny's nephew arrived and led the way up the dirt road, heading toward Buffalo Gap. We stopped at a latched gate in a wooden fence in an otherwise nondescript part of Cuny Table. Owen Cuny unlocked the gate and closed it after we passed through. There was no road at all on the other side of the fence, only a giant field of three-foot-tall grass as far as the eye could see. People were standing up through the roof hatch in the drivers' cabin of both buses. We were heading toward Sheep Mountain Table, and the race was on.

The pickup truck led the way through an undulating sea of yellow grass. The truck drove fast, so the tires would not get stuck in the soft earth, carving a path through the dry grass. The bus rolled across the treeless prairie, on a wild joy ride up to our campsite on the top of Cuny Table. The buses followed the pickup, driving faster and faster; faster than I thought was safe. The tall grass blinded us to the contours of the land. We drove over hidden bumps that lifted the seated passengers off their seats and threw the dancers off their feet. Everyone had to hold on to something or someone, including Driver Chris, who had to hold onto the steering wheel with both hands just to keep him in the seat. People were slam dancing wildly, and falling all over each other laughing, whenever we hit a dip in the fields.

The music was blaring, and everyone was enjoying the thrill of the mad-capped race to the top of Sheep Mountain Table. I was standing in the stairwell holding onto the dashboard handrail with a white-knuckled grip, bracing myself against the cushion of the front platform. I was blown-away by the feeling, and it seemed like everyone was dancing and grooving with it, and no one cared. It was amazing what these buses were doing, driving across those fields of grass at such high velocity.

I was staring bug-eyed at the yellow grass only a foot below the windshield, searching for hidden obstacles. We were rolloping across this giant field. I was in love with this bus, amazed at what it could do. I was in awe at the skill and precision with which Driver Chris piloted the forty-foot monster bus across the fields, fields where the Buffalo roam. This was his finest hour. His face was full of joy and his eyes could not have been more open.

Every so often, the ground below us would drop away, hidden by the illusion of tall grass. Driver Chris would react with lightning speed, and we'd all lurch forward as the brakes were being applied, and then BUMP, OOP, for an instant all of the dancers would be piled on top of me in the front stairwell, but then, TSSSS, and we'd hear the air brakes go, and everyone would lurch backwards, and the dancers would just start dancing naturally in rhythm again.

I could see the other bus racing right beside ours, as Driver Chris yelled over the party noise, "Going slowly is the one sure way we'll be stuck here forever in the soft mud."

We drove another mile at least until the grass thinned out and the slope of the land increased. The grass became sparse as we climbed the big hill. We stopped at the top of the hill at the edge of a cliff overlooking the most beautiful canyon I had ever seen in my entire life. This was Sheep Mountain Table.

We were out on a peninsula of land that dropped off the edge of the prairie into the canyons of the Badlands. We parked on the edge of a canyon full of the same gorgeous formations that we had hiked through that morning. This time we were well off the beaten track; there were no paths for hiking. Only this one road in and out. Together they were one road that we ourselves had made. We could see the new road behind us that we had made an impression in the grass. The grass had gotten matted down in two crooked Tortoise trails.

Out near the cliff, the buses parked strategically in a V shape, so that they would act as a wind block. Owen and his nephew said goodbye and headed home. "Just lock the gate when you leave in the morning," Owen told us.

It was early in the evening and the night wind had already started to blow. The near corner of the V stood only twenty feet from the edge of the canyon. On the bottom of the canyon, a huge herd of Buffalo were feeding on lush fields of green grass. The sunlight was filtered through puffy orange clouds on the western horizon. It felt like we had driven into a dream. So vast was the horizon, for the life of me, there was nothing to see but the emptiness of the Great Plains, and the beautifully sculptured formations of the Badlands.

14
Sheep Mountain Table

The moment I arrived at Sheep Mountain Table I was overcome by a profound sense of awe. Dozens of passengers from both buses staggered with me to the edge of the cliff overlooking the entirety of Badlands National Park. The light-colored sandstone reflected the sunlight, making it a very bright place even at twilight. Off to the east a group of surrealistically shaped sandstone pinnacles and peaks were glowing in the orange-tinted light of the summer evening. With the sun close to the horizon, all the colors were morphing, and the shadows were growing. The sky was a dome of deep blue that did not fade until the edges of the world, making the visibility seem endless.

A creeping miasma of haze floated above the canyon floor where herds of Buffalo mottled fields of green grass. Beyond the fields a vast patchwork of jagged sawtooth sandstone formations stretched out to the north east for over thirty miles. I turned around to get a better sense of our position on top of the grassy plateau. The fields of forever blanketed the earth as far as the eye could see in a landscape barren of trees. Over the edge of the cliff lay our own private canyon, featuring a menagerie of bright gray and sand-colored formations. The vertical walls were etched like otherworldly sculptures while the milder slopes were as smooth as sandcastles.

Deutsche Mark and Guitar Johnny stood by my side taking-in the majestic view in solemn reverence. Out of the corner of my eye I caught a glimpse of Jewels skipping toward us in a flowing sundress that caught the light. She greeted the three of us with a joyous smile.

"A vision of l... l... loveliness," remarked Guitar Johnny.

Jewels put her arm around him. "This place is so wonderful, Johnny. Don't you feel it? I feel so connected to the earth, this land and everything around us."

"W... w... w... well, I'm feeling something, but I don't know fuck all about that."

Yülia came running up behind us and startled Guitar Johnny with her hand on his back. "Wunderbar! Wunderbar!" She put her arm around him on the opposite side of Jewels next to Deutsche Mark.

"I'm a bit n... n... nervous about falling off the edge of this b... b... bloody cliff." We all laughed a little as we looked over the edge into the canyon. It was quite a drop. I gave Guitar Johnny a knowing look.

"I feel so connected here," Jewels continued. "My spirit feels so free."

"This one view is worth the whole trip," Deutsche Mark commented.

"Wunderbar! Wunderbar!" exclaimed Yülia.

Guitar Johnny rolled a cigarette in the pouch of tobacco in his waist-pack. Before he finished Deutsche Mark said, "The Indians smoke tobacco in ceremonies. It seems appropriate here." He watched the Englishman lick the paper and motioned with his head. Guitar Johnny passed him the cigarette without hesitation and started rolling another.

"I'll take one too, if you don't mind," I said.

"Bloody hell! Anyone else?" he asked snidely. The girls both declined.

"Thanks, man," I said.

It was too windy to light cigarettes even with a cupped hand, so Guitar Johnny showed us a trick where he put his head inside his shirt to light the first one and we jump started the others.

While we stood there unceremoniously smoking our cigarettes, Jewels told Yülia, "I'm going to smoke weed later if you want to try it."

"I'd love to try it," the German girl answered cutely. "I smoked hash once before when I was young," she revealed, "but I never tried smoking the flowers." We all laughed.

"Is that what you call it in Germany?" I asked with a smile.

"No," she said innocently. "We call it grass, but grass is the flowers, right?"

"Grass is the flowers," Deutsche Mark confirmed. "We call it wied in Holland," he added.

"We call it weed in America too, honey," Jewels informed her young friend.

Deutsche Mark sounded dejected. "I'd smoke weed with you guys, but I rolled my last bone this morning."

"I'd smoke, if you have enough," I added.

"I'm trying to conserve," reported Jewels.

I smiled and said, "Dave might be able to hook us up. He's pretty cool. I'll ask him." Then I asked Guitar Johnny, "Do you smoke weed?"

"N... n... n... no thank you," He stuttered. "It's not my bag. Wacky backy makes me n... n... n... nervous and my legs get a bit wonky," he explained.

"That's cool," I said patting him on the back. "We wouldn't want to make you nervous. We want to keep you singing."

"Your music is spectacular," crooned Jewels.

"I love your songs," observed Yülia gleefully.

"See," I said. "You make everyone happy with your music, man. That's just cool."

"J... J... Jeez, thank you, John," he said, kicking his boots and taking a drag from his smoke.

"I feel like I love all of you guys, especially here, and now," Yülia revealed. "I'm so happy now!"

"I definitely feel good energy," said Deutsche Mark. He put his arm around her to share warmth.

"You guys are awesome," grooved Jewels. "I've never felt so comfortable with white people before," she revealed. "Everyone is so warm and accepting. It's like skin color doesn't matter on the bus. That's rare in the states," she opined.

"Your skin is wunderbar!" proclaimed Yülia. "I want your skin. Look how white I am." She displayed her paperwhite forearm. "I'd do anything to have your color." She hugged Deutsche Mark again. It was getting chilly in the constant breeze.

Jewels was so pleased with her friend. She rubbed her arm behind Guitar Johnny's back. His face lit up with joy too. So, I moved in close and put my arm around Jewels. We stood arm-in-arm for a while on the edge of the windy cliff, overlooking the Badlands on Sheep Mountain Table, contemplating the universe and everything. (SOUNDS OF WIND).

It was getting cold standing there out in the open, so we decided to find Big Dave. We found him on the bus seated in his normal spot at the dinette. When I asked him about hooking us up, he made a strained face. He only softened when Jewels offered to contribute. He put his hand to his breast pocket, and a wave of revelation swept across his face. "I need to find Michelle," he told us. He got up slowly without saying a word and walked past us down the aisle toward the door.

I'll help you find her," I offered, getting up to follow him out. He hobbled down the steps and said "Woe!" when the blustery wind met his bearded face. He stopped just outside the door and looked surprised.

Mother Michelle walked up from the direction of the cliff like a waif in a loose-fitting white dress. "Don't you look lovely," he intoned deeply.

She held out her hand and said, "Nice tent, Dave."

He took his pipe with a grin. "There's room for two if you're so inclined," he offered. "No strings attached. I assure you I'll be on my best behavior."

"I just might take you up on that," she responded. "I suspect it's going to be a late night around the campfire, and I won't be able to stay up that late. I guess it depends on the noise level. I'll let you know."

"I have to warn you," he said. "I snore like a moose."

"So, do I," she said with a laugh and she floated away in her lovely dress.

Berndt Toast had walked up while they were talking. Now, he said, "I hear you guys are gonna smoke."

"How many people did you tell?" grumbled Big Dave.

"He's the last one," I said tentatively. "There's no one else coming, right?" I asked him.

"It's just me," the German guy confirmed.

The three of us went inside, closed the door behind us and took seats at the dinette table. The two Julies and the Dutchman closed all the windows and sat close by. Big Dave unfolded his red bandanna and spread it out on the table. He removed a big bud from a tobacco pouch and began breaking it up, using the bandanna as a weed tray. Under these circumstances, nobody cared that he used his bandanna to wipe sweat from his forehead.

Jewels placed a big bud on the bandanna and the big man broke it up while we passed her bag of weed around for a sniff. Yülia wanted a better look at the marijuana, so she slid into the seat next to Big Dave, watching closely as he broke the buds into a pile. I gave a knowing look to Deutsche Mark. The pile of weed was growing. He noticed and said, "Right on, dude." We were all psyched. Much to our surprise Berndt Toast produced his own bag and dropped a pair of buds onto the bandanna. This made Big Dave smile and seem more relaxed, but then a knock came at the door.

"Who is it now?" grumbled the big man.

The Dutchman jumped up off the drinks cooler and said, "I got it." He went to the door. "It's Josh's mom," he informed us.

This made Big Dave smile broadly. "Let her in you fool," he commanded.

"This looks fun," said the Hippie mama as she approached in her flowing white sundress.

"The more the merrier," Big Dave said with a romantic smile.

Her eyes sparkled back affectionately. She took a seat on the drinks cooler and made room for the Dutchman to sit beside her. As Big Dave continued this meticulous work, he told us about his pipe in a slow and low voice. "I bought this pipe from an Indian twenty years ago."

"It's beautiful," Jewels raved.

"Yes," he agreed, holding it on display. "The Buffalo calf carved on this side represents the earth that feeds us," he informed us. "The eagle feathers engraved on the stem signify the sky and the twelve moons." He handed Jewels the pipe. "Check it out," he said fondly. She had a good look and passed it around. "Soapstone doesn't conduct heat," he informed us. "So, it never gets hot even after prolonged smoking."

"I'm up for some prolonged smoking," joked Deutsche Mark. We all laughed and agreed. We all watched eagerly as Big Dave packed the pipe. He showed us how the carburetor worked and put it to his lips to smoke. All the windows on the bus had been closed, but the air was still whipping through the cracks in the frames. The flickering flame lit up our faces and made shadows that danced in dark bus. He took a hit, inhaled, and passed it to Mother Michelle on his left. She took a hit, held her breath and passed it to the Dutchman. Around the circle it went.

Yülia held the pipe hesitantly. All eyes were on her. "I don't know," she said cutely.

"Awe, don't be afraid," Jewels encouraged her.

Big Dave pointed out the carburetor and worked the lighter to make it easier for her. The petite German coed took a tiny little hit, squeaked like a mouse and held her breath. A few of us giggled, but then she said, "Holy Mole!" This made us all laugh. She tried to contain herself, but a giggle slipped out that triggered a spasm of coughs. She coughed and coughed for the longest time. We all laughed as the pipe continued around the circle. We spent a long time talking and laughing. It was an enjoyable time.

I began to want to move again, so when the conversation ebbed, I suggested, "Let's go grab some cushions and blankets and go watch the sunset out on the cliff." The response was unanimous except for Big Dave and Mother Michelle. The big man needed to rest, and he wanted nothing to do with the cold. Mother Michelle was happy to hang with him inside the warm bus. Guitar Johnny took his guitar, I took my drum, and we marched down the steps like the seven dwarves stoned to the gills on our communion weed.

We stood in a semicircle facing the cliff overlooking Badlands National Park with the sun at our backs and a light wind in our faces.

The plateau we were standing on cast a shadow over the Badlands that visibly moved as we watched. The shadows of the two Tortoise buses stretched over the edge of the cliff. A lane of sunlight illuminated the golden grass between the buses opening onto a massive bonfire. Beyond the buses lay the bleak expanse of the Pine Ridge Indian Reservation, bathed in the light of a blood-orange colored sunset.

Guitar Johnny approached along the cliff playing his guitar like a strolling minstrel. The wind stole the sound as soon as he plucked each note until he stood close before us. Jewels' hair was flying about, so she went with Yülia to get jackets and a shawl. The men braved the cold while they were gone, but we were happy when they returned with mattresses and a pair of sleeping bags.

Deutsche Mark and I laid down on our sides spooned with the two Julies under the blanket on the foam cushion a few yards from the edge of Sheep Mountain Table. The lip of the cliff created a pocket of dead air low to the ground near the edge of the canyon that took the edge off the wind. The addition of the blankets made it cozy. I cuddled with Jewels on one side and Deutsche Mark cuddled with Yülia on the other with our legs all intermingled. Guitar Johnny sat on the edge of the mattress leaning against us with our faces next to his knees.

Guitar Johnny played American Pie by Don McLean and he sang.

> A long long time ago
> I can still remember how
> That music used to make me smile
> And I knew if I had my chance
> That I could make those people dance
> And maybe they'd be happy for a while

When Guitar Johnny finished singing the song, we clapped for him and he stuttered, "I take it you guys are high?" Self-deprecating to a fault he had just finished singing the complicated lyrics flawlessly.

Jewels responded soulfully without taking her eyes off the canyon. "I'm feeling so good." As always, she stressed the good. "I feel the energy radiating from the Earth. I feel so in touch with myself and you guys and everything." She asked him, "Do you feel it, Johnny?"

"Oh my! Do I ever," he spat sarcastically. "My head is spinning, and I feel absolutely scrummy." We all laughed.

When Driver Brian happened by, Jewels lifted the edge of the blanket with her foot invitingly and said, "Why don't you join us?" Without much encouragement he curled up on the grass with his head resting on Jewels' lap. We hung-out on the cliff talking and laughing,

Sheep Mountain Table

absorbing the magnificent spectacle of the Badlands being slowly engulfed by shadow.

My eyes swam through the liquid landscape submerged in the ocean of darkness as my spirit diffused outward into everything. The mild current of wind floated my voice past the others, "What an awesome place!" I commented.

We sat high upon the cresting wave of Earth called Sheep Mountain Table, in the sacred land of the Sioux, flanked by the emptiness of the Great Plains and the ancient shells of two Tortoise buses. We were in a place that defied the words map and compass. To get where we were one would need a different kind of guide. One would need to triangulate the soul and create a new reality. This was a once in a lifetime experience. We were on hallowed ground.

The Buffalo on the grassy floor of the canyon were on the move, flowing across the ancient marsh, through the darkened valleys of sculptured time. The shadow of the earth had already darkened the green pastures below, but the shoulders and heads of the nameless sand mountains in the east were still on fire with orange light.

The line of shadow crept up the spine and shoulders of the distant formations, devouring every inch of light in its path, mounting the brilliantly burning peaks one by one. The curve of orange melon cresting over the mountains behind us, painted peach in the yellow grass and tangerines on Yülia's cheeks. Her whole face beamed with the auburn fire of bent light. The glowing mountains no longer seemed so far away, as if we could now access their texture in the shadows.

A tremor of energy shook in my limbs like the power of the living land was alive within me. Struck with a sort of physical telepathy, I could feel the Buffalo moving over the land below us, connected to us, with a certainty as strong as the wind on my skin, and as sure as the pounding in my chest. My mind was blown with a tempest of sudden comprehension, where lightning flashes illuminated the web of being.

The soft angled light of the orb of dusk breathed a living palate of rouge up the nape of the neck into the cheeks of the land, as the dripping death of dark shadow laid its body down to rest. Cuddling under our blankets together, we watched the shadow of the sun slowly engulf the canyon, moving across the formations of the Badlands like an eyelid over the globe. Accompanied by the distant sound of drums at the bonfire, from our feet to the end of the world, we witnessed the setting of the sun in the forms of both light and shadow cast over Mokosica. The red sun dipped below the sacred mountains and all present entered the cathedral of silence.

The fuzzy light of the netherworld vanquished the hollow wind-swept land, thinning the light-painted sky with the liquor of night's darker shades, morphing blue into the gossamer colors of night, giving way to the dark vacuum of space that sucks the twinkling diamonds of time from the currents of celestial velvet. The Badlands were illuminated under the residue of ancient starlight. I was filled with wonder and a profound sense of harmony within the sacred web of everything.

****

We headed back toward the buses, where the fire was now blazing warm. Deutsche Mark was rapping about Black Elk with Yülia while Jewels was gushing with enthusiasm for the sunset. "I've never seen so many shades of pink, and that red near the end didn't even make sense. I mean, like, I saw something like that in a painting one time, man, but I never thought it could be real." Everyone was inspired by such floods of expression. "I feel such love for life, and the planet, and everyone," she emoted. "I'm so connected with the Earth and all you people like we're part of something bigger."

I could not have agreed with her more.

Big Dave added, "It does seem like the earth is speaking to us here."

To which Guitar Johnny responded by saying, "It sounds like a load of bloody b... b... bullshit if you ask me!" He turned away from the group and lit up a smoke in the wind by pulling his leather jacket over his head.

We walked out into the clearing, between the two buses, where the passengers had dug the giant fire pit. A huge pile of wood from Loon Lake was stacked off to the side of the fire waiting to be burned. Water buckets were lined up around the pit to douse the grass if the embers wafted onto the thin grass.

Our group walked through the crowd of sixty people standing around the bonfire. Both buses were fully intermingled in conversation, music, and laughter. Peruvian Ursula was dancing like J-Lo, swinging her curvaceous hips to the music blasting on the rooftop speakers. Flip-flop was stomping up a dust cloud with Driver Hal. Eventually, Guitar Johnny and Chicken Jim took seats on the communal mattresses and they played their best songs and sang, while Deutsche Mark and I drummed, clapped, and chanted. We sounded better than ever, and the whole crowd got into it. The rhythms flowed out of my hands like the heat of the fire.

The passengers and drivers were dancing barefoot in the dust. Sun dresses were getting thrown up into the air like veils. We danced foot-stomping dances, making Indian war whoops, and howling into the night. It was easy to be full of wonder, frolicking like happy children on the highest hill overlooking the South Dakota Badlands. We were all shaken out of the ruts of normalcy high atop Sheep Mountain Table.

Driver Hal had taken an interest in Flip-flop ever since the dinner party at Cuny Cafe. She was so full of energy and good cheer; it was easy to see why everyone liked her. All night long they led the festivities in dance and song. At one time they lead an epic conga line around the massive bonfire with about sixty passengers in tow. Even Peruvian Ursula marched in the conga line, unaware that her traveling companion who was getting drunk with Driver Chris. As she got drunk Flip-flops dancing grew more provocative until it became obvious that she and Hal were going to hook up.

Guitar Johnny made every attempt to entertain us with his skill on the guitar. He had a large repertoire of songs he could play on request. He kept asking Jewels, "Is there anything else you'd like to hear? Can I play something to tickle your ear?" It became clear that he was interested in getting to know Jewels better. Every time he sat down, he took the closest open seat to her and Yülia. He was like a moth to her candle whenever she clapped or raved about his playing. Driver Brian also hung close to Jewels most of the night.

It was also heart rending to watch Chicken Jim get shot-down serenading Fräulein Vera with the lyrics of the Beatles "Blackbird." All she did was curse his name and repeatedly and walk away as he followed her around.

When the moon rose over the horizon, again we were silent and reverent. When the music started Jewels convinced us all to get up and dance. Jewels moved provocatively with Driver Brian in a Moondance during Chicken Jim's rendition of the Van Morrison song by the same name. Jewels raved about the Moon coming out of its cave as she danced. This was a legend in her native culture. Evidently, the Moon sleeps in a cave during the daytime.

While we danced, the moon grew like a giant melon on the horizon, turning orange then yellow, like a pumpkin, and then silver! The near-full moon rose out amongst the tremendous multitude of stars in the Milky Way, and we danced like pagans around the blazing fire.

****

Late that night, we were some of the last passengers awake around the campfire. Among us were Deutsche Mark, Jewels, and Yülia. A few of our other friends were awake too, including Guitar Johnny, the Irish Twins, Fräulein Vera, and several people from the other bus. I had long since stopped drinking, and I was ready to get some rest.

Deutsche Mark's eyes twinkled in the firelight as he held Yülia in his lap. She was smiling a huge face of happiness. Her skin looked amazing in the moonlight. Jewels was in a marvelously empathetic mood after she puffed on her pipe. "Would you like to hear a story?" she asked the group.

"Y... yes, I'd like that very much," said Guitar Johnny. "I'd love to hear your story."

"Wunderbar!" exclaimed Yülia.

"Of course," I responded. Everyone seemed entirely in tune with the idea.

The wind died and it was quiet on the prairie. Our group sprawled out luxuriantly in a formation of intertwined bodies on our communal mattresses. Yülia's head rested on Deutsche Mark's stomach with Jewels bent legs over her knees. Driver Brian was sprawled out on her far side and so on. I sensed that we were all connected by touch when Jewels began telling her story.

The New York schoolteacher spoke in a voice we could all hear, enunciating every word at a quick pace as the story progressed. "This is the story of 'Hermes and the Origin of Music,'" she told us. "According to legend, the first musical instrument was the tortoise shell lyre." There were lots of oohhs and aahhs when revealed this was. A feeling came over me, like a muse of the Ancient World was visiting me, and I let my consciousness slip away into the flames. Jewels' words flowed like the wine of the ancient world, filling my ears like goblets.

> "When Hermes was born, his mother knew right away that he would need special care. His potential for intelligence was as equally great as his potential for trouble. His mother watched him closely, but Hermes was always wandering off and getting himself into all sorts of predicaments."
>
> "One day, when Hermes was still only a baby, his mother was traveling with him through the desert, when she rested for a moment by the bank of an enchanted river. Baby Hermes crawled away from her and found a magical Green Tortoise."

Our spirits and voices rose like doves before she continued.

> "Now, mind you Hermes was a difficult baby. That kid was always on the go. His mother only put him down for a second."

Mother Michelle raised her beer and said, "Here! Here!"

Sheep Mountain Table

Jewels continued without delay, "Before his mamma could turn back around, Hermes was gone. He had climbed onto the back of the magical Green Tortoise, and snap! Just like that, had crossed over into the Realm of the Gods."

"In the blink of an eye, Hermes Traveled around the World for many lifetimes on the back of the magical Green Tortoise. Hermes and the Tortoise became the best of friends and grew to love one another. Hermes had great adventures over many more lifetimes in every part of the world on the Tortoise. Together they mastered every subject and discovered the secrets of the universe."

"As his mother turned her head to look for him, she caught a glimpse of baby Hermes riding the Tortoise out of the corner of her eye. Without hesitation she snatched her child from the Realm of the Gods back into the human world calling upon the greatest power of the human realm, the power of a mother's love."

She paused before adding. "Her baby was saved."

There was a collective sigh.

"Sadly," Jewels lamented. "Without Hermes the Tortoise died of a broken heart." Jewels snapped her fingers. "And just like that there was nothing left of Tortoise accept an empty shell and fond memories."

"Hermes could not just leave the Magical Green Tortoise's shell behind, so he cried a fierce cry that frightened his mother until she understood, and she allowed him to take the Tortoise shell out of the desert with them."

"Hermes was still just a baby in his mother's world. So, his story would have to remain a secret for a while, at least until he learned how to speak. Hermes knew it would be difficult for his mother to comprehend the gift of consciousness that he alone possessed as a human, but he still wanted her to see more than anything in the world."

"Hermes mourned the loss of his friend. He wanted the spirit of the Magical Green Tortoise to live on forever. So, when Hermes got back home, he lay the Magical Green Tortoise shell over himself, and cried. He cried a thousand tears into the shell. He cried so much and for so long that the shell filled with tears and transformed into a magical Lyre, strung with the heartstrings of a child."

"The magical music put his mother's mind to rest and after he played it for a while she fell into a deep sleep. The Tortoise came back to life, and while she slept peacefully,

Hermes was able to slip away and travel around the world on the Magical Green Tortoise again."

"Hermes learned a great many secrets of the realms of the gods. He knew how much better human life could be, if we humans could only attain a small fraction of the consciousness that he so fully enjoyed. He began to seek a channel for the communication between the mortals and the divine."

"He saw before him a vision of Apollo's splendid herd of cattle. Hermes knew his mother would appreciate such a gift. Certainly, Apollo would not miss just one head of cattle among thousands. He watched Apollo carefully, having learned to sneak out stealthily from his friend the Tortoise. When Apollo sat down to rest Hermes played the Magical Green Tortoise Lyre and lulled Apollo to sleep."

"Instantaneously, Hermes was back on earth playing the Lyre at the foot of his mother's bed. She was lying awake, unable to understand who the grown man was standing in front of her. Not only was Hermes now an old man, but the room was full of Apollo's cattle. The herd was so big cattle filled every room and surrounded the house."

"Unbeknownst to Hermes, Apollo stormed the cosmic realms of the universe looking for his lost herd of cattle."

"Hermes sacrificed one of the supernatural cattle in the name of his mother. As a direct result she was granted higher consciousness, and she no longer feared for the safety of her child. A muse whispered the epic of her own rebirth in her ear, and she became conscious of the energy of her own womb, and her place in the web of life."

"Hermes felt at peace in the world of the gods, so he shared the music of the Lyre with mortal man. Before the Lyre existed, music was something that only the gods could create. Hermes played the Lyre for every human being that wanted to listen."

"Meanwhile, Apollo had still not given up his search for his herd of cattle. He zealously searched every field on Earth. Apollo dreamt dreams that bridged the supernatural world with the divine, and he found himself listening to the Tortoise Lyre at the feet of Hermes mother. Apollo heard every note in his dreams. At one magical moment, sweet music was brought unto the human world and simultaneously shared with the gods."

"A muse whispered in Apollo's ear, and for the first time a god felt how joyful a human's life could be, and in the same instant he saw how painful it was to be mortal and to have to face death. Apollo loved the music of the Lyre so much that he wanted to share the music with the other Gods. Mortals had never given a better gift to the gods, the gift of divine song, and the gods wanted to listen. Apollo called for Zeus to come hear the music."

"Apollo gave his entire herd of supernatural cattle in exchange for the Magical Tortoise Shell Lyre, with its mortal heartstrings, and Zeus made Hermes into a god and granted him eternal life, enlightening mortal man with consciousness. In both heaven and on earth the gods and humans can hear the sweet music of the Lyre. In heaven, it teaches the gods how important life is when faced by mortality. On earth the music of the Green Tortoise Lyre reminds mortals of the fleeting nature of life. We live each moment and breathe each breath knowing that our lives are like a magical song that will never be heard again after we are gone."

Jewels went silent. There was a light smattering of applause, thanks, and praise. Jewels told her story with such passion I would not have been surprised if Hermes himself had paid her a visit around the bonfire earlier in the evening. After that everyone remained silent and I drifted into a peaceful sleep, conscious of a deep connection with the Earth and all my new friends.

15
American Prayer

[Whistle of wind, faint drums and Indians chanting.]

Nature called me awake in the darkness before dawn on Sheep Mountain Table in the Badlands of South Dakota. I wiggled my way out of my sleeping bag and rose to my feet. I stretched my spine and took a deep breath. The cool moist air startled me. I turned and surveyed the hillside. A veil of fog was moving over the land, billowing down from above my head, covering the downslope of the plateau. I breathed again with a rush of appreciation for the forces of nature.

I walked barefooted past the prone bodies of my friends, around the smoldering embers of the campfire, through the gap between the two Tortoise buses, to the edge of the highest cliff in the Badlands. Carried by a steady wind curling up the lip of the wide plateau, a fog bank rolled up out of the canyon like a vertical wave until it broke far above my head in the prevailing wind.

As if falling into a dream, I had stepped into a pocket of clear-air below a twenty-foot-high wall of windborne fog. The tumultuous force of moisture flowing up out of the canyon churned as it crashed in the upper reaches, spreading out above Sheep Mountain Table like frothy water cast upon a beach. The fog settled to the ground ten yards from the edge of the cliff where it thinned out down the slope of the hill like water sinking into sand as it retreated into the sea.

I strode effortlessly alongside the mystical wall of fog in rapt amazement, following the lip of the cliff toward the East. As I walked in the pocket of clear air, I felt like a surfer riding in the tube of a wave.

American Prayer

I peeled off a dozen yards away and stood to make water with my back to the wall of fog.

I felt a presence in my chest. Then I looked up, I got the unsettling feeling that I was not alone. I peered into the fog. Someone or something was out there. I could feel it. I was inexplicably drawn forward without fear to the edge of the clear air where the fog started falling back to the ground.

I recognized the shape of a Buffalo partially obscured in the broiling mist. It was standing perfectly still on the hillside facing the cliff farther down along the edge of the canyon. The lone Buffalo stood on the slightly downward slope of Cuny Table with hooves planted in the ancestral earth. I felt compelled to step closer through the zephyr of mist. The fog thinned as I drew near, revealing the broad head and silhouette of a female Buffalo, identical and no less formidable than a full-sized male. She faced into the wind breathing billowing clouds of breath from her nostrils. Her eyes were open, but she did not so much as blink. The Buffalo appeared to be sleeping with her eyes open.

It was still dark in the distance, but I had crossed the veil into a brighter world where celestial light penetrated the atmosphere, as if a new sunrise had breached the horizon of the stratosphere. The other eye had gone partially out of view with the proximity to the Buffalo's massive head, still some twenty feet off.

"Oh my God!" I spoke out-loud, doubting my own sight. "No way!" Beyond the Buffalo at the center of my vision, another Buffalo stood shrouded in the veil of mist. I fell forward a few more steps, letting my eyes adjust in the distance. The deeper into the fog I walked, the more shapes I could see obscured in the light haze on the hillside below. Spaced at twenty-foot intervals, a pattern of massive Buffalo stood facing North into the wind, spread out across the entire plateau down the slope of Sheep Mountain Table. Visibility was better along the ground farther downhill, partially obscuring Buffalo a hundred strong. All remained motionless, except for the billowing plumes of visible breath wafting in the wind. Somehow, I understood there to be a great herd standing out there in the fog beyond the boundary of my perception.

All the while the wind continued to swirl up the lip of the cliff like a standing wave, rising above Sheep Mountain Table before dumping fog over and down the plateau. I imagined the timeless scene replaying itself for countless centuries on that very hillside whilst the Badlands slowly took shape, sinking gradually into the earth like sand melting in water.

Down the hill a good distance from the edge of the cliff in the middle of the prairie, one Buffalo appeared to be sitting down. "No!" On further inspection it was a tent. I took a few more steps downhill and focused my eyes in disbelief. "That's not good," I said aloud. One of the Green Tortoise passengers had pitched a tent right in the middle of the herd of Buffalo.

I took another few steps and a chill ran up my spine. "Holy shit!" I exclaimed. There appeared to be a Buffalo lying next to the tent. "No!" It was no Buffalo; it was a person sleeping on the ground on a Green Tortoise bus mattress. Judging from the size of the lump in the sleeping bag, it had to be a big person. In a whisper I gasped, "Dave!" It was Big Dave! No one else would choose to sleep way out in the middle of the prairie like that.

No doubt the Old-Growth-Hippie was sleeping outside his tent having given it up for Mother Michelle and her son. I grew nervous for them, contemplating worse case scenarios. If one of them startled the Buffalo, they could be gored or trampled to death. It was unsettling, but I shook it off. The Buffalo remained unmoved by my presence, so I kept moving closer along the cliff through the swirling clouds of mist.

Suddenly, I felt a whisper of Buffalo instinct that impelled me to stop. Naturally, I heeded the call and stood perfectly still. The magnificent Buffalo's eyes opened, and I could tell She was now aware of me. I remained frozen there, standing face to face with her. She was magnificent, like the Lion King on the mount, looking proud without hubris, sacred without ceremony, dignified and true.

Waking them up did not make sense. If they do not bother the Buffalo, the Buffalo will not bother them, I surmised. Maybe Dave is communing with the Buffalo, I thought hopefully. Either way, I did not want to take the opportunity away from him, so I stood perfectly still, not wanting to disturb the formidable animal now fifteen feet away.

The rich black fur on the face and head of the Buffalo was wet with moisture from the broiling mist. Her earthen-brown body shone with an equally rich luster. The spear point of her massive dewlap dripped on the ground below her chin. Her humped shoulders rose up in a powerful, prominent, permanent pose.

There She stood, Her Eminence, the Free-Range American Buffalo, with hooves grounded in the Ancestral Earth. I came fully into the moment with this peak life experience. This was no wooden nickel bullshit; this was a Sacred Woman Buffalo, the Matriarch of us all! To think I share genes with such a Creature made me love myself even more. She was magnificent. Thank you, Mother Earth. Wow! What a moment!

Marveling at the girth and immensity of the enormous Animal, I became transfixed in wonderment, staring at the zephyr of vapor blowing from her huge nostrils. I took a deep breath enjoying the moisture. Exhaling, I could see my own breath billowing plumes before me. My hair stood on end as I felt a deep connection with the Buffalo.

I was close enough the see the sheen on her moist eye, reflecting the soft glow of the fog. I looked into her all-telling eye to see if I was disturbing the honorable creature. I could feel her powerful presence. She was aware of me, very aware. She was watching me as much as I was watching her. I felt humble and thankful that she was letting me stand so close to her. I had done nothing to deserve such an honor.

A wave of awareness washed over my mind. There was no past or future. I was a young man standing on a remote hillside with the Mother of All Buffalo. I had stumbled blindly into her world, and now all was revealed to me.

I recognized the Lady Buffalo as a Sacred Being with dignity and rights equal to that of a Human Being. I understood that I was her equal. I stood not above her as a human being but shoulder-to-shoulder with her as a Fellow Creature of Earth. The land beneath our feet nourished our bodies and fed our spirits.

I realized that our physical bodies consisted of the same basic components. Our lungs breathed the same air. Our hearts beat the same rhythm, keeping us warm. Blood was pumping through our veins, even our minds worked in similar ways. The same fog was mixing with the air that filled our lungs. Visible breath came forth from our nostrils.

I had never seen myself as a sacred animal before. My self-esteem had bottomed out before the trip to the point where I had wished I was dead. Now, here I was having this peak experience feeling wonderfully alive. How lucky to have befallen this fate for having serendipitously wandered down the path less chosen on the Green Tortoise.

I could see a faint reflection of myself in the Buffalo's glistening eye. I fell into the eye, trying to discern detail in my tiny reflection. I was in there somewhere. The eye blinked. I could feel her watching me. My skin went all goosey with an invigorating chill.

From this new perspective, looking at my tiny reflection in the eye of the Buffalo, I began to have a vision.

> A single cell gestated in the ripe womb of life at the moment of conception. The cell at first resembled various single-celled organisms. Cilia formed and it began to move like some primitive protozoan life form one might find in the primordial soup. Still with flagellum it developed a solid nucleus and intra-cellular components like organelles and mitochondria.

The cell split, went to four, then eight and so on. Hints of the building blocks of more complex organisms began to appear. As the life form continued to evolve and grow, symmetrical arms and legs burped out of the cellular blob like the branches of a tree. The primitive buds of hands and feet sprouted from the tips. A transparent heart pumped fluid through veins like those on a leaf. The heart grew solid with visible pulsing of fluid. The circulatory system became visible in the arteries pumping blood to the extremities. The lungs expanded with breath, filling with fluid.

Shadows of bones appeared in the four limbs, and a brain grew from the top of its spine. The shadow of a primitive skull appeared, changing shape as it morphed into the form of a bird, a fish, a frog. The shapes of animal skulls many in number appeared, fluidly adopting the features of creatures great and small. It evolved rapidly, taking on the familiar shapes of all-manner of creatures, as if undergoing the entire course of human evolution.

Still with a tail, the fetus continued to morph into different animals with four limbs. Various shapes appeared and disappeared resembling countless other species. The spine arched and elongated. The fetus morphed into both familiar and unfamiliar shapes. For a moment, the skull resembled a large cat like a mountain lion. The jawline extended resembling that of a fox, a horse, a deer. This evolution happened quickly, seamlessly morphing from one species to the next.

The tail faded away to a nub. Its jaw shortened and the skull transformed into the more familiar shape of a bear, then an ape, then a Neanderthal, then a Cro-Magnon, finally taking human form. The limbs of the embryo began to conform to human proportions. The size of the fetus doubled quickly, continuing to develop all the harbingers of a human male, including a penis.

The fetus kept many of the aspects and qualities of the various forms and shapes from which it had evolved. It was as if this human fetus embodied all the diverse aspects of the sum-total of all the living creatures and plants of the world. It was like all the creatures of earth had morphed into one being possessing the genetic material of every living organism.

The fetus grew into a full-sized baby, kicking its legs and contracting. The baby was delivered unto the world by human hands and held up in the light. The child was given to its mother to suckle. The boy got bigger and bigger, first crawling then standing, then walking on two feet. It quickly transformed into a young boy. The boy grew into an adolescent child, an awkward youth, then a young man.

Suddenly, my mind opened with infinite clarity. I sensed the same eminence, dignity and sacrality in this young man as I had discerned before in the Buffalo. I was a sacred creature of the earth of no less stature, standing on an even footing with this sacred being. I felt proud with no hubris and sacred without ceremony. For a few moments, my entire being glowed with the light of the world. With a profound sense of awareness, wisdom, and conviction, I knew the land and all the plants and animals were One.

The fully-grown person in my vision bore a remarkable resemblance to myself. It was like I was looking upon myself from outside of my own body. Behind him was a billowing wall of fog that broiled above his head and fell to the ground as mist in my face. I suddenly realized that the young man born of the embryo was standing before me in the broiling fog on Cuny Table. Indeed, it was me that I was gazing upon!

A zephyr of visible breath billowed forth from my enormous nostrils. I watched my nostrils flare at the end of my nose as I inhaled, but there was something very strange about the sides of my nose and my face. My whole countenance had changed. My face was covered in short black fur. With wide eyes, I could see the billowing plumes of my breath coming from a big black nose at the end of a hairy snout.

I realized in that moment; I was the Buffalo! I was no longer Myself looking at the Buffalo; I was the Buffalo looking out of her eyes onto Me. I could feel my hoofs planted in the Earth and feel my massive body breathing. I was a Buffalo looking at Myself as a Human Being.

Had I been wiser, stronger, and more deserving a man, I may have lingered in this alternate reality for a while longer, but I was weak. I got scared. I began to resist, to doubt, to turn my back on the ether world, to deny what I was seeing. My father's voice played inside my head. "Believe none of what you hear and half of what you see." His voice screamed, "Wake up!"

I broke the spell and came out of the trance. Once again, I was a young man looking out through a veil of fog hovering over the land atop Sheep Mountain Table, in the Badlands. Nonetheless, I was left with a lingering sense of the sacred nature of life. I identified myself as part of the sacred hoop.

I had never read a word of *Black Elk Speaks*, but I was sure I had just had a vision. Why this happened to me was a mystery. Certainly, I was not worthy of such a gift, but I knew right away that I had to tell the world what had happened. This made me nervous at first. Who would believe me if I told this story? I was an ignorant kid from the East Coast. My mother had taught me that the truth will set you free, so I made a solemn vow to remain truthful in the telling of this tale, lest I betray the meaning of this gift.

I decided to honor the Buffalo by stepping back so She could return to sleep. I needed to return to bed and get some sleep myself. Big Dave would be fine sleeping amongst this sacred herd of Buffalo high atop Sheep Mountain Table. I began to back off, taking steps backwards toward the bus, still facing the Buffalo. I backed out of the mist until I could see just the One.

I stood motionless for a long time, peering through the haze, watching, and thinking, building my resolve to remember what had happened so I might share what I had seen. At some point I walked back, through the gap between the two buses, around the smoldering embers of the campfire, past the piles of blankets and bodies. I found my mattress and wiggled my way back under the blankets into a comfortable position, surrounded by my friends.

16
Champagne for Breakfast

A whiff of campfire smoke awakened me from my astral slumber high atop Sheep Mountain Table, in the Badlands of South Dakota. I lay awake for several minutes, alone on the communal mattresses encircling the smoldering bonfire. The morning air was cool and refreshing. The sun had already risen above the horizon, so I got out of my sleeping bag to avoid overheating. I lay there for a while watching and listening to the sounds of Green Tortoise camp. Passengers were moving about in all directions, busy with breakfast tasks, packing gear, seeking privacy with shovels, loading mattresses on the bus, sipping Cowboy Coffee, collecting trash, and conversing happily. The orange juice looked especially appealing.

I heard Little Josh yell, "I got it!" He was playing Frisbee along the cliff with a couple of passengers from the other bus. The other players were playing keep away from him because he sucked at throwing. He kept running from side to side trying to catch the Frisbee, shouting, and pushing the other players as they snatched it away from him.

I stood up, stretched my arms over my head, and took a deep breath. Only a few passengers remained on the massive circle of mattresses surrounding the smoldering bonfire. Juliano was still in bed but he was not sleeping. To my dismay, he was making love with one of the girls from the other bus in plain sight of more than fifty people. The South American stud was really going at it, grunting, and huffing like a snorting bull pawing the earth. One of the other girls Juliano had been entertaining the night before lay beside them less than three feet away, resting on a bent elbow, watching them intently.

I looked around to see who else might be watching. The Irish girls, Fräulein Vera, and Flip-flop were staring right at them, casually sipping tea while they enjoyed the show. Judging from the telltale strings dangling over the rims of their mugs, they were drinking Ireland's finest. Their relaxed postures and jovial conversation made it clear that the shock had already worn off on them. Apparently, Juliano and present company had been going at it for quite some time.

An errant throw floated the Frisbee into the camp kitchen where it skipped across the food table on which people were cutting fruit salad with sharp knives. There was a burst of laughter, but no one seemed to mind. Little Josh tore into the crowded kitchen area at top speed, bumping into people and creating a stir. Driver Chris picked up the Frisbee and gave Little Josh an unspoken look. He threw the Frisbee so far that the game moved away. He was aware of the South American's fireside free show, and he had been watching the boy to make sure he remained unaware of the double backed beast.

The girls drinking tea giggled as Mountain Girl walked straight up to them. She picked up a sleeping bag and draped it over them, and shouted, "Get a room!" Juliano lifted his head with his back arched in surprise. The girl beneath him looked horrified. She glanced at Mountain Girl, then her voyeuristic friend, then she pulled Juliano back down on top of her and hid beneath the blanket. The teetotalers held their bellies laughing and Driver Chris guffawed.

I stepped off the mattress onto the cool dusty ground close to the still-smoldering embers in the fire pit. I was conscious of the Earth beneath me, as if my bare feet penetrated the soil, rooting me into the land. The fine dust between my toes was like a conduit of heightened awareness. I could sense my place on the earth like I was looking at myself from space. I was standing on the same land where the hooves of Buffalo and the feet of Indians had certainly passed. It was then I recalled my vision. I had seen myself out of the eyes of a Buffalo.

I strolled around the curve of smoky, gray ash, between the buses, past Juliano and company, out to the edge of the cliff. The Buffalo were gone, and the fields were dry and yellow with sunlight. I gazed over the expanse of Badlands National Park, struck again by the magnificence of the sacred land. I stood silently enjoying the powerful feeling of being connected to something so magnificent. From horizon to horizon the Badlands lay before me as a testament to the beauty and power of the natural world, and I knew that from that day onward, Sheep Mountain Table would always be with me, connected to me, wherever I might stand.

Looking to the east, my eyes were drawn to the place where Buffalo had stood in the fog the night before. I passed along the cliff, retracing my steps, mystified, and perplexed by what I had seen. Buffalo Dave was gone. He had already packed up his tent.

I felt very alone for a second, a little frightened, so I spun around to reassure myself that my friends were still there on the cliff. Mother Michelle stood sipping coffee at the edge of the canyon with her eyes fixed on the distant horizon. "Good morning, Michelle," I said as I walked up and stood next to her.

"Good morning, John," she said softly, turning toward me, moving the mug away from her lips. "How are you feeling this morning?" Michelle looked rested, and happy to be standing right there where she was, gripping her plastic coffee mug, contented.

"Oh, I feel fine." I paused thoughtfully looking out over the Badlands National Park. "I've never actually felt better in my life." I sighed. "I've been looking for Buffalo Dave. Have you seen him this morning?"

"Yes," she said, spinning around on one heel on the dusty soil. "He's around here somewhere." She peered left and right. "He's been up for a while now."

"Was that his tent out there in the middle of that field over there?" I asked, thumbing over my shoulder with a tone of disbelief.

"Yes," she informed me. "He packed up early."

"Did you sleep out there with him?"

"No," she responded. "He was so gracious. He let us sleep in his tent while he slept outside on the ground." She smiled and took another sip, and asked, "Why?"

"I'll have to tell you later," I told her. "Something awesome happened."

"Good luck finding Dave," she said, looking away again out onto the canyon.

I found Buffalo Dave at the back of our bus, washing his face with his handkerchief in a bowl of water, using the engine compartment door as a shelf. I said, "Good morning, Dave."

"Good morning, John," he intoned in his always deep and slow voice. I looked at him reverently. There beside him, leaning against the bus was his cane. He finished rubbing his face with his handkerchief and started combing his blondish-red hair. He was still wearing his signature denim overalls, but he had donned a fresh T-shirt underneath. He was a beautiful man, bald on top with a wide freckled nose. His thick beard made his cheeks look like chops. His mustache turned up at the corners. His hair stuck out over his ears, wet, and matted down after being combed. His eyebrows seemed a little heavy, as if he had seen a lot in his life and it concerned him that he was doing the right thing.

With a cocked head, I asked him, "Dave, you slept out in the field last night?"

He confirmed the fact with a nod. "Why, yes John, I did."

I turned, looked over my shoulder, and pointed toward the field saying, "Out there, man?!" I looked back at him with wild eyes.

He said, "Indeed, I did." He stopped wiping his face. "Why do you ask?"

My eyes widened, "There was a whole herd of Buffalo out there last night! Did you see them?"

He stopped moving altogether and remained stoic; transfixed in the mirror like he remembered a dream. "There were Buffalo out there last night?" His question lingered. He looked at me and we both turned and looked out into the field. I felt a little spooked. I nodded my head furiously, unable to speak for a second, snorting breath.

"Oh my God, yes, there were Buffalo out there last night! A whole herd, stretching out as far as I could see. They were sleeping. I just wanted to, like, wake you up and warn you or something, but it seemed dangerous. One of them was standing right next to your tent, dude."

I looked him in the eye. It was like a trance or something. I was in a different place. I had a vision last night, I swear. It was amazing." He looked excited and seemed to believe me right off. He nodded. "For a few minutes I could see out of the eyes of a Buffalo," I nodded convincingly, so he knew that I was being serious and that I had no doubt about what I had seen. "I became a Buffalo last night, man. I swear, I looked right out the Buffalo's eyes, and I knew everything. I was so connected; I've never felt anything like that before. It was so real."

Buffalo Dave came to life for a few seconds, shaking his comb in the water. He was thinking. Then he looked me straight in the eyes, combing the cowlick behind his ear, as if he could not have been more pleased in all his life. "Good for you, John. You're a lucky man. Consider yourself blessed." He smiled and looked at me. "Congratulations, John. You communed with the Buffalo." This pleased me to no end. He nodded knowingly, and he could tell that the experience had moved me. "I thought I sensed something out there last night," Buffalo Dave marveled. "But I didn't see anything; I slept straight through the night."

"I'm struggling to believe my own eyes," I confessed.

He looked once again out into the golden grass. "I took a walk early this morning." He motioned with his chin toward the fields. "I found a bunch of fresh Buffalo chips. Now I know how they got there." He said, "Thanks Johnny," and we both stared out into the distance.

Champagne for Breakfast

Deutsche Mark was blown-away when I told him about the vision. "This is a sacred place, dude" he informed me. "Native people have been having ceremonies up here for thousands of years. That's why Driver Chris wanted to camp up here. He had to get special permission from the Indians." He patted me on the back and told me, "I am totally jealous, brother. I wish I had a vision."

"I'll gladly trade," I told him. "It's left me feeling unsure about everything."

"You'll figure it out, bro," he reassured me. "Try to tap into that universal consciousness."

"Yeah right," I scoffed. "I feel weird enough as it is."

Driver Chris was anxiously making breakfast, running around, directing traffic, overseeing passengers who were cutting fruit and preparing the feast. People were catching things thrown off the roof by Chicken Jim, who seemed a little disoriented. Driver Chris took his "Hospitality Competition" for all he had, and he had just begun. The drivers had bought four cases of Champagne. Mimosa was served in a giant bowl with bagels and lox for 65 people. It was a gorgeous spread, a banquet for all.

The driver of the other bus, Raoul Hafwirth as he called himself, also rose to the occasion, baking brandy collier, a medieval, spirit-laced breakfast treat made of peaches, brandy, vodka, sugar, cinnamon, cloves, and coriander seeds. Two large Dutch ovens were heating in the smoldering embers in the fire pit. Much to our enjoyment, the Driver's competition was fierce.

Deutsche Mark and Yülia were lapping it up. He poured me a cup of mimosa and said, "Be sure to have a few of these before they're gone."

"I'm on my third," tittered Yülia.

"Drunk this early in the morning?" I chided the Dutchman. "I like you more each day."

"Yülia," he coaxed her. "Tell Lovebus what you told me about how much fun you had last night."

She leaned into me, she said, "I had a wonderful time last night. I love smoking flower pot."

The Dutchman and I cracked up laughing, although she did not seem to get the joke. We conversed for a few minutes. After recalling the story Jewels told about the tortoise lyre, Yülia said, "We have to help with the dishes now. I don't want the drivers to get thick necks."

I raised my mug and they walked away. Our wonderful, late breakfast was ready. With a bagel and lox spread, and a bowl of fresh cut fruit, I sipped mimosa out on the edge of the cliff, thinking about the vision I had experienced the night before.

Eventually, I returned to help with the clean-up and ate the last few peaches at the bottom of the large cooking pot. As I scraped out the last little bits, Flip-flop's eyes suggested that she wanted a taste, so I held out the oversized spoon and she took a bite. "That's so good." I took the very last bite nodding. "Now that you finished it you can wash the bowl," she teased.

"That would be just peachy," I commented.

"Ha!" she laughed before she turned on her heel and walked away.

I brought the big cooking pot over to the wash buckets near the other bus. It took another hour to do the dishes and load up. We had to shake the dust out of everything. We packed up every bit of trash, even more than we created, picking windblown garbage out of the bush near the rim of the canyon. We poured water on the fire pit and we the engines revved. Flip-flop took the buddy seat on the other bus next to her new friend Hal. The race was on.

Having gained a new perspective on the ride up, I knew the best seat in the house was to not sit at all. So, I stood on the bus steps in the door well close to the windshield, staring into the undulating fields. The race down the hill began with a jolt. We went much faster downhill with the confidence gained from blazing Tortoise trails through the grass the previous day. As the bus rose up and down the passengers were rocketed off their seats repeatedly, sending passengers flying into the air with flailing limbs amidst a bus full of laughter.

Each time my feet left the floor, my eyes grew like saucers and my inner child smiled. When I got on the bus in Boston, I was seeking to recapture a lost sense of childlike wonder and here it was right in my face, coming at me like a freight train. I loved it so much; I could see myself driving the bus. I could just picture it. I asked myself, "What do I need to do to make it happen?"

I studied Driver Chris' expression. He was having a ball. His countenance glowed with the energy of the land. Complete focus and determination washed over his face in the reflection of yellow light shining off the golden grass. Much to our dismay, he took one hand off the wheel, reached under his seat, putting all his strength into the other hand to maneuver over the next undulation in the field. He precariously removed his cassette collection from below his seat. He threw the case to me. "Pull a couple of the tapes out of there for me, man," he said to me.

With one hand holding on for dear life, I picked up the case, unzipped the zipper, put the case on the floor with a bang and we launched into the air again. I rode the stairwell, looking through his tapes, with my feet rising repeatedly off the floor.

"Grab the Van Morrison, dude, the one with 'Gloria.'" I handed him the tape.

Once the music began, people started dancing and singing along, holding on to the bars bolted to the roof for support, slamming into one another in a provocative monkey dance. I danced and stomped rhythms on the hollow floor like I was in the jungle. The stairwell filled with the playing of my rhythm and the music thumping in the speakers. We hit another large bump and entered the air again, on purpose this time, stomping our feet together in rhythm, making loud thumping sounds on the hollow floor of the bus. This heightened the experience of music, nature, and song, filling my whole body.

We were all getting off on each other, having a wild, frolicking time, bouncing, and shifting in intimate rhythm with the braking and lurching of the Green Tortoise bus. Soon there were others in the stairwell with me, dancing, crazy, giant bumps, music thumping... and then the road through the tall grass flattened. We had beaten the other bus to the gate, and there was a cheer. I could see Flip-flop sitting next to Driver Hal on the other bus as it pulled up alongside.

At the gate to Sheep Mountain Table, Driver Chris stopped the bus, turned the stereo down and made an announcement. "Both buses will be stopping at Cuny Cafe on the way to the mud hole to drop off our trash and, as Nelly Cuny says, to make a courtesy stop. Now, she is a very gregarious and giving woman. There are port-a-potties there, but only one flushable toilet, so please do not overstay the Cuny's favor and use that toilet to death. I repeat," he shouted. "Do not line up at the flushable toilet; we're not gonna let you do it, so don't even try it. The men must use the port-a-potties, ok? Get me straight. We don't want to ruin her septic system. Anyone who doesn't understand, please translate."

Behind Driver Chris, the long, bare legs and sandals of Driver Brian came stepping down the ladder at the driver's window stealthily. Driver Brian stuck his head through the window and tried to kiss him before Chris even saw him. Everyone laughed. Driver Chris dodged the attack, screaming in mock fear, just out of Brian's reach. He blew the air horn several times in succession.

The music came back into our ears, and we continued to dance, as Driver Brian unlatched the gate. The bus crawled through the gate, listing severely as we breached the edge of the dirt road, throwing the dancers into a pile one last time.

The bus started rolling with the door still open and Driver Brian ran to catch up. They let the other bus latch the gate, because we were trying to beat them to Cuny Cafe. We were all aboard now, and Driver Brian joined me in the stairwell. I closed the school-bus-style swing-arm to close the door and the dance party rocked on.

****

    The road to Cuny Cafe was a wild, dancing time. The bus kicked up a huge trail of dust that choked the other bus and left them in our dust. Out of respect, Driver Chris drove slowly down the driveway, as not to choke the Cunys in a cloud of dust.

    "Hey, John!" Driver Chris asked me, "will you help me pass the trash down off the roof? It might be easier if you go up there, you know, uh, through the roof hatch in the driver's cabin, but, you know, do me a favor, man, take your sneakers off on the bed, you know, man? Sandrine freaks out when there's sand on the mattress." He looked and smiled his leprechaun smile. "I think Josh is the real culprit. He's in there all the time."

    "Right on," I said. "I'm on it." Driver Chris nodded with scrunched eyebrows of approval.

    After my shoes were off, I made my way past the smiling faces of the passengers, stepping on the cooler in the center aisle, surprised to see some of the people from the other bus tucked in lovingly among our group and up in the racks. People still clenched glasses of mimosa, so I stepped carefully between the sea of legs and knees. I walked, shoes in hand all the way to the driver's cabin. I slid the wooden door open and pushed aside the blankets. Driver Chris' cabin was dank, and the sheets were moist with morning dew. I climbed across the sheet on all fours and pushed the roof hatch open.

    I was still trying to wrap my head around what had happened the night before. I wondered if Owen Cuny would be around so I could ask him some questions. I put my head out the roof hatch of the Green Tortoise bus, as it rolled to a halt at the end of the driveway at Cuny Cafe. What a view! I saw Owen Cuny exit the kitchen door and I suddenly felt full of hope for an explanation.

    I passed down the first trash bag to Chicken Jim. He taught me how to slide the bags against the bus, so he could catch them without much effort. Soon, all the bags were down, and my shoes were on, and I was sliding down the outside of the back of the bus, using the technique Driver Chris had taught me.

    "Nice one," Chicken Jim clucked. We each carried four bags of trash toward the front of the bus.

    Driver Chris was speaking with Owen Cuny by the tailgate of his dilapidated Ford. The Indian man nodded, and our driver said, "Thank you," and went inside to use the phone. A line had formed at the door as we approached. I could see Driver Brian directing people, mostly men, away from the farmhouse, pointing toward the port-a-potties.

Owen Cuny told us, "You can load that trash right into my pickup." He smiled a toothy smile. "Thanks for the help."

Chicken Jim and I placed the trash in the bed of the truck and Owen held a hose for us to rinse our hands. I dried my hands on my shorts and stepped toward the dignified Indian with my hand outstretched. I shook his hand looking him straight in the eyes. "Thank you so much," I gushed. "Sheep Mountain Table was amazing."

"Where you camped last night is a sacred place," he revealed. "Few are the white people who know it by that name. Most people know this area as Cuny Table. Sheep Mountain Table is a Lakota name. There are other names, too, sacred names." Owen seemed to know that I had something more to say. He looked into my heart and asked. "Did you see something up there last night?"

The words leapt from my mouth, "I saw Buffalo in the mist last night, a whole herd of Buffalo in the middle of the night. I mean, it was more like early this morning, but it was still dark and there was mist. It blew my mind! Is that even possible?" I let his hand go, after what seemed like an eternity.

Owen Cuny spoke slowly, "Many people have seen Buffalo on Sheep Mountain Table," he said.

"Well," I sputtered. "There was mist blowing up over the lip of the canyon and the Buffalo spread out as far as I could see into the distance. I could see them breathing. I think they were sleeping." I said with incredulity. "I think I had a vision."

Owen's eyes lit up. He nodded. "Many people have had visions on Sheep Mountain Table."

"So, you think it was real, then?" I asked.

Owen nodded slowly, speaking carefully, "Visions are as real as the grass, as real as the breath of the Buffalo, very powerful. It has been years since I had my teepee on Sheep Mountain Table. Of the many times I have camped there I have never received the call."

"What call?"

"Many who have had visions hear the call to do what we Sioux call 'walking in a sacred manner.'"

"I'm not sure about a call, but what I experienced was very powerful," I reported. "I felt like I could see out of the eyes of a Buffalo. I feel like she was trying to send me a message."

"What did you hear?" he asked.

I answered excitedly, "That all living things are One, the grass, the trees, the birds and all animals, big and small."

"You have seen the truth," said the dignified Indian man before pausing in thought. "You have been given a gift. You are young and have much to learn. Keep your mind open and listen. Many who have had one vision have more visions. Listen to the wind. It is something that you cannot stop."

"Thank you for letting us camp out there Mr. Cuny. You have a wonderful home here. I'll never forget it," I told him.

"You can call me Owen," he told me. "You are family now."

"It's my honor," I said. "Very nice to meet you, Owen."

Driver Chris came out of the Cuny's house looking relieved. Owen invited him over with his hand. The driver motioned with his head for the passengers to get back on board. I began to back away, but something in Owen's eyes kept me from moving far. The red-bearded driver came up to us said, "Nice to see you, Owen." They embraced.

The middle-aged Lakota man turned his eyes to the ground and his brow dropped with concern that bordered on anguish. "I have some sad news," he groaned.

"Is something wrong?" Driver Chris spoke with concern.

Owen lifted his stark countenance and locked eyes with Driver Chris. "The park service called this morning. They saw your fire burning from park headquarters last night, and they were worried that there was a wildfire."

"What do they care?" Driver Chris was stymied. "There's nothing to burn up there but grass," he scoffed. "It's a bald hill."

"Yes," the Lakota man said slowly, pausing respectfully while Chris shook his head in consternation. "We can't let you camp up there anymore. They forbade it."

"What?" Driver Chris was exasperated. "That's ridiculous." His eyes locked with Owen's. "Did you tell them to go to hell?"

Owen's eyes dropped. "No, no, no," he said mildly. "The park service people are our friends. They have been friends to us. We don't want to start any trouble with their superiors."

The young driver put his hand on the Lakota man's shoulder. It was like his eyes dove into his soul. "That is your land, Owen. They have no right to tell you what you can or can't do with your own land."

Owen's shoulders dropped as if the weight of the young man's hand was all he could bear. "They have been telling us what we can do with our land since before I was born," he huffed. "The seasons have changed but the air is still thick with the smell of gunpowder and the blood of our ancestors." I felt pain in my heart for Owen Cuny.

"I'm sorry you feel that way," reacted the distraught driver. "So, there will be no more camping on Sheep Mountain Table. That's too bad."

"I'm sorry," he said somberly. "We can't allow it."

I shook my head in disbelief as I walked away. I was greatly saddened by this show of modern disrespect for the rights of the Lakota.

Champagne for Breakfast

I slowly climbed up the steps of the bus, looking back several times, until Driver Brian started calling people to board.

I mindlessly took the first seat by the door across from Peruvian Ursula. PAC-MAN was sitting somewhere in back. She seemed carefree and at ease. Her gruff exterior had vanished, at least for the moment.

The other bus arrived at the café. Driver Brian was eager to beat them to the mud hole, so the two drivers rushed people aboard and started rolling away with the door still open. Flip-flop jumped on board at the last second anxious about getting separated from our bus.

While the bus roared down the Cuny's driveway the red headed Irishman stood next to the buddy seat to make an announcement. "I have some good news to share about my brother," he shouted.

There was a cheer from our group, and many of us expressed our happiness by clapping.

"What's the good news?" shouted Yülia.

Driver Chris held the chrome support bar behind the driver's seat. "My brother came out of the coma last night," he announced. "He woke up on his own."

There was a cheer of elation throughout the bus.

Yülia exclaimed, "Wunderbar! Wunderbar!"

"That's great brother," Driver Brian cheered.

"That's awesome," said Maid Marian.

"Groovy," crooned Jewels.

"That's great news," Flip-flop concluded.

"Spot on," said Guitar Johnny.

The consensus was universal. The whole bus was feeling good about the news. This was awesome. "I'm happy for you," I told him.

Driver Chris thanked each person in turn and put his hand up to speak. "My brother is not out of the woods yet, but it sure looks good, so you can all relax. The trip will continue as planned for the time being."

There was a huge cheer and lots of happy consolation.

Driver Brian came forward and put his hand on his shoulder. "Awesome news bro. How is he functioning?"

Our driver lowered his voice and his brow dropped in consternation. "It's pretty much like they said it would be. He can't speak very well, and he doesn't recognize anybody yet. He seemed to recognize one of his firefighter friends, but that could have just been the uniform. He always wanted to be a firefighter. His first words out of the coma were, 'That's not a knife. Show it to me. That's not a knife.' So, we're pretty sure he was mugged. He kept saying that over and over."

Hearing this Jewels stood up abruptly. She sighed and said, "People are sick." Then she walked away down the aisle toward the back.

Driver Chris continued, "My sister said he looks scared, like he's trapped inside himself and he doesn't know what's going on. He was only awake for a short time and they had to sedate him again because he started getting combative. They said that's normal too, so it's a waiting game, but at least he's awake and alive."

"How's your dad?" his partner asked.

"Great, "Driver Chris said. "He was in good spirits on the phone."

"That's awesome."

"My father didn't have anything negative to say in the few minutes we talked. He actually remained civil throughout the entire call."

"Even better."

"There's a first time for everything," he scoffed.

"It's a good day then," his co-driver cheered him.

"Let's go get dirty!" Driver Chris exclaimed in a loud voice for all to hear.

There was another cheer.

Driver Brian said, "I'll drive," and he jumped into the seat.

Driver Chris ran down the aisle and dove onto the back platform into a sea of loving bodies and everyone hugged him.

I turned my face in the open window and made eye contact with Owen Cuny. I was still in the throes of disbelief that the Park Service would have the audacity to tell the Indians how they could use their land. Owen's eyes remained locked with mine even when his dog ran up to him looking for attention. We locked eyes until the bus pulled away.

17
Mud for Dessert

In a remote corner of Badlands National Park, there is a little swimming hole hidden behind a clump of trees across the street from the White River Visitor Center. The bus passed through a small gate, down a dirt road, and parked in a field beneath two massive oaks. Past the trees, through a row of thick bushes to the left, we could see a shallow and slow-moving river about twenty feet wide. Behind the row of thick bushes to the right, a muddy creek joined with the little river, creating a delta full of grey mud. The mud had collected in the creek bed, covering an area about ten feet wide by forty feet long.

It was hot and everyone was excited to swim. When we got to the edge of the mud, no one really knew what to do. As he started to undress, Chicken Jim informed us, "This is the best mud in the whole country, right there. It's mostly volcanic ash and sediment that erodes out of the Badlands when it rains." Berndt Toast took a seat on the rock and started removing his prosthetic limb. Little Josh, Mother Michelle, Australian Sheila, and Chicken Jim all wore bathing suits, but everyone else got naked.

We all stood sheepishly by the edge of the mud for several minutes and no one had the guts to go in. Our drivers knew just how to break the ice. They both came running through the bushes naked, yelling and yahooing, and they jumped right into the mud, feet first, landing like bombs, throwing handfuls of mud as our group scattered. After testing the depth of the mud in several places, the two drivers found spots they liked and began wiping mud all over their bodies. Driver Brian made ape sounds and painted lines on his face like war paint. Driver Chris dropped into a seated position making a loud squishy sound with his ass. It looked fun. Soon passengers began jumping in, and I followed suit.

Out of the bushes we heard another thundering roar. "MOOOO!" To my amazement it was Buffalo Dave. He came thundering like a mad bull out of the bushes bent over at the waist with fingers pointing in the air like horns. "I'm a Buffalo!" he shouted. "MOOOO!"

"Look! It's Buffalo Dave!" I yelled.

Passengers darted out of the way to clear a path as he arrived. As the massive man's body came to a halt at the edge of the mudhole, his feet slipped in the mud sending him careening down the bank of the creek like a Buffalo on water skis. He stayed upright all the way off the lip of the foot-high embankment. His feet kicked out from beneath him as he launched off the wall. Time seemed to suspend itself as we stood there naked watching his giant form land like a hairy bomb in the wettest part of the mud hole. His ass explosively threw mud in every direction for twenty feet. Mud splattered the bystanders like shrapnel, freckling naked forms with flecks of grey. There was a universal cringe and a groan of communal pain. Considering the force of the explosion, the massive man's ass must have been jam-packed with mud.

Silence befell both tribes as we held our collective breath like a parent after hearing a disturbing thud at the bottom of the stairs. Hardly anyone knew about his spinal injury, but it was obvious he was feeble and limited in his ability to walk. A moment later, Maid Marian rushed to his side and urgently asked, "Are you alright?"

Driver Chris asked too. "Are you okay, big guy?"

The Old-Growth-Hippie checked himself. He wiggled his toes. He straightened his back. "I seem fine," he intoned.

There was a big cheer. "Woohoo!"

"Hey Chicken Jim," Little Josh called out. "We have a new bus name over here. He's Buffalo Dave!"

"Well, that name's gonna stick," Buffalo Dave bellowed with laughter.

"Ya!" Shouted Fräulein Vera. "You will call him Buffalo Dave."

"Get him!" shouted Yülia.

"Get him!" shouted Jewels.

Spontaneously, everyone in the group stepped into the mud, picked up a handful of silky-glop and showered Buffalo Dave with mud bombs. When the onslaught was over, I slapped a good-sized wad of mud between his shoulder blades, covering the last white spot. "Nice one Dave," I commented.

Little Josh threw one last mud bomb intended for Buffalo Dave, but he missed, and it hit me. I threw mud back at him and this triggered a chain reaction. Who of us could resist throwing mud when more than thirty bare-ass targets were now standing knee deep in the gray goop? Together, we succeeded as a group to rediscover another one of our most primal instincts: War!

This peace-loving group of world travelers turned quickly into primal warriors in the ancient mud. A sprawling mud fight erupted, involving everyone within throwing distance, sending passengers running in all directions, up both banks, through the row of thick bushes, screaming, laughing, and plotting revenge. Teams formed strategically on both banks as if by some unforeseen force. Compatriots joined forces and began defending their own kind. Naturally, the British, Australian, and South African ladies ended up on the same bank.

The American drivers had a small camp in the center of the skirmish, and they were the common enemy. Some rogue states fought alone, while other predators seemed to travel in packs, hiding behind the bushes like gorillas, attacking easy targets, fighting among themselves at times. Sorties were flown in every direction. With every successful raid and with each target hit there was always the counting of coup. The coup was counted in the form of whoops and hollers and war cries with great open mouths panting laughter. The adrenaline was flowing. The more mud that was thrown, the more the laughter grew.

We were bonding, literally, in mud that dried quickly under the hot sun. We became adhered together by this sticky, grey substance, pushing and shoving and flailing in the slippery creek bed. So many countries at war, so many mud missiles in the air. A battle royal of mud wrestling broke out in the center of the skirmish. Men and women from different countries clashed in physical mayhem, a fierce, bohemian rhapsody of belly bumping, knee slapping, muddy combat. We had escaped from reality. Humiliations were wrought in mud and vendettas were forged in muck. Bodies hammered into each other, slamming each other into the goo, making a racket of sloppy, sloshing, slippery sounds. Warriors were jumping off the banks into the crowd as if they were pro wrestlers launching off the turnbuckle. People slam danced in the mud in rhythm with the laughter and sloshing sounds.

Buffalo Dave was not throwing any more mud. He was defending himself, though, and he now seemed a bit hurt from his earlier impact. "All wars should be fought with mud," he intoned before adding, "naked as the day Adam was born."

Mud was in the air constantly, and laughter abounded. It was a magnificent Greco-Roman wrestling battle. For fifteen solid minutes mud flew, bodies slammed, and bellies slapped, until we were beat up from laughter. Battle-worn and exhausted, a truce was drawn. When it was over, I had mud in every orifice. I could not stop laughing with mud packed in my nose, and I had to breathe heavily through my mouth for a while, just to catch my breath. All I could taste was mud.

The good thing about this kind of mud is that you truly wear it. As soon as everyone settled down, they started making their own tailor-made mud outfits, and in a few minutes, we could not tell who was who anymore. At least twenty people from our bus were now coated in mud from nose to toes. The luxurious silky-smooth mud was primarily gray with a touch of blue, and it clung to skin like latex paint. Nothing feels better than that mud dried on your skin, baked in the sun, and then washed off.

Chicken Jim was swimming in the river, washing mud out of his eyes when he yelled, "The other bus is coming!" He commanded, "Attack the other bus!"

Now, we were all enlisted on a new crusade. Everyone stood up and grabbed as much mud as they could carry. The troops mobilized as a unit; the common enemy united us. Before the other bus came to a halt under the massive trees next to our bus, mud was flying from the bushes and splattering loudly against glass and steel.

Muddy scouts had already broken through the tree line before the infantry arrived to confront the new enemy. Soon the invasion of foot soldiers followed the assault in the air, lobbing grenades of mud at the windshield as warriors advanced. Driver Hal slid his window shut.

The other team seemed to unify very quickly, defending the motherland with real passion and zeal, blocking open windows like human shields with bellies and sets of breasts until the windows could be closed. When the last window was shut, things grew incredibly quiet in the field beneath the massive oaks.

With her arms extended out by her sides, Australian Sheila pressed her naked body against the bus, covering the words Green Tortoise with a mud angel, creating little roundels of mud where her breasts pressed against the Tortoise. Having used up all our ammunition achieving our dirty objective, I yelled, "Retreat!" The mob ran back to the mudhole.

Soon, a contingent of waring passengers from the rival bus ran through the bushes and jumped into the mud ready to fight back. They looked at our group in disbelief shaking their heads as they began throwing mud. They had fallen into an ambush. We were already covered in mud from head to toe, making their efforts futile.

The rest of the clean passengers reluctantly moved through the bushes to join in the filthy fun. Deutsche Mark and our two drivers flanked them and took prisoners, grappling them forcibly into range of our warriors who pelted them with mud bombs. There was a lull in the action, and we all heard Little Josh crying. He had mud in his eyes, and

Mud for Dessert

he swore at one of the unsullied soldiers in the ranks of the opposing force. "Fuck you, assholes!"

Mother Michelle got angry with her son. "You're not the only one with mud in your eyes mister, and I warned you about that filthy mouth of yours." The soldiers looked at the boy and laughed because he was getting in trouble. Little Josh raised his middle finger at the spotless warriors, thinking that his mother could not see.

The guy gave him the finger back and Mother Michelle's eyebrows rose. "Come here, Josh," she prodded. The boys finger rose again. "Come here!" she demanded. Reluctantly, he trudged through the mud to her side. "Pick up that mud," she commanded. "Both hands!" He filled his hands with mud while she did the same. As she bent over, she whispered, "On the count of three let's attack him together." The boy smiled joyfully. "One... two... three, Attack!"

"Attack!" screamed Little Josh, "Get him!"

Our entire bus joined-in and pelted the clean guy into submission. We counted coup naturally, eliciting fear in the hearts of the enemy. Little Josh was in his glory. This small victory inspired our army to a decisive victory over the enemy. The captives were allowed to strip, and then all of them were lovingly hand-painted from head to toe.

Flip-flop extended the olive branch and crossed the line with open arms to embrace Driver Hal. Her whole body was covered in mud, but he picked her up off the ground and gave her a big hug. This resulted in great laughter when everyone saw the mud prints of bare breasts left on his chest. Driver Hal waved his hand like a white flag and shouted, "We surrender!"

After the war was won Mother Michelle consoled her son, "Come to the river and I'll clean your face and help you get that mud out of your eyes." She waded out into the river with him and did the needful. She stretched out in the shallow part of the river and bathed the mud off herself.

When her son was clean, she sent him back to the bus.

"I don't want to go back to the bus," he complained.

"You've seen enough naked girls for one day," she told him. "I'll make it up to you later. Maybe I'll let you get McDonalds." He was gone in a flash.

****

The Pink Panther arrived at the mudhole au naturel, but her manservant, Cato, was still wearing his new bathing suit, although, for once, he removed his Ace Bandage, tossing it over on the bank of the mudhole. The two of them faced away from the rest of us and proceeded to cover their bodies with the luxurious grey silt.

When they turned around, I could not resist peeking at the Chinese guy's man-boobs. Although they were coated in thick mud, I could plainly see why he might want to hide such a disfigurement. It probably caused him great embarrassment. At least his Ace Bandage covered them most of the time. I wondered if he ever had injured ribs in the first place. It didn't matter though. The people on the bus were cool. Nobody gave a shit in any way shape or form.

The Peruvian painted her face expertly like a mud mask at an expensive spa. Her body was amazing. I was not the only one who noticed.

When she caught Juliano looking at her body, he said, Você está deslumbrante."

"Desenmerda-te," she snapped at him.

I felt bad for the little bro. I was like, "What did you say?"

"I said she was gorgeous," he explained.

"I take it she wasn't happy with that," I said.

"She told me to unshit myself," he huffed. I laughed and laughed.

I heard Jewels tell Yülia, "Ursula is really nice when she isn't all up in PAC-MAN's business." Evidently, the Chinaman's bus name was catching on quickly. Many of us were now going by our bus names.

After the remaining passengers from the other bus joined us in the mud, Driver Hal shouted, "Everybody line up for a mud massage!"

I took a seat in the cool mud and got ready for peace.

Peruvian Ursula stood above me surveying the disorganized massage line with her hands on her hips. "This isn't going to work. You need to sit closer together," she advised me and the next closest person. "Who's in charge here?" she demanded. "We need more bodies over here," she called out. As the line began to form, she barked orders at passengers from both buses. "You need to sit here. You need to sit there."

I was happily painting my face with mud when she asked me, "Would you sit behind me please? You're the only one I can trust."

This caught me off guard, so I said, "Sure," without thinking.

She sat down in front of me, then PAC-MAN sat in front of her, falling into her lap with an audible squish and a giggle.

"Would you like a massage?" I asked her.

"Certainly," she said with a grin. "Just don't get any funny ideas."

I laughed and said, "No worries. I am always a gentleman."

Mud for Dessert

"We'll see about that," she quipped. I could not believe it. I was sitting in the mud massaging the Pink Panther.

PAC-MAN invited Yülia to sit in his lap for a massage and she giggled when she plopped down in his lap. I giggled when she giggled because it was so friggin' cute and we all giggled again. Yülia in turn extended an invitation to Deutsche Mark. A girl from the other bus sat in front of him and soon she was massaging our red-bearded driver. He put his hand out to a stranger from the other bus who turned out to be the girl who had been lying next to Juliano earlier that morning. "You're the cutest thing on the planet," he told her as she sat down. Juliano took the hand of his new lover and sandwiched himself in between her and the German girl, and so on down the line.

French Sandrine was upset because the voyeuristic girl had taken her seat. This left her standing there looking dumb, not wanting to sit with anyone else. Driver Chris remained unmoved. I did not remember a single word of French from grade school, so I whispered a question over Peruvian Ursula's shoulder, "How do you say, 'Your name is mud' in French?"

She answered in a mock French accent, "Je m'appelle mud!" We all giggled together. It was not long before a good-looking guy from the other bus sat in the cute girl's lap in front of Driver Chris. This allowed French Sandrine to sit in front of him and say, "Oh, la, la! Lucky me! You're the most handsome man in the world." After she sat down, she turned and gave her lover a nasty look.

We had to sit awfully close to one another, because as Driver Chris explained, "If you don't squeeze in tight, the line will get too long and then we won't have enough room for everyone."

Driver Hal led Flip-flop by the hand through the mud, guiding her into line behind me. She rubbed her hands over my chest with mud and boasted, "I'm a trained massage therapist."

"I did not know that," I said. "Today's my lucky day."

Suddenly, she hugged my back and leaned in to hide her face from someone who was snapping pictures. I felt her hot breath in my ear, "I don't want naked pictures of me falling into the wrong hands. I could end up on the Internet."

"That would be bad" I proclaimed. She was sitting so close to me that I felt like I was her new boyfriend, but then Driver Hal tucked in behind her and she started to moan with delight.

"Hey Ursula," Flip-flop asked suggestively, "Is Johnny Lovebus any good at massage?"

The debutante turned around to see who was asking. "Oh, it's you," she said fondly. "He's not a pro like you," she assessed. They both giggled.

Driver Chris directed everyone to move closer together in the massage line. "Hey, guys, we're running out of room at the front of the line here," he spoke in a loud voice. "If everybody sits closer, we can all fit in one line and set a new record. Let's see how many people we can get in a line. Pass it down." We passed the message down, although everyone had clearly heard Driver Chris, and we made room for more passengers by pressing in even closer together. There was a lot of sloshing and farting noises as we tightened ranks.

Driver Chris yelled, "Tighten up the line!" We all budged up even closer until Flip-flops breasts were touching my back and my private parts were bumping Peruvian Ursula in the tailbone.

For a few minutes, I got a double massage from Flip-flop and Driver Hal, but then the Bostonian moved her hands to Peruvian Ursula's shoulders, so in turn I bypassed her and went to work on PAC-MAN. Hal was good at massage, but he had nothing on Flip-flop's skills.

"Oh yes!" crooned the Peruvian. "Your hands are lovely Jen. That's so much nicer than Mr. Big Hands back there." She giggled. This drew laughter from many others in the line.

I went to give it another shot, but PAC-MAN objected. "Don't stop. I like it!" he complained. The Peruvian must not have been doing a respectable job. So, I rubbed his shoulders for a while longer while we all giggled. Driver Hal's strong hands dug into my shoulders and I moaned too. Eventually, everyone was moaning. I switched back to massaging Peruvian Ursula directly in front of me, but it was hard to concentrate much effort into my big dumb hands.

Flip-flop was performing magic from behind, working her strong fingers all over my shoulders and chest, down over my stomach, pressing her chest against my spine to grab at the muscles of my thighs and legs, massaging me with her whole body. The mud made the perfect massage lotion. I could feel her silky nipples touching my muddy skin in rhythm with her movements. I moaned every time her fingers dug into my flesh. She was Sporty Spice all right! Her massage skills were a constant source of distraction from the main event happening in front of me.

In my lap sat the hot tight Latina, the Peruvian Pink Panther wearing a lovely suit of mud. She was a walking talking Jennifer Lopez with motorcycle hugging curves, light mocha skin and a totally empowered personality. She was half Polish and half Peruvian, think sausage meets supermodel, and here she was, inexplicably seated in my lap, demanding a topless massage. Life is good on the Green Tortoise.

I felt equally attracted to both women simultaneously. I could not turn either one down. The wheels were already greased. I loved all the girls at that moment. I was having my first feeling of being

Mud for Dessert

polyamorous. Far more walls would need to be torn down for me to feel free to love whoever whenever, but for the moment I dug right in.

I rubbed Peruvian Ursula's back and shoulders with as much skill as I could muster. She seemed to be enjoying it, but she could hear and feel what was going on behind her. She grabbed my hands, squeezing them affectionately and then placed my hands on her pillows of womanliness. Her breasts felt like over-ripe melons in my hands. I massaged them gently with my fingers, brushing her soft springy nipples with my muddy wrists.

Driver Hal's hands came back, only this time on my chest. Flip-flop's hands followed down my arms until she realized I was massaging the Peruvian's breasts. She shooed me away and took over massaging the Peruvian. I in turn moved my hands to Pak Chan's chest. He writhed uncomfortably when I grabbed his man-boobs and Peruvian Ursula slapped me on my wrist. I withdrew my hands and went back to his shoulders. Although this was painfully awkward, everything went ahead as before.

Driver Brian then took over as director of the mud line because Driver Chris was not doing a respectable job. His partner had given up trying to break the Tortoise record, choosing to focus instead on the cute girl from the other bus sitting in his lap.

"He's just trying to get in your pants," warned French Sandrine.

"I'm not wearing any pants," was the cute girl's response.

Driver Brian sat at the very front of the mud line, where the mud ended in the river. So, there was no room for anyone else to sit in front of him. This forced Jewels to sit behind him which worked out for Guitar Johnny who was sitting behind Driver Brian when she arrived. Judging from the love songs he sang to her on Sheep Mountain Table, the guitar player had a crush on the soulful teacher from New York.

Driver Raoul sat in the last seat at the far end of the mud hole where the mud ended below an embankment. This meant that all latecomers had to squeeze in-between those already seated, resulting in a hilarious symphony of slippery, slushy, farting, mud sounds, accompanied by painful cries and squeals of delight. Fräulein Vera screamed and much giggling ensued.

In the end, sixty-three people sat in the densely packed mud line where we relaxed in each other's arms, groaning with a mixture of pain and pleasure.

Buffalo Dave was sitting half a dozen places in front of me in the mud line with Mother Michelle massaging his aching back. He was in his glory, judging from his deep pleasure-full laughter. His massage partner was one of the young girls from the other bus who had no problem letting him explore the hills and valleys of her body.

I was beginning to feel a generalized love for all the Tortoise people, even the passengers from the other bus. We were all taking care of one another, nurturing one another. We cooked and cleaned for each other. We had come to know one another intimately. It was so real, so honest, and so deliciously dirty.

Yes, it is true, I was inspired by love in the mud. I felt like it was time for a celebration. I excused myself and ran like an indigenous tribe member through the bushes back to the bus. I grabbed the last four bottles of Champagne and ran back to the mud hole.

Driver Brian gave me a knowing look as I handed him the first muddy bottle. "The champagne," he exclaimed, "Chris! We forget about the champagne."

Driver Chris said, "Oh shit!" He started to get up, "I'll get it."

"I got it," I said as I handed him the second bottle over his shoulder.

"Right on, Lovebus," he cheered. "We'll make a driver out of you yet!" I beamed a face full of joy at the thought.

Chicken Jim said, "Hey, man, you're making me look bad."

"It's true," Driver Chris hissed at Chicken Jim.

The trainee gave me a look of disdain.

Driver Brian laughed. "I can't believe we totally forgot the champagne."

Driver Chris popped the first cork into the air. POP! He put the bottle to lips and foam ran down his beard. With a laugh, he passed the bottle to the cute girl in front of him. After taking a sip she passed it to French Sandrine, and so on down the line.

I passed the other bottles to eager passengers and took my seat between Flip-flop and Peruvian Ursula. I uncorked a bottle of champagne, took a drink, and passed the bottle forward. Soon, everyone in the mud massage line was enjoying the cool, refreshing champagne. The champagne did not last long with that many people drinking it, but it cleaned the taste of mud from my mouth and left a taste for something different. The magic carpet was unrolled, and we were flying high.

After lounging in the mud and massaging each other's bodies for what seemed like hours, the sun baked the mud dry on our faces and warmed our bodies so much that it started getting uncomfortably hot. One by one, we all left the mud massage line and went for a luxurious swim in river, washing off the gritty mud, adding to the silt in the river with our own dirt. The mud was difficult to remove, and it stuck like glue when it dried, so we all helped each other clean the mud off our backs and pointed out spots where we had missed cleaning.

Soon we were drying off on the banks of the river, enjoying the heat of the sun, getting dressed, and saying goodbye to the people

Mud for Dessert

from the other bus. I left the mud feeling like I had visited an expensive, outdoor, natural spa.

Letting other people touch your naked body requires a shift in consciousness that can only happen in a community where there is a great deal of trust and respect. Once we understood that nothing bad was going to happen, that we were all looking out for each other, our group began to develop a that sense of trust. Many of the inhibitions present in our daily lives were gone.

After the mud, everyone seemed more free-and-easy about pretty-much-everything. We were able to lean against each other more and touch each other more without feeling weird. Most of our tribe piled onto the back platform, laying in one another's arms, relaxing with our legs draped over each other. Unbelievably, Peruvian Ursula curled up on my lap and we talked and cuddled on the way to Wounded Knee.

18
Wounded Knee

Out in the middle of the Pine Ridge Indian Reservation, where nothing but yellow grass grows in the hot summer sun, there is a humble monument to the Massacre at Wounded Knee. As the Green Tortoise rolled slowly down Big Foot Trail toward the site, a gigantic plume of dust rose in its wake.

Deutsche Mark shook my shoulder excitedly, until I woke up in the bunk where I had been napping, "We're here, man!"

My mind was clouded in the midst of vision, and I could taste the dust of the road in the air. I yawned and stretched. "Where's here?" I muttered.

"This is the place, man. We're at Wounded Knee. Come on, get up, man!" He bent down to look out the window for a moment and then popped his head back up again.

I got down from the bunk and sat next to the big man at the dinette to put on my boots.

Deutsche Mark waved a small paperback book in my face enthusiastically. He spoke with a passion I had not seen in him before, blurting out words as fast as his tongue would fly, "I just finished reading *Black Elk Speaks* on the way here. It was awesome."

When Buffalo Dave heard this his eyes lit up. "What is that fine piece of literature?" he intoned.

"*Black Elk Speaks* is like the Indian Bible, dude," Deutsche Mark told him. "Hold on a minute, I'll show you what I mean." He quickly rifled through the pages, ran his finger up and down, found the passage, and read to himself a little. "This is Black Elk speaking about Wounded Knee," he prefaced before reading the following passage aloud.

Wounded Knee

> *When I look back now from this high hill of my old age, I can still see the butchered women and children lying heaped and scattered all along the crooked gulch, as plain as when I saw them with eyes still young. And I can see that something else died there in the bloody mud, and was buried in the blizzard. A people's dream died there. It was a beautiful dream.*
>
> *And I, to whom so great a vision was given in my youth, - you see me now a pitiful old man who has done nothing for the nation's hoop is broken and scattered. There is no center any longer, and the sacred tree is dead.*
>
> John J. Neihardt - Black Elk Speaks page 270.

Deutsche Mark was clearly inspired; "See, man? I told you this was the coolest book ever."

"Might I read that when you are done?" asked Buffalo Dave.

"I already promised it to Johnny," the Dutchman responded.

"I'll pass it to you next," I told him. "If I can read fast enough to finish before we reach San Francisco."

"If you leave it on the table here, I'll take care of it," the big man offered. "That way I can read when you're not using it."

"Agreed," I said.

Mark handed me the paperback book. The image on the cover depicted a middle-aged Indian man with a rack of elk horns and a feathered headdress. The title read: *Black Elk Speaks* with the subtitle, *Being the Life Story of a Holy Man of the Oglala Sioux*. A third line read: *As told through John G. Neihardt (Flaming Rainbow)*.

"I had friends in the AIM movement who took part in the occupation here in seventy-three."

"What's the AIM movement," I asked.

"The American Indian Movement," he answered. "I was a big supporter of Indian rights back in the day," he told us. "They were fighting for the broken treaties to be acknowledged, but the feds just shot them to shit. They were forced to take their own kind hostages, or else they would have been run into the ground by federal troops. It is so ironic that it happened here at Wounded Knee. It is a shame so many people had to die when hardly anything came of it. The government said they would honor the broken treaties. They promised to give the Indians back their homeland, but they lied again. All they ever wanted was the Black Hills. Instead, they gave them this." He motioned with his arms. "Pine Ridge is the poorest community in the entire US."

"I never heard any of this before," I contended. "I'm eager to learn about it."

English Tessa spoke up, "Surely, you must've had lessons on Wounded Knee in primary school?"

I shook my head from side to side. "You know, I can honestly say that I can't remember ever learning about Wounded Knee in school, all the way through high school. There was no class in Native American history."

"No way!" Deutsche Mark was shocked. "We spent a whole week on Indian history every year in high school."

"In Holland!"

"Yes," said British Sue, "they seem so proud of killing them all off, it's hard to believe they don't teach that."

I shook my head and shrugged my shoulders sheepishly. I found it hard to believe our country keeps these facts hidden from us. We all heard the familiar pop and hiss of the air brakes and the last few rumbling coughs of the engine as the dust cloud cleared. Sure enough, we were out in the middle of a barren wasteland on the Pine Ridge Indian Reservation. A tiny barn-red church and a small graveyard sat together on a slight rise in the fields, surrounded by nothing but golden prairies and a few sparse trees. In the distance a lone Buffalo stood motionless in the sea of wind-swept grass.

Driver Chris seemed ready to give a speech, and he waited for everyone to quiet down. He spoke in a loud voice from where he stood, leaning against the dashboard in the stairwell, "As you can tell there's not a whole lot to see out there, but when you learn the history of this place as it is written on the monument over there, I hope you will understand that this is one of the most important monuments in the United States."

"Can we do this outside? It's bloody hot in here?" complained British Sue.

"This will only take a second," Driver Chris continued. "Before you leave, I'd like to tell you a few things it doesn't say on the monument. In all probability, if the Indians did not give up after Wounded Knee, they would have been wiped out of existence," he continued with passion. There were a few whispered comments as he nodded his head to gain consensus. "Much like Hiroshima and Nagasaki, the victims of Wounded Knee were killed by the ultimate weapon of its day, the Gatling gun." He labored to breath in the heat. "The Gatling gun is a machine gun that fires fifty caliber bullets at two hundred rounds per minute," he explained. "To put this in perspective, the Geneva Conventions of War prohibits the use of fifty-caliber rounds on human beings because it is considered inhuman to use bullets that make bodies explode."

He breathed again waiting for silence. "The Indians believe that the spirits of their dead are left to haunt the earth when they are not buried right away. Given that exploded bodies are not easy to bury, it should not come as a surprise to find out that the remains of the victims of Wounded Knee were left to rot in the snow." People were upset to learn this detail. "So, please be respectful to the people here," he pleaded with us. "Keep your voices down, and don't do anything you wouldn't do in a graveyard." He looked around outside momentarily before continuing. "This whole place is graveyard."

With that he opened the door and left abruptly without another word. The wind blowing through the open windows provided little relief to the intense heat, so we were all dying to get off the bus.

Across the dirt road a footpath ran through a short stonewall, under a brick archway with a cross overhead. Several Lakota children were standing in the shadow of the brick archway, trying to keep out of the midday sun. A man, who appeared to be their father, leaned against the grill of an old beat-up pickup truck parked close to the wall.

As the passengers began to move about and get ready to go outside into the fields of nowhere, Driver Chris poked his head inside the bus again and spoke at the top of his voice, "There are some Indian kids over there selling jewelry, and it helps them if you buy stuff, so get your money out and don't be stingy."

The children presented jewelry to each traveler that passed through the archway, men and women alike, but when I approached them, the children grew quiet. They neither approached me nor held up any jewelry. They seemed to recognize me, as if I was one of their own. It was like they were looking right past me.

Deutsche Mark trailed a few steps behind me. His presence broke the trance. Suddenly, the Indian children became animated again, holding up the jewelry, shouting out prices, blocking Deutsch Mark's path as he tried to pass.

I walked up to the chain link fence that surrounded the gravesite. A tall Indian man wearing a dark purple shirt and a cowboy hat was bending down putting flowers on a grave. The dignified man stood up and looked over at me. He faced the grave again, making the sign of the cross, and then approached me, as if he had been waiting for me to arrive. His ornate silver bolo swung back and forth above his matching belt buckle as he maneuvered carefully between the graves. Time seemed to slow down again as he approached.

"Hello, friend," he spoke softly with power in his voice, "I am here today visiting the graves of my ancestors, and if it would please you, I would like to share the story of my grandfather and the wisdom of the elders, with you and your friends, so that you may understand the history of Wounded Knee."

"I'd like that very much," I responded, nodding again. I felt reverence for the great strength I could see in his eyes. I swallowed hard and nodded, glancing at Deutsche Mark before looking back at the Indian beneath the five-gallon hat.

"Yeah, that would be sweet," added Deutsche Mark, as a murmur of agreement went through the group and several others gathered behind us to listen.

British Sue had not been listening and she approached the chain link fence popping bubble gum and remarked, "I thought this was supposed to be an Indian burial ground or something? What are all those Christian crosses doing there?"

The enormous Indian smiled broadly, standing before us in the bright hot sunlight, and British Sue's eyes grew wide with silent embarrassment. "Some of you may be surprised to see Indians buried in graves marked with the Christian Cross." He examined each of our faces as we looked at all the crosses in the graveyard. "What most white people don't understand is that the ancient religion of the Sioux is very similar to Christianity, especially the stories of creation and the concept of a savior. My ancestors knew about the savior, but they did not know that he had arrived on earth, that he was crucified, and that he had risen from the dead. That is important to realize when you hear the story of my ancestors who are buried here under the Christian cross."

The Indian man seemed to be looking right at me, and his energy focused on me. "My people have experienced a lot of pain and great sorrow," he professed, "but no insult was worse than Wounded Knee. What happened here can hardly be classified as a battle, but it has been called that all of these long years."

I could see the energy of his spirit glowing within him, and he seemed to grow in stature as the story came into him. "Chief Big Foot and his band of three-hundred and forty braves, women, and children had been walking for weeks in the snow, heading for the town of Pine Ridge, which is not far from here." He turned his head to the southwest, and then looked straight back into my eyes.

"The Big Foot Sioux were starving, near to death and bitterly cold when they surrendered, unconditionally, at Porcupine Butte on December 28th, 1890. Soldiers on horseback then escorted the band to Wounded Knee Creek, where they made camp in that small valley over there." He gestured, sweeping his hand and pointing. He said, "Over there." We all turned and looked at the field of dried grass behind us and I tried to imagine the scene.

The great Indian seemed to be recalling images from personal experience, as if his ancestors were speaking through him. He continued, "On December 29th, five hundred soldiers arrived early in the morning to disarm the Big Foots before moving them into Pine

Ridge. It should be remembered that to the Indian his rifle was his plow; his means of livelihood and a cherished possession indeed. It was no small wonder, then, that the Indians did not readily comply with this request, requiring the soldiers to search the teepees for firearms. They had already surrendered, but the soldiers were still afraid, and they surrounded the Big Foots on three sides with wagon-mounted cannons and 50 caliber machine guns. Most Big Foots had already surrendered their weapons in a pile near the tent of Chief Big Foot, but the soldiers were searching all the tepees, and trashing the camp."

"Yellow Bird refused to give his rifle to a military officer who approached Chief Big Foot's tepee with a pistol drawn. The officer wrestled Yellow Bird to the ground and the officer was shot dead with his own gun. As soon as the shot rang out, another soldier entered the tepee and killed Chief Big Foot, in his bed where he was lying sick and unarmed." The Indian speaker paused in reverence and bowed his head. My friends and I remained silent. I could feel the sweat beading at my temples.

From under the rim of his cowboy hat the Indian's eyes engaged mine once again; only this time, his eyes looked right through me into the past, into the souls of the ghosts of his dead ancestors. His lips moved again, and I heard his voice, but now the voice seemed removed, as if it were hollow, like an echo across the open gulch. "One of the soldiers saw the end of a rifle sticking out from under a blanket and he called out to the other soldiers, that the man had a gun. As the soldier started forward to take the rifle, suddenly the rest of the federal troops raised their guns and fired right into the band. Many were shot dead right where they stood. The fifty-caliber wagon-guns began firing into the crowd of my relatives and family, and now everyone was fleeing. Unarmed and submissive, then running and frightened, they were fired on and executed as they tried to get away. The women ran with their babies and children up the dry gulch but were shot dead as they ran up the hill."

He pointed in front of him at the flat dry gulch below the little hill and said, "The bodies of women and infants fell right here, dead from bullets." We could see the tears welling up in his eyes. He paused, looking all around him with fear on his face. Everyone else followed his glance and looked around, but I could not keep my eyes off his expression. His eyes returned to mine as if I was his relative. "The surviving Indians now started to escape to the bluffs and the canyons," he continued. "The artillery guns were turned upon them, and the battle became a hunt really, on the part of the soldiers, the purpose being the total extermination of women and children." He paused for a great while. He breathed in a great breath through his nostrils and out through his mouth like a collective sigh of the ancestors. "This broke the will of my people. This nearly ruined us all."

Except for the sound of shuffling feet and the whisper of wind blowing over the hill through the graveyard and past our ears there was complete silence. Even the boys selling jewelry were sitting silently in the shade. [Sound of wind]

To my amazement Deutsche Mark spoke up enthusiastically, "Is that when Black Elk rode in?"

The Indian seemed pleasantly surprised, "Ho," he said, with a chuckle and a smile. "You know of Black Elk." He spoke louder than before. "Yes, it is true, Black Elk and his band of twenty Sioux heard the big guns and rode over from Pine Ridge." At this my eyes grew wide and I looked at Deutsche Mark, who nodded in recognition. "They carried no guns or weapons," the Indian man informed us. "Only Black Elk carried a sacred Bow with no string and no arrows. They rode into the dry Gulch between gunfire and exploding artillery rounds. Cavalrymen were hunting down the groups of fleeing women and children who were running and hiding."

Deutsche Mark nodded, focusing all of his attention on the Indian as he continued, "A group of women and children were being held at gunpoint as they were shot one by one. Black Elk and his men rushed these soldiers, and the soldiers shot at him and ran away. These women and children were my relatives. They were taken into safety, and none of Black Elk's men were shot." The powerful Indian man looked up at the sky as if to thank God.

He continued. "Two of the Big Foot boys were rescued from the gulch. They had been killing soldiers with guns they recovered from the gun pile. One of those boys was my grandfather." The man pointed over at the graveyard and said, "I have come here today to visit him."

He paused, and then continued with a new spirit. "Black Elk charged into battle, holding up his sacred bow, and the bullets did not hit him at all that day. He found a baby girl lying alone at the head of the gulch. He wrapped her up in a shawl and put her in a safe place. Then Black Elk found another baby. This one was trying to suck its mother's breast, but the mother was bloody and dead. Women, children, and babies were lying dead and wounded in the dry gulch. Many of the bodies were cut in half by machine guns. The massacre was ended only when not a live Indian was in sight."

Again, the Indian seemed to reflect into himself. "Eighteen members of the Seventh Cavalry received the Congressional Medal of Honor for their actions that day."

[Sound of wind.]

The wind washed over and around us on the barren plane and no one spoke for several moments.

[Sound of wind.]

The Indian man spoke slowly, taking off his hat and holding it at his hip as he continued. "It may be hard to imagine, because it is so hot here today, but after the massacre, a heavy snow fell and a hard wind blew, blanketing the bodies in snow, in a line of bloody snow that stretched all the way up the gulch to the top of this hill. The chill was so fierce; it did not thaw-out until spring."

The Indian put his hand out and braced himself against the gate of the graveyard, and said, "This was the greatest dishonor, to the dead, to my family, and to our people." He paused with a painful smile, looked up at us and said, "May God bless you," as he made the sign of the cross." His eyes met mine and our souls introduced themselves. I felt his pain and he understood mine. "Thank you for listening," he concluded.

"Thank you," I said. A chorus of thanks and praise was offered and given. As the others stood around talking about what had just happened, I politely stepped forward and offered my hand to the speaker. We shook. "Thank you for the history lesson, your passion, and your prayers." I looked him in the eye as I spoke. "I find myself weighed with grief for your people. I regret the passing of your relatives and anyone who died here." I made the sign of the cross. "God rest their souls."

"Thank you," he said with eyes that spoke to my heart.

"I don't want to offend you with my ignorance, but if you would permit me, I would like to ask you a question."

"You may ask me anything you like," the Lakota man responded. "I can always choose not to answer."

"Thank you," I said again.

He nodded approval and said, "Go ahead."

"I'm an American and I have lived in the United States my whole life, and to be perfectly honest, I never heard about Wounded Knee or Pine Ridge or the Black Hills, until I came here today. How is that possible that I never learned about these abominations in school, or even in college?"

The dignified Lakota man inhaled deeply as he gathered his thoughts. He stood up straight, looked me in the eye and said, "The sins of the past are often overlooked because the white man does not want to suffer, especially at the hands of their forebearers. The Lakota see the past and the future and all experience as one continuum, so this is hard for us to understand."

He paused. So, I made an observation. "Well, as an American, I feel ashamed of these atrocities," I told him.

Again, he paused in thought, but I could tell he intended to speak, so I remained quiet. "You needn't feel ashamed for the sins of the past. The crimes against Native Nations continue today! The Federal Government continues to break the laws designed to protect us. They refuse to uphold the Treaty of 1868, granting us the Black Hills, even though the treaty was signed by the president and every member of the house and senate, in agreement with the Native Nations in Washington DC. A crime is being committed each day the Federal Government fails to uphold that treaty."

"How can they get away with that?" I exasperated.

After a few moments he proceeded. "They claim that subsequent deeds override the Fort Laramie Treaty, but any such documents were signed under duress. The threat of genocide twisted the arm that touched the pen, and no subsequent deed was signed by the president, house, and senate."

"Why don't the Indians sue the government for Genocide against a sovereign nation? That happens all the time in other countries."

"We have tried," he revealed. "When they refused to reopen treaty negotiations in 1973, we staged a revolt right here at Wounded Knee. It was part of the American Indian Movement, much feared by your government at that time. They treated us like terrorists on our own land."

"I'm ashamed to say, I was never taught that either," I admitted. The Lakota man had passionate beliefs. I extended my hand and said, "It has been my honor sir."

"I hope I've helped answer your question."

"Very much so," I told him. "I wish there was more I could do."

"You've made a good start here today," he said.

With that he walked toward the gravel turnout where he met an Indian woman coming down the hill from the direction of the church. They walked together and climbed into the back of the beat-up pick-up truck and sat down, leaning with their backs against the cab so that all I could see was his five-gallon cowboy hat.

Driver Brian called us back to the bus, and we all climbed on board. No buddy check was needed because the area was so barren and devoid of trees. As we moved slowly along Big Foot Trail away from Wounded Knee, I realized that the Green Tortoise Adventure Bus left more than just a plume of dust in its wake. I had left a piece of my heart and a whole lot of ignorance behind me that day at Wounded Knee.

I sat at the dinette table facing the front of the bus with my legs in the aisle, across from Buffalo Dave and Mother Michelle. Deutsche Mark handed the former Hendrix roadie the book *Black Elk Speaks*. "Read the postscript," he instructed.

The big man opened the paperback and read. "I can't believe my eyes," he muttered. He turned to Mother Michelle to explain. "We were camped right where Black Elk had his visions."

"It's true," I confirmed. "Owen Cuny granted us special permission to camp up there. It was Driver Chris' idea. He's the one who gave Deutsche Mark the book."

Buffalo Dave read aloud the first words of the Author's Postscript. "After the conclusion of the narrative, Black Elk and our party were sitting at the north edge of Cuny Table, looking off across the Badlands." As the others reacted in disbelief, a chill ran up my spine and tears welled in my eyes.

"My gosh! That's unbelievable!" Mother Michelle stammered. Buffalo Dave was also excited.

I opened the first chapter and began reading. It was like the words were written in my soul. I read aloud as I wept, "My friend, I am going to tell you the story of my life, as you wish; and if it were only the story of my life I think I would not tell it; for what is one man that he should make much of his winters, even when they bend him like a heavy snow? So many other men have lived and shall live that story, to be nothing but grass upon the hills."

19
The Return of Crazy Horse

North of the Badlands lies the highest mountain range east of the Rockies, the Black Hills of South Dakota. Surrounded by the sparsely treed sea of grass called the Great Plains, this 1.2M acre island of majestic mountain forest is gorged with aspen, birch, bur oak, white spruce, hazelnut, and Rocky Mountain ponderosa pine. The web of life in the Black Hills supports many species of fish, plants, and wildlife found nowhere else on earth, such as the Black Hills red-bellied snake and the Black Hills flying squirrel.

Known to the Lakota and Dakota Indians as 'Paha Sapa,' meaning 'The Heart of Everything that Is,' the Black Hills live within the collective spiritual consciousness of the Great Sioux Nation. This land has forever been contested even among the Indians. The Black Hills is like the Indian Holy Land; the Lakota and Dakota cannot exist in a sacred manner without the freedom provided by the Black Hills.

In the Black Hills National Forest, where the black road crosses the red road on the map, at Custer, South Dakota, the bus turned uphill, rising into the cool mountain air. I was entranced by the verdant landscape filling the view out the windshield. The girl from Boston was on the buddy seat talking with Driver Chris. I grabbed hold of the support bar and positioned my head over the driver's left shoulder so I could see out the windshield. The big green bus was roaring up a winding, tree-lined road in the top of second gear.

"What's with you and Sandrine?" Flip-flop asked Driver Chris bluntly. "Are you in a relationship?"

He gave her a sideways look and said, "We're just friends."

"She sleeps with you, but you're just friends?" Flip-flop marveled.

"She's not allowed to sleep anywhere else because, technically, she's here as my guest," he answered matter-of-factly. "The Tortoise just assumes she's my girlfriend."

"So, she's not your girlfriend, but you're sleeping together. You're just not having sex?"

"Oh no!" he corrected her. "We have sex all the time."

"I thought you said you were just friends?"

"We are," he responded.

"How does that work?"

"Just fine," he answered slyly.

"That's not what I meant," she said with a smile. "You're in a relationship, obviously."

"I know what you're getting at," he said smoothly. "It's cool. Most people don't understand that kind of sexual freedom. Most people are sexually repressed, or at least they start out that way, especially on the East Coast."

"Why do you say that?"

He gave her a serious look. "I don't want to offend anyone, but most people are in denial when it comes to embracing their libido, their real sexual desires. To them sex is a sin you pay for in Hell. So, they block their urges, they block out the thoughts, they block their natural desires."

"That's so true," gushed Flip-flop. "I feel that way myself a lot of the time." He had a quick look at me in the mirror, and then he looked at her and said, "It all comes down to honesty. The truth will set you free."

"So, Sandrine knows you're just friends then?" she quipped.

"Of course, what do you expect? I'd have to be a robot not to love all you guys."

"Right on," she said.

"The only way to make it right is to be honest about everything," he revealed. "So, I freely admit that I am a sexual being, and I refuse to lie about it."

"That's good," she commended him. "Most guys are less than honest when it comes to their feelings."

"I wear my heart on my sleeve," he said proudly.

"So, you and Brian are both polyamorous?"

"No," Driver Chris said shaking his head. "I don't consider myself polyamorous. Historically I have been monogamous every time I've been in love. I'm not in a committed relationship with anyone. If I was in a committed relationship, I'd probably be with that person alone."

"Oh!" her voice fluttered. "So, you're not polyamorous. I'm sorry."

"Don't be sorry," he said with a laugh. "I'm comfortable with my sexual identity. I prefer to be honest about who I am."

"It's refreshing," she observed.

"I had good teachers," he told her.

"You had sex teachers in school?" she queried.

"No," he clarified. "On the bus. Mostly women, and it wasn't all about sex."

"They taught you about relationships?" she asked.

"Yeah, totally!" he grooved.

I looked at him in the mirror and said, "Teach me something."

He grimaced and nodded in thought. "You don't need to constantly be on the prowl searching for a woman who digs you, Lovebus. You just need to be yourself, and they will come to you."

"Yeah, right," I scoffed. "That didn't work at the high school dance; why would it work in everyday life?"

"You can't just lean against the wall, unless that's who you really are. You've gotta get up and dance. Let it all hang-out. Get your groove on."

"Put your best foot forward," added Flip-flop.

"The ladies want to see you strut your stuff," Driver Chris revealed.

"Do they?" I questioned Flip-flop.

She pouted her lower lip in contemplation. Then she tilted her head in a shrug. "How else would we know you're a good dancer," she quipped.

"So, all you need to do is dance, and the women will flock to you?" I asked.

"No, dude, you need to be more patient than that," he instructed me. "It takes a while to gain confidence in yourself, but once you learn to love yourself, you can develop an aura that is very attractive to the ladies."

"So, I need to work on my aura?" I questioned.

"Your aura is not something you can work on directly. You just need to work on being yourself," he explained. "I had a passenger once named Bruce. This guy was cool. His aura was almost visible. The ladies were attracted to him like he was some kind of cult leader." He laughed. "We all were," he admitted.

"Was he religious?" I asked.

"Na. This guy didn't have an agenda. He was just Bruce." He nodded in contemplation at his own words. "Bruce never pushed himself on anyone. He was very relaxed and jovial all the time." He smiled in recollection. "He was always calm and happy. It was catchy."

"So, he had his way with women?" I commented.

"More like they had their way with him," he replied with a chuckle.

"I appreciate confident men," reported Flip-flop. "Their confidence makes me feel safe."

"Was it confidence?" I asked the driver.

"That's one way to describe it," he replied. He wrinkled his brow in thought. "Come to think of it, he never did anything to attract the attention of women; they just gave it to him. It was like he projected good energy and love in all its forms. He was Bruce. We all wanted to be part of it." He smiled and laughed at himself. "If he were here, I'm sure he'd tell me it has nothing to do with him, that we are all part of it, and we take it wherever we go."

"I'm sorry. What are you talking about?" Flip-flop refocused. "I drifted off there a second."

"Where did you go?" he asked her.

"I was picturing myself with Bruce," she admitted. "He sounds awesome."

"Ha!" Driver Chris laughed. "His aura got you, even though he's not here."

"That's a powerful aura," I observed. "I'd love to adopt his philosophy."

Driver Chris perked up. "You can dude! Bruce gave me a card. It's floating around here somewhere. I swear I saw it two seconds ago, but I forget where I saw it. Michelle found it when we were cleaning the bus in Boston." He searched his surroundings and said, "It's the size of a business card."

Flip-flop and I searched the area. She scoured the dashboard, but that was a lost cause with so much crap piled on top of more crap.

"Hey Michelle!" Driver Chris called out.

"Yes darling," she responded, pretending to be the perfect wife.

"Where did you put that card, you found in Boston?" he asked her. "The one with the five secrets of love."

She looked puzzled for a second, then thrust her pointed finger at him in the mirror and said, "The secrets of love!"

"Yes!" he concurred. "Where did that go?"

"I have no idea," she said flatly. "I put it on your seat. That was the last I saw of it."

Something caught my eye when I looked up at Driver Chris' face reflected in the glass. A wheat-colored business card was tucked into the edge of the mirror. I was surprised I had not seen it before, having looked in the mirror countless times conversing with the drivers. "Is that it?" I suggested, pointing.

"That's it!" said Driver Chris. He snatched it off the mirror and read the five lines of text aloud as he drove with excitement building in his tone. "Love without condition, give without expectations, comfort without control, guide without direction, support without carrying."

Flip-flop marveled, "Wow! That's so cool." Our driver handed her the card to read. She handed it to me, and then I passed it to Mother Michelle.

"These are words to live by," she opined. Mother Michelle handed the card back to me. She made suggestive eyes at the Bostonian and whispered, "You should practice on her. She's perfect for you."

"Look! Mountain goats!" shouted the driver. He pointed. "Those things are intense."

I leaned down so I could get a better view out the windshield from the first seat by the door. I spotted two shaggy mountain goats with incredibly long white beards and thick white coats, clinging to a steep rocky outcropping. The beasts were unlike any creatures I had ever seen before. "They look like giant albino Monopoly dogs," I said out loud. Laughter gave way to the oohhing and aahhing of amazement, followed by a barrage of questions.

I heard Guitar Johnny stuttering, and then made out the tail end of what he was saying, "The Mountain Goats are a folk-rock band from California," he insisted.

The roaring sound of the engine echoed off the rocky outcroppings as we passed by, turning the head of the mother mountain goat, causing her to usher her youngling away. I chose the sign of the day: The Black Hills Mountain Goat.

Eyes forward again, scanning the roadside for more wildlife, we passed a sign for Mount Rushmore. "We're going to Mount Rushmore!" Flip-flop cheered from the buddy seat.

"No, we're not," Driver Chris informed us.

This caused another barrage of questions directed at our driver, who ignored the inquiries until Flip-flop spoke up again. "Why aren't we going to see Mount Rushmore?" She asked, looking at the map.

This frustrated Driver Chris. His face went all disconcerted almost annoyed. "Mount Rushmore is an abomination. It's an insult to the Indians."

Flip-flop shrugged and asked, "Why?"

"I might as well tell everyone, he miffed. He turned to see how many passengers were listening. He had our attention, so he lowered the music and began speaking loudly. "We will not be going to Mount

The Return of Crazy Horse 391

Rushmore," he announced. This drew some complaints and sparked some heated rumblings. Driver Chris continued, "You have to understand something, the Indians see Mount Rushmore as a desecration to the Black Hills." He gave Flip-flop another quick look of distaste for opening the can of worms. He went on. "We carved the faces of our presidents into a mountain on land they hold sacred, where the Indians have buried their dead for thousands of years, and now a million visitors a year crash their graveyard."

More questions were hurled into the air, too many to answer, and none came across clearly in the crossfire. Driver Chris just shook his head in disbelief, listening, and waiting for a chance to speak again. "Please let me finish," he pleaded. "You really need to understand the Indian's perspective. We carved our presidents faces in their most sacred mountain."

A few of us made sure people remained quiet. "Let him speak," Jewels urged. "Quiet down," she pleaded.

Just then a gigantic logging truck laden with fresh timber came into view around the curve ahead. In a tone of voice that clearly meant business, he shouted, "Hold onto your hats!"

Everyone looked out the windshield at the same time. A candy-apple red tractor trailer truck was bearing down on us at high speed, pulling a double length trailer full of tree trunks averaging six-feet in diameter.

"Time for evasive maneuvers," he informed me. "Watch how fast the tachometer drops when I shift on this hill," he encouraged. His left knee rose up and he stomped the clutch. In one fluid motion his foot came off the accelerator and he bumped the stick into neutral. We all leaned forward as the bus slowed down. "There's no room for error," he said, as he jumped back on the clutch and jammed the stick simultaneously. He floored the fuel and the bus roared at the top of second gear going twenty-seven miles an hour.

Yülia rushed forward to the top of the stairwell. "That truck looks dangerous," she observed lightheartedly. "Are we all going to die?"

"All bets are off if he rolls over and loses his load," Driver Chris explained.

"That's what she said," touted Chicken Jim from several seats back.

"Say your prayers people!" shouted the lovable German girl.

It was easy to imagine the truck tipping over on the downhill curve. Everything about it looked dangerous. If those giant logs cut loose and rolled our way it meant certain death for everyone. I looked back at the faces of the passengers. Maid Marian made the sign of the cross, but the rest of them looked perfectly calm. They had faith in our driver. We had all come to trust his ability behind the wheel. He drove with complete confidence, like Neal Cassady on the road to the La Honda House in the Hippie heydays.

He turned slightly into the narrow breakdown positioning the driver-side wheels on the other side of the white line close to the edge of the road. Driver Chris' eyes focused on the white line like a laser as the truck's engine brakes engaged, growling with all the sound and fury of a freight train.

"Hold your breath!" shouted the driver.

As the truck passed us it created a powerful gust of wind that pushed the bus hard to the left, sending passengers reeling back from the open windows. We all heard the disconcerting sound of sand getting kicked up into the wheel wells. We all feared for our lives for a moment as grim fate loomed over the steep edge of the road. Driver Chris expertly turned the steering wheel to compensate. The wheel wells went quiet.

Several passengers gasped for air and there was a collective sigh.

"There but for the grace of the Goddess go we," prayed Jewels.

"Ya!" laughed Yülia. "You prayed after it was too late."

Jewels answered coyly, "Pagans believe shit happens, then we pray." She was so cool it was ridiculous.

"I saw lots of logging trucks like that on my cycling tour in the Great Northwest," I commented to Flip-flop. "They're still cutting down redwoods in the last remaining groves of old-growth forest."

"That's right!" our impassioned driver announced. "Those were old growth trees, stolen from the Indian's sacred land." He began again after a pause. "All of this land," he shouted, "everything you see, this entire mountain range, eight thousand square miles, all of it legally belongs to the Sioux."

Flip-flop made a poignant observation. "How ironic would it be if we were all killed by trees going ninety-miles-an-hour."

After he finished addressing the passengers, he said, "Thanks, Jewels."

"For what?" she questioned.

"For helping me get their attention so I could get my point across," he explained.

"I'm used to being talked over," she scoffed. "It's so disrespectful.

"Your students don't pay attention?" he questioned.

"Yes, in school for sure," she answered. "But it happens outside school too. It's especially bad for women. We are conditioned to listen not talk. If we talk more than a quarter of the time we're seen as 'dominating the conversation.'" She paused to see if he had something to add, then she said, "You seem different though. Most men talk your ear off. You listen and ask a lot of questions. That's nice. It's like a breath of fresh air."

Deutsche Mark came forward to use the pee funnel, but Driver Chris told him, "Not here. We'll be stopping in a few miles." The Dutchman acquiesced but stayed in the door well for the rest of the conversation.

The forest around us appeared to be especially magnificent along this stretch of the road. Our driver informed us, "The Black Hills are the birthplace of the ancestors of the Indians. According to legend, the Black Hills is the Eden of the American Indian creation story. This is their Mecca, their Mesopotamia, and there is evidence to suggest that Indians have lived here for more than ten-thousand years."

"Oh my gosh. They must have come from somewhere," reacted Flip-flop. She had been hanging on his every word since she took the buddy seat. She was sitting with her hands folded under her chin and her elbows resting on her knees, looking up at his with starry eyed admiration. It seemed that her brief fling with the driver from the other bus had given her a new sense of respect for Driver Chris. She was impressed with him. Hell, we all were. He was an amazing person in every way.

Without missing a beat, he answered her question on the fly, "They migrated from Asia across the land bridge at the Bering Strait."

"Ooh!" crooned Flip-flop. "That's extremely cool."

"Actually, it was extremely cold." Driver Chris continued smugly. He laughed and Flip-flop giggled. He then took his eyes completely off the road and smiled into Flip-flop's eyes for what seemed like an eternity. Everyone watched him do this and it made many of us feel uncomfortable, but nobody said a word.

Flip-flop's face lit up and she seemed to melt slightly. She put her feet up on the seat and tucked her other knees below her chin, hugging her legs and her shoulders lifted with glee.

Driver Chris turned his eyes to the road again and continued where he left off, "The first time the government entered the Black Hills they immediately recognized this land as the homeland of the Indian. A proclamation was issued that promised the indigenous people that the Black Hills would always remain under their control. Despite this act of congress, settlers crossed the land and built outposts. When the Indians fought the invaders, the government sent troops to protect the settlers and to secure the land. That action led to the Powder River War, where the Indians fought fiercely for the Black Hills and won claim to the land again. That war was the first military conflict the feds ever lost."

Driver Chris adjusted himself in the driver's seat. The mountain air was cool and fresh, and the scenery just kept getting better as Driver Chris kept our attention. "After the War," he explained, "the Indians were promised the land again, and a treaty was signed by the president, vice president and every member the House of Representatives and the Senate. They were all there because they wanted to see the Indians all dressed up with headdresses."

Deutsche Mark interjected enthusiastically, "Yeah, dude, the Treaty of 1868."

"Right!" said Driver Chris.

"One hundred years before I was born," I said softly, thinking out loud.

Driver Chris' words rolled on, "Then General Custer arrived, and his scouts reported seeing gold from the riverbanks, and Custer demanded the Indians sell the land."

A bunch of comments were thrown into the air and someone pointed out that we had just driven through the town of Custer.

Driver Chris listened, waited, and continued with passion in his voice, "The Indians defeated Custer's army at the Little Bighorn."

Deutsche Mark interjected, "Yeah, dude, Custer's Last Stand."

"Yes," said the driver. "The Indians defeated the feds twice, but once word about the gold was spread, the gold rush started, and the treaty failed to keep the prospectors out."

Some of the European passengers were visibly upset, while others cursed the government and Maid Marian blamed greed. This was clearly an injustice.

Driver Chris turned, taking his eyes off the road for a second time to inspect the group gathered to listen, and added, "The Indians only gave up after Wounded Knee broke their spirits. Since then, they have been stuck on the shittiest piece of unusable land in the entire country, the Pine Ridge Indian Reservation. They went from having millions of acres of rich mountains, forests, and hunting grounds to a few square miles of lifeless flat desert."

There were objections to this injustice also. People were really appalled. Australian Sheila's golden ponytail popped into view and she asked, "It just seems so unfair; can't your government do something about it?"

Driver Chris shot her a quick look, "They tried to make things right once in the seventies. After they removed a hundred times the gold in Fort Knox, they offered them a hundred million dollars in nineteen-seventy, but the Indians would never take money. They just want the Black Hills back."

The Return of Crazy Horse

Australian Sheila sat back down with a raw look of horror on her face and muttered, "A hundred million is nothing but a slap in the face?"

Guitar Johnny spoke up, "a bloody joke is what it is."

"Well, whatever it is," said Driver Chris, "that's why we're going to Crazy Horse instead of Mount Rushmore."

Chicken Jim piped up proudly, "We're going to Crazy Horse!" he shouted, clucking with laughter.

****

The bus listed from side to side as the road snaked around outcroppings in the rocky hillside. With her head out the window, Flipflop's eyes sparkled with the reflection of the sky and Ponderosa Pines. There seemed to be a natural energy given off by the land, making me think that the land itself was alive. Driver Chris spasmodically changed gears, and the bus slowed down and listed as it turned into the wellsigned entrance to Crazy Horse Monument.

Cars were in line stopping briefly to make donations at the visitor's entrance. Entrance to the park is free, but all visitors are invited to donate to the non-profit project, the largest sculpture in the world. When the Green Tortoise bus rolled up to the entrance booth, Driver Chris killed the engine and got up out of his seat. An elderly woman arrived outside the bus door as he opened it to receive her. "Hello, Mrs. Ziolkowski," our driver greeted her warmly.

"You're always so polite Chris, but you know you can call me Ruth." She spoke with surprising familiarity and they hugged like she had known him for years. As she looked into his face, she said, "I haven't seen you since last summer, what took you so long to come back?"

"Well, this is the first northern crossing of the season," our driver told her. "I came back as soon as I could." Evidently, they had known each other for years, but it was remarkable how well she remembered him considering the thousands of people that visit Crazy Horse Monument each year.

Our driver turned to address the passengers and in a loud voice he said, "I'm pleased to introduce to you my good friend Ruth Ziolkowski." At this there were many greetings of hello Ruth exchanged. Driver Chris continued the introduction. "Ruth's husband Korczak was the famous sculptor who started carving Crazy Horse more than forty years ago. And Ruth, if you don't mind speaking, I will leave the rest to you."

Accustomed to addressing large groups of bus passengers, Ruth smiled at Chris and shouted, "In the museum you will see a model of the Crazy Horse sculpture that shows what the mountain will look like someday. We started carving Crazy Horse in the 40's with the first blast removing 10,000 tons of stone from the top right of the sculpture. Sadly, my husband, Korczak, died in 1982. For many years I struggled alone to keep his dream alive, but recently all ten of our children and their families have come back to help carry on his work."

Ruth Ziolkowski turned back around to Driver Chris and said, "I think we need to wrap this up because we are blocking other visitors from getting in."

"I'll come up to speak to your group in a bit after you find a place to park," she said. "My granddaughter will drive me up."

"Oh, for sure," Chris said, and he stood up again and said, "Ladies and gentlemen, Ruth Ziolkowski." The whole bus exploded in applause. Ruth waved and stepped off the bus.

Driver Chris exited the bus and donated money for us. Whatever he gave her made Ruth happy, and she came to the driver's window to say something personal before the bus pulled away. After about a mile we passed the visitor center on the right and turned left up a small hill into a gravel parking lot. Driver Chris parked in an area with exceptional views of Crazy Horse. Several passengers rushed to one side of the bus and crowded the open windows facing the memorial, craning necks to get their first look at Crazy Horse Monument.

Intent on seeing Crazy Horse for the first time from outside the bus in the open air, I waited patiently for the aisle to clear. A feeling that had been growing within me since we entered the Black Hills slowly took hold of me and a whole cache of emotions welled up to the surface. I knew about Crazy Horse and the mountain carving since my early childhood. The legend of Crazy Horse had painted my childhood dreams. Flip-flop came back to find her boots.

"Hey." I got her attention with a smile and told her my personal history. "My cousin's a writer, and he wrote a book called *The Return of Crazy Horse*," I told her. "When I was a kid, he used to send us his children's books. My mother read me the story of Crazy Horse a hundred times."

Flip-flop looked impressed. "So, writing runs in your family?" she asked.

I nodded and said, "I suppose it does." I had not written anything substantial at that point in my life.

Guitar Johnny sputtered, "What kind of a book is it, history or fiction?"

I smiled warmly at Flip-flop and answered Johnny's question, "It's a children's book, with great illustrations: it's about the Legend of Crazy Horse and the sculptor who was carving the mountain." I could

The Return of Crazy Horse

still vividly remember the images and the powerful story. "It was one of the first books I ever read. Legend has it that when Crazy Horse is finished, Crazy Horse will ride again."

Guitar Johnny said enthusiastically, "I'd like to get my hands on a copy of that." He then asked, "Has he written anything else, something we might have heard of?"

I felt a little embarrassed, but I answered, "Yes, actually, he wrote the novel 'ET, The Extra Terrestrial.' Steven Spielberg asked him to write a novel based on a screenplay by the same name, and the novel became the new screenplay."

"Spot on!" Guitar Johnny patted me on the back, "There's one we've all heard of; he's famous then?"

"Not so much," I remarked. "He's a relative of my mother's side of the family in Pennsylvania. He's a recluse."

The line to get out the door had formed, but the door itself remained closed. Driver Chris had been talking on the phone with Driver Brian in the driver's cabin. He set the white handpiece on the receiver and stood up to address the group. "Welcome to Crazy Horse." He bent down for a second and peeked out the panes of glass in the door, as the people closest to the front took their seats again. "It looks like we got lucky with nearly perfect viewing conditions today. The last time we came here it was raining, and the fog made it impossible to see anything, and you can't go any closer because it's a blasting zone."

"Did he say Blasting zone?" shouted Little Josh. "I want to see it blow it up."

Driver Chris smiled and leaned against the support pole next to the driver's seat, "Ruth Ziolkowski is on her way up to tell us more about the monument. Please try to remember she's 80 years old so speak up when asking questions. As you can tell she's a really sweet lady with a ton of class. She's one of the strongest women I have ever met." Driver Chris looked out the window again and lowered his voice a bit, "Mrs. Ziolkowski has been a friend of the Tortoise for twenty years, so please treat her kindly and try not to talk about her husband too much. She has her hands full running this place and the last thing we want to do is upset her."

Driver Chris heard the phone beep and reached over quickly to pick it up before it beeped again. He spoke with Driver Brian briefly and hung up. "Ok everybody, Mrs. Ziolkowski is on her way! Wait for her outside and please be polite." He spun around and cranked the swing arm and opened the door.

There was a rush to the door; feeling the excitement building, I was pushed up against Flip-flop in line. She turned and looked at me. I was so happy tears were welling in my eyes. She hugged me in the thrill of the moment. I bounded down the steps behind her, laughing joyfully. A feeling of revelry had infected the entire group. I looked up for the first time in my life at Crazy Horse Monument and became transfixed in awe and reverence.

I could hardly believe my own eyes. The mountain was over a mile away, but to my surprise I could make out the pupils in the eyes of Crazy Horse. I really had no idea how incredibly huge the sculpture actually is. A lifetime of childhood memories flashed on the screen in the theater of my mind, and I was speechless. I felt a joyful rush of wonder.

The likeness of Crazy Horse is being carved out of a mountain six-hundred feet long and five hundred feet high. The monument depicts Crazy Horse seated on a wild bronco, pointing south toward Wounded Knee. The entire right-hand side of the mountain shows striations from where hundreds of feet of rock have been blasted away.

The enormity of this undertaking and the raw power of the experience made me feel in awe, like I could imagine a father feeling at the birth of his child. No longer an abstraction gestating in the womb of thought, Crazy Horse was now alive in my world, living and breathing in front of me. Like a father holding his child for the first time, my responsibility became obvious. I understood my calling with great clarity. The meaning of my vision became clearer.

I could feel the course of my life changing under my feet, moving to the beat of ancestral drums. Tears of joy welled up in my eyes and rolled down my cheeks. "The tree of life is not dead," I thought. "I refuse to believe it. There is still hope in the world because Crazy Horse will ride again." The embryo from my vision at Sheep Mountain Table flashed in my mind, and I knew in an instant that this was what it was all about.

It all began to make sense to me, now. America needs to grow up and face the corruption of the past. As a nation we must abide by the Treaty of 1868 and return the Black Hills of South Dakota to the Indian people whose ancestors are buried there. I felt compelled from that moment forward to tell the story of my vision and to spread the glorious legend of Crazy Horse as my cousin William Kotzwinkle had done before me.

Ruth Ziolkowski approached our emerging number, walking from the car at a commanding pace. There was an air of dignity about her, despite her simple country dress. Driver Chris stepped forward to greet her, meeting her with a warm smile. "Hello Ruth. Thanks for giving us the VIP treatment."

"Oh, I always go the extra mile for our friends at the Green Tortoise. She smiled at him before adding, "Especially you, Chris."

The Return of Crazy Horse

He beamed a leprechaun smile from behind his red beard. "You have my deepest respect, Mrs. Ziolkowski, ah, Ruth. It's always an honor and a pleasure to be in your company."

She caught me beaming a huge smile with wet eyes and she nodded in acknowledgement. I was moved by her personal power. She sure had magnetism.

"It's always nice to have you, Chris." She turned and greeted our group again with a broad smile and a dignified wave. "Hello everyone. It's so nice to see all of your smiling faces." She spoke with distinction and a refined sense of decorum. "I am the caretaker of Crazy Horse Memorial and the Chairperson of the Crazy Horse Foundation that runs the museum and the Cultural Center." She gestured toward the group of buildings with a set of large iron gates. "The footpath through those gates is lined with reproductions of some of Korczak's best sculptures."

"When my husband, Korczak, died in 1982, I was so distraught; I did not think I would have the strength to continue his work, but the Lord blessed us with ten children, and they have all returned to answer the call. They have done a mighty fine job too, I must say; better than I could have ever hoped for. In fact, last June we reached a milestone that I thought I would never see in my lifetime. We completed the carving of the face of Crazy Horse.

There was a cheer before she continued. "It was a wonderful time. We had a great celebration where we opened up the mountain to visitors, allowing them to hike all the way up to the platform in front of the completed face." She turned and looked behind her, so that we all looked up with her at the mountain, observing the amazing detail of what is already the largest sculpture in the world.

Compliments emanated from various sources within our group, and someone asked a question I did not hear. Ruth nodded and humbly said, "Well, you can't hike up there today because we are actively blasting. We have a big blast scheduled for later this evening. It goes off at 8PM. I hope you get to see it." She smiled broadly with an air of hope. "Our work here is a group effort and everyone who comes here contributes, so thank you all for coming today. Your donation will be used to continue carving the monument."

Ruth paused, and put her hands on the hips of her light blue rose-patterned dress. "A different world cannot be built by indifferent people, you know," she said with authority. "The way I look at it, we all share a common goal here. We're all carving Crazy Horse, each in our own way." She bowed her head slightly, closing her eyes in thanks. "Your contributions and all of the proceeds from everything you buy here today, go directly toward paying for the blasting and carving."

Ruth turned all the way around to face our group again and spoke even louder, "We are a non-profit organization and we are proud to have never taken a single dime of federal money or state money or any money from any government source; even though that would surely speed things up, we have refused their repeated offers." She nodded as our group voiced approval and respect for her integrity. She smiled, and spoke again, "We have plans to build a university, free to all Indian tribes. Someday when the carving is finished, Crazy Horse Monument will be the cultural and spiritual center for all native people. By then hopefully, the Black Hills will be returned to the Indians."

When Ruth stopped speaking, Mother Michelle spoke up from close to where Ruth stood, "When will the carving be finished?"

Ruth grinned broadly, looked patiently at Mother Michelle, and answered, "At the current pace, the carving will not be finished for many generations, perhaps when your great-grandchildren have great grandchildren."

"Wow!" I said to Flip-flop. "Talk about putting your life into your work." Several other questions were asked and answered, but I found my attention drawn to the great mountain being carved by human hands, here in this peaceful wilderness where the fresh mountain air lifted one's spirit. My ears perked up when I heard Ruth mention Sitting Bull.

Ruth recounted the historic details, "Sitting Bull had never left the Black Hills in his entire life, but he led a delegation of Indian Chiefs to Washington DC to plead before Congress for the Black Hills to be returned to the Indians. Sadly, his argument fell on deaf ears. On the return trip the delegation attended the World's Fare in New York City where they saw my husband Korczak's sculptures on display."

Ruth pointed down the hill toward the buildings below, "Replicas of the World's Fair sculptures line the path to the visitor's center behind those iron gates, she informed us. "Korczak was not in attendance at the World's Fair, but the Indians understood that he had worked on Mount Rushmore, and that he was the right man for the job."

Several comments were interjected, and Ruth held up a finger and widened her eyes. She paused to wait for silence and began again with a renewed energy, "Since the delegation of Indians could not reach Korczak directly at the World's Fare, they held a sacred ceremony to contact him through a spiritual dream."

People reacted with astonishment, and several people made remarks to each other.

"Korczak had a very vivid dream that weighed heavy on him for a long time. He never shared the details of the dream with me, or anyone else for that matter. The dream pulled him in many directions

The Return of Crazy Horse

until he decided to visit the Black Hills once again." We were all blown-away by this miraculous story. Ruth explained further, "Of course, Korczak didn't know that the dream had been sent by the Indians until he arrived here. Sitting Bull and the other chiefs told him that they had been waiting for him. They were happy that he had finally arrived because so much time had passed. Sitting Bull feared the message had been lost."

"What was the dream about?" asked Yülia, in a soft voice few could hear.

Ruth responded, "Korczak did not speak about his dream very often; he was a very private man when it came to spiritual matters, and he didn't talk about it much, but it clearly moved him for the rest of his life."

Driver Chris made a motion like he was slitting his own throat to silence us, and Ruth continued after a moment when silence returned, "The Indians guided Korczak around the Black Hills when he first arrived, suggesting several smaller sites more along the lines of Mount Rushmore, but Korczak's vision was grand. Even the Indians had not imagined a project this enormous. Korczak and Standing Bear were certain that they had found the perfect location, because the mountain points due south directly at Wounded Knee. So, when the sculpture is finished it will stand as a permanent reminder of what happened there. Our hope is that someday the Black Hills will be returned to the Indians, so they may be free to live here once again on the sacred land where their dead lie buried."

The wonderful woman was growing emotional and seemed weary from standing, so Driver Chris took the opportunity of the long pause that followed to thanked her warmly, then he shouted to the group, "Ok, everybody; how about a round of applause for Mrs. Ziolkowski."

The Tortoise passengers applauded loudly, and I rushed forward to say more personal words of thanks to Ruth as our motley group followed behind her. She and Driver Chris lead the procession down the gravel road from the parking lot through the cast iron gates. We all marveled at the incredible row of sculptures lining the path into the Visitor Center.

I took this opportunity to speak with the widow of the sculptor. "Mrs. Ziolkowski," I addressed her formally.

"Please call me Ruth," she prodded gracefully.

"I think it's great what you and your family are doing here," I told her. "I have dreamed about coming here since I was a child. I learned about the carving of Crazy Horse from a children's book my cousin wrote, called "*The Return of Crazy Horse.*"

"William Kotzwinkle is your cousin!" Ruth marveled.

"Yes," I confirmed. "You know him?"

"Of course, we know Mister Kotzwinkle," Ruth Ziolkowski scoffed. "It was Korczak's favorite book. He read it to the children all the time, more than any other book. It sits on the mantle above our fireplace."

"Isn't it great," I cheered along with her. I was floored. "I'm so glad your husband liked it. What are the odds of that?"

"It was one of the first books ever written about Korczak," Ruth informed me. "That makes you family in my book."

"Thank you," I said being a smile.

"Heck, we're all family," she said, linking arms with me and Driver Chris. "I'll have to see what the ladies in the kitchen can drum up for you."

"That's too much," Driver Chris dissuaded her. "We brought plenty of food."

"It's the least I can do for family."

****

After checking out the visitor center with Flip-flop, we watched a short film about the history of Crazy Horse, I viewed the six-foot-tall sculpture of Crazy Horse superimposed in front of the mountain sculpture a mile away. Later, I walked back to the bus with Flip-flop and Guitar Johnny.

When we arrived, the kitchen scene was abuzz with the rhythmic chopping of knives. One crew was peeling and chopping garlic, and another was chopping pan-loads of onions. The mushrooms and melted butter sizzling in the sauté pan sounded like a round of culinary applause. Thinly sliced garlic was sprinkled over the top of the onions, creating a very sweet smell. Deutsche Mark was on top of the bus taking commands from Driver Brian, who was directing the dinner crew. The Dutchman seemed frustrated, "I'm not seeing any potatoes," he shouted.

"Keep looking," instructed Driver Brian. "They're up there somewhere, or else we are in for some pretty weenie potato soup." He looked around in a big circle at the horizon, "Has anybody seen Chicken Jim?" He spun around looking for the rookie, spotted me and said, "Lovebus! Would you mind helping Deutsche Mark find the potatoes up on the roof?"

"I know where they are," I replied. I walked around the bus to the driver's side window and climbed the green ladder welded to the side of the bus.

"Hey Dude," the Dutchman greeted me. "I can't find the potatoes."

The Return of Crazy Horse

I opened one of several paper bags from the grocery store in Minnesota and removed a bag of potatoes. "They're right here," I said with a laugh.

"Damn!" said Deutsche Mark, "I was looking in the wrong place." He picked up two bags, held them over his head triumphantly and yelled, "I found the potatoes!"

We tossed down the potatoes to Driver Brian who spread them out in front of the eager row of knife-wielding passengers. "We need these chopped pronto!" he commanded. The water was already boiling." He looked up to us on the roof. "We're gonna need all twelve bundles of asparagus and pass down the cayenne pepper from the spice box. We're gonna kick it up a notch."

Driver Brian stirred flour and milk into a buttery roux in a five-gallon cooking pot floating in a huge silver bowl of boiling water. The huge double boiler was balanced on the blaster with flames licking up to the rim. "You have to cook the roux just right," Driver Brian explained to his helper, Jewels. "You can't let it get too hot or it will turn into mush."

"That's what she said!" Chicken Jim shouted. He howled laughter.

Much to the chagrin of Guitar Johnny, who had a thing for Jewels, the two of them kept tasting the batter-like mixture off each other's fingers. Once it passed Driver Brian's final inspection, he added a healthy sprinkle of cayenne pepper to the roux, and then slowly whisked in two more gallons of milk. "If you add the milk too quickly," he warned Jewels, the flower will fall out of suspension and we will have a loaf of potato cheese bread instead of soup."

While the potatoes boiled, the salad crew got busy chopping and dicing the ingredients for an amazing salad. Fräulein Vera Lead the team with terse commands, directing the Irish Twins to wash and shred three types of lettuce, telling Maid Marian to diced tomatoes, mandating Mother Michelle to cut carrots, prodding Chicken Jim was to skin and chop cucumbers. She even compelled Peruvian Ursula to cut crowns out of radishes with the paring knife. When the work was done, a small wheel of blue veined cheese was broken-up and mixed in a bowl with virgin olive oil and balsamic vinegar.

On top of the bus, I got a chance to catch up with Deutsche Mark.

He said, "You know what, man? I'm over her. I'm moving on."

"There are plenty of fish in the sea," I told him, but I was still feeling a bit hurt. I'm sure he was too. I spotted the box containing the elk skull that I was bringing back to California to return it to the woods where I had found it. "Do you want to see that Elk Skull I was telling you about?"

"Sure," Deutsche Mark said enthusiastically.

"You are going to freak when you see this, dude," I warned him. I positioned myself over the large cardboard box, opened the folded flaps and removed the huge skull. "Check it out! It's a grandfather Elk."

He was awestruck as expected. "Whoa," he gasped, "That thing is awesome. It's way bigger than I thought," he marveled. "You found that in the wild?"

"Yeah, in California," I told him nodding, "in the Redwood Forest at a place called Elk Prairie."

"Holy shit!" He gasped. "It's amazing."

"Dude, it called to me the moment I saw it," I told him. "I knew I had to take it with me, but now I think I should return it to the forest where I found it." I handed the skull to Deutsche Mark, who held it by the antlers. "I had it hanging over the desk where I write. Sometimes it inspires me, but other times it gives me the creeps, like it has powers that I don't understand."

Deutsche Mark held the skull over his head so that he looked like an elk-headed Dutchman. "This thing is sick," he marveled. "How do you know it's a grandfather?"

I laughed a little at the elk-headed Dutchman and explained, "The lady at the park headquarters said she could tell by the teeth that it was a very old elk, and that only bull elk live that long. So, she surmised that it must have been a grandfather that died of natural causes."

Deutsche Mark spun the skull around by the antlers and looked into its mouth, "I can't believe you had this up here when we were up on Sheep Mountain Table. What are the odds of bringing a Grandfather Elk skull to the same spot where Black Elk had his visions?"

I agreed with wide eyes and added, "What are the odds of being there on the one and only occasion when the Tortoise was allowed to camp up there, now that the park service told Owen Cuny to never allow camping on Sheep Mountain Table again." A chill ran up my spine, despite the sweltering heat.

"Yeah man I know," he said looking me in the eyes. "In Black Elk's day, the braves would return to the village after a vision quest, and the elders would interpret what they saw. Even today, Sheep Mountain Table is a sacred site for the Lakota. That's where they go to pray and to seek visions of the future."

I slack-jawed in amazement. I put the elk skull back in the cardboard box. Driver Chris was coming up the hill followed by

The Return of Crazy Horse

Peruvian Ursula and PAC-MAN. Each of them was holding a large tray wrapped in tinfoil.

"Oh good, the cornbread is here," Driver Brian seemed genuinely pleased.

Driver Chris explained to the curious as he approached with the others, "Mrs. Ziolkowski made us cornbread." There was a big cheer for Mrs. Ziolkowski, the wife of the great sculptor.

Mark and I felt the bus pitch to one side as Buffalo Dave emerged from within, "Did I hear someone say cornbread? You baked fresh cornbread? That's my favorite food in the whole world. Cornbread, oh, I just love it!" Buffalo Dave had not helped with many meals thus far on our journey, he mostly did dishes, but he took charge of cutting the cornbread and he made sure Chicken Jim did not steal a single piece.

After dinner I worked on the clean-up line and helped Chicken Jim pack the roof box. From that lofty perspective, I noticed Flip-flop sitting with Driver Chris on the opposite side of French Sandrine. His self-proclaimed girlfriend had her arm wrapped around him like she was trying to keep him away from her, even though the Bostonian's fascination was clearly platonic.

When the cleanup was completed, several passengers sat up on the roof with me and Chicken Jim with our eyes fixed on the mountain to the east. The sun was dropping behind the mountains, painting Crazy Horse with the long angles of light, illuminating the sculpture of Crazy Horse in amazing colors that blew my mind.

As the clock ticked down to eight o'clock, we all kept our eyes glued on the sculpture of Crazy Horse in the distance. At exactly eight o'clock a loud blasting siren wailed and a few seconds later we saw a plume of smoke on the horse's head. The plume instantly billowed into a huge cloud and then the sound of the explosion reached us. "Wow, what a sight!" I gasped in awe.

As our departure time approached everyone started brushing their teeth, unfurling sleeping bags and getting ready to sleep. The Miracle Conversion was performed before we rolled away, transforming the front platform into a bed.

Peruvian Ursula took the Buddy Seat next to Driver Brian. He did most of the talking, telling driver stories, but she spoke one time about her personal collection of animal bones she called the Curiosity Museum. A few times their voices dropped to a whisper, but the wind blowing through the windows made it impossible to hear.

I watched the pine trees pass by in the moonlight as the bus rolled downhill until we reached the town of Custer. I sat against the window reading *Black Elk Speaks* for the last few minutes before the lights were turned off on the front platform. I remember reading how

Black Elk recognized his story to be a story of his tribe, lest it not be worth telling if it were just about him personally. This rang true. I made a promise to myself to keep my stories real.

Before falling asleep, I reflected on the previous forty-eight hours. In the wee hours of the morning, I witnessed the sunrise at Badlands National Park. I saw my first Buffalo roaming free at Prairie Dog Town. I conversed with a dignified Indian couple at the Longhorn museum in the ghost town of Scenic, South Dakota. We got to meet Strong Shoulders and listen to him sing his special song. We had dinner with the Indians at Cuny Cafe.

We camped overnight on top of Sheep Mountain Table where I had a vision. I saw a reflection of myself in the eyes of a Buffalo, evolving from an embryo into a boy connected genetically with all creatures and plants big and small. Owen Cuny confirmed our camping spot to be where Black Elk himself had his visions. We heard an impassioned retelling of the history of Wounded Knee by a Lakota man who's relative died in the bloody snow.

To top it all off, we ended the day in the Black Hills as special guests of Ruth Ziolkowski at Crazy Horse Monument. She made us cornbread for crying out loud. This fulfilled for me a childhood dream induced by a children's book written by my cousin, William Kotzwinkle. After an amazing sunset we had seen an explosion, sculpting part of the largest and most important sculpture in human history.

The message was clear. America will never have a clear conscience over our treatment of the Indians, but we still have a chance to make things right. Exactly one hundred years before my birth, the President of the United States, the Vice-president and all the members of the house and senate signed the Treaty of 1868, unequivocally granting stewardship of the Black Hills of South Dakota to the Indians. It is their sacred Holy Land as much as Israel is to the Jews. We must honor the Treaty of 1868 and give back their ancestral homeland, so the Indians can once again walk in a sacred manner on the land where their ancestors have been buried for thousands of years.

John Mernick is a storyteller of Irish and German descent.

Made in the USA
Middletown, DE
06 February 2026